ChangelingPress.com

Sympathy For the Devil

Stephanie Burke

Sympathy For the Devil
Stephanie Burke

ISBN: 978-1-60521-866-3

Publisher:
Changeling Press LLC
315 N. Centre St.
Martinsburg, WV 25404
ChangelingPress.com

Printed in the U.S.A.

Editor: Treva Harte
Cover Artist: Bryan Keller

The individual stories in this anthology have been previously released in E-Book format.

Table of Contents

Charle (Sympathy For the Devil 1)
Stephanie Burke

Reporter Charle Lexington is covering the last leg of Abadon's American tour. Charle's no uptight stick-in-the-mud, no matter what his ex has to say. After a confrontation at a concert, he loses himself in a one-night stand. Now he's finding it hard to forget the stranger he screwed, even if he never saw his face.

Abadon is a Rock god... literally. Announcing he's taking a break from performing, Abadon discovers a way to ease his depression -- mindless sex with complete strangers. But now he can't forget the man who played his body just right, delivered up a powerful jolt of pure worship, and left him wanting more.

Chapter 1

"You just plain suck." Charle Lexington stared at his ex, and the bitch he'd cheated on him with... and the friend of the bitch he had cheated with's best friend, whom he was also fucking.

Now would be a good time to let the floor open up and swallow him whole.

"Maybe if you learned to do that a bit better, I wouldn't have to go and find Andy and Candy."

Instead of opening his mouth and letting the asshole have it with both barrels, Charle rolled his eyes, crossed his arms over his Iron Man Pony T-shirt, and silently imagined the worst happening to his ex.

Then something, a strange awareness in him, poked him hard in the self-esteem. He couldn't let the spray tanned asshole get away with embarrassing him like this. He was better than that wannabe Dr. Dre any three hundred sixty four and three-fourths days of the year. He wanted war? He was going to get it.

"Well, if you had something a little bit bigger than a thumb to practice on, maybe I'd be better," he mused aloud, giving Dick a bright smile that showed all of his surgically corrected teeth. "I'm not saying you have a small dick, but when the whole thing fits in my mouth and can't even reach the middle of my tongue... well..." He let his words trail off as he grinned at his ex-Dick. "You're the only Richard I know who wants to be called Dick. Overcompensating much?"

"Bitch," Dick growled, rising to his feet in an attempt to be intimidating, but it was kind of hard to be intimidating when you had to wear lifts in your classic throwback Adidas to reach the coveted six-foot height... a height that guaranteed that not too many people would notice his receding hairline.

Except Charle was six-feet three inches in his bare

feet. Sometimes life was good.

"Yes, I am," Charle purred. "I learned it from watching you."

"Like anyone else would want you," Dick growled as the twins twittered from behind their hands, their matching neon nails making glowing trails that threatened to give him a headache in the low light of the venue.

The Stage was a small studio/auditorium that catered to the elite in the rock world. Everyone from the Stones to the Who, from Prince to Snoop Dogg had played private gigs there. Usually the invitees received an email on the same day as the event, inviting them to come and take place in the making of history. Established bands used the venues to announce tours, introduce their hottest new discoveries, showcase new or replacement talents, or to just kick back and jam without the complications of stage make-up, rock personas, and screaming groupies to get in the way of the fun. Tonight Abadon had taken the stage to announce the last leg of their American tour and that they would be taking a small hiatus afterwards to create a new sound.

Charle had gotten his email late, as he was out interviewing the latest stripper- turned-female-rap-sensation, and didn't get to check his emails on his phone until his three hours were up with Miss Thang.

She was surprisingly intelligent and forthright about her career goals, her past, and what she intended for the future. She also demanded his full attention as she strutted around the basement studio of her new house, complete with stripper pole, while they talked politics and fashion.

He had raced to get to The Stage and had missed the performance and announcement by minutes. But that was okay. He could still interview those who were invited, pick up a press packet, and watch The Other, Abadon's warm-up band, perform. The Other was a small alternative rap band, kind of like Twenty One Pilots, that was gaining quite the name for itself. The members were entertaining as hell to watch on stage. They kind of made the audience feel like they were part of one big joke instead of condescending to them.

Charle didn't think that Dick would be here or, with misplaced sarcasm and snark, he would intercept Charle on his way to find a seat.

"Oh, a lot of people want me, Dick," he snickered, while trying to control the inner bullshit meter that was ringing quite loudly in his head. "It's hard to be so sexy."

Charle had been dateless and even worse, sexless since he discovered Dick fucking the twins in the backseat of his car years ago. His '69 Pontiac Firebird was his baby and to have it so defiled by that fool in the velour sweat suit sitting there...

He mourned the abuse of his car far more than he mourned the explosion of their relationship. He did have fun marching up to his studio apartment and activating his LoJack, reporting that his car was the victim of a break-in, which it technically was. He had never given Dick the keys or permission to even breathe on his car, let alone set his cheap materialistic ass inside of it.

Dick had not been amused when the police showed up and arrested him for breaking and entering, public nudity, lewd behavior, and engaging in sexual acts in public. Charle got to play shocked lover who had no idea that his boyfriend of three years had broken into his car and was cheating on him.

The officers, who were very sympathetic even if subtly grossed out, were all too happy to arrest Dick and talk to Charle about pressing charges. No, Dick didn't live with him. He did not have permission to be at Charle's apartment or in his car. He was a reporter who had been covering Aerosmith all week and had only moments before arrived at his home. See? There was his plane ticket and photographs of him and Steven Tyler at breakfast that morning. They all agreed that it was a passive-aggressive way to break up and from the way Dick was cursing at him, it could turn violent. Tall, thin Charle would be no match for his thicker, angry ex in a fight, so maybe he should go upstairs and let another nice officer take his statement and see about a restraining order.

Charle did that before he took his car to get deloused and detailed.

Dick's shocked face would have been almost comedic if it wasn't so tragic as a trio of officers cuffed and stuffed him in the back of a police car with just his long T-shirt covering his modesty while the twins were taken away in a second car with a lesser charge of accessory to breaking and entering and public lewd behavior.

Ever since then, he had been singing Pink's *You and Your Hand Tonight* to himself. Then there was his Bob... Battery Operated Boyfriends were the best. They didn't cheat on you or defile your most prized possession, and when you were done with them, you cleaned them off and threw them in a drawer.

Now he was kind of regretting that as he really didn't have a final comeback for Dick or the ability to lie worth a damn.

"You couldn't get laid if you bend over, spread your cheeks, and tattoo cum dump around your asshole. You are pathetic, Charle, a pathetic sad, lonely old man in a twig of a body."

Charle could respond in kind or he could be mature, walk away, ignore Dick, and try to enjoy the music that was coming.

And there was the third option, throwing a punch.

Charle decided to throw a damn punch. The drink

that Dick spilled all over him and his companions was just a bonus as far as he was concerned.

In the midst of the squealing and bodies flying around -- the twins -- and blood gushing from noses -- well, one nose that belonged to Dick -- Charle ducked down and slipped away in the darkness of the gathering crowd.

No one in their right mind would think that prim and proper Charle Lexington would throw a punch much less get into any conflict. Charle was considered a good guy, nonconfrontational, maybe even sweet and innocent, definitely not one to start trouble. Security moved right past him and he ducked into a quiet dark room, hoping to find a place to chill out while Dick ether settled down or left. The rich producer had already taken a beating in the papers after his arrest and the reasons for it were made public and even though years had passed, he couldn't afford another scandal, especially one involving a so prim and proper, upstanding gay black man like his poor cuckolded ex.

He had no idea the room was occupied until the first moaned complaint reached his ears.

* * *

"If you're going to fuck me, then fucking fuck me hard!"

Abadon thrust harder into the soft feminine body beneath him as he turned and glared at the weak fuck who was trying his best to do a number on his asshole... and failing... miserably. He arched his back and used his backward thrust to knock the weak fucker on his ass while keeping the fucker's hard dick deep inside him. "I'll do it myself."

He sat down hard, grinding on the cock beneath him while pulling the groaning woman onto his lap for a good hard ride. He had no care for the man below him groaning at the extra weight on his bent knees. He wanted to bust his nut and leave.

The man's nails raking at his back as he clenched down hard on him added to his already growing frustration. The woman on his lap squealed and shuddered around him, gaining her own release, so he eased out of her, tossed the condom aside and sat back down on the dick that was going limp even as he grumbled in frustration. He was so horny his balls hurt. He looked up as the door opened and the woman blew him a kiss as she walked out.

"I'm so sorry," the man behind him whispered. "Give me a moment, baby. It happens to us all."

"No, it doesn't." He was about to really let loose on the guy when another man peeked in the door. When he didn't run away screaming and a camera didn't flash, Abadon gave him some consideration.

It was too dark to make out any features, but he looked tall and slim. He cocked his head to the side and something about him... yeah. He stood up, letting the other man's limp dick slide out of his ass as he motioned to the man in the doorway. "Get in here."

The newcomer froze while the man behind him stuttered excuses.

"In or out," Abadon called out and the man behind him stopped making excuses and slid out from behind him.

"What?" the man asked but Abadon noted that he wasn't leaving.

"I need to be fucked in the worst kind of way."

"But --" his failed fucker stammered and Abadon ignored him. He ran his hands through his hair before he slammed his fists on the desk.

"Get the fuck out," he snapped and the man slunk out of the room, shame wafting off him in palpable waves.

"You really need it?" The voice that spoke from the

door was deep and precise. It spoke of someone who did a lot of public speaking.

"Get the fuck in me or get the fuck out." Heat was coiling through his belly and need was tearing at his gut.

"Sex?"

"No. I need a mani-pedi," he growled in his frustration. "Get in here and fuck me or so help me I'm gonna spank your skinny ass until I feel better about the situation."

The man stepped inside and closed the door. "I think I can satisfy you."

"You'd have to be a blind one-armed chimp to do worse than that NBA no balling asshole."

The man snorted in laughter then there was the clink of a belt buckle being undone.

"About fucking time."

"Condom?"

"On the desk," he reached for one and held it out. "We give this shit out like candy. Play safe or go home."

This was kind of wicked, not seeing faces. A good nameless faceless fuck might be what he needed to get him back on track. His managers said he was going stale and needed to change direction. He'd resisted but they won the argument. So here he was, announcing a break and the confusion was eating at him. He'd thought a good fuck would clear his head and get him back to business but no. He had to run into Limp Dick Larry.

Hopefully this guy was better.

The condom was plucked from his hand and there was a rustle before the smell of oranges filled the air.

"Lotion," he explained. "Not oil-based."

"What the fuck ever." Abadon's hole was twitching. He needed to be filled. That other guy started his engine revving but this guy… he had a good feeling about him.

"On the desk?" he asked as he moved closer and ran his hand over Abadon's chest. He purred in delight at the feel. The man had soft hands.

As he kicked the chair aside and pressed up against his back, Abadon got a feel of the latex covered battering ram he called a dick. "Please tell me you're over twenty-one." He had to ask. Responsibilities and all of that.

"Way past that. I'd show you ID but that means I would have to let you go."

Damn, there was command in his voice. Then those hands gripped his hips, urging him forward. Eagerly he spread his legs and bent over the desk. Finally he was going to get fucked right. And if this one couldn't stay the course, he was going back to his hotel, order up a dildo, and do the job himself. It has been some time since he got rogered and his hole was hungry for hot cock. He was going to be really pissed if he had to settle for latex. "So fuck me," he demanded and then felt two fingers slide inside him and spread out.

"Yes," he murmured, dropping his head toward the desk as the delicious feeling of being spread filled him. He moaned softly and pushed back on the finger spearing him.

"Eager."

"Horny. Stop talking and fuck me."

"Your wish, my command."

He felt the latex covered head at his hole and then...

"Holy fuck," he hissed. This dude was built. The cock was hard and fat and... why was he pulling out?

"What are you doing?"

"Too much?"

"If I needed a safety word I would have given you one. Fuck me now!"

And then that perfect cock was slamming back into him and the man behind him was cursing. "God damn," he murmured as a spark of something flowed into Abadon. It burned almost as deliciously as the ache in his ass. Then the man was pulling out only to slam in deep.

"Open that greedy hole for me."

That was too pretty a demand not to obey. Abadon reached back and gripped the globes of his ass. He spread them wide and growled as the man sank in deeper. "Yes," he hissed. "This is what I needed. Give it to me hard and fast."

The man pulled out and then fully inside again.

Fuck, their balls were bouncing together and the friction in his ass was incredible. He was babbling, he knew it, fucking back on the man and it wasn't enough. "Harder!" he demand. "Make me come."

Instead of answering, the man reached under him and gripped his dick in his fist. "Holy hell," he breathed and another jolt of pure energy hit Abadon. "How many are there?"

The piercings? Was that was he was talking about? He didn't get a chance to answer before the other man was fingering them, tugging at them and groaning as the metal heated in his hands. "Fuck, that's so hot."

Abadon didn't get the chance to say anything because the man began to fuck him like it was his job. He slammed in as deep as he could go and then ground his hips in circles, touching places that set off more fireworks in his brain.

The man was going for gold, picking up speed as his hand worked his dick. "Yes," he encouraged. "Just like that. Fuck, just like that!" He could feel his climax rising, feel it taking over his body as his fucker moaned into his shoulder, nipping at the tight skin.

"So fucking good." The man was working it in deep, slamming into him, and fucking him like a god needed to be fucked. His hand was not shy about tugging hard at his Jacob's Ladder piercing even as he took the time to work the shaft. The other one pushed into his hair, holding it.

His scent covered Abadon, bright with oranges and

something indefinable as the man began to grunt with each thrust. And all the while this crazy energy was pouring off the guy, feeding into Abadon, building up to something so intense it was blinding him. He adjusted his stance and the man's next thrust slammed directly into his prostate.

"Fuck!" he screamed and the man repeated his actions.

"Found it."

"Fuck, yes," he managed before the man's grip in his hair jerked his head backwards, the slight pain adding to the overwhelming pleasure that filled him.

This was fucking at its most primal and he loved every second of it.

Again and again that spot was hit just right until he couldn't hold on any longer.

"Gonna come," he panted.

"Please?"

That did it. A jolt of energy hit his head while his body exploded in pleasure. He could feel his ass clench around the solid mass in his ass as his balls snapped up to the base of his cock. He cried out as his cock spurted his release across the man's hand.

"Yes," he shuddered, feeling it from the top of his head to the bottom of his feet. This was the best orgasm ever. He pushed back onto the man just as he slammed forward, using his weight to push Abadon flat on the desk. In a series of amazing thrusts against his overly sensitive prostate, he felt a liquid heat fill the condom as the man got his release.

"Fuck," he breathed, laying against Abadon for a moment.

Abadon closed his eyes as the man pulled out, relaxing on the table fully. The electricity in his brain was still buzzing. He hadn't felt a jolt like that in centuries. Not even his best performances garnered that type of a worshiping buzz.

Who was this guy?

By the time he gathered himself together enough to stand up and ask, the door was already closing. His mystery fucker was gone.

"Damn," he muttered, feeling as if something important had just gotten away.

"Lyin' in my bed... can't get you out of my head... head."

Abadon chuckled at his own arguably bad sense of humor as he tossed off the rest of his clothing. His shoes had gone away the moment he entered his hotel room and the rest soon followed as he hummed a tune in his head and played with lyrics.

"Head would be good right about now," he mused as he flopped across his bed and curled up on his side.

He'd been sporting a semi ever since his mystery man had walked out on him. He wiggled, grinning when the pleasant soreness in his ass reminded him that the guy who did him was a huge motherfucker.

After he rolled out, Abadon had gotten himself together and limped back to the greenroom with a huge smile on his face.

The others noticed his improved attitude and gently ribbed about him fucking it out of his system. He wanted to join in on the rest of the drinking and merrymaking but he smelled of sex. The others made no comments and a few partygoers gave him knowing looks but... Orange and spice.

The scent lingered through the smell of cigarettes and booze. It was stronger than the perfume that scented the air. It was more powerful than the smell of sweaty bodies as people danced and made merry around him.

And now lying in his bed, all he could smell was the mystery man, oranges and spice. He rolled to his back, his hands trailing over his still hard nipples, feeling the pull of the stranger's fingers.

"I'm getting obsessed," he decided as he gave one a good hard tug and felt his dick jerk in reaction.

Chuckling, he ran his hands down his stomach and undid his pants. His fingers danced on the pricks of soreness left on his hips that signaled bruising from his shadow lover. He looked down and saw ten little purpling finger marks and the sight ignited something primal within him.

He wiggled, feeling the odd emptiness in his ass as his dick sprang to full mast. He recalled the feel of the man hovering over him.

Abadon could have broken him into pieces but instead he allowed himself to submit to the pleasure of his thick cock and his aggressive presence. It was a trip knowing that at any moment he could have turned the tables and put the fucker in his place but he instead chose to swallow down his instincts for the second time that night and take what was being offered.

The man was so damn confident. He couldn't see the expressions on his face, but he imagined that he had sneered at the asshole fuck-boy who promised ecstasy and couldn't deliver. He could imagine the look of disdain as the boy slunk past, tail between his legs. But it was the man's actions that had him lost in memory.

He ran his hands over Abadon's body as if he had never touched anything so precious and then in the next moment he was trying to manhandle him, to get him where he wanted him to be. He wasn't intimidated at all and yet he still asked for permission and consent in his own rough way.

It had been so long since he had been fucked so hard that the emptiness in his ass was starting to annoy him.

He moved to the bag on the nightstand, pushing aside his complimentary fruit basket, and pulled out his dildo, the one he he'd been so glad he didn't have to settle for earlier. But it looked like he was going to have to settle for it now as he was hung, horny, and empty as fuck.

It was a good dildo, long and thick with realistic veins and a set of balls attached. He pulled out the pump bottle of lube that always went with him when he traveled and lightly coated the rubbery flesh.

He wanted to still feel some burn, just like he felt when his shadow lover slammed into him at full force.

He made himself comfortable, thighs spread wide, feet flat to the mattress and gave his cock a good hard stroke.

The tugging from the myriad of rings that made up his ladderback piercing made him start to leak like a faucet. The guy had loved these rings tugging and pulling at them as he rode his ass hard. It was one of the reasons he put them in. He loved the burn and tug when he fucked someone or when someone struggled to swallow his cock down and bit at the jewelry. He wasn't a masochist by any stretch, but he was a warrior and pain just added extra to anything he did. It was a quirk of his nature.

He sang and growled his lyrics until his throat burned and he had to heal himself a little to make it to the next show. He loved it. He pierced his body because he liked the look and loved for the piercings to be played with roughly. He grew his hair long so it could be pulled and jerked as he moved about his day. It was a form of fighting in his mind, of battle, of endurance that challenged him personally on a level that he was not allowed due to the lack of sword battles on open fields.

And now he wanted to be fucked and he wanted it to burn.

One hand tugging at his rings, he pressed the rounded head of his dildo to his straining hole. No, he wasn't going to stretch himself out more. He was still pretty open from when the guy worked his ass over good.

He wasn't going to add more lube because he craved this intimate burn. He wanted to recreate the feelings the mystery man pulled from him and he hungered for it now.

Abadon threw hack his head, hissing as he forced the dick in. He didn't want to do himself any lasting harm so he went slow but steady.

He could feel his guardian muscles part as the latex slipped inside prying him open as it slid in deep.

"Fuck..." he groaned as the feeling of being split open grew more intense.

He closed his eyes, imagining his fucker pushing him down on his back, pressing his thighs wide until the muscles burned, then diving in deep.

He recalled how those slim muscles felt grinding against him as the dildo bottomed out. He grunted at the burning pleasure as his walls clenched around the fullness that parted them.

He slowly began to jerk his dick, fingers sliding over the rings made slippery with the amount of pre cum he was spilling.

His heart began to pound as he slowly pulled his dildo back, not fully out, but enough so that there was a delicious slide against his prostate.

Fucking himself never felt so good and with the echo of his previous lover brought back to the forefront of his mind, this session was just about perfect.

He began to fuck himself faster, his hips arching up and he opened his mouth and let all of those hungry sounds roll from his throat. He loved being loud, not holding himself back in expressing anything, let alone his own pleasures. So he roared as he thrust upwards into his hand, making sure to let go and caress his jeweled balls, tugging at the rings there too.

He moved his hand faster, fucking himself harder and he got lost in the memories of the one who got away.

He could hear his teasing words and feel the rough slap to his ass as he was plowed but good. And the smell... again he could smell the scent of oranges and it only amped up his enjoyment.

This was good. "So good," he muttered as he pulled his cock again, jerking himself faster as sweat began to fall from his body.

"Fuck yeah," he was muttering as he felt the phantom touch of his lover caressing his skin, felt his hands sliding over his back, felt his fingers pulling at his hair.

He was losing control and he loved it.

His ass was sore, his muscles clenching around the fake dick as it hit his prostate and filled that empty feeling within him just right. And then there was the words he wanted him to speak...

"I will never forsake you," his man growled in his ears as he pounded into him harder, deeper, faster. "I will offer you up anything you wish. Take my ass. Take my cock. Take all of me to do with as you will." He could picture him panting, beginning to whine as he reached his peak. "I'm yours."

"Mine," Abadon shouted as he felt his balls draw up and his control start to shatter. His dick swelled to its fullest and with a few more pumps of his dildo, his ass was clenching around the hard latex. His hips thrust up spraying his load over his chest and hand.

He was panting and trembling from the hard climax when he realized what he had said. Then his eyes popped wide open as the scent of oranges and sex filled his nostrils. When had he ever thought of a fuck as his? This was so not right.

He ignored the burn of overused muscles in his ass as he pulled his dildo free, shuddering as the latex bumped the rings in his balls. He shuddered as pleasure spiraled up his spine and that reminded him of those thin knowing fingers traveling over his skin...

No, he decided, standing up. He was not going to do this. He was not going to let the memory of one good fuck stick with him. Nope. He was not going to start down this road. One good lay did not call for him wishing for more. Even the thought of the word relationship made his dick want to crawl back inside his body where it would be safe. Mystery man was a one-off and his body had better not forget that. And he would aid in the forgetting by removing the piercings.

And after showering three times, he called down to the concierge to remove all the oranges from his complimentary fruit basket. And when the scent of oranges would not go away, he shaved his crotch. Orange scent apparently stuck to things.

And when he kept feeling twinges of the guy's dick in his ass, he healed himself fully. A one-off was a one-off. There was no going back... no matter how much he wished he had gotten his number. Maybe a second round would have satisfied the emptiness that was suddenly filling him.

Fuck. It was five in the morning and all he could do was think about the one who got away, the mystery man.

Hmm... Mystery man. That was a good name for a song.

Chapter 2

They called him Abadon.

Really, it was a good choice, because he looked like the devil incarnate.

Charle looked at the man, no, the creature that he was supposed to be following on the last leg of his American tour and knew that he was going to be in for it. The creature himself stood there sneering at Charle's comfortable khaki cargo pants and his long sleeved AC/DC band T-shirt.

That was fine. Charle eyeballed him, starting at his tight leather pants, moving up to his wild abandon of long black hair, then down again to his bare feet and his chest. Charle found himself less than impressed as well.

The man he banged last night was so much better... At least he thought he was. The night had gotten kind of hazy after stranger anger sex, but Charle had to admit it was because of last night and his mystery man that he was feeling a lot more calm when dealing with this impressive...

Okay, maybe Charle was a little impressed, he decided as he watched the man's muscles flex as he moved. It was obvious that between the drinking, the partying, the womanizing, and the reported drug use, Abadon also found some time to work out.

I work out too. But Charle knew it was just to stay in good enough shape in a world where he spent a lot of time eating fast food with whatever band he was covering or sucking down whatever the catering service supplied back stage. It was obviously nothing like what Abadon did to get those abs rippled enough to scrub Charle's T-shirt, the one that the rocker so easily dismissed, clean as hell.

The biceps weren't bad either. Slinging a guitar and screaming at the crowds of adoring fans who paid upwards of ninety dollars for a nosebleed seat must really be a workout.

After trailing his gaze up from his black painted toenails to the red-rimmed black eyes staring at him, Charle cleared his throat and got back to the mission at hand.

"Hello," he forced cheerfulness into his voice. "I'm Charle and I'll be following you guys as you hit your last three cities before you all head off to Europe."

He lifted an ID badge and press pass that someone so kindly hung on a steel lanyard for him. This was not his first rodeo. Charle had done jobs like this before under different circumstances and had learned to keep his credentials handy.

Charle didn't offer a hand because it looked like Abadon wouldn't shake his anyway. So he stood there staring at the singer, hoping that he would wash his feet after they boarded his tour bus.

"What kind of a name is *Charle* for a grown man?" Abadon asked, his forehead wrinkled in what had to be confusion.

Okay. The lead singer's not all that bright, though his voice is very familiar. Must be from all the sample songs I listened to in order to get ready for this job.

"A grown-ass man should be Charles or Chuck. Not Charle," Abadon continued. "Never a diminutive that makes you sound like a twelve year old girl."

"And what kind of name is Abadon?" Charle asked, as sweetly as he could. "It sounds like the name of an aging rocker from the eighties trying to reclaim his youth or maybe his throne among the lost Emo Kids set -- the ones who wore black eyeliner and wrote depressing poetry about how no one understands them and how they wish they were never born while thinking that cutting *would* give them the attention they deserve."

Charle offered him a smile. It didn't have to be war between them, but there was no way he was going to take any shit from the great Abadon either. He just wasn't in the mood. He had only taken this job because he needed to get away even before the incident with Dick. Abadon was not going to mess this up for him.

"Ohh," Abadon purred, his black eyes looking interested for the first time since they started this conversation. "*Charle* has some fight in him."

There were chuckles and Charle turned around to see that Abadon's three band members had somehow managed to sneak up behind and now had him surrounded.

There was Hash and the name was appropriate. The man was a mountain of muscle squeezed into a black T-shirt two sizes too small and a pair of black jeans. His skin was so dark it seemed like every color of the rainbow was reflected in his skin. Seriously, the man had perfectly dark skin without a blemish that Charle could see. His hair was braided into a multitude of waist length cornrows that had some iridescent beads interspaced throughout. It was a striking hairstyle as the sun picked up the color of the beads and there was an explosion of color surrounding him every time he moved his head.

Hash was snorting at Abadon and shaking his head, looking rather amused.

Beside him was Apollon, also called the golden one. His skin was so pale Charle finally understood what a watered milk complexion was. His arms were covered in bright tats in shapes and swirls of bright red and blue, that made it look like fire was flowing up his arms. He was rather thin, but not skinny. Fortunately he didn't look like a cracked out rendition of a young Axl Rose. If Charle had to choose a word to describe him, it would be elegant. He looked like he would be right at home in a tux being catered to by eager masses. Instead his stick straight platinum silver hair was pulled back into a thick ponytail. He was smiling broadly, and Charle puzzled at one of his incisors that was rather fang-like. You'd think with all the money this band brought in, he could afford to get that fixed by a dentist.

The last one, Python, was openly chuckling. It was his laugh that had made Charle turn around. He too was shirtless like Abadon and his arms were thickly corded with muscle. Although he was cut, he was not as cut as Abadon. He too was covered in tattoos, but it was clear he was not trying to copy the lead singer and guitarist. Python had his own style, and that included shoes, thank God, and a pale gold-white python that was draped around his body. His hair was a riot of red curls that bounced as he laughed, his hand absently petting the head of the snake that rested on his right shoulder.

"Charle-boy has teeth," Python chuckled as he moved closer.

It was about the time that Charle noticed that he was literally surrounded by a mountain of men. Seriously. He considered himself to be tall at six-three. These guys had to be around six-foot five each. Did they meet on a basketball court or something? Did they choose band members by height? This was ridiculous.

"He bites back." Apollon's voice was surprisingly deep.

"This is going to be one hell of a trip," Hash added, his voice deep and almost hypnotizingly mellow. "Oh yeah, this is going to be fun." Then Hash went on to introduce each band member as if Charle didn't know them on sight. "That's Python with the snake. The snake doesn't have a name because Python's a lazy ass who won't think of one."

"Hey, man. His name has got to be epic," Python rumbled. "Like Snake --"

"No," Apollon snorted. "I thought we had this sorted years ago."

"Well, at least he got over calling it Human," Hash

chuckled. "That was a stupid name."

"Was not," Python protested. "It was ironic."

"Whatever man," Hash rolled his eyes. "That's Apollon," Hash pointed to the gravel-pit voiced blond. "He's rather normal besides sounding like his balls are made from lead."

"Brass, I keep telling you," Apollon rumbled. "I get it from my mom, brass balls and the voice to match."

"And that says what about your dad?" Hash joked.

"That he was an incredibly brave man."

Even Charle had to chuckle at that one and that made Hash break out into a smile.

"If we are done?" The imperious tones of Abadon again drew Charle's attention to the star monkey of this circus. "We need to get on the road. Ohio is not my favorite place in the world. Too... Bible-y."

"Dude," Python laughed as he stepped closer to Charle to comment. It was a good thing he had gotten over his fear of snakes a long time ago. "Did you see the ten commandments on the roadside billboards last time we drove through? And the God who's watching you just after the last commandment posted?"

"It was a bit of church on the road. It was like you're going to get a dose of religion whether you want it or not."

"This is the bible belt," Charle pointed out. "Be thankful you missed the pissed off looking Jesus about to do a back flip on I-71. Butter Jesus burned down a few years ago and the church hasn't put him back up."

"Butter Jesus?" Apollon rumbled as he turned his brown eyes toward Charle.

"Yeah, he was made out of insulation foam or something and looked like he was carved out of butter. He seriously looked like he was going to do a back flip into the reflecting pool behind him and then he was going to smite some serious ass as soon as he made that last dive."

"He was going for no splash, I assume." Python snickered.

"The world will never know," Charle intoned, lowering his head and peering at him from underneath his lashes. "He was struck by lightning and that was that. There's even a song about it... I Can't Believe It's Not Jesus... Olay, oh Lord."

The band cracked up at that, and Charle felt any worry about getting along with these guys starting to melt. Like butter.

"Just take it on the bus, please," Abadon sneered at them before brushing past Charle and climbing aboard the huge black bus that would be home for the next few weeks.

"And wash your feet," Apollon called, turning to enter behind him. "No telling what you walked in on the way over here and I'm not getting sick because you want to play rock star."

"Rock star?" Abadon tossed back his red-striped black hair and took a pose that had Charle's breath catching.

There was a sudden breeze that made his hair swirl around his body that looked like it was ready to launch itself into greatness. His eyes were glittering and his smile was beautiful and arrogant at the same time. He slowly licked his full lips, leaving the bottom one glittering as he threw back his head and basked in the fingers of wind that first covered his body with his hair before it blew it back, as if offering a gift to humanity by exposing perfection to mortal eyes. "I *am* a rock god. Now get on the fuckin' bus."

Chapter 3

The tour bus was unbelievable.

Charle had been in his share of tour busses but as he sat in the plush recliner, he was at a loss to describe such opulence on paper. But he was going to damn sure try.

There was definitely enough space for the four musicians and the annoyed reporter that he was turning out to be. The guys seemed to be okay or a bit more intelligent than the usual heavy metal rockers he was used to, but the star of the piece, the one who had requested him because of his work with Dragonforce no less, had yet to make an appearance.

"We keep a lot of space for, you know, propaganda."

"Sure," Charle rolled his eyes as he stowed his bag beside him. For two days this seat had been his bed and his front row seat to the insanity that was the band Abadon. He was grateful the damn thing was so comfortable.

"All the propaganda that my magazine sent me out here to find was not for me to revel in, I'm sure. Because no one else has ever spread any rumors about this bus. And word has it that no one's ever allowed on this bus, not even your manager."

"Well," Apollon rumbled, "We make it a hard and fast rule that there are no hos in the bus. You wanna fuck, you get a hotel or get the orgy started in the green room. No rumors at all? Damn, the propaganda machine's failing, big time."

"Sure," Charle rolled his eyes again as a thought floated through the back of his mind.

Sex in back rooms was never the cleanest. He thought back to a few nights before and fought down a blush. He wondered what had happened to his dark-haired fucker? He was suddenly wishing that he had left his number for him, just in case he wanted to hook up again. Then he remembered what they had done in the back office of that club... on that executive office chair, and the desk... He hope they cleaned and fumigated those chairs frequently because he was sure that he left more DNA there than he had intended to leave anywhere that could become a crime scene.

"We party here, yeah," Hash interrupted his musings. "But we made a pact, man. No sex on the bus. We live here way too many months out of the year for that shit."

"Can you imagine the used condoms that would litter this place if we hadn't?" Apollon rumbled. "Not to mention the bodily fluids," he chuckled, then paused to frown at an apparently disgusting thought, before snickering like a kid caught saying a dirty word.

"Yeah," Hash added, a chuckle of his own on his lips. "Remember those squirting twins we picked up in Baltimore? Yeah, I was ready to go surfing on the tides." He threw his fist out for a fist pound, which Python, sitting in his own chair, was quick to give.

"Damn man, we were nearly flooded. She sat on my face and I nearly drowned."

Charle shifted in his seat, uncomfortable with the turn this conversation was taking. Sure, he'd had sex with women before, and even gotten off on it, but there was a reason he preferred sex with men. Too much natural... lubrication. And it smelled. He had taken three showers and still couldn't get the smell of pussy out of his then scraggly beard or his sheets. Nope, women were awesome friends and some of the most talented human beings to ever walk the planet. Didn't mean he wanted to fuck another one or talk about their sexual... juices.

So here they were hurtling down the highway at god knows what speed, their driver Max appeared to be just about as insane as the rest of these guys, and all he wanted them to do was change the subject.

As a somewhat closeted gay man, the last thing he wanted to talk about was pussy.

He glared at the snickering and joking beings and for the umpteenth time wished he had the power of mind control. If he did, he would make them shut the hell up about pussy and put on some damn clothes.

Let me set the stage. He pulling out a pen and scribbling on a pad he kept nearby to document his thoughts while he was working. *Me in my dancing chili pepper lounging pants (no judgment), a plain black tank, and my lambskin slides. Hey, being on the road don't mean that I have to give up creature comforts and for two days I'll be like the strange awkward friend you bring along because your mommy says you have to. I'm sitting with my tablet at one of the four window seats with a desk. The other three are filled by Apollon in front of me, and Python and Hash across from us.*

From the moment I whipped out my pad to take notes, the beefy boys decided now would be a good time to visit the writer. I mean there are three couches, two bedrooms, two full sized bathrooms, a full kitchen and a TV area, but they had to sit with me. And to make matters worse, they were all in boxer-briefs. Personally, I lived in hope of a tip slip with the dick prints I could see through the undies as they laughed, flexed, and basically showed their bodies off with no shame. But I am a professional. I can't let my inner joy at the sight ruin the job I was hired to do.

"Oh look," Python, who had his snake draped around his body like a stole, "Charle-boy don't like pussy jokes." Charle stopped writing and glared at the larger man.

"Ohh," Hash chuckled. "Looks like you pissed him off. Are you pissed off Charle?"

"Charles," Charle growled through gritted teeth. "My name is Charles while you guys act like fools." He bent down to reach for his bag, wanting nothing more than to storm away to one of the lounging areas, but that would be too much like giving in. So he sat back and looked at the grinning assholes, crossing his arms in front of his chest.

"Charles in Charge." Python gave him what he was sure was supposed to be a good-natured buddy smile, but looked more like an evil smirk, the ginger bastard. His accent was more pronounced and Charle still could not place it. "Look at his face turn red. I wonder how far down that blush goes?"

"Maybe he don't appreciate good pussy?" Apollon chuckled. "Do you, Charles? Do you like good, tight, hot wet pussy?"

Bastards.

"I prefer a good hot tight asshole," Charle tossed back, hoping to unnerve them a bit. "All silky and smooth..." He was quite sure they never would have thought of anyone just coming out and admitting to being gay. Most rockers that he had interviewed over the years would run from the g-word like it was a close twin of the words one hit wonder.

"You didn't say wet," Hash tossed out without missing a beat. "Do you like to go in dry, Charles? Man, that's cold."

"Yeah, buddy," Python tossed over his shoulder as he swirled his chair back and forth. "Lube means love. Or do you tell them to bite down on a pillow before you start tearing it up?"

"That's just mean, man." Apollon laughed. "At least use spit --"

"I am talking about men," Charle had to clarify because it seemed the intelligence he had earlier attributed to them was a mistake. Were they really this dense or were they fucking with him?

"That just means the screams of pain start lower when you tear that ass up," Python laughed. "No, *Charles!*" he shouted in his best scared voice while thrusting his hips up. "Use some lube!"

"Fuck you," Charle shouted at them, losing a bit of his cool before he managed to rein himself in. He was a pro, damn it, and was used to dealing with this type of shit. Maybe the recent incidents in his personal life were starting to affect his working one, and that meant it was time for him to reevaluate his goals.

"Not if you don't use lube," Apollon rumbled back. "That's a hard and fast rule of mine."

Charle felt himself blush red hot as they exploded into laughter, the damn hyenas. He was sure the torture would have continued but a completely naked Abadon slammed in from one of the bedrooms.

"Why don't you all shut the fuck up?" he roared, glaring at them through a wild mane of red/black hair. Charle found myself staring, nearly choking on his spit as the beefy boys erupted in laughter again.

"I'm trying to create in here," Abadon snarled and Charle had trouble bringing his eyes up to his face with all of that flesh on display.

His fingers itched for his camera as he watched Abadon's flaccid dick bounce as he shifted his weight from one foot to the other. Oh yes, the rumors were true. The bus lights reflected off of the silver of his PA piercing.

The dude who had fucked him last night preferred the rings of death running down the back of his dick. The rock god seemed to like a nice modest bar. He was an impressive man naked and his tattoos swirled along his body in an ever-moving wave of black and gray. His tattoos looked alive and they trailed over his body, surrounding his shaved cock. Apparently, he was a believer in the no body hair and for once Charle found a shaved groin that didn't look like a plucked chicken skin.

For some strange reason, he kept comparing him to the man he had screwed through a desk and a chair before they departed. That man had a nice soft down of dark body hair and a neatly shaved thatch just above his cock.

"Bitch, you just mad 'cause you missed the joke." Apollon laughed and Abadon rolled his eyes at him.

"I have to finish this new song and you jackaroos aren't helping."

"New song?" Charle winced even as the words left his mouth because suddenly all that rock god-wrath was directed at him.

"Oh yeah. I forgot about you. That's why I wanted the blood-sucking media with us."

Well, that was flattering.

"Well, I was invited to report on this leg of the tour before you go back to Europe, remember," Charle countered, hoping that his lounging pants were baggy enough to disguise the erection he was growing as he watched the naked man. "And something like this is what you wanted reported, instead of the usual wild goings-on that probably develop around you every time you step outside of your door. So, in lieu of having the paparazzi chasing you down and reporting half-baked rumors, why don't you give a dog a bone and tell me what you're working on? It's kind of my job to be fair and impartial and I can't do that if you don't give me anything to work with."

"How long has he been here?" Abadon asked of Hash.

"Two days, man. We're one day out from our next gig. You better get it together."

"Right." He turned away from Charle as if he didn't exist and stormed back into his bedroom.

"And that's why we ignore his crazy ass," Apollon grumbled, and Charle jerked in his chair as he turned to face him.

He knew his eyes were still wide as he tried to breathe normally after getting a look at that rounded muscular ass. Squats must be pretty good to him. "Is he always like that?"

"Nah, sometimes he curses more." Python laughed.

"Great," Charle mumbled to himself. He was trapped on a bus with three men who thought it was fine to play fuck with the gay reporter and one man who reminded him a bit of his ex from the constant glares and the silent treatment he was receiving when he decided to pay any attention to his surroundings. So much for this job getting him away from it all.

"Buck up." Hash rose to his feet, his boxer-briefs clinging to his body like a second skin. "He's like that to everyone when we're on the road. He'll be better once we get to Indiana."

Great. One more day with these guys before he could get off this damn bus. After two days of the silent treatment from the star of this rodeo and interesting conversations from the trio of asses that he called friends and bandmates, Charle would do anything to catch a break.

"Are you cooking again?" Python added as he rose to his feet. "'Cause I could stand to eat."

"The kitchen's there." Charle pointed.

"But you're so much better at it than we are." Apollon grinned showing all of his fanged teeth.

Who finds that shit attractive anyway?

But he bucked up and moved to the kitchen. It was no problem to cook extra and he was really bored as hell. Charle had already framed his preliminary article and he was just waiting for insights, first-hand experiences, and impressions from the group's fan base. Anyhow, he was just throwing ramen noodles in with some boiled eggs and frozen veggies. If one or two packs more got them to eat and then go away, he was willing to do it. So much for the theory that rockers ate like pampered celebrities while on the road.

There was a problem, though. So far the only thing

he had to report were inappropriate sex jokes at his expense and temper tantrums.

The life of a rock god was so glamorous.

* * *

Abadon sat back at his desk and ran fingers through his hair, tugging at the red and black strands absently.

Why, suddenly, was his life so complicated?

It was a fling, a fling that really didn't mean anything.

He was horny, he'd wanted to get laid. He got laid. End of story.

So why was it that he found himself pining away for a man that he never got a good look at, never met before, and would probably never see again. He barely remembered the woman. When did she leave?

Abadon had had plenty of men and women in his life. When he was known as Nargal, he ruled all with an iron fist, his seven pleiades warriors answering his every call, even if it was in the bedroom.

He missed those days when life was simple. You made war, you defeated your enemy, you took a lover or three, humans worshiped you, and repeat. It was easy in Ancient Sumer to coexist peacefully with humans as long as they did what you told them to do and generally they were too scared not to.

His people lovingly worshiped his body and increased his power base tenfold, giving him the power to escape his crazy wife, Ereshkigal. Arranged marriages were a thing, but he had to defeat that woman or lose his head. So he pulled her off her throne by her hair and took what he wanted. Nargal always took what he wanted. And he wound up ruling the underworld until he got bored.

So he got away from crazy and went back to causing plagues against the humans when they got too plentiful and mouthy or coordinating battles so that the humans could kill each other off.

Truly, one of the reasons he still existed, along with a host of other war gods, was that humans really loved killing. They loved it almost as much as they loved fucking and that was saying something. They worshiped those who led them into battle.

That was why one of the legendary deities of the Babylonian empire was now a rock star...all the worship.

One concert singing about carnage could give him a power boost that he hadn't felt since he was leading his warriors into the slaughter, getting covered with the blood and guts of his enemies.

The man he'd allowed to fuck him so good was not into the sex for what he could get out of him. He wasn't thinking about money or reputation or the praise he would get from bragging to his friends. There weren't many people alive who could say they fucked the god Nargal... now Abadon, god of plague and destruction, and that he was one few that who fucked him out of sheer joy and the pleasure of the act. That was something Abadon hadn't experienced in years.

He wanted more.

He was becoming obsessed.

He looked down at the words he had written, the words that were coming from his heart, not modernized epic battle tales of gore, and he wondered where this was heading.

He wondered what his seven would do.

Of course his Pleiades were still alive. The vicious little buggers were now his managers and lawyers, tearing down the entertainment world so that their god would always rise above the rest. He loved them dearly, but they were the reason he had been attempting to take the band in a different direction.

The band wanted to appeal to a more feminine demographic and that meant ballads. He hated ballads.

The break after their American tour was supposed to be all about developing a new sound. It was something that he fought against but if he wanted to keep free and easy worship, he had to conform, to adapt of die off the way that so many hard rockers and gods had done before him.

Of course Hash, or rather Nabu, was all for it. Abadon rolled his eyes at the thought of the god of wisdom and writing and his opinions on how to move the band forward. He was all about the romance and flowers and sharing courtly love. The women ate it up. It made him want to puke. But Hash had enlisted Apollon, and the god of mischief and intelligence had seen an opportunity to make his life difficult. Enk was an asshole, but he was intelligent and he loved to create new things. A new sound for the band was right up his alley.

Python couldn't care less. He was Sin, the god of the moon and all he wanted to do was stay up and party all night.

So the band was going to mix up their usual catalogue and he wasn't in the best of moods about it.

That night at The Stage, he just wanted a good hard fuck to help him forget that he was going to be doing something he loathed and making that announcement made it a done deal.

That brought him right back to the human he allowed to fuck his body a few nights ago.

He wished he had gotten his name.

There was something so uninhibited about that man. It had been dark in the room and he had just walked in.

It scared the weak fuck who was doing his best to work a number on his ass into a permanent state of limpness. But the stranger had eagerly took the limp fucker's place, something not many men would do without convincing, and had exceeded expectations.

Abadon even made sure he got the woman he was

fucking off before he lost himself in the other man.

The guy touched him like he was vulnerable, something that could be easily hurt, something delicate. Even his lover Laz had not treated him so tenderly and she thought he was made of sunshine and flower petals.

His mysterious fucker had traced every crevasse of his body, tenderly nipped at his neck, massaged his muscles, and damn near ripped his hair out of his head in the most loving way possible.

He gave him such a fucking buzz and Abadon erupted like he hadn't since the orgies he hosted thousands of years ago.

Now, that human was gone and he left no way to contact him.

He could place an ad in the paper, *Rock god seeks to reconnect with the guy who fucked him through the desk backstage at The Stage. Tall, slim, with fat dick. You filled in where the other guy couldn't. Me, fucked into ecstasy. Call me, maybe?*

The tabloids would have a field day and his seven would try to have his balls.

So here he was, stuck on a tour bus writing out his feelings about some guy he didn't know other than in the biblical sense and going mad because of it.

He looked down at the paper, at the title, *The One That Got Away*, and shook his head at his own sorry state of affairs.

All this upheaval because of a good fuck. Maybe it was good that he couldn't find the guy, because if just screwing around did this to him, who knew what prolonged exposure could lead to...a boyfriend? Monogamy? A real relationship?

Yeah, maybe it was better that the mystery man remained a mystery. Too bad he couldn't get him off of his mind and ignore the small voice in the back of his head telling him that all mysteries were created to be solved.

Chapter 4

Essential to every Rock Star is his entourage. But strangely enough, Abadon doesn't subscribe to the notion of having scantily clad groupies following them wherever they go. They make do with each other, their driver, and a strangely huge albino python once named Human.
~Charle Lexington, Abadon, the Fallen Ones

Charle Lexington was going deaf.

Seriously, he was sure he had lost his hearing by the second sound check. Despite the ear protectors that the management of the arena insisted he wear, he could hear the screaming of the guitars and the even louder screaming of front man Adabon as he went through his set for that night's show. He had never been so happy as to get out of that confusion and to a nice quiet hotel room.

He, Abadon, and the gang, were staying at a hotel not one mile away from the venue, that promised hot tubs, a full bar, room service, and most importantly, a bed without wheels. Sleeping on a pullout couch was no fun at his age and Charle's back was making its displeasure known. So knowing that he was going to sleep in a real bed in a real building was a godsend.

They had been rushed into the hotel via a service entrance in the rear, then rushed up to the floor that was reserved in their honor.

Charle could understand the need for a whole floor for security issues, but the guys behaved as if their safety was a forgone conclusion and nothing would ever do them any harm.

"Hotel floor party," Apollon called out as they exited the massive freight elevator that was reserved for employees and people sneaking in and out. The manager proudly led them ahead once they exited the huge metal box, a wide grin on her face. She rambled on as she was followed by the crew of heathens plus Charle, as she spoke of amenities they could offer.

"We have private masseuses and massage therapy specialists who can be called upon any hour of the day or night. Happy Endings not provided," she snickered.

No one laughed.

"Oookay...You have a personal chef who has already been made aware of food preferences and any medical needs that you may have. Your manager was really specific about your need for fresh unfiltered spring water. Chemicals get to you, huh? Ruins you vocal cords?"

Abadon glared down at her from his advanced height and her smile slowly began to dim. Charle almost felt sorry for her... almost. Bubbly people need to learn to not be so bubbly when the folks you're talking to look like they are dead on their feet.

"Well, your floor has a balcony with privacy screens, an outside Jacuzzi and infinity pool that overlooks the beautiful manicured gardens --"

"If you do less talking and more walking, I'm sure we can all go do better things with our time," Apollon spoke, his deep voice rumbling like the rock of ages, and the manager blushed a little patting her perfectly tight and perfectly respectable hair knot.

"I was just informing you of all the --"

"Inform us of our room numbers and please know that we thank you for your time and efforts on our parts. But we are really tired, we went right from the road to practice, and we need to rest up for tomorrow's concert."

Python was polite and professional -- who knew? -- and the tension that was building in the manager visibly eased.

"I'm so sorry," she gushed a little as the redhead winked at her. "You all must be exhausted and here I am going on..."

She trailed off as they reached what Charle assumed

was the middle of the floor. There was only one wide set of double doors. He looked to the left and right and unless there were other doors further down the line, it looked like access to everything was achieved through one entranceway.

"Your tech people arrived earlier and are on a floor below yours," she said as she pressed her palm against a glass window and opened the double doors with flourish.

"The only one who can use the palm print access in staff is me. "She spoke as she typed at a keypad located on the foyer wall. "And if you'll indulge me for a moment, I can get your prints on file so there will be no need to key or card access, though you will be supplied with a key card as well."

She stood back and one by one, like good little schoolboys, the guys stepped up and pressed their palms against the window until it happily beeped and flashed green.

Charle was about to start examining the room when Abadon himself spoke to him.

"Charles. You need to get your hand scanned,"

Charle blinked and spun round in surprise. In the three days he had been with the band, Abadon had not bothered to have a conversation with him, let alone speak his name. The sound of it spoken in that dark purring tone threw him for a moment so he didn't immediately respond.

"Charles? We don't have time for this bull. Get over here and press your palm to the window."

Jumping, Charle complied, and he must have looked a little dazed because Abadon opted to explain further.

"Look, I know you have to be around us but I refuse to have to drag my ass up here every time you feel the need to shit in private or beat one off because you need to relate to yourself."

"I can relate," Apollon called out, always the biggest

asshole.

Abadon continued, "It just makes sense to set it up so you can come and go as you please. We have a two fucking days here and I'm not going to cater to you like you're some pampered princess. So press your fucking hand to the window so we can find a bed. I'm wiped."

Narrowing his eyes, Charle ignored the small meep from the manager as he slammed his palm to the window.

"First of all," he began, his patience at an end, "I know how to take care of myself. I don't need you to hold my hand as I go about my job. I can adapt because that's how we survive. That has never been my issue. And if you think I need your permission to jack off --"

"It's not like you got anyone to do it for you," Abadon growled and for a moment a shaft of pain flew through Charle's heart. Was he really turning out to be that unfuckable? Granted, he was wearing sleep pants and a band T-shirt, but he cleaned up pretty well.

Bravado to the rescue once again. "If I wanted someone, I could get someone." He glared harder at Abadon, not seeing the rocker but a taller larger version of his ex.

"Yeah, right," Abadon sniffed. "People talk, your producer boyfriend talked, and I research. I know all about you, Charles Lexington, and your lack of a social life. One of the reasons we chose you is we didn't have to worry about you fucking around and bringing groupies back to fuck on our reputation. Not that someone as uptight as you would."

Oh, that tore it as far as Charle was concerned. "Fuck you, Abadon," he growled, taking a step closer to the glowering tower of muscle and flesh.

"Not even on your best day."

"Okay," the manager interjected, looking from the amused faces of the band to the irate expression on

Charle's face, to the downright annoyed one on Abadon. "I'm just gonna put your key cards on the table and leave you to sort out your room assignments. There are five bedrooms in this suite as requested and I want you all to have a nice stay here with us. Bye now."

Then she was gone and with her went a lot of tension in the room, though Charle and Abadon were still glaring at each other.

"You have got to be the most annoying fucker I ever had the misfortune to be around." Charle's parting shot was heated as he snatched up a card and stormed into the suite, ignoring the band as he slammed into the first room he saw.

"Fuck them," he growled. "Fuck Abadon and fuck my fucking life."

He threw himself face down on the bed and contemplated screaming into his pillow but that was a bit too juvenile. Talking himself down was all he could do to stop himself from going back there, throwing a punch. He'd get his ass kicked for being unprofessional and starting a fight with a man who looked like he bench pressed Buicks as a hobby.

This job was going to kill him.

He lay back on the bed, closed his eyes and dreamed of his mystery man.

God, he remembered how perfect he was. Those very good thoughts had the wonderful effect of giving him another outlet for his frustrations. His dick grew hard in his pants as he thought of the perfection of that encounter.

It was dark and hot in that room, but all he could remember was the feel of that silky flesh underneath his hands, the softness of his hair, the way his body opened and accepted him as he fucked him through the desk.

Before he could think twice about it, his pants were down around his knees and his hand was pumping his dick dry. God, yes the burn was beautiful.

He remembered the sound the man made as he sank into that perfect hole. He thought of how hungry his ass was as he pulled his cheeks apart to get him deeper.

How such a huge, powerful man submitted to him.

He didn't have a face, only the shadows, but it took very little for him to imagine Abadon on his knees before him. Yeah, he would love to shove his dick into that smart-assed mouth and choke him with it.

No, he wanted to make him suck it, make him beg like his mystery man. Make him plead and whimper as he slapped him in the face with his cock. He wanted to slide his balls into that hot wet mouth and make him suck them hard. Abadon was beautiful, but he would look so much better on his knees sucking his cock.

His hand was moving faster as he pictured his nemesis begging for it, gagging for his cock. Yeah, he would give it to him, too. He would take him face to face so he could stare into those black eyes and see them hungry for him. He would take it so good. He would beg and cry, tear at the sheets as he offered his body up to Charles. And he would fuck him right too, make sure he hit his sweet spot, make him see stars as the tight body bounced under him.

Yeah, to hear that perfect voice scream his name...

He was arching up into each thrust now, making no effort to stifle his own moans. He tugged at his balls, rolling them in his hands and hissing at the slight pain that only enhanced his pleasure. Precum was flowing easing his movements as he threw back his head and gave into the fantasy. Yes, he was dominating that man, closing his smart-assed mouth while his friends looked on in awe. Abadon was clawing at him, begging for more as he threw his legs over his shoulders and slammed deeper, slapping at that perfect ass as he made sure he wouldn't sit comfortably for at least a week. Yes, Abadon with his mouth open, panting, writhing in ecstasy only he could give...

"Fuck," he hissed as he felt his orgasm rush over him. His hips locked up and his ass clenched as he shot his load over his stomach. He pumped himself through his release, finally relaxing back on the bed without an ounce of shame or guilt.

He really wanted to fuck that man senseless if only to get him to stop talking.

* * *

"I'm just shocked by the lack of prostitutes, and groupies, and drugs." Apollon snickered.

"Hotel party later?" Hash asked as the others nodded and a silent Abadon stalked ahead of us toward his own room.

"Yeah, now's the time to cut loose and swing wild. We have fun now that the work's done," Hash intoned, the beads in his braids clacking as he turned to look at Abadon.

"Not that Buzz Killington over there --"Apollon pointed to their front man --"would know anything about that."

"I have fun," Abadon growled back, pausing in his flight for privacy. He was dressed in a plain black T-shirt, a pair of worn-out looking jeans that cupped his ass just right, and a pair of sheepskin slippers.

"If you consider fun fucking with the one person who has never done you wrong," Apollon sing-sang as he moved deeper into the room. "Nice digs."

The suite was nice. It was huge, but nice. There was the foyer where they were standing and then deeper into the room was a step down living room complete with fire place.

On the other side of that was a huge bar, the promised balcony with the swimming pools, hot tub, and a pretty view.

Inside, there was a library, an audio corner complete with speakers and a small stage, and on top of that, there were several sitting areas laid out with couches and tables, all nice and semi -private.

"He's annoying," Abadon grumbled, not sure what it was about the tall skinny man that set him off.

"Only when you fuck with him."

"You fuck with him," Abadon pointed out and Apollon rolled his eyes.

"With, as in I only give as good as I get. It's all done in fun. You, on the other hand, seem to have some vendetta against the poor bugger. Let him do his job and stop riding his ass so hard."

"It's not like you." Dash stepped in, his beads in his braids clanking as he took his keycard and stepped further into the room. "Have you been working too hard?"

"I -- I am working --"

"Look, if you need help with the lyrics, all you have to do is ask." Dash was magical like that. "I know that we write most of the lyrics together, so if you need a spotter, man --"

"No," Abadon shook his head before running a frustrated hand though his hair. "No. I can do it. It was my decision to allow The Seven to do this and if I'm going to be singing from the heart, it has to be from my heart."

"Okay," Hash nodded, turning down the hall to hunt for his own room. "But if it gets bad don't take it out on the kid. I think he has enough problems without you throwing his past up in his face."

"Problems?" Abadon hadn't noticed that.

"You're right, we did the research, but we just didn't listen to what the money people said. He's a solid reporter, never did a hatchet job on anyone he interviewed. He's fair and objective and that comes from

- 45 -

some of the big names he has on his resume. His problems are social and he didn't need you throwing that up in his face."

"His ex was at The Stage starting some shit," Python added, petting his snake. "Rumor has it that he threw a punch after the guy called him frigid or some bullshit. Charle-boy broke his nose and then slipped out the back."

"Charles Lexington?" Abadon asked, eyebrow rising in disbelief. "The man who just threw a tantrum and flounced out of here?"

"Yes, Charle Lexington, and from what I understand, it was deserved."

"Charle's not so bad." Apollon moved over to the bar. "Got a real sense of humor on him, once you get past the façade. That man is going to snap if he doesn't stop repressing himself. He just needs to let go and that's hard to do when you have an ex spreading rumors around. I mean our world is small, relatively, and Charle's a part of that world. He can't get men interested in him if a major player in our sphere keeps fucking with him."

"He doesn't need you adding to the pressure." Hash moved to the bar beside Apollon and reached for a bottle of rum. "You requested him, so treat him with some respect. Betrayal is a real fucked-up thing and I'm not even getting into the crazy ex…"

That was something Abadon could relate to, betrayal and the crazy ex.

He sighed deeply before turning towards a door that would lead to the master bedroom.

Maybe he would go and apologize. Just because his life suddenly seemed so confusing didn't mean he had to make someone else miserable too. Tomorrow morning he would make it right.

Chapter 5

There was a party going on and Charle was proving just how boring he was by editing in his room.

Not to say that it was irresponsible of him. It was his job to report events as they happened with the world's most famous rock legends. Still there he was... sitting in his room and revisiting parts of the *AP Guide* to make sure his copy editor didn't have fits.

"What the hell is wrong with you?" he muttered to himself before rising to his bare feet. He went to his window with its beautiful views of the back forty and cracked it open only to be hit with a wave of sound that almost knocked him flat on his ass.

True to their earlier promises, the boys of Abadon were cutting loose.

He could hear the laughing of men and women, the clanking of glass bottles, and the sound of a good time happening.

And still he was sitting in his room contemplating jerking off for the third time.

Images of his fantasy man made him grin.

He had pulled on that long hair, slapped that plush round ass, and fucked that hole into next week.

He did everything but get a good look at the man's face, but somehow the darkness made the event more mysterious and dangerous. It made him feel more alive.

Charle knew himself and knew that he wasn't a one-night stand kind of guy. Ultimately, he wanted a solid relationship. He wasn't talking marriage and kids, because he wasn't sure he was the type, but he wanted to come home and have someone waiting for him, someone who he didn't have to break out the condoms for, someone he could trust.

His past relationships were proof enough that he wasn't good at choosing partners who wanted a little longevity in their lives.

But that in no way, shape or form meant that he had a stick up his ass or was ultraconservative.

He wasn't like that at all, he just wasn't one for the whole sex, drugs, and rock and roll thing.

Yet he was sure that there was sex, drugs and rock and roll taking place outside his door and he had yet to go out and seek out the truth of the matter.

Abadon's words stung and as much as he would like to say he was filled with bullshit and tattoo ink, there was a ring of truth to his words and that's what hurt the most.

Abadon was wrong in one major respect. He could get laid if he wanted to.

He thought about it for a moment, and then decided yes, he was in the mood to get laid.

Time to sexy up.

Charle was in no way vain about his looks. He knew he was a pretty average looking guy, but he knew how to play up his hot points.

He stripped off his loose T-shirt and replaced it with a tight tank top. He was slim, not skinny, and all of his stress relieving work outs had given muscle to frame. He was tight and toned and his six pack was nothing to sneeze at. He had one thing that most guys worked their asses off to get, the low ring of muscle around his lower hips, the treasured Adonis belt, and his was defined.

So to that end, he pulled out a loose pair of plain gray sweatpants sans underwear.

He slid the soft fleece up his corded thighs and his rounded ass, letting it settle just below his navel, giving a good look at his shocking musculature and the tiny treasure tail of thin hair that ran up to his navel.

That done, he ran his fingers through his hair, pulling it out of the tight bun he habitually wore to keep it all contained. He let his wild afro puff up to its fullest, tugging at the coiled locks of hair which seemed to take on a life of its own, picking up red and gold in the dark brown color.

A quick application of coconut oil and shea butter lotion on his elbows and hands, after all no one found dry ashy skin sexy, and he skid his narrow feet into his slippers.

He made sure his emerald stud earrings were in place, two sets in each ear, and he was ready to go.

Confidently, he stepped outside of his door... and immediately wanted to run back.

Why was he doing this? He had nothing to prove to anyone. He was a grown man and... and... was that the buzz of a tattoo gun?

He always wanted to get some ink. He was the only one in the office with virgin skin and he had wanted to change that for years.

The draw of body modification drew him in. He wanted ink.

He sped down the hall and into what a roman orgy must have looked like.

Every flat surface was filled with food and booze. There were several of the most beautiful people he had ever seen standing around in all levels of undress, some only a throw pillow hiding their lack of modesty. The music was pumping.

Someone had brought in a DJ and he was spinning tunes in the corner, a mixture of rock and hip hop, and strange electronic music. He hated EDM, it always gave him a migraine, but there was that tattoo buzz.

"I hate to see a man without a drink in his hand." Charle jumped as a woman who smelled like flowers and weed whispered in his ear.

He jerked around to see her with a bottle of Jack in one hand and an empty glass in the other.

As he watched, she poured a generous amount of the golden liquor into the glass and held it out to him.

She was really pretty. She had big brown eyes and a clear dark complexion. Her ass was round enough to make him want to drop and do squats and her breasts … in another life, he would be goo-goo gaa-gaaing and trying to get one in his mouth. Her tits were high and firm and jiggled just so under her thin dark tank top. Her nipples were perky.

Stunned that women like this existed outside of music videos, he stared.

"He won't take it," a gravelly voice snorted and Charle looked to his left to see Abadon in all his glory, in repose on a leather settee. In repose was the only way to describe the man who lay there like a barbarian king. He leaned up against the lone arm, his muscular body on display in a tight pair of leather pants and that's all. His feet were bare again and there were several golden toe rings encircling the long narrow toes.

Around him were several beautiful men and women imbibing only god knows what while their beady little eyes were judging him.

"Charles's straight edge," Abadon continued, tossing back a shot of some clear liquid and smirking in his direction.

"Fuck you, Abadon." Charle growled before grabbing the bottle from the amused woman and taking a huge swig.

"Way to go, Charle!" Hash called out from his corner where he was spinning a drumstick in one hand, making it dance between his fingers.

"You show him what for!" Apollon called from his spot between the knees of some woman who was playing in his hair. "You do what you want, man. I'll back you up."

Rolling his eyes, Charle took another swig from his bottle and the woman who approached him shrugged and took a sip from the glass before making her way back to Abadon and taking the coveted spot leaning against his chest. His hand dropped around her waist and he raised an eyebrow as he stared back.

Putting the asshole out of his mind for a moment, Charle turned toward the sound of the tattoo gun.

Like a moth drawn to a flame he moved in closer, the bottle swinging loosely from his hand. All thought of getting laid was pushed aside for the siren call of body art.

Charle wanted to ink up his person. He didn't need a full body monstrosity that created a confusion of color and shape. That wasn't for him. He knew he was thin and if anyone envied him for his metabolism, he would gladly trade places with them. Oh, to be warm in the winter… but that was going completely off topic.

Charle, for as long as he could remember, wanted art on his body. When he was a teen he was too nerdy and frightened to venture into the shady world that was tattoo shops. His only experience with them had come from fiction novels and action movies where the tattoo shops were always seedy dives with rough talking biker stereotypes doling out ass whippings and bright red ink.

In college he learned the truth, that tattoo shops were cleaner than some of the hospital rooms he'd been in. Then the holdup was the cost.

He was a starving student and couldn't afford off-campus housing, food, books, and the occasional part for his Firebird. Good ink cost, he discovered when he worked up the nerve to talk to a tattooist.

Ink was again put off because he was too busy flying out and doing interviews and then it just became habit to push tattoo plans on the back burner. But if someone was slinging ink right this very moment…

He moved closer and saw that the tattooist was a blue-haired pixie of an Asian man with the cutest pair of Buddy Holly glasses and a small ring in his bottom lip.

The woman squirming under his gun was getting the Abadon symbol tattooed on her back. Charle thought that she was going to regret getting that in a few years if the band fell off or her taste changed, but he was wise enough to keep his mouth shut. The gothic-looking viking sword wreathed in ice blue and glowing green looked bad as hell though.

"Tell me you don't want to get the same thing in a tribal band," the artist grumped, looking up from the small of the fangirl's back. His gloves were a bright purple, the same color of his eyes.

"Uh --" What to say to that.

"He won't get it done." Abadon's voice coming from behind him made Charle leap about a foot in the air before he turned around and glared at the singer.

"And why is that?" Charle asked.

"Because you're not the type."

"Like you know --"

"Oh, I know," Abadon ran his hands through his hair before looking back over at him. "I know your type, Goody-goody. Never done anything daring in your whole life."

"Fat lot you know," Charle sneered. "I've done a lot of wild things."

"That second piece of cheesecake at dinner don't count."

"Why are you riding my case?" Charle asked, sincerely now. "Do I remind you of someone you hate?"

"No," Adadon huffed, giving himself an all over shiver before his shoulders sagged and he began to speak again. "No. You... just... I don't know. I tend to get a feel for people and you're trouble in khaki pants and a polo top."

"Oh no you just didn't put me in the uniform of the alt-right --"

"Those assholes? If I even thought that you were like

that you wouldn't get a foot anywhere near me. You just... you're just too good."

"I am not."

"Stop pretending to be someone you're not," Abadon growled. "That's the thing that pisses me off the most. You all come in with your uptight ways trying to blend in with the rest of the Locusts --"

"Wait! What?"

"Locusts." Abadon grinned then, showing all his perfect teeth before standing and waving his arms, gesturing to everyone who filled the room. "Locusts!" he shouted.

"Devour! Devour! Devour!" The room chanted before exploding into claps and cheers.

"Those are my people." Abadon spun in a small circle and Charle swore he grew about a foot taller as he basked in the cheers from his adoring fans. "I need them and they need me. We feed off of each other and we are honest about what we want."

"Right," Charle snorted. "Like there aren't some doctors and school teachers in this crowd."

"Probably are," Adabon allowed as someone called out, "I'm a psychologist!"

"I'm a proctologist!" the hot chick with the afro called out and for a moment, Charle just stared. Did she own a strap on? She would have no problem finding the prostate --

"Point is," Adabon pulled Charle's attention back to himself as he moved next to him. "They are honest about what they want and what they are here for. They are not pretenders. You -- I don't know. You seem like a pretender."

"So, your highness, you came all this way over here, leaving your throne and your proctologist, just to get in my face? Don't you have a life or something?"

"I'm trying to figure you out."

"Figure out this," Charle snapped, growing angry at Abadon's assumptions. "I'm living my life, doing my job, and occasionally, I have been known to let my hair down --" he ignored Adadon's laughter, growing more angry by the second. "I happen to be a fun person."

"You look like fun," the tattooist commented, sitting up from where he was hunched over the woman's back, wiping her down with a paper towel after spraying a sharp smelling fluid on her back. "Especially if you don't want another Abadon flaming sword."

"He won't do it." Abadon smirked at the tattoo on the girl who spun around so that the artist could tape some clear film over her tattoo. "He's not the type."

Charle could feel the heat rush to his face as his inner voice demanded that he put this so-called rock god in his place.

Abadon leaned in close and whispered, "You're the type to run crying in your pillow while your ex fucks anything that moves. You have done nothing exciting or spontaneous in your whole damn life. You got the high-impact action-filled job but don't do shit but kiss stars's asses and scold them like babies when they do stuff that you don't like. You're a poser, Charle. A god damned cold fish who judges people. I look at you and wonder how such an okay body and a kind of cute face could have such a dead personality. You're dead inside, aren't you, Charle-boy? Just a little old scaredy-cat standing on the outside, too weak to ask to come in. You watch the others and are jealous, aren't you, Charle? You want to be what we are but that's a fucking joke because all you are is dead inside. All the want, all the desire and no drive to get it yourself, waiting for a hand to invite you in. But guess what, Charle-boy? That hand will never come. You gonna be forever on the outside wanting in. That's why you took this job, isn't it? To be close to what you want but will never have. Am I right, Charle, or am I right?"

Charle froze as his heart began to pound in his chest. Suddenly he was very afraid and felt very stupid in his clinging tank top and loose sweat pants. He *was* scared. He had the high powered job, but always stood on the sidelines, existing on the fringe. And Abadon saw that clearly. His eyes burned and he had to resist the urge to cry. He was a fake, a fraud, and there was nothing exciting about him. Maybe Dick and the others had been right. He was cold and stiff and no one really wanted him.

He felt something inside him snap and shatter as he realized that what Abadon said was true. He wanted to run and hide. He could feel the eyes of all in the room watching him. They couldn't hear what Abadon said to him, but he could imagine they knew, that their god was calling out an infidel in their midst. Too quiet, too strange, too queer, he would never fit in.

Slowly, he lifted the bottle of Jack with his shaking hands… and poured that shit all over Adadon's head.

Fuck him.

Yup, that voice inside him was back and it screamed Fuck Abadon sideways with a chainsaw.

He heard the Locusts gasp in horror as Abadon jerked back, his eyes wide in shock as whiskey dripped over his head and face, making him look like the victim of a low budget water sports scene in a really cheap porno.

The look suited the bastard.

"Told you he had balls," Apollon called out in the stunned silence of the room, quickly followed by Hash's booming laughter.

Snorting, Abadon threw back his head and roared with laughter. "Now it's a party!" he shouted and the Locusts began to chant, "Devour! Devour! Devour!"

Flinging his whiskey-fragrant hair back, Abadon stalked from the room, leaving a stunned Charle standing in front of an equally stunned tattoo artist, an empty bottle of Jack dangling from his fingers. That was a shame because now he could really use a shot.

"Fuck, dude," the blue haired pixie laughed. "After that, anything you want on your body will be bad ass! You can get a purple and pink unicorn fucking over a rainbow bridge while dicks explode in the background and it would be fuckin' metal."

"I --" Charle stammered as Python, with the ever-present nameless snake wrapped around his neck, pounded him on the back with approval.

"You gotta get some ink, dude, commemorate the moment."

"I -- I don't know what --" Charle stuttered, but tattoo guy took over.

"Let me give you an original piece," he all but begged. "I'm seeing a tribal piece on your shoulder, asymmetrical, with a hidden lion crawling up your arm because you are fierce! You are fire, dude, so some red accents and some green... the lion's eyes. They have to be green to match yours."

"I don't --"

"Yes!" Apollon was suddenly in his face. "Yes! Do that, Siou! No matter how long it takes!"

"But..." Charle tried to speak again, What the hell just happened?

"You beat Adabon at his own game," Apollon laughed. "I don't know what he said to you, but it looked like he deserved it. And now he's in the corner licking his wounds."

His fans were actually licking off the whiskey that dribbled down his bare chest. Why were all the beautiful ones assholes?

At that moment, Abaadon looked up at him and smirked, and that voice inside his head came roaring back with a vengeance. He turned to the blue haired Siou. "Let's do this."

Those around him roared in approval and Python, in one movement, ripped his tank top from his body. It happened so fast, Charle looked down to see if he still had nipples attached. The remains of his shirt were tossed into the room and he was urged down into a chair.

"Gonna do this freehand." Siou grinned at him. "Somebody get this man a drink. He's going to need it."

Chapter 6

He didn't know why he was fucking with the kid so much. It was a compulsion.

Abadon sat on his settee, surrounded by those who worshipped at the altar of his stardom, and contemplated the kid getting his body inked.

While he enjoyed the attention and the praise that was being heaped upon him, he couldn't help letting his mind wander to the curious puzzle of Charle.

There was something about the kid… maybe the way he smelled or the way his eyes seemed to peer into his soul, but he was undeniably drawn to the son of a bitch.

He should not have taunted the little bastard like he had, but seeing him standing there, looking all kinds of scared and desirable and so freaked… he had to do something.

He hadn't meant to insult him like he had, but the devil in him made him want to destroy him, just a little.

There was a goodness in Charle, a determination that he hadn't seen in many a century and that for some reason annoyed him.

Maybe it was his voice.

Yeah, that was it. There was something of it that reminded him of his one-night stand.

He sighed and leaned back as someone he didn't know won the privilege of sucking the whiskey off his chest. He lay back and let it happen, noting that the soft tongue on his nipple was agile and knowing, but nothing like what his one that got away could do with his.

That was a night to remember. He felt his pants get much tighter as his cock began to bloat with the memories.

His lost lover had been amazing, his slim body writhing like a snake. The feel of the high rounded cheeks of his ass flexing as he fucked into him…

Maybe that's what it was. The kid was a similar build.

My Lost One... that was a good name for a ballad. Goodness knows he suddenly had a lot of experience with regret and letting the good one go.

That big night had been crazy. He'd been angry at the seven, tired of touring, and in a general bad mood.

The muscle boy in the greenroom looked like sin wrapped in leather so he eagerly took him up on his obvious invitation to get laid, thinking that maybe a good solid fucking would make everything all right.

From the way the fuck-boy licked his lips and palmed at his crotch, he thought that man knew what he was about. He had never been so disappointed that the packaging didn't match the advertisement. The man couldn't even keep an erection, blew off ten seconds after he got him in his mouth and started palming his hard round balls.

No bragging, but he knew he was that good so he exerted a tiny bit of power to bring him back to full hardness and with the edge off, he thought that he would be getting a wild ride.

But hard muscle didn't mean he knew what he was doing when it came to sex. Great sky, the man was bad. He choked pitifully when he slid his dick into the sucker's mouth, and sucker was being generous. He whimpered and licked a little at the head of his cock, like he was scared and then tried to impale himself on the rest. Abadon felt obligated to stop him before he threw up in his lap. Then when he reached back and touched the guy's tight ass, he tensed up, stiffened as if Abadon was trying to ram a tent pole up his hole when he'd barely even touched him.

Abadon could smell his fear and that made him want to kick the fool out because the mixed signals were killing his erection.

But the man begged to stay, said he could show him a good time, that he was merely intimidated by everything that was Abadon, so he did something he rarely did. Be it desperation to feel anything but the depression building up in him, he agreed to bend over and take a dick up his virtually virginal ass.

And what a disappointment that had been. He expected to top from the bottom, so to speak, but he didn't think he'd be getting Romper Room: Sex Edition. The man was horrible. He fumbled the condom, lost his erection just from the sight of Abadon bent over the desk fucking the chick. It was the main reason he turned the lights off and he had to prep himself with lube because the fool went off again after sinking one finger into his ass.

He got him up again, got a fresh condom, and with a determination to get some kind of stimulation out of the fucker, pushed him in the office chair and tried to take a ride on his cock, tried being the operative word. The fool had no rhythm and no idea what to do with his dick. Abadon was all set to kick him out and get himself off before frustration killed him when his Lost One walked in.

Lost one. That was a good song title too.

"Ouch!" The shout from Charle pulled him out of his musings and he sat back to at least enjoy this show.

He ran his hands though the hair of the person in front of him. It was the pretty little thing, whose afro reminded him of Charle's, who was nested between his legs and lapping at his nipple.

He had to admit he deserved the whiskey shampoo but he didn't think that Charle-boy'd had it in him, not when he smelled his fear. But he had rallied and dumped the whole fucking bottle over his head. It wasn't the worst thing he had ever been doused in over his centuries of life, but it was shocking that Charles would defend himself in this matter. All the people he talked to said that Charles Lexington was a good guy and a bit of a pushover, but that wasn't the vibe he was getting.

"Not the nipple!" Charles was frowning at Siou as the tattoo artist diligently worked over his light-brown skin, the tattoo gun buzzing somehow louder than the music that the DJ was spinning.

"I'm not," Siou insisted, never pausing in his inking. "I'm saving that one to be pierced --"

"Pierced?"

"Shh," Siou soothed. "It'll be bad-ass. Now stop moving. You're gonna make me mess up my lines."

Abadon chuckled as Charle froze, obediently allowing the tattoo artist to go about his work.

The kid had a wild streak. Maybe he would help bring it out, develop it more, help the kid reach his full potential. Yeah, that sounded good to him. And maybe that would help him forget about his Lost One.

That sounded like a plan. The education of one Charles Lexington was about to commence, whether he wanted it or not.

* * *

Charle endured.

Tattoos hurt, though he would never let any of those watching know. That would be bad for his new reputation as a wild child.

Right now, he maybe wanted to shed a few tears, but that was okay. For the past few hours this man had used his body like a pincushion and that was okay too. He was going to be topical if it killed him.

"Done." Siou, the blue haired tattoo artist finally sat back and shut his gun off. He rubbed at his back a bit and allowed Charle to shift from where he had been sitting.

His muscles ached and the right upper hemisphere of his body felt sunburnt, the parts that weren't numb. And his nipple... God help him, when he made noise about it earlier, Siou paused in his tattooing to actually clamp and pierce his nipple, much to the delight of the watchers.

He didn't say no though, thinking a little metal would be a great souvenir of his trip and unlike the tattoo, he could take it out later.

"Four hours man," Siou was saying, grinning like a loon as he got out the stinging spray and began to clean his arm, chest, and shoulder one more time. Frankly, the cleaning hurt more than the tattoo. "This is some of my best work."

"What do I owe you?" Charle felt compelled to ask.

"Not a damn thing. I've known Abadon for years, done this at his parties, and you would not believe what they pay. That's in addition to what I charge these assholes who keep getting flaming sword and locusts tattooed all over. Man, once I had to tattoo an anus. I don't care if it was bleached and cleaned beforehand, that was fuckin' weird."

Charle blinked at those words, truly not believing what he'd just heard.

"Oh yeah, it happened," Siou chuckled, pulling out a large hand mirror and holding it up so Charle could finally see his work. "Charged her an extra two hundred to do it too. She paid up so it was all good in the end. In the end, get it?"

Charle would have laughed at Siou's words but he caught a glimpse of his ink and his mouth fell open.

There was an elegant swoosh of a wave surrounding his nipple. It rose up and blended with other waves up over his chest to his shoulder where they began to form the most intricate and dainty celtic knots that he had ever seen.

There were sharp lines that emphasized the size and shape of his pecs, but the lines were not so thick as to make his tight frame look skinny. There were blank places of flesh that the black ink didn't cover and they made an interesting pattern on his upper pec that did resemble a roaring lion. The wave and knot pattern continued over his shoulder and down his bicep, encircling it and making it look decidedly masculine despite the use of the swirls and thin lines. The knot pattern got thicker as it trailed down his arm, stopping just below his elbow, the pattern original, elegant, and powerful as hell. As promised, the tattoo was done in all black and gray, the only spot of color was as promised, the bright green eye of the lion that perfectly matched the color of Charle's eyes.

"Wow --"

Then there were camera flashes that blinded him after Siou put down his mirror and pulled up a camera.

"I know, right?" he chuckled. "I always get some of my more interesting jobs here but you were a pleasure to work with."

More people began walking over and asking to take shots of his arm and Charle, in a daze agreed. He was staring down at his arm and shoulder, amazed that he could be wearing such beautiful art, when a hard hand patted him roughly on his back.

He looked up to see Hash standing there, a wide grin on his dark face.

"Somebody get his man a drink. He has heart."

There was a cheer and a glass was pushed into his hand.

"To virgin skin and having his ink cherry popped!" Siou called out and the room roared.

"To bravery, 'cause I would sure as hell not go through all of that in one sitting." Apollon called out to everyone's amusement.

"You should have gotten a snake," Python added, stroking his ever-present pet. "But that looks good."

And it did.

Charle felt something building inside of him as he stared down at his tattooed arm. It was an amazing feeling. He felt... free.

For the first time in a long time he felt like he was rebelling. No, this wasn't like taking journalism classes when his parents wanted him to do hard science. It wasn't like buying his dream car and getting her painted a cop magnet candy apple red. It was more profound. It felt like something deep inside of him was finally getting let out of its cage.

That little voice in his head, the one that had been urging him on this whole time was growing louder, taking over. That part of him that had frightened him into behaving like society wanted was gone and he was finally paying attention to the real him.

He was Charle Murdock Lexington, damn it, and he was not to be ignored anymore.

He was ten times better than any of those people who sought to hold him down and put him in his place. He was the hero of his own damn story and it was high time he started acting like it.

He hefted that shot in the air and tossed it back before demanding, "Another!"

And the crowd went wild.

For the first time since punching his ex in the face and fucking a complete stranger he was trying his best not to get hung-up on, Charle felt like he was his own man.

Charle Lexington was getting a life and nothing would stop him.

It felt glorious.

Someone handed him another drink which he downed. A joint was thrust at him and he toked. Some strange woman grabbed him by the back of his hair and pulled him down into a kiss filled with tongue and fire. The woman was pushed away and an even more enjoyable kiss delivered by some strange man with a mohawk and a pierced tongue. The party began to swirl around him.

There was dancing and coughing -- really he had never smoked weed before -- and more drinking. He was being passed around like a party favor and he was fine because he was doing quite a bit of passing himself.

His arm was sore, and his right nipple was throbbing, but he was having the time of his life.

And in the corner, he noticed Abadon on his throne of leather surrounded by his throng o' worshipers, watching in approval.

Then an idea so wicked, so nasty, so delicious took root in his head.

If he was going to go out, why not go out all the way.

He was going to fuck Abadon, his nemesis, and he was going to make the man love it.

Chapter 7

"I didn't believe you had it in you."

It was approaching something like dawn and he had no idea where he was. Charle decided that maybe it was a good time to open his eyes.

Open his eyes… Open…

"Where am I?" Was that twiddled dry croaking thing his voice? Damn his mouth was dry.

"Cotton mouth, huh?"

Cotton mouth? Oh yeah. From the drinking and the liberal use of non-medicinal weed.

"Here."

He felt something cold press against his hand and deciding that it might be a good time to make his eyeballs work, Charle squinted them open and immediately regretted it.

"Nope," he gasped and meant it. The sun was trying to kill him.

"Come on, Charle-boy," the voice taunted. "It's time to open those pretty green eyes. They were all kinds of wide open yesterday."

That voice… So Charle tried again and this time was more successful in keeping his eyes open, but most of his awareness had to do with a burning along the right side of his body and a powerful need to pee.

"There. We'll make a party boy out of you yet."

Very slowly he turned his head to the side and saw his worst nightmare.

"Not you," he croaked. "Too early for you."

"Now you've gone and hurt my feelings."

Abadon was going nowhere.

"God, what did I do to deserve this?"

"Fifteen shots of various liquors and those two joints you smoked."

Maybe that had something to do with it, Charle

reasoned, finally trying to rise to his feet. It was a painful process as his body just wanted to lay there and rot, but Charle persisted and soon found himself sitting upright on a lounger overlooking a pool.

He was in a suite with the band and there was a party and...

He looked down to his left, the bottle of cold water from Abadon lay cradled in one hand and saw his right arm was covered in plastic wrap.

The tattoo.

A grin pulled at the corners of his mouth as he placed the bottle on the chair beside him and began to unpeel the plastic from his arm.

It looked as badass as he remembered.

"So, you gonna survive?"

That voice drew his attention back to Abadon and any sarcastic thing he was about to say disappeared as his mouth dried out even further.

He had seen the man barefoot and defiant. He had seen him naked and irritated. He had never seen him freshly showered, wearing a pair of slippers and in a pair of thick cotton sleep pants.

His hair was damp and pulled back into a demure man-bun -- yes, a fucking man bun -- and he managed to wear it well.

With a few tendrils of hair falling down to frame a face free of makeup and arrogance, Abadon looked oddly vulnerable. It made his plan to fuck him seem crass, but that wasn't going to change his mind.

"Yeah," Charle shook his head and tried to answer. "I think I will."

"How's your head?"

"Oddly enough, my head's fine. Just thirsty." As if to demonstrate, he uncapped the bottle of water and turned it up, moaning in appreciation as he swallowed until it empty.

"I'm surprised at you, Charles. You hung in there with the big boys and partied like a rock star. Didn't think you had it in you."

"Shows you," Charle snorted, ignoring the fact that the man's crotch was merely feet away and at eye level. Pulling his eyes away from the soft bulge, he forced his eyes up to meet the man's face. "I told you I could party when I wanted to."

"Party?" Abadon chuckled, taking a seat on the lounger beside him. That was easier as Charle, didn't have to strain his eyes looking up but that also meant that he was now getting a closer look at those bulging muscles and the solid ink, and the pierced nipples. Can't forget the pierced nipples. His mouth went dry again and he looked down a little pitifully at his empty water bottle. "That wasn't a party."

Charle's eyes opened uncomfortably wide.

"That was a gathering of some friends and associates. That wasn't what I'd consider a party."

Abadon laughed as Charle continued to gape at him. Charle tried to ignore the way his Adam's apple bobbed and his broad shoulders shook as he roared in amusement. The man was too handsome by half.

Charle wanted to push him in the pool, but he knew he would have to get a running start and he didn't have it in him yet.

"It was an intimate party."

"Party!" Abadon laughed a little softer this time as Charle stared on in disbelief. "You're gonna learn."

Of course it was a real party. There was the drinking and the drugs. At some point there was dancing and finger foods. There was nudity and two guys tried to out-twerk two girls. Charle distinctively remembered bending one guy over and dry humping the hell out of him to the beat of the music as doe eyes stared back at him and he was sure that person was his tattoo artist

Siou.

He was quite sure at some point, he had his dick in someone's mouth while he observed two girls and a guy on the floor prove that hetero sex was just as moist and juicy as he remembered. And there were body shots! Of course it was a party.

Everything had quieted again but this time Charle felt like he was being zapped with electricity as Abadon's black eyes stared at him.

"You really wanna party, Charle-boy?"

There was a change in Abadon's tone, his voice was deeper, his attention fully on him. There was something dangerous dancing in those odd black eyes and Charle felt his heart drop.

There was the swelling in his groin and for a moment he wanted to drop his hands and hide his growing erection.

But that's what the old Charle would do. This new Charle wanted to take that bull by the horns and ride him off into the sunset. The voice in his head was cheering him on and the old him quivered at the thought of letting go fully.

"'Cause if you want, I can make that happen."

"What's the cost?" He wasn't foolish enough to think that anyone got something out of this world without paying. He just wanted to know if he was going to be financially, emotionally, and morally bankrupt by the time this job was done.

"Why do you think there's a cost?" As he spoke, everything around them seemed to freeze, time seemed to be holding its breath and Abadon's look got more intense.

Suddenly he wanted to be honest, to lay all his cards on the table. Something within him was urging him on.

"You don't make a deal with the devil and not expect to be burned."

Abadon's body shook as he chuckled, drawing

attention to his tattoo filled chest, his hard downturned nipples with their tiny bars running through them, then back up to the wicked smile that was slowly spreading his lips.

"So very true, Charle-boy," he purred. "And what I want is simple really. I want to take your virginity."

"Too late," he smirked in return. "And I think you know that. You saw me with my dick in some guy's mouth --"

"Oral don't really count and that was not the virginity I'm talking about."

"I've been fucked before --"

"And fucked over, but still not what I'm talking about here."

"Then what --"

"I want to be the one to take you down and show you the ropes, to show you the proper way to party."

"Safe, sane, and consensual?"

"If you must," Abadon was back to sounding amused again. Fuck, it was a sexy look on him. Charle wished he had his camera. Reaching down into his pocket, he miraculously found his cell phone. Without thinking about it he whipped it out and snapped a few photos of the singer.

"I'd better get copies of those," Abadon smirked. "And I want you to give yourself over into my keeping. Let me show you how to really party, how to have a good time, to unleash the inner beast you keep chained up. I want to be the one to set you free. That's my cost."

"Why?" Charle knew he was being blunt and he tried to hold back the excitement he found growing his chest. This was everything he wanted. No man in his right mind would hesitate. Abadon was a legend in the rock world. The band was known to play as hard as they worked and you didn't get to become rock legends... rock gods without putting in a lot of hard work. There had to be a catch somewhere.

"I need inspiration," Abadon allowed, nodding in Charle's direction and running an absent hand over his chest.

Charle had to bite back the words 'I can do that for you,' when Abadon absently rubbed at a pierced nipple. He found himself biting back a moan, imagining what it would feel like to have that nipple, gold piercing and all, in his mouth.

Man, screwing that guy in that office obviously did something to him. He'd never been interested in body jewelry before. Now his mind flashed back to using his tongue to tug the ring that other guy had piercing his nipple. God, his moans had been delicious... and the way his whole body shivered in the dark, the way sweat made his hands glide softly over that muscled perfection --

"Inspiration?" he choked out, pushing those cherished memories back until a time he was alone to jack it off properly.

"I'm writing some new things trying different angles and I need something to inspire me."

"And me partying will inspire you?"

"No, you doing something for the first time will inspire me. I need to see joy, fulfillment, ecstasy... I need to see the joy in losing something, Charles. I need the experience."

"Sounds like you need a good hard fuck." He bit back the 'I volunteer as tribute!' that was dancing on the tip of his tongue and tried to consider Adabon's point of view.

"I can get that anytime --" no lack of confidence there --"But I want to see something real and new. I want to see discovery and I saw some of that in you yesterday." Abadon paused before he admitted, "And I was an ass to you --"

"No shit --"

"And I want to make it up to you," he continued as if the flash of anger in Charle's eyes was nothing when it came to meeting his goals.

"You want to make it up to me? An apology would be a good start."

"I'll not apologize for telling the truth."

"What?" Charle squawked, again the urge to smack the shit out of a rock star rising.

"You wouldn't have dumped that whiskey over my head or gotten that tattoo if it weren't for me driving you on."

Charle nodded as there was some truth to that statement. "You don't --"

"I do know."

"Okay. We finishing each other's sentences now?"

"I saw it in your eyes, Charles. That little voice telling you it wasn't safe. You were ready to run back to your room and write about what you saw. You're good at that, standing on the sidelines, staring at the big glass window, and watching from outside waiting for someone to invite you in. Without me you never would've let go last night, experienced life, instead of living it vicariously while dreaming of actually joining in, and you know it."

Charle swallowed hard. Damn the man for being right.

"Last night, I got to see a virgin accept his first kiss. But it was only a brush with what you're truly capable of, Charles. I want to see you cracked open like a ripe fruit. I want to see you consumed by what you can be. I want to see you running wild. I want to see the real you emerge from the ashes of your former self. I want to watch you become. What do you say about that, Charle?"

Well, Charles first wanted to slam Abadon against the nearest flat surface, roughly opening him up with his fingers and a hell of a lot of lube, and fucking him in front of the Locusts. He wanted to feel the burn as he struggled to take all that dick, feeling it splitting him wide open and riding Abadon like there was no tomorrow.

I want it all, he wanted to say but instead he squeaked out, "Sounds like a plan?"

"You telling or asking?"

He blinked and pulled himself together. "It sounds like a plan." Why was he suddenly so breathless? Damn, Abadon was getting to him. It just reinforced his goal of having that man before this tour was over.

"Awesome," Abadon purred and the world began to breathe once more.

With the spell broken, all Charle could murmur to himself was "What the hell did I just get myself into?"

* * *

Fuck, it was loud.

Charle stood back stage, phone in hand typing down his observations as fast as he could in the flashing lights and smoke of the back wings.

He had a good seat having had Abadon himself plonk Charle down on a special VIP chair between an up-and-coming musician and that night's Wish Maker guest.

The Wish Maker was a ten year old black girl with aspirations of becoming a rock star before her predicted death in three years. She was brave in her wild tangle of an afro and her personalized smaller stature bass guitar slung around her neck. Apollon himself was going to bring her out later and they were going to tear up the strings and put fear in the frets, or whatever new term she came up with as she absently muttered to her guardian. The girl -- Shi -- had style, spunk, and a continuous drip pain med dispenser attached to her hip. Back in the green room, Shi had been dueling Apollon while the others in the band made sure the room was PG for their young guest. She had been chattering away, fingers flying as they played the blues until Abadon himself walked in. Shi had frozen, eyes wider than dessert plates, before she pushed her guitar at Apollon and launched herself at the rocker.

"How do you get your voice to go so low?"

"I'm a man."

"Yeah, but voices that low are unnatural."

"It's not deeper than Apollon's."

"Yeah, well Apollon's unnatural. No one should be able to play bass that fast."

They both ignored the bassist's deep. "Hey!" as Shi proceeded to hug the stuffings out of Abadon. Somehow he wound up sitting on his ass on the ground before her chair while she proceeded to braid the tightest braid he had ever seen in several sections of his hair. A helpful Hash handed her beads periodically and before he knew it, Abadon had several clanking braids in his red highlights. Shi was amused. The official photographer was enchanted. Abadon was resigned.

"I have to keep these in?"

"While you're on stage," Shi insisted. "It'll give you character."

If Shi beat the odds and made it to adulthood, she would have any person she wanted wrapped around her finger.

The up-and-coming musician was a rather tall trans girl who was currently tearing up the charts in the alternative market and a bit defensive about selling out.

"It's not really selling out if you can afford to eat at the end of the day," Hash pointed out and she gave him a frown.

Callista, as she was known, did it all on her own. Following in the footsteps of the late great Prince, she produced her own shit, thank you very much. She wrote her own music, played all the instruments, edited, promoted and put her own sound out there for the world to like or lump. So far, the world was liking it and she didn't use her trans status as a gimmick.

"I could," she told Python as they both sat on a couch in the greenroom and played with the snake. "But then it wouldn't be my talents getting me ahead. No one knew I was trans until a reporter tried to make an issue of it." She gave Charle an eye so side it was almost adjacent and he shrugged. Some of those in his profession didn't value privacy as much as he.

"You have talent and a great pair of tits," Python pointed out and watched as she blushed.

"Want the number of my surgeon?" she asked. "If I give a recommendation, I get a discount off of my next surgery."

The two delved into the mysteries of personal physical change as Charle learned more about inverted penis and hormonal changes than anyone not considering a change. Python seemed to be in the know, giving out helpful advice, common sense tips and more importantly, an understanding ear with no hint of judgement.

"I'm familiar with change," was all he said when Callista asked him.

"Someone you love or you?" the lady asked and Python smiled. "A few I'm close to," he admitted. "Change's natural. If something in you doesn't fit, you change what you can to give your life balance."

No one asked who he knew that transitioned. It was too personal. Instead, Python gave her tips on promoting, shady venues to avoid, and the names of several venue owners who would be gratified to have her perform.

Callista who started that night as defensive, relaxed and even started joking with the others in the band while Abadon got his new hairstyle.

Now Charle was seated between the two, watching as Abadon tossed his braided hair about and roared into the mike. Today, he was playing bass with Apollon, as he dominated the stage. The lights loved him. The Locusts chanted, and his voice reached heavenly highs and devilish lows.

And when Shi joined him on stage, he put down his bass and let her play in his place.

The sounds that little girl could wring out of a guitar...

In the end, all four band members bowed to her majesty and she got a roaring leaping ovation from the watching crowds. Her smile was ten miles wide even off the jumbo screen. Her happiness was a palatable thing as she took a final bow, then curtsied Abadon but not before Abadon stopped the show so that they all could autograph her guitar and drown her in praise.

Callista joined the band for one of their signature songs and one of her favorites, *Bay At the Moon*, while the roadies brought out a second drum kit. When the song about transformative magic was complete, she was invited to battle Hash on the drums.

The two performed for fifteen solid minutes before the rest of the band joined in and performed a rather raunchy version of their newer hit, *Pound it Out.*

It was all sex, primal instincts, and savage imagery set to sound.

The audience loved it. Shi was screaming along with some rather inappropriate lyrics, and Callista was loving life, singing sexual innuendo with Abadon and shimmying her way around the other band members one by one, paying close attention to Python who welcomed her by laying the dirtiest, wettest kiss Charle had ever seen outside of a porno, on her lips when she was ready to leave the stage.

After that, Shi was whisked away. It was after her bedtime and her guardian didn't want her overtired. After three encores the band ran backstage and the real party began.

Chapter 8

It started when someone handed him a drink.

He didn't know what it was but he decided to screw the rules.

He tossed it back and then... the colors.

The world disappeared in a sensory explosion. The sights, the sounds, the feelings, they all blended into a kaleidoscope of sound and motion that kept his head spinning.

He recalled Abadon was by his side for most of the night, introducing him to people whose names he wouldn't remember and shaking hands of fans he would be glad to forget.

The music was turned low and the after-party was taking place in a separate ballroom behind the venue. It was there that the first dare happened.

"Charle!" Some scantily clad pretty-boy walked up to him and got in his face with breath that smelled like cinnamon and apples. "I dare you to take off your shirt."

Charle snorted. That dare was easy enough. With his hair in its wild afro, wearing leather pants that Abadon somehow acquired for him and a tight solid black thin silk button down that he already owned, he didn't much look like the same reporter who met the band only a few days ago.

Abadon had burst in his room brandishing the pants and an eyeliner pencil at the start of the night. The result was that his green eyes popped under the careful application of kohl and a few locks of hair at his temples were now braided and beaded while Abadon had looked on in approval.

"Gonna show you how to party right," he declared before Charle's feet were stuffed into his favorite black boots, a leather bracelet with the band's logo, the flaming sword, embossed on the front was strapped on his wrist, and his VIP pass was placed around his neck. Then there was a quick meal of steak and salad before they were rushed by limo to the venue.

The beefy-boys heartily approved of his new gear. In fact, it was Hash who demanded he unbutton his shirt to damn near his waist to tease all the boys.

"Not the ladies too?" Abadon asked and the boys all shook their heads.

"Charle's into tight hot asses... though from the blow job he got last night from that chick with the blue hair --"

"That was Siou," Python corrected. "But he was kissing that chick with the afro. The pretty one who was all over Abadon. She kind of looked like you," he said pointing to Charle.

"Hey! Just because we are both fair-skinned black --"

"That's not it," Python interrupted. "Green eyes and an Afro."

"Plus she was tall and thin... shapely though." Apollon added with a grin.

"Yeah, Abadon latched onto her as soon as she came up. She's the proctologist, right?"

"Yes," Abadon seemed a bit taken aback by that for a moment, before he shrugged and the conversation continued around them. "She's a friend."

"A friend who loves whiskey. Didn't she lick it off of you?" Apollon asked, before turning to grin at Charle. "Good work, by the way. You achieved total hair saturation and missed his eyes. That's not easy to do."

"And he deserved it," Hash added, glaring at their lead. "Whatever he said to you --"

"I already apologized." Abadon threw his arms up in a placating gesture. "I was wrong and I admitted it. Now Charle-boy and I are becoming friends."

Charle felt his dick lurch at that statement because it immediately brought to mind Abadon, stripped down and giving him a warm friendly embrace...then abasing the wall… with his dick.

Charle blinked that image away and forced a smile.

Getting his hands all over that body was still the ultimate goal. He'd just have to prove himself wild enough to hold his attention. No boring talks by the fireplace right now. This was going to be all about raunch and heat and all the things that rockers reportedly liked.

And sitting around a dinner table in the middle of the afternoon eating steak with the band seemed a bit tame. But Charle chalked it up to ritual and party prep. Better to have some food on your stomach to soak up the alcohol.

And now with this twink in front of him daring him to undress in public, he was glad of that heavy meal. He wasn't nearly as drunk as he should have been, but was loose enough to put his plan in action.

"What do I get if I do?"

That caught Abadon's grinning attention as he turned to face the pair of them, black eyes glittering in amusement.

"I'll let you take off my shirt."

"Bitch, please," Charle scoffed, looking at the neon threads that at one time may have been a T-shirt. It was fashion now to dress like you've been through a shredder but when the material of your shirt hid nothing, there was really nothing to disclose. "I can see your everything right now. Nice belly ring. And is that a bite mark around your right nipple?"

"Okay, okay," he agreed. "You take off your shirt and I'll do an upside down hand stand."

"Done!" Charle would have held out for more but that sounded pretty awesome to him.

"And you have to stand on a table to do it."

Charle looked around the room. The music was pumping, the lights were dim, and the place was packed with crazy fans and sponsors who were all paying them little attention. Abadon had made the rounds early with Charle at his side so his job now was to get good publicity and charm the fuck out of the money people so that they would keep giving money.

"Oh, this I gotta see," Abadon smirked. "It's an essential to your party-boy development."

Charle looked up at Abadon and smirked before tossing back the drink in his hand and shoving it at the twink.

"Hold on to that, Doll," he all but growled in his sex voice. Yes, he had a sex voice and he discovered it while screwing that hunk of a one-night stand through that desk a short while ago. It seemed to work well so he was adding it to his repertoire of seduction techniques.

Abadon jumped, eyes wide, and Charle made a point to use that voice again around him, if it was getting that kind of reaction. Hell, even the twink fanned his face as he fumbled with the glass.

"And you have to be creative," the pretty boy warned. "I'm also gonna be upside down with my ass in the air. You better make it worth my while."

Charle snickered as he looked around. The money people had left. The other bands had headed out for other parties for the night. The party had slowly become smaller, more intimate, wilder.

Looking over at Abadon, Charle knew he had one shot to impress. With the steady flow of liquid courage filling his system, he reached up and tapped Abadon on the full bottom lip.

"Watch this," he whispered, wandering over to a table that had at one time been filled with buttons, and scarves, and other swag.

Pushing back the unsteady feeling that was apparently part of the getting-drunk- in-a-wild-party experience, he gave himself a full body shake and then made his way to the table pushing people aside as he moved.

Of course his deliberate moves garnered immediate attention from the remaining Locusts and they began to follow.

His target in mind, Charle swept the remaining swag from the table and for a moment, wondered how he was going to sexily get up there. Was crawling considered sexy when men did it? Of course if you looked like Channing Tatum in *Magic Mike* then excellent, crawl away. But if you were a rather thin though tightly muscled reporter whose last dance excursion developed into some kind of cross between the Running Man and the Lawnmower, you start to have second thoughts about your life choices.

But despair or second thoughts were not allowed in this new Charle... nor was the ability to change his mind and beat feet for safety because Abadon was there.

Before he could blink, the larger man wrapped his hands around his waist and hefted him atop the table, muttering, "You got this." Charle fell to his knees, a combination of shock and sudden painful arousal.

If him shoving people out of the way didn't garner attention before, Abadon's voice carrying across the room sure did. Suddenly there were more eyes upon him, some eager to see what was happening, others who just couldn't wait for him to fail. Judging eyes and loud drunk voices... they were everywhere.

He wanted to crawl off that table, damn being sexy, and go back and hide where it was safe. There was not enough alcohol in his system for this!

When his courage was about to fail, he got double slammed with his inner voice suddenly noticing how awesome it was to have all this attention. It felt good to have all those eyes on him. Were they undressing him? He really hadn't had a shortage of compliments during this whole party and the sexual innuendo ran hot. Those people in the know, those party girls and glamor boys, wanted to see him. The second thing that shook his world was Abadon himself leaning forward and whispering in his ear once again, "You got this, Charle-boy. Do it for me."

Thank God that leather pants were so tight because his chubby turned into a full fledged hard-on in about two seconds. The blood flooded to his dick so fast he almost fell off the table in a giggling dizzy mess. But that acute horniness factor could work for him some part of his psyche decided, since suddenly he had confidence he'd never known before.

There was something about Abadon's voice... it was like hot sex in a summer storm. It was like lust was made physical and reached inside his body to caress his cock from the inside out. It was soul-sucking and it was directed at him.

He could do this.

With the driving beat of the music making his hips sway, he slowly rose from a kneeling position to his feet.

The lights were blinding and the music nearly drowned out by the sudden cheers from the watchers, but either way, Charle Lexington suddenly knew he was a sexy being, worthy of lust, and more importantly able to pull any person in that room for a good hard fuck. He closed his eyes, imagining that it was only he and Abadon in the room that he was naked and hard, dick in hand and waiting to see what Charle had on offer.

He opened his eyes and turned to stare at Abadon for a moment, before running his hands through his hair, peering between his arms and biting his lower lip. What did the man taste like? Suddenly he wanted to know. He deserved to know. He was one sexy bastard and he was going to seduce the rock god on his terms and prove to the world he could be more.

* * *

- 82 -

Abadon felt his stomach clench as he stared at the reporter on the table and wondered for at least the fifth time that night, what the fuck was he doing.

He was taking a mild-mannered reporter, his very own kind of cute kind of annoying Clark Kent and turning him into... this. Damn this was so much fun. He was already composing lyrics in his head. Maybe the ballad could be all about sex...

He had looked so adorable backstage doing his job with the huge ear protectors on. He had spoken to Shi and Callista, taken notes and all the while looked like he belonged. It was amazing to see and surprisingly enough, Charle-boy was holding his attention. He had been cute the way he interacted with the folks in the green room, the photographers and the guests. He wasn't intrusive, but something about him kept drawing Abadon's eye. He found his gaze straying to him while he was on stage but that could easily be attributed to him checking on his special guests.

There wasn't too much info out there about Abadon other than his penchant for partying hard and driving his band relentlessly in the pursuit of perfection. People knew him for a hard-drinking, hard-ass of a man who indiscriminately took partners, had no problem with public nudity and sex, and that was a reputation he carefully cultivated. There was more than one type of worship than praise. Those who wanted to be him gave him a powerful jolt and he made sure he gave them reason to be envious. Oddly enough, he didn't get that from Charles Lexington. The man was out to prove something to himself and it was odd that he wasn't really trying to fawn all over Abadon. Charle's actions couldn't even be read as selfish. He wanted to change something about himself and Abadon realized that he was lucky enough to be in on the transformation. And now with the sexy young man's eyes on him, he was beginning to discover something about himself. He could still feel want on a personal level and it was something he had not experienced in years.

Looking up at Charle he was again taken back to that special night and to that moment of pure worship. There was something about the man that was drawing him deeper in.

And now as those green eyes flashed at him, as that full bottom lip was nibbled on, Abadon wanted to reach up and jerk him from that table and protect that special spark he was becoming.

The other part wanted to fuck him on that table in front of everyone, to mess him up good, to fuck that perfect mouth and pull out and blow his wad all over that face, to mark him and keep him only for himself in a way so public that no one would even dare to touch... look all they want, but not touch.

Where the hell did that come from? Abadon was questioning himself and his priorities when he turned back to Charle. What was it about this mouthy prick that had him in a mental uproar? He couldn't understand it.

Then he started to move and Abadon felt his mouth dry out.

Charle's body suddenly became a graceful thing of beauty as he rolled his body to the beat of the music, his hips thrusting in time with his pumping arms. He bent at the knees and showed the world how he fucked.

His thighs were bulging and sliding teasingly outward as his body rocked with the diving beat of the music. His tight round ass bobbed teasingly as he dropped his body, his thighs spreading further as be bent back and thrust up.

The Locusts were screaming, saluting him, throwing money at the table and Charle licked his lips and basked in the glory of being worshipped.

He bent forward, dropping lightly to his hands and

knees as he threw his ass in the air, his face showing ecstasy as his eyes dropped to half-mast and he spread his lips and hissed, just like he was being taken from behind.

He began to grind his hips, his knees spreading wide then teasingly sliding shut. Abadon could picture him doing this naked, looking teasingly at him over his shoulder as he urged him to fuck him harder, his hard dick swinging between his thighs.

Charle's head began to drop as his ass went higher and he swooped his body down and brought himself back up before kneeling on the center of the table.

Slowly, he ran his hands over his chest, tugging at the remaining buttons before he carefully slid them free. Teasingly looking out over at the sea of eager faces watching him, he allowed the shirt to slide off his left shoulder, exposing his slightly red looking tattoo and the gold bar through his left nipple.

Abadon knew it was there but to suddenly see it in this context made the ink stunning. His eyes were drawn to the single green eye of the lion and the glint of the nipple ring as the light bounced off of the jewelry. His permanently hard nipple was suddenly looking obscene and sexy as hell.

Jumping to his feet, Charle tore the shirt from his body and spun around, swinging it in the air as he threw back his head and laughed.

As Abadon watched, Charle began to lose himself and transform into a being of pure lust.

He threw his hands in the air and ran his hands over his chest, pinching his nipple and barking his teeth in a growl so lustful that the twink holding his glass exclaimed, "Damn."

Bills showered down as the watchers began to squeal in excitement while he put his tight body on display, spinning and twisting, helicoptering that shirt over his head before he let it fly. It flew directly at Abadon, landing on his shoulder and filling his nostrils with the scent of a young man in heat.

He bent at the waist, showing an impressive display of flexibility that made his ass look all kinds of perfect before snaking his way upright again, before dropping hard to his knees and crawling across the piles of cash raining down, toward Abadon.

Once before him, he rolled onto his back and popped two fingers into his mouth. The way he sucked and worked his tongue around those two digests should be illegal. Abadon felt a jolt of lust as his dick sat up and paid attention.

He crossed his arms over his chest in an effort not to touch, and stared down at Charle, fighting the urge to drag him off by his hair and fuck him into next week. He inhaled once, taking in an oddly familiar scent wafting up from the damp shirt, before he smelled himself for what was going to happen next.

"I wanna get fucked." He mouthed the words and Abadon suddenly felt his heart start to race in his chest.

But the crowd, the watchers, roared in approval, and suddenly there were so many hands there, so many grabbing, lustful hands, and Charle Lexington fell back into the masses of sweating flesh and hard human desire.

* * *

Abadon fled.

He tucked tail between his legs and he ran as fast as he could, completely oblivious to a pair of hungry green eyes that watched him as he fled.

Hunched over, moved away from the flashing lights and the sounds of the party raging behind him, he made for the comfort of the first open office door he saw.

Not caring that the door wasn't closed all the way or that he hadn't moved very far from the teeming masses that exuded the stench of sex like it was perfume, he tore at his belt buckle, trying to loosen his suddenly too tight leather pants.

"Fuck," he hissed when he ripped at the zipper, pulling it down to allow his swollen cock to spring free. He hissed as the cool air hit his damp tip. He was leaking precum like a faucet as he leaned back against the huge desk that sat off center in the room.

With shaking hands, he reached down and cupped himself, even though he knew there was no way he was getting his dick back into his pants until he took care of the persistent throbbing that made his dick hard enough to crack nuts.

Charle-boy was on fire, the fucking tease.

What was all that fuck me bullshit he was whispering? If he was looking for a way to get even with him for messing with him so much, Charle had found the perfect weapon.

Abadon's whole body was trembling as the ache in his groin threatened to become actual pain. He hadn't felt this aroused by anyone since the mystery man rang his bells just right until he decided to forget the encounter and move on.

Maybe that's why he was reacting so strongly to Charle. In his sex-deprived mind he had put the two of them together. After all, he was helping Charle get his groove back, so to speak, because he was trying to forget the mystery man. It was just all messed up in his head... and in his groin. Knowing that relaxed him a little but did nothing for the killer erection that would not die.

"The things I do for you." He spoke down at his dick which leaked another drop of shiny precum, making its head glisten in the dim light coming from the hall.

He had to grin though. Charle-boy could be one sexy beast when he wanted to be.

"I did that." He gave himself the credit even as he lazily fisted his dick, stroking it softly to the beat of the music he could still faintly hear.

He got the boy dressed up real pretty and letting go of his inhibitions. He was responsible for bringing out the wild child in the quiet reporter.

Wild Child... that would be a good title for a song. It would be a song about a man tearing free of social constructs and embracing the sexual beast within himself.

Like the way Charle crawled across that damn table, licking his lips and flashing those eyes at him.

Yeah, he would dearly love to see that play out when it was just the two of them. Fuck, he would choke that bitch on his cock. Maybe bitch was too strong of a word, Charle-boy was just breaking out after all. No, Charle would be a good cock slut. Yeah, he would whimper and beg for it.

He recalled those full lips forming the words 'fuck me' and tightened his fist around his dick, rolling the foreskin down and exposing the shiny metal of the one piercing he left behind. He ran his thumb over the tender head of his dick and allowed the full body shudder to work through him. Lust was making his knees weak and his toes curl in his boots.

He could close his eyes and picture Charle choking on his dick, those huge green eyes staring pleadingly up at him as he tried to swallow him whole.

Those slim fingers would rub at his balls and grip at his hips when he started to fuck his face. Charle would be down for the face fucking as he put that wicked mouth and that sharp tongue to some actual good use.

He closed his eyes and fisted himself faster. This was going to be a fast and dirty ride. He needed to get himself off and then back out to the party. He paused long enough to whip his T-shirt over his head before he determinedly gripped his dick once more. He was going to enjoy the hell out of this.

So he braced one hand on the desk, leaned over, and

began to fuck his fist as hard as he could. The slick precum he gleaned acted as an adequate lube and made it easier for him to glide his callused fist up and down his shaft more comfortably, but it wasn't enough to take away the full burn.

He closed his eyes, humming softly as he threw his hips into the action, using every part of himself to fuck up into his hand all the while imagining he was sliding into Charle-boy's tight throat… or better yet, his tight ass.

Charle had a nice high and tight ass on him. He remembered watching the material of his sweatpants slide between the quivering globes as he danced around at the hotel party. His boy wasn't wearing anything under either as his bloated dick slid across the front of his pants, showing the world that he was built to fuck and be fucked.

And Charle-boy had a nice tight body which could only be topped by that nice tight ass.

It had been a long time since Charle had been fucked. He knew it just by looking at him, reading the cock hunger in his face. He wanted to be fucked but that didn't mean he was going to give it up to just anyone. He needed someone strong and capable and for a moment Abadon pictured himself as that man.

His fist slowed down as he imagined those eyes wide in shock as he slid inside Charle's luscious body in one long slow thrust.

His balls began to tingle as he could almost feel those thighs wrapping around his waist as he slid balls deep, his hips confined by the nice plush cheeks of his ass.

The look on his face when he pounded into him, slamming into the slick wall of his ass, as his hole tightened and milked him as he pounded him through his stress… the way his moans and gasps would match each thrust as his nails tore at his shoulders, and he begged, as he screamed his release as he…

"Fuck," Abadon gasped as his climax washed over him. He closed his eyes as the dark office was washed away, as his brain shut down with the influx of pleasure that took over. His stomach ached, his back burned and his cock throbbed as it shot a creamy load over his fist and onto the desk that was not supporting his weight.

His hand kept moving as he wrung the last of his orgasm from his quivering body and his muscles began to grow weak.

"Damn, that was good," he panted as he looked down at the mess he made of the desk. Chuckling, he looked around until he found a box of tissue and hastily cleaned himself up before tucking his sated cock back into his pants. He cleaned up the desk as best he could, tossing all the used tissue into a waste paper basket.

He looked down at his discarded T-shirt and shrugged. He would leave it there as a thank you for whoever's office he'd just defiled.

Running his hand through his sweat-dampened hair, he left the room and made his way back to the party.

He didn't even notice the person who ducked around the corner when he left or walked into the office when he was out of sight.

* * *

"What the fuck did I just witness?" Charle was tipsy but he wasn't sure if maybe someone hadn't also slipped him some mind-altering substances.

From his crowd of admirers, he had watched as Abadon quit the room after his little table stunt and wondered what had been going on. From what he remembered of their hotel party-not-a-party, what he had done was pretty mild for the rocker. Did he push too hard too fast?

Making up a pee-break excuse and ignoring the one guy who volunteered his face as a urinal, he made his way through the heaving dancing bodies and followed

Abadon discreetly.

When he ducked into the office, he couldn't help but remember the time he peered into another dark office and the pleasure that awaited him there. Curiosity being stronger than his common sense, he peered into the room and had to shove his fist into his mouth to stop himself from moaning out loud at what he saw.

Abadon the great was jerking off, casually as you pleased, inside someone's office.

He watched as his tight pants grew tighter as he freed his massive cock from his pants and -- mercy -- Charle got to see him full and hard.

Fuck, the man was too good to be real and his dick was pretty. What the fuck? Who has a pretty dick? Well, Abadon had one and it was prettier when it was hard.

He had to be packing a good nine and a half inches of prime beef with its pierced tip.

Charle never paid much attention to dicks in general, unless it was his or one he was dating, but Abadon's demanded attention.

He was uncircumcised, Charle knew that, but when he was primed for action, the foreskin slid back to expose the plum colored heart shaped head that leaked prettily of precum. Leaked was too weak of a word. When aroused, apparently Abadon dripped like an old faucet.

Charle licked his lips as he watched the object of his desire whip off his shirt and without a by your leave start beating off his meat.

His eyes went wide and his mouth dried out as he watched all of that perfection in action. His hands slid down to the crotch of his pants and he began to stroke his own hard cock as he watched.

Voyeurism was a turn-on for him, his porn collection paid truth to that fact, but there was something about watching someone he lusted after live and in person getting himself off... that was taking his kink to a whole new level.

He watched as Abadon closed his eyes, cursing softly to himself as he began to fuck his fist. There was no self-consciousness about it either, he was getting himself off and enjoying every hard-wrung second of it. He was fucking his fist, putting his whole back into it and it made Charle's hole quiver in hunger to imagine the man putting that work into getting him to scream his name.

'Cause... just yeah, if Abadon was working him like that, he would be screaming his name, scratching his back, promising to have his babies... fuck... he would do anything to get taken like that by the man.

Abadon's hips rolled like a snake, a powerful testament to his grace and strength. His motions were controlled and mesmerizing to watch. Sweat made his skin glisten in the dim light cast inside by the cracked door and it made his moves all the more erotic.

He threw back his head, growling, and Charle found himself cupping his balls, massaging them as the ache in his groin grew to spread to his back and up his spine. He was moving his hips in sympathetic thrusts with Abadon's, doing his best to stay unobserved while he rubbed his swollen cock harder through his pants.

His whole body was shaking and Charle just knew he was going to be caught any second but somehow that only added to his desire. He gripped the door harder, his eyes tearing up. Hunger and want tore through him.

God, he wanted to go into that room and offer himself up, to drop onto his knees and offer his ass for a pounding. He could almost feel the heat from Abadon's body, feel his sweat drip down onto him, smell his sex and desire.

Just as he was about to say fuck it and rush into the room to demand to be fucked, Abadon stiffened, threw back his head and groaned as he blew his load all over his fist and the desk.

Charle moved to the side, leaning against the wall beside the door as the man chuckled inside and breathed heavily.

There were the sounds of him adjusting his clothing and before Charle could scamper to safety with his bloated dick in pants that were two sizes too tight, the door swung open and Abadon, a shirtless Abadon, casually strolled out, like he hadn't just filled Charle Lexington's spank bank with enough material to get him through the rest of his life. He didn't look back but strolled back toward the party, all satiated languid grace.

Charle slipped into the dim room, closed the door, and inhaled deeply.

Fuck, it smelled like spice and sex and Abadon. It was too fucking much.

In an instant, he had his pants whipped open and his hard dick in hand.

He fisted himself, roughly jerking hard as the images of what he just witnessed ran through his head.

He leaned against the desk, still warm from Abadon's body, and groaned his frustration as his cock begged for more.

He pulled back long enough to spit into his palm and used that as lube as he began to pound his own flesh.

A picture of Abadon, head thrown back in ecstasy as he sprayed his release over himself, floated to the front of his mind. He had to shove a hand on the desk to keep his knees from buckling and he touched something soft, damp, and warm.

The scent hit him before he realized what he was fisting. Abadon's shirt was in his hand and it was still hot from his body. Charle whimpered as he brought it up to his face, inhaling the more concentrated scent of Abadon as his fist fairly flew up and down his shaft.

His whole body was shaking as his balls drew up and --

"Fuck!"

He shouted it. He didn't care who heard as his release tore through him. "Fuck, fuck, fuck --" he gasped as each spurt of his seed erupted from his cock. His balls burned and he dropped to his knees, each inhalation bringing more of the pure scent of Abadon.

"Fuck."

His vision whited out and he slumped against the side of the desk as the last of his climax ran through him.

He was a shaking, sweating mess and oddly enough, he had never felt so relaxed.

Yeah, he was going to get that man to fuck him hard. Charle chuckled a little to himself before common sense invaded the mush that was now his mind. He could get caught at any moment. He had to leave.

He looked down at the shirt still fisted in his hand and with a perverse sense of delight, he used it to clean up his sensitive cock and balls before tossing it aside and tucking himself away neatly.

He rose shakily to his feet and inhaled the combined scent of Abandon and sex and now the smell of himself added to the mix. Grinning, he tossed the shirt into the trash can and moved toward the door.

He now had a concrete plan in mind to draw the man into his web and he wasn't letting him out until he got what he wanted. He would have the man he desired and he would prove to himself and to anyone who cared to watch, that Charle Lexington was fucking worth it.

Adabon didn't stand a chance.

Abadon (Sympathy For the Devil 2)
Stephanie Burke

Abadon becomes obsessed with the snarly reporter who's covering him and decides showing Charle how to party will be the perfect distraction from the one who got away. Now Charle's getting out of control. Abadon is falling hard, but Charle just wants to have fun.

Abadon has created a monster -- a monster he wants to keep. Will someone please offer a little sympathy for the devil, especially if he and Charle have to part ways?

Chapter 1

"Oh, God, that feels so good --"

Charle was on his back and moaning. He had never felt like this in his life. People wanted him. They were touching him, stroking him, joking with him... For once he was in the in-crowd and there was no feeling like it.

He was seated in a huge leather chair, surrounded by people who just wanted to be next to him. He was sipping on a glass of something that burned going down and he was certain he had a contact high from the weed someone was smoking.

At the moment he had no idea where he was and really, he just didn't care. Some guy was stroking his bare chest and another was playing with his hair. His new tattoo stung when people pressed against it, but even that small amount of pain bled into pleasure.

His crotch was a heavy weight that many had pawed at but when he told them to back off they did, so being this aroused and admired for it was cool.

God, he had danced so much his thighs were burning. He was sure what he was doing wasn't real dancing -- he just applied knowledge of the latest rap video girl's dance moves, altered them for his more masculine frame and let the music do the rest. Right now the handstand twink was sitting in his lap and he absently slapped his hand as he reached for his nipple ring again.

"It's new," he warned. "Stop that."

The pretty boy pouted, but Charle bent and gave him a peck on the lips and he was all smiles again. Charle lay his head back into the body behind him, loving that he was being petted and it felt so good.

He had achieved one of his goals. He had gone out there and done something wild and crazy, something that the old him would have been too afraid to even attempt.

Had he taken it too far? Maybe a touch, seeing that he didn't know where he was, or what time it was for that matter, but so far he hadn't regretted anything that he had done.

There was a lot of blow jobs happening in this group, he noted, and most were desirous of blowing him. Who was he to say no?

But now that voice in his head was poking at him. The ultimate prize had yet to be had.

"I'm so mercenary," he thought out loud and the warm nest of bodies surrounding him giggled and chuckled and added their own commentary.

He had no idea how long he sat there, lost in his own thoughts, when the door opened and a familiar head popped in.

"Yo! You in here, Charle?"

The group shifted in excitement as Hash stuck his head in. "You know we were looking for you, man?" Then he turned out toward the hall and called out, "Found him."

Hash moved into the room, making way for the rest of the band.

Immediately the squeaking and squawking started, but when Abadon himself stuck his head in, the crowd went wild.

Charle was damn near dumped on his own head as the group raced toward the stars. Fame is fleeting he thought from where he landed on his knees, and shrugged to get upright. It was then that the room decided to start to spin.

"Back to the bus."

He barely remembered Hash throwing him over his shoulder and taking him from his adoring fans...

"But there was more," he whimpered, bouncing over the big man's shoulder while the rest of the group laughed and Abadon looked on with tacit approval.

"We gonna stop the bus every night so that Charle-boy will learn to live like a rock star."

"Damn straight!" Charle managed to lift his head and gurgle. "What?"

"Tomorrow will be better," Abadon promised, patting him on the shoulder as a camera flash damn near blinded him.

Funny, but suddenly he didn't feel quite so sick anymore, just really, really tired. Maybe he was tense with all those strangers... well, as tense as one could be after popping pills and drinking and smoking whatever the hell they gave him. Maybe it was just that he trusted Abadon to see him safe. Yeah, that had to be it. Abadon would keep him safe.

And when he opened his eyes later that day, he was sprawled out on his chair in the bus feeling amazingly hangover free. Maybe he did have a tolerance like no other.

The boys from the band were teasing him, showing him photos of what he had been up to but couldn't remember. By all rights, he should have felt shame and embarrassment. But when he saw himself dancing like a madman in a pile of pretty people, he couldn't find it in his heart to disavow what he had done. He was finally living. Charle Lexington, at damn near thirty years of age, was finally getting a life.

* * *

"I hope you know what you're doing."

"Relax." Abadon reclined in his favorite chair in his room on the bus and began to feverishly write on his tablet. "I know what I'm doing."

"And just what the hell are you doing? How about you clue the rest of us in?"

"Writing a song called *Runaway Train*. It's about discovering yourself and exploring parts of you that you never knew existed."

"Oh, like the selfish twat that you're turning into?"

Abadon stopped typing to glare at his friend and compatriot. "Wanna run that by me again?"

"You have been acting funny since we started this trip, Nergal. Hiding out in your room, changing the way you look... Python is Sin and says change is inevitable and all that shit but his aspect is the moon. Apollon seems to be just playing Enk and is getting a buzz out of whatever you're planning. But I am worried for the kid."

"Relax. I'm not going to let anything happen to him. I think I kind of like him."

"That's funny because you have been nothing but a little bitch to him since he got here. You deserved to get doused at that party. If it were me, I would have decked you."

"Look." Abadon placed his tablet on his desk and watched as Hash took his spot on the king-sized bed. They were rolling down the road to their next destination and he'd already told Max to stop at the largest town in Indiana. Where the hell were they anyway? But it didn't matter. He was going to see to it that Charle-boy had his fun and he was going to watch every second. "I mean him no harm. I'm protecting him. He wanted to party, so I'm going to show him how to party right. He needs this."

"He needs to find better boyfriends," Hash argued. "This can't possibly be helping him."

"It is. He's more confident. He's more demanding. He's more like... well, he kind of reminds me of..." his words trailed off as he glared at his friend Hash, also known as the god Nabu. "He isn't what he thinks he is. And with a little push he could be... well, amazing."

"Or more like the guy who fucked your ass good and put you in a bad mood."

"I'm not in a bad mood."

"Sulking. You're sitting here sulking. You're ruining that boy because you're sulking over the one who got away."

"I am not sulking or doing any ruining, Nabu," Abadon defended himself. "And I'm not letting one good fuck affect me... a lot. Okay, I should have got his name or number, but he rolled out when I was still trying to remember my name. It wasn't the sex... okay the sex was amazing, but that's not all. I didn't get the usual power rush from him, Nabu. It was like... it wasn't him praising me for what I could do for him. He was just praising me for being. It's hard to explain."

"Pure worship. You got a taste of pure worship at last."

"I don't know what you're talking about. I've been given pure worship before --"

"Tainted with fear or want or desire or need. This guy didn't know who you were but he was praising you for what you shared. That is powerful indeed, Nergal. I understand your reaction a bit better now. The first time I got a jolt of pure worship, I took to my temple and created the basis for the alphabet. It's a rush."

"Hmm..." Nergal closed his eyes and shuddered at the remembered feeling of the rush. It ran down his spine and made all the nerves in his body tingle with a golden light. He had gasped, clutching the table to not hurt the human fucking him just right but that feeling, it was like an all-over body orgasm and it was something he had never felt before in his long life. "Maybe."

"But you won't recreate it by agitating that poor kid sleeping it off in there."

"I am not trying to recreate it with him. He's a project. Simple as that. It's a coincidence that he's roughly the same size as my pure worshiper, but other than that, they're totally different. My guy was confident and demanding --"

"And you're trying to change young Charle into him."

"I am not," Nergal denied. "Really, I'm not. The kid wants to break free and I'm just helping him. I won't let it get out of control and I'm not trying to turn him into my mystery worshiper."

"If you're sure…"

"I am, Nabu. In fact, when we're done, how about we make a quick stop back in Baltimore so I can look for him."

"That would be a song worth singing," Hash agreed. "Just be easy on the kid, will ya? All of this is new to him."

"You got it," Nergal agreed. "I'll treat him with kid gloves."

But Nergal didn't really count on the mechanical bull.

Chapter 2

"What the hell?" Abadon was trying to move toward his project, but there were people in the way.

"Hey, Abby!" Charle called out from his place on the floor. "What's shaking?"

Abby? What's shaking? Abadon ignored the few people that crowded around, whipping out their cell phones and taking photos. "Do you know how long we've been looking for you?"

"No idea." Charle righted himself and smiled up at the larger man. As he wasn't thinking about it Charle raised his arms and, groaning in frustration, Abadon bent and picked him up. It took a moment for Charle to gain his feet, and even then he swayed, but he grinned up at him, looking all kinds of guileless and guilty at the same time.

"A day and a half."

"Abadon!" One squeaky voice called out and the feel of the energy that came from the naked drunk man only annoyed him further.

"Bitches out!" he roared and ignored the offended muttering as the five in the room walked out.

"Abby --"

"Abadon," he corrected the still grinning Charle. "And you have some explaining to do."

He had no idea when he lost sight of the man, but he never expected something like this to happen.

The stripping on the table was a fun bit of nothing, even if Charle-boy started channeling the ghosts of strippers past. It was fairly innocent, something he had done at bars before and was really nothing to Abadon at this point. After the dancing though, he was sure that someone handed him a spiked drink, but again, as long as he was with his little protégé, he could protect him from anything they threw at him. That's what being divine was all about. The problem was he had to be near Charle-boy to be effective and Charle-boy didn't like to stay where he put him.

He turned his attention away for one moment, for just one fucking moment, and Charle was off playing *Never Have I Ever* with an array of interesting looking drinks.

Still no big deal, right? Well, it wasn't until the hooting started. Who knew there were drunken big dick contests or that Charle could win?

At that point, Abadon still didn't know what was going on so he sent Hash over to find what Charle-boy was up to and Hash came rushing back telling him he had to see this to believe it.

Charle was packing a lot of dick for someone with such a small frame. A nice fat dick even at half-mast from what he could see, but that was something Charle Lexington should not be doing.

"Abadon, look at this!" he called out, his voice a bit slurred but proud as he posed before a man with a tape measure with the band logo on the side. They gave out tape measures? The Seven were working overtime. "Dick sling!" He waggled his slim hips from side to side and his wang... well, waggled beautifully. It was obscene, it was arousing, and it was one of the funniest things he had ever seen.

"If you could get it hard --" the man with the tape measure interjected, his head moving from side to side with the movements of Charle's cock, tape measure ever at the ready.

"Well, the eye candy has arrived so --" He leered at Abadon as the crowd grew quiet.

"Really?" Abadon grumbled and Charle's grin grew wider.

"Sing something sexy to me... "

Rolling his eyes, Abadon thought, "what the hell"

and started to croon.

"Is it the way you walk? Is it the way you move? Is it the way you rain down fire with the flash of your eyes and punch me in the gut with your sincerity? Can you understand what you do to me? The way you slide into me? The way you fuck me up by fucking on in and making me weep these alkaline tears? The way you caress my fears and grind my soul… The one who got away… "

There was absolute silence and for a moment, Abadon had never felt so exposed. He had no idea why he was singing this unfinished song to his work in progress, but there was something in him that called out to the kid. Maybe he was more like the one who got away than he wanted to admit.

As for the kid… "That was new," he breathed and licked his bottom lip while giving him drunken come-on eyes.

Yeah, no. The kid was nothing like the one who got away. Even as he thought this, the kid's dick grew and grew until the guy with the measuring tape called out, "Ten and a half! Winner!"

In some ways, it appeared that Charle and his mystery fucker were exactly alike. "Proud of yourself?" he called to Charle, who began to waggle his dick in his direction again while the band and the Locusts, Abadon's worshipers, watched.

"See something you like?" he returned, his voice dropping into an octave he had never heard from Charle-boy before. Bam! Charle's words were familiar and startling and slammed him in the solar plexus.

That voice in which he purred them… it was like sex and Abadon looked down as he felt his tight leather pants get tighter.

Pushing down the urge to walk over and stroke the monster that Charle had been hiding in his pants, he managed to get the fool dressed. "I'm not interested in your religion or you catching a cold. Button up man. You already put the rest of them to shame, now time to be adult about your win."

Charle pouted, but pulled his pants up and got everything tucked away. How, he would never know. Abadon had enough trouble with his own pants and his didn't have a twenty-nine inch waistband.

He turned to see if his people were ready to leave the backroom of this very exclusive club when someone handed the well-hung idiot a pill. Before he could stop him, the Ecstasy was down and Charle was getting higher than a kite.

"The fuck?" he raged, snatching Charle away from the dog pile of sycophants as he tried to talk some sense into him. "You can't go around taking pills."

"He said it would be fun. I've never done this before. You think it was too much?"

"I think it was too much. That's the kind of shit that can get you dead."

He tried to talk to the man, but all Charle wanted to know was if he had ever done things like this before. "You know you have," the drunk man argued and Abadon couldn't get his wiggling Charle to calm down long enough to pull some of the effects of the drug from him. He could keep the idiot from OD'ing, but he was going to have to suffer some of the physical complaints that came with the drug.

"Of course I have," he snorted before he remembered he was supposed to be cautioning Charle about doing too much too fast. "But I'm not you and you're not me."

"Well, I'm a grown man," Charle declared and shook off his concerns. "You said you were going to show me how to party --"

Grunting, Abadon pushed a bottle of water in his face and used a touch of divinity to remove the drug from Charle's system as he finally stilled.

He had done the same thing that first night when he found the determined little man passed out on a lounger next to their private pool. For some reason, he didn't want the young man to suffer the effects of his first foray into real partying. Now he wished he had.

"You need water, idiot. And I never take anything that didn't grow from the ground." He tried to get another bottle of water and ignore the judging looks he was getting from his band.

Maybe a hangover would have taught him about moderation, a lesson that he sorely needed, but as soon as Abadon's back was turned, Charle was gone again. That's right. Ladies and gentlemen, Charle Lexington had now left the building.

* * *

"Idiot." Charle grumbled as he stormed away from the man he really, really wanted to get his claws into. "He called me an idiot."

"Well," the voice of reason in his head interjected, "You are getting a little out of control."

Even his wild voice agreed. Popping pills was really a stupid thing to do.

"But nothing happened," he grumbled to himself.

Okay, for a moment there the music got real intense and the colors... man, it was almost like that spiked drink he had on the first day of party, but more intense. And just as quickly it faded away, leaving behind a powerful thirst and him not quite in control.

Bright lights and the loose, hazy feeling were addictive, but not really what he wanted. For a moment, though, he'd kind of felt out of control and the only thing that grounded him was Abadon's touch.

Abadon's touch always seemed to make things right with him.

"Fuck, I'm a fool, an idiot," he finally accepted as he turned for the nearest exit. He just wanted to get some air, to cool down a bit. Suddenly it was too tight in the place, too many people, the air perfumed with too many scents. It was starting to make his head hurt.

He made it out of the club to a rather clear alley where some people had gathered to smoke. It wasn't much better than being in the club surrounded by the perfume and cologne of sweat and desperation.

This partying shit was getting old. How did people like Abadon keep it up? The paps were always snapping photos of glamorous celebrities having the times of their lives and he had always envied them. And now that he was in the thick of things, so to speak, it didn't seem to be a lot of fun. It was a lot of damn hard work.

Oh, he was having a grand time, no mistake about that, but to keep this up day in and day out? How did anyone survive?

And although he had set out to impress Abadon with his wildness and claim the grand prize of having the ultimate bad boy in his bed, it seemed like he was slipping on the battlefront.

He'd known he was making progress when Abadon crooned that song to him. It was romantic cliché bullshit, but his unique voice singing those words low and deep had touched something deep inside of Charle... his libido.

He could close his eyes and imagine that voice begging him to fuck him harder... kind of like the mystery man. Yeah, he could easily replace the mystery man who set his world on fire with Abadon. It was great to have a face to a fantasy, even if it were only for wanking sessions.

And then he blew it with the drugs. Until that point Abadon had been all in and participating eagerly. Then he called him an idiot over a pill.

Yeah, he was an idiot. His mind circled back to statistics of people dying from drug overdoses and excessive drinking and he thought that maybe he was pushing things a bit. Maybe it was time to use other means to get Abadon's attention.

He was considering his next way to strike when the doors opened and the man with the tape measure and a few of his friends poured out.

"Charle!" he called and Charle could not hide the grin that spread across his lips. This guy, Jessie, he thought his name was, ambled over, his girl under his arm. "Man, we're about to beat feet to another party. Wanna join in?"

"I don't know." He absently took another bottle of water that Jessie's girl handed to him.

"This place is getting out of control and I know Abadon is gonna split soon. He and his die-hard Locusts don't get caught. Well, the wannabe's do all the time, but he always rolls out before the cops roll in. And in this town, Sheriff Brown... I know, dumb name, is kind of a hard-ass about things. And with Abadon on the move, the key players are going to split. Soon this place will be a meat market."

"Like you don't have a tape measure in your pocket."

"That was for fun... to give the kiddies something to talk about."

"You gave them a lot to talk about." Jessie's girl giggled. "I guess it's true what they say about skinny men."

"I'm not skinny." Charle snorted. "And I thought you were going to say that about black men."

"Oh, I know that's not true... all the time." She snickered. "Besides, I think you brought up another question. Length or Girth. You have some awesome length."

"Yes, you do." Jessie dropped a kiss on top of his girl's head.

"You didn't mind handling it, as I recall," Charle pointed out, wondering what Jessie was going to do now that they were no longer in a club surrounded by people of ambiguous sexuality.

"Relax," he snorted. "I ain't choosy. So long as a body is willing."

"And that brings us back to girth," his girl said. "I know a place where we can answer that question."

"You do?"

"Oh yeah, I do. It'll be a real party."

Charle looked back over his shoulder at the place where he was losing Abadon's attention, the party that was winding down, and thought *fuck it*.

"Sure. Let's get out of here."

"Charle!" Jessie exclaimed. "My main man!" He got a hug and a kiss on the cheek from his girl, and then they were off.

There was nothing to see here anyway. The moment had passed. Now maybe after a few more drinks in him, he could find a way to get the man's attention again and this time hold it.

"Where we going?" someone else in the small group asked.

"To hell if we don't pray!" a smart-ass called out.

"Nah, going to have some fun," Jessie's girl called back. "Boys and girls, I'm about to take you to Paradise."

"So long as you get me to my bus on time," Charle warned and there was agreement all around. "Awesome. I don't want them to leave without me."

Chapter 3

"I'm going to fucking kill him."

Today was a frustrating time of trying to track Charle Lexington down. Abadon had turned his back for a moment and then poof, the bastard had done a runner. Now guilt was starting to set in and he wondered if they would find a dehydrated corpse in leather pants instead of the kind of cute, irritating, and well-hung porcupine that was their resident reporter.

It was his fault that Charle was trying to be something he was not so Abadon had to slow him down, at least a little, to fix the mess he was becoming.

A little excitement was one thing, but Charle-boy was going the full monty and, for some strange reason, it disturbed him. Okay, his full monty was impressive but that was beside the point. He was getting out of control. It's not like Abadon wanted to put the man on lock-down or anything, he just wanted him to be careful and for Abadon himself to be there guiding him... protecting him.

He didn't know when this urge to corrupt became the urge to protect but the feelings were there and he wasn't going to do anything to stop the instinct. His instincts had meant the difference between life and death for far too many generations for him to discount them now. Everything in him was telling him to protect Charle with the strength of all that he was, but that protection wouldn't mean shit if he couldn't find the man.

Charle-boy was off to the races, nowhere to be found, and he was left postponing their exit from this dinky little town so he could find the cute little idiot.

Trying to sneak around this town while staying relatively incognito was damn near impossible when you were a household name. He had to tie his hair into a tail, glamor away his tattoos and markings, dress in mundane clothing, and walk among the people.

He fucking hated walking among the people.

He was a god of destruction, but damn, these people were doing the job for him. Class divisions, racial divisions, social divisions... who needed to pray for destruction when humanity did a better job than he could ever do.

His Hunt for Charle started when he didn't show up at the bus. Someone had mentioned he went off with the tape measure guy and friends, and Abadon assumed that he just went to get his rocks off. Okay, he had to bite down on some anger at those thoughts, since he really didn't want Charle fucking around with strangers. It was dangerous. But he pushed back his anger and concentrated on trying to find the guy.

All morning he made phone calls and called in favors. He started getting a photo stream off Instagram called Afro Gone Wild and wanted to curse himself for being seven kinds of a fool.

There was Charle, his Charle, trying to breakdance... nude. There was one of him on his knees taking a beer luge from two busty drag queens. Then the photo of him shirtless and being used for a body shot. There was Charle in bondage gear spanking some laughing man across a sawhorse, and Charle getting his lower back licked by a set of very attractive twins with the caption reading, "Fuck You Andy and Candy! Real Twins Rock!" There was Charle in a mosh pit, Charle spinning liquor bottles while a leather clad daddy watched on in approval, and Charle napping between two male strippers while a third painted his fingernails emerald green to match the pop of color on his tattoo. There was even a few of him at the first party with his junk swinging around that caught Abadon staring at him with a hungered confusion on his face.

Well, at least now he had a few leads to follow.

"Corrupted, huh?" Hash asked, snickering as Abadon glowered at his phone. "Looks like he could teach you a few things or two."

"No orgies… yet," Python called out from where he was eagerly following the photo feed. "And they found out who he is. His name is starting to pop up and some who know him are saying it's fake news."

"Fuck, I hate that term," Apollon called out from where he was saving the photos to his laptop. "I bet you're getting a buzz off of this," he told Abadon. "'Cause I know I am."

"This is getting out of control," Abadon grumbled when a new photo popped up on what people deemed "Charle Hunt" and this time he was being taught to do the splits on a stripper pole. Who knew the little bastard was that flexible?

"Well, he's trending." Hash laughed. "And look, we get a mention too. When did you give him your snake, Sin? There is video of him trying to do the Selma Hayek dance from Dusk to Dawn. He ever take belly dancing? He's got some moves."

"Yoga," Abadon grumbled. And when everyone stared at him added, "What? It's in his profile."

"You created a monster." Apollon chuckled. "Go you."

"I didn't want him to go this far," Abadon protested.

"You're just jealous because you aren't out there with him. He did this all on his own without the help of big brother."

"I am worried that he may kill himself." He shot Hash a death glare. "And I don't think of him as my brother."

"That's for sure," Python pointed to the photo that was going to be infamously now known as Dick Sling. "You're practically drooling right there."

"I am not."

"You want him." Hash took the reins again. "You're like a little boy tugging at his pig tails."

"I am not."

"Just admit it. You like him. He's different and you like that."

"He's..." Abadon was always truthful with himself and the gods that shared his pantheon, honest to a fault actually. "Okay, I kind of like him. He reminds me of the one that got away."

"Thought so." Apollon nodded. "Glad to see that you can admit it."

"I wanted him to party a bit, to find himself. I didn't want him to go full Charlie Sheen on me."

"Well, he's not screaming about tiger's blood so maybe you have a shot at finding him before he hurts himself."

"Or fucks someone else," Apollon cheerfully interjected.

"I hate you, Enk," Abadon snapped and the god of mischief laughed.

So now Charle hung... hunt...was in full swing. The boys broke up, each taking a different part of town to try and track the young man down. No one was successful.

The sun had set and the photo streams had stopped and Abadon grew more worried.

After tracking down a few hints from the partygoers from that first night, he tracked Charle down, at last, to a gay bar where he was going shot for shot with some locals.

"Time to call it a night at this place," he urged but Charle disagreed.

"It's only nine o'clock and I'm having fun."

"Where did you sleep last night?"

"Between Richard and Heath... I think. Well, there was a nap. And then there were kiddie pools... and jello."

Chalre looked and sounded dazed and confused.

Abadon reached out to touch him, and relaxed when he only read exhaustion and a heavy buzz. There were no drugs harder than weed in his system.

"Jello? You aren't sticky."

"Well, there was a shower... and someone cleaned my pants with water but they got tighter."

"That will happen." Abadon tried not to laugh in relief. Charle was still Charle.

"And I lost my shirt. But someone gave me with one... gave me one with unicorns. I like unicorns. I may be a bit drunk."

"I can see that." Charle was hanging onto the bar in the middle of a collection of very attractive men and a few beautiful ladies. "Know where you are?"

"No." He blinked adorably up at him. "Someone said the music was good and the drinks were strong and here we are." He waved his arms around, barely missing hitting the person pressed up close behind him trying to order. "Where are we?"

"*Bottom's Up.*"

"Strange name."

"Reported the best gay club in the area."

"Well shit, this is a gay bar?" He blinked owlishly up at him and Abadon threw back his head as laughter rolled from his throat. "I always wanted to go to a gay bar. As a gay man, this should have been a rite of passage. You ever been to a gay bar?"

"I own a few in Europe," Abadon said.

"Well shit." He looked around and then grinned up at him again. "Where's the rest of the band?"

"Shh." Abadon was quick to shush him. "They are around, probably back at the bus. They were looking for you. We all were looking for you. They probably got tired and are doing their best to make up for the sleep they lost by trying to out-party you."

"Why aren't you with them?"

"'Cause I'm here with you, Charle-boy. Someone has to make sure you don't get in over your head."

"You said head." He snickered and offered his drink up for tasting. "It's good. It's a bit sweet."

Rolling his eyes, Abadon turned to the bar and ordered whiskey straight, tossing a credit card on the table. "I got his virgin highness over there too."

The bartender's mouth dropped open and he placed his finger across his lips, the universal sign of keep this a secret... which of course meant that the world would know in about two hours. It would take that long for the owner to realize who was standing in his bar and spread the story or someone with a cell phone to take a photo and send it off to social media. Either way, the bartender was going to get a big tip because he nodded and saucily set up the tab all the while pretending that an international star wasn't hanging out in a gay bar in the middle of nowhere.

"Not a virgin!" Charle protested, then leaned in to him, squeezing his arm a bit. "You are big."

"You are drunk."

"I'm tickling the bottom of tipsy," he corrected in a scholarly voice. "There is a difference."

"So long as you don't pop any more pills unless I check them out."

"I didn't like that. No more pills. For a moment the world went crazy out of control and I didn't like that."

You would have liked it even less if I hadn't pulled it from your system, Abadon thought but he nodded in agreement. Out loud he said, "Then don't take anymore. If you wanna do anything, stick to weed. Stuff that grows out of the ground is your safest bet."

"You know your weed?"

"I own a dispensary." He chuckled. "It pays to diversify."

In a few years he would have to pack it in as a rocker

before anyone noticed he hadn't aged in a while and he wanted to be settled with a tidy nest egg before that happened. Sure he had money to burn, but he had people he needed to take care of, like his seven.

"Wicked." Charle then tossed his drink back like a pro and ordered another, petting Abadon's arm all the while. After two more drinks and a fair amount of time petting his biceps, Charle turned and smiled endearingly up at him.

"You're sooo big," he purred. "How'd you get so big?"

"I work out."

"I work out." He lifted his arms and flexed a little, pouting when a firm but not overly large bicep popped. A drunk Charle was an increasingly adorable Charle.

"I swing a giant sword and breach castles." Not lying about that.

"That would do it." Charle turned and watched as the same sex couples danced on the packed dance floor, drank companionably in groups, and just did what folk in a bar do. "It's not different."

"Pardon me?" Abadon tossed back his drink and tapped the bar for a refill. The bartender was right on the spot with it.

"The gay bar," Charle explained, eyes wide, his head still bobbing around as he watched the patrons. "It's like any other bar."

"Because it is like any other bar."

"I expected it to be different."

"Why? You're gay and you're just like any other guy, Charle-boy."

"You're right," he declared sitting upright. "I'm just like any other guy. So why don't I get treated like any other guy, huh? Abby, tell me."

Oh great. Charle was a self-pitying drunk. "Stop calling me Abby and maybe I will."

"Well, that's the only name I could find on record for you. Your people are good, 'cause I'm a research god."

"Call me Nergal." It was the first time he uttered his true name to a human in decades. Like his past as a warrior god and all the sacrifices offered in his name, he had cast that aside as he grew and changed with the times. "And you're just like other guys, Charle-boy. But if others don't treat you like the rest of the boys, it's because you're not like them and that is fine."

"I'm just as good --" Indignant, his green eyes flashed and that, too, Abadon found adorable.

"I didn't say that. I said you are different. Hell, I am different, Charle-boy. That's what makes you you and me me."

"But no one wants me." He pouted. "Not the real me. Not really."

"Then you find someone who wants you for you. Don't settle." Like me, he bit back. Instead, he tossed back his drink while Charle sipped at something that was garishly orange and smelled like pure sugar and oranges. "Your exes were asses."

"Ohh," Charle purred. "Song title. My Exes are Asses... You can keep that one."

"Thanks, I'll pass." He snorted.

He reached out and touched Charle's arm, drawing away some of his intoxication and an infection he could feel building in his nipple ring. He was a god of destruction so he could feel and manipulate destruction in its many forms.

"Dance with me."

Before he could protest, Charle dragged him out on the floor and started jumping and bouncing to the tech-swing that was blaring from the speakers. What happened to the sexy dance from before? 'Cause really, it was so embarrassing and uniquely unapologetic that Abadon stood there and enjoyed the show, glaring at anyone who approached like they had something to say. They backed off quickly when they saw the expression on his face.

Soon though, they were separated when some pretty little thing latched onto him and, screaming, pulled him into a conga line.

Abadon shook his head and went to retrieve his card. They were done drinking here. In fact, he was growing bored. He looked up at a laughing Charle and felt a tug at his heart. Well, it wasn't a tug, it was more like anger. Yeah, he was growing angry. He brought Charle there and the tart was out...

Nope, he shook his head, shocked at what he was feeling. He was not jealous. He couldn't be. But there was something familiar about him... the way he rubbed his arms, that caress felt familiar. He shook his head and reached for the credit card. He signed his name and left a hell of a tip for the bartender and winked when the man gasped in shock.

"Outta here," he whispered before wading in to pull Charle from the middle of a pretty-boy sandwich. "Time to go."

"But --"

"Paparazzi," he intoned. "You know they're coming and we need to be gone before they get here."

"Scared for your reputation?"

"No, don't want a warrant for punching someone in the face."

"But you're not ashamed --"

"I fuck men and women."

"But you --"

Before he could say anything else, Abadon decided on the swiftest means to get the man out of the building before he really did punch someone. He bent down and kissed him.

Charle tasted of sugar with a hint of fruit and a deep

rich flavor that had to be all Charle.

It was new and familiar at the same time. He slid his tongue into the warm cavern of his mouth and had to bite back a groan of his own at the feelings. His spine tingled and his poor dick grew hard once more. Charle moaned, his lithe body squirmed against his, those tight muscles rippling deliciously against his own. Fuck, he was a warm tight armful and that large dick -- He could already feel it sliding inside him again--

He jerked himself away. No. Charle was for corrupting... Okay, he could really corrupt the kid in bed just to see what happened, but Charle deserved better. He didn't want to corrupt his soul.

"Next bar." He declared and the shocked, sad look turned eager.

"Yes! Next bar!" he declared, thrusting his arm into the air. "With music you can dance to. I like dancing."

"You can't dance. You blew the stereotype."

"But I want to move!"

So they wound up in a country and western bar... with a drunken Charle... on a bull.

Chapter 4

They were at *24-Hour Beautician and Scarification While You Drink Spa*. No, really it was a place--a hair salon/barber shop/day spa/bar/tattoo and piercing parlor. And the ladies that ran it were offering up waffles.

The waffles were amazing. Charle was struggling a bit. A fresh tongue piercing could do that to a man. Nergal helped out where he could, drawing away some pain and increasing his body's ability to heal, but he couldn't magic it all away. There was always a price to pay for body modification when you weren't a god and Charle, barely sober and struggling to chew his blueberry waffles, now he knew that.

"Why did I let you talk me into doing half those things?" he complained and Abadon chuckled into his Bananas Foster waffles. "It's not funny."

"I didn't talk you into anything. You did it on your own. I just watched."

And it was the funniest thing he had ever seen. Charle with his mouth hanging open while the piercer dotted ink onto the perfect spot. He looked like the victim of a low budget porn cum-shot, his eyes wide and a "just get this over with" expression. He squeaked a little as the needle went through, then he gave a little cheer when he realized it didn't hurt as much as his nipple. It was almost as funny as listening to him whine when the ladies took exception to his hair looking like a rat's nest, their words, as two descended upon him, cornrowing his hair until he was deemed fit for human interaction. By then his buzz was just about gone.

"And you paid. A lack of cash would have stopped me from doing much and I left my wallet in the bus. Thank God, I still have my ID."

"But I was having fun watching you," Abadon admitted, taking another bite while he contemplated getting his nails done. One of the ladies who escorted them back to the restaurant portion of the mega business looked like she gave a mean hand massage and playing guitar sometimes caused the tendons in his hands to cramp up. "I like to watch."

Charle blinked at him, then ran his new tongue ring over his upper lip. Instantly, Nergal's pants were too tight.

"Tease."

"I am not," Charle protested. "I never offer what I don't plan on delivering."

Nergal choked a little, then glared. He was getting really tired of this game. He had chased this boy all over... Indiana? He still had no idea where they were, but he chased him everywhere, protected him, helped him, and the kid was still fucking with him.

"You don't play games like that, kid. It's not you." As wild as Charle had become, there was a line that he refused to cross. There was so much integrity in him.

"I don't play games."

"You don't do one-night stands."

"I got blow jobs --"

"Party trick for the rich and famous." Abadon waved it away. "It's no big deal."

"It is to me."

"And there, I proved my point." He was feeling frustrated and mean and the urge to poke at Charle was growing.

"I'll have you know, I have had a one-night stand before. And I have to admit, it wasn't all that."

"The sex?"

"Fuck no." The kid looked reverent. "The sex was amazing. The experience let me know that there were things out there for me that I haven't tried."

"Really?" He knew he sounded doubtful but--

"Really. I was going to walk away when I opened

- 121 -

that door, but something made me want to be someone else. I walked in when the guy called to me. I mean he was a big guy too, kind of like you, and he was gagging for it."

"So you walked in on someone jerking off--

"No. He was getting fucked and it was all wrong. There was some woman who left happy enough but the guy, the man fucking him, didn't know what he was doing."

Nergal froze with his fork half-way to his mouth. There was no way...

"Stop looking at me like that. I was safe. In fact, I have to thank you for getting me laid. The band had promotional condoms. So I slipped one on and... fuck it was so hot."

"And so dark you could barely see."

"Yes." Charle looked excited to finally be sharing. "Yes, it was so dark and so hot. The other guy kind of slunk out of the room and he must not have been very big because I had to stretch the guy's hole open before I split him in half."

"Lotion for lube." He dropped his fork and sat back. "Orange-scented lotion for lube."

"It was all I had and --" Charle stopped. "How did you --"

"I told you to get the fuck in me. I told you I would spank your skinny ass if you didn't --"

"It was you!" Charle all but jumped up out of his seat as he ran a shaking hand over his face. "It was you."

"Well fuck."

Nergal sat back in his chair and tried to resolve this situation in his head. Well, he finally decided, that was why Charle fascinated him so.

He inhaled deeply, trying to place his scent and although there was a hint trace of it, probably the thing that had him running after him in the first place, but the rest of his memories were tainted by the scent of that orange lotion.

"I-- I --" Charle took his seat again and stared. A few people in the place snapped photos as Charle's outburst garnered them some attention.

"Okay. I think we need to get out of here. In a few moments we're going to be surrounded."

Even as he spoke, a man with his hair freshly cut...those lines were on fleek...walked up to their table. "Hey, aren't you --"

"Abadon," Charle sighed, as the man blinked and turned to stare at Nergal. "I was going to say that reporter gone wild but damn..."

Then he was snapping pictures of them both.

"Time to leave," Nergal gritted out as he rose to his feet and grabbed Charle by the hand. He reached into his pocket and threw some money on the table before dragging Charle back through the tattoo shop and piercing parlor. Their piercer waved and they rushed out the front door. Charle was still looking rather dazed.

"It's a ways to the bus so we're going to have to walk and talk fast."

"It was you," Charle repeated. "I-- wow."

"I knew there was something special about you," Nergal admitted. "I was writing all those songs about the one who got away and there you are. Fuck me."

"I did."

Nergal turned to glare at Charle for a moment, ignoring the smug look on his face, before they hurried down the street. "Yeah, you did. And I don't allow that to happen often."

"But why did you?"

"You ever been in a rut?"

"Like right now?" Charle's sarcasm was clear even if he wasn't looking at the faces Charle was no doubt making behind his back.

"Well, I was tired and depressed... changing the focus of this band is not easy even if this is more like an addition. I'd rather sing about disembowelment than sing about emotions."

"So that led you to getting fucked in the backroom of a venue?"

"Not really," he sighed, slowing down a little. They were making good time and it didn't look like anyone had followed them. "I mean... I didn't know what I wanted and the guy and the woman with him offered. He was hot and I was horny and she was satisfied and then I was disappointed."

"And then I came along." Yeah, he was reading smug in that voice now.

"Yes, you came along, Charle. How didn't I know it was you? I mean, how didn't you know it was me?"

"It was really dark," Charle defended himself. "And I was riding on cloud nine from making you come without touching your dick."

"It was a good night," Nergal admitted. "And I have been trying to recapture it ever since."

"Well, it was the reason I wanted to explore, so to speak." Charle started walking beside him, adjusting the dragging grip on his wrist to holding Nergal's hand. "And I wanted you. I wanted to go back and find you, but I fell asleep and then you were gone."

"Really?" Nergal hated that hopeful tone in his voice but shit, he had regretted leaving without contact information too.

"Really. And I decided that was the perfect jump-off point for me to try something new with my life. I just never expected you to be such an asshole, Nergal."

"I was dealing with losing you," he admitted. "And I never really had you. Ain't that some shit?" How do you explain to a human that the rush of power he got from him, unselfish power, was like taking a shot of the finest whiskey and feeling the burn for hours?

"I was chasing what you made me feel and look!" Charle jerked his hand as they closed in on the bus. They were making good time and he was pleased to see his end point in sight. "The thing I was chasing was right here."

"You were out getting blowjobs and drinking."

"I was trying to get your attention and I thought --" Charle looked rather bashful all of a sudden "--I was trying to be what you wanted. I wasn't joking. I wanted you."

"I thought you wanted the stranger in the backroom."

"You made me feel like that stranger in the backroom was with me again. You must know you're hot. And after getting to know you a bit... well, I was serious. I wanted you. Still do."

They had reached the bus and Nergal beat on the door twice. Crazy Max popped it open and Nergal dragged Charle past the other band members who were eating something, ignored their hooting, and made for the master bedroom in the back.

Once there, he slammed the door shut just to have a place to press Charle. He needed to feel his body against him again... and knowing that here was the man who upset his world, who had him writing ballads and bemoaning fate... was right there... He was hard and throbbing in his pants. Charle was pushed face-first against the door, Nergal crowding in behind. And that ass, fuck, that perfect ass was pressing up against his hard dick.

He bent down to nuzzle at the back of Charle's neck, lapping at the tender skin there before nipping him, making Charle gasp and push his ass back into him. He gripped the smaller man by his hips and began to grind against him hard.

"Fuck, you feel so good..."

Charle's hands were pressed against the door, and he was arching his hips back as he moaned softly. He looked over his shoulder, his pupils blown, and he licked his upper lip, then nipped his bottom lip.

That was enough for Nergal to bend down and take that mouth the same way he wanted to take that body. He forced his tongue inside and decided he loved the flavor of Charle with blueberries and syrup.

Charle was eating at his mouth just as hard as the air heated up between the two of them.

Nergal couldn't help but run his hands over that perfect body, slipping his hands around to the other man's chest, tugging at his nipple ring just to hear him gasp in shocked pleasure.

One hand went down into those tight leather pants and he cursed lightly when he discovered that Charle-boy was sans underwear. He gripped at the shaft of his dick, his thumb teasing the head as he spread around the generous amount of precum Charle was producing around the slit.

Charle sighed deeply and sagged back into him, his hands leaving the door to latch into his hair.

"I gotta have you," Abadon whispered, pulling back to spin Charle around as he dropped to his knees.

A few tugs and the leather pants were open and Charle's fat cock was springing out.

"Delicious," he declared before bending lower and just sucking the whole thing in his mouth.

"Nergal," Charle breathed. "Yeah, baby. Just take me down."

The hands in his hair were not demanding or jerking him forward, they were just there and they helped ground him in the moment.

Nergal laved his tongue along Charle's hard length, sucking as much inside as he could while playing with the thick vein that ran up the back of his dick. Charle was still growing. Abadon's hole burned as he remembered the feel of it splitting him in half.

He swallowed deeply and sank down on Charle lower, going until the head of his cock bumped the back of his throat. It was a little uncomfortable as he was not used to doing this, but he knew that he could deep throat him as soon as he got used to the delicious feeling of being stuffed.

God, there was nothing like a good fat dick in his mouth, taking control of a lover and dominating him this way. He was the power over his pleasure and as he cut his eyes up to stare into Charle's eyes, he read awe and shock as he got another little jolt of pure worship. It really was an addictive feeling.

"Oh my God, Nergal." Charle was panting, his hips rocking gently, trying not to choke him. But that wasn't what Nergal wanted. He wanted to be gagged on that dick, he wanted to stuff Charle down and take him so good that every other lay he ever had would be obliterated from his mind.

It was time to get real.

He gripped the perfect globes of Charle's ass and jerked him forward.

"Fuck!" Charle shouted as his head slammed back against the door. He uncontrollably slammed his hips upwards, sliding down Nergal's throat just the way he wanted.

One of his hands went to his pants and soon, Nergal was stroking his own hard dick in time to the head bobbing pace he was setting on Charle, trying to ease up the pressure that was building in his lower back.

The man's knees were starting to shake and he was babbling in his cute shocked voice as Nergal finally pulled off.

"Why'd you stop?" he demanded, rolling his head back against the door, his fingers massaging Nergal's scalp.

"'Cause we need the bed."

Charle moved like he was on fire and before Nergal could rise to his feet, Charle was naked and sprawled across his bed.

Nergal kicked off his boots and shimmied out of his pants while moving toward the bed. While his hands were over his head tugging off his shirt, he felt Charle strike.

Charle was a generous lover as he remembered when the younger man wrapped his hands around his neglected cock, bending forward to examine the ring going to the head of his dick. "I remember more of them," he muttered, running a finger gently up the back of his shaft.

"I took them out..." He purred, tossing back his head as Charle's fingers danced over his hot flesh. He could feel his balls swell at his lover's touch, and yes, Charle Lexington was going to be his lover.

Once he took him, he knew he would never get enough of him. Charle had to be his. He had to possess him, those bright green eyes, that perfect body, that attitude. He wanted it all.

"Those were the best parts." Charle's breath caressed the damp head of his dick as he moved closer. "But look how wet you're getting for me."

It was true. Precum was beading up and dripping down the metal bar that ran through the head of his cock, making the metal gleam in the dim light of the room.

"What're you gonna do with it, Charle-boy?" He was not a nice person by any means so his hands cupped the back of Charle's head as he ran the wet head of his dick over his face.

Charle was up for the challenge because he looked up at him with wicked eyes as his tongue lashed out and caught a clear droplet as it hung on the ball of his bar.

"Mmm," he purred, moving closer, running his stubbled face over his dick, painting himself with Nergal's scent and taste. The shiny snail trails over his cheeks made Nergal hiss before he reached down and pulled Charle up until they were face to face, so he licked himself from Charle's soft flesh.

"What do you want, baby?" he whispered as he lapped at Charle's lips, swallowing his moans, holding Charle closer to his bare body as Charle shivered.

Damn, the kid was beautiful, trembling and needy.

"I wasn't kidding." His voice was low and intense. His hands again went to Nergal's hair, pulling at the locks, urging him closer, begging for any contact.

Their cocks were rubbing deliciously together, their shared precum acting as lube as they began to grind against each other. Nergal's hands went to that perfectly rounded ass, pulling him closer as he gave in to Charle's demands and took sipping kisses from his lips.

"I want you to fuck me."

Somehow Nergal managed not to come all over himself after hearing that. Struggling for control as another jolt of pure worship flowed to him, he got Charle on his back at the head of the bed and his finger on the lube stored in the bedside table.

"You're so going to get it."

"I told you I wasn't a tease." Charle placed his feet flat on the bed and spread his knees wide, reaching down to hold his balls out of the way, exposing his twitching hole. "I want you to fuck me. I dreamed about taking that fat dick deep inside of me."

There was no stopping him after hearing that.

Nergal swooped down and took Charle in a demanding kiss, his tongue invading his mouth before he pulled back and bit at his lips.

Charles mewed, arching his hips upward, making his hard dick flop against his flat belly.

The kisses moved down to his newly pierced nipple, Nergal tonguing then, tugging at the gold bars.

"Fuck, that's intense," Charle growled, his own hands going to Nergal's back, tracking down his skin and making his own back arch under Charle's addictive touch.

"Not as intense as it's about to get."

Nergal abandoned his peaked nipples and went straight for his cock again as he popped open the lube. As he took him into his mouth, he looked up to see Charle staring at him, awe and lust in his face.

"You're so good at that," he breathed. Then Charle hissed as Nergal slid one well -lubed finger into his ass.

He groaned at the silky soft feeling when Charle's muscles seemed to suck him in.

"Fuuuck..." Charle's head went back into the pillows as his whole body shuddered then relaxed.

Nergal swirled him deep as he worked him open on his fingers, adding a second then a third as he loosened up nicely.

"Eager."

"Been so long." Charle panted, grinding down on his fingers, riding them in ways that made Nergal's cock jump in anticipation.

"Time to end your drought, baby." Nergal purred as he moved in between Charle's legs, placing them on his shoulder and spreading him wide.

"Condom!" Charle gasped and Nergal pulled back to reach into his drawer and pull one out.

"Better safe than sorry," he agreed and pulled back long enough to don one.

Then he was pressing the head of his dick against the stretched pucker's opening.

Sliding into Charle was like sliding into heaven. He was tight and slick, heated, and all for him.

"Fuck!" Charle was gasping, his nails tearing into his

back and that made Nergal have to clamp down on his own control so he wouldn't just slam into the giving body beneath him.

"Shh." He struggled to sooth, his own body trembling as the inferno within him blazed brighter. "I'll go slow."

"Fuck going slow!" Charle protested, lifting his head up to glare. "Get in me now! Move, Abadon! You're in my ass. Fucking destroy it!"

Charle's legs slid down from his shoulder and both legs climbed down around his waist with a strength he never knew he possessed. He slammed his ass upwards and then groaned as Nergal's cock sank in deep. Only when his balls were slapping against Charle's ass did the younger man relent and ease back onto the bed.

"Fuck, Charle-boy. Didn't that hurt?"

"Yeah," he breathed. "So fucking good."

The words Power Bottom flashed across his mind as Charle tightened his legs around his waist, his heels digging into his ass. "Move!"

Nergal moved.

And Charle roared. He clawed and bit and scratched at him and all the while the low hum of pure worship flowed into him.

It was a double whammy, the hot perfection of his body sliding up and down his cock while his praise and emotions flowed into his body and mind, raising him to heights so extreme he thought he would go mad.

"Fuck, Charle... Fuck..." He could only gasp as his hips pistoned harder and harder.

Charle was demanding and wild in bed. Once someone had him, how could they ever let this go?

Damn, it was so good.

He slid his hands between them and wrapped Charle's dick and began to pump it hard.

His lover let out a wail that damn near burst his

eardrums as his whole body began to quake and tremble.

"Harder." Charle panted, his beautiful face slack with ecstasy. His nails dug into Nergal's shoulders as he threw back his head and wailed.

His cock thickened in Nergal's hand just before Charle's hot release coated his pumping hand in thick white spend. Charle's insides were rioting -- grasping and milking at Nergal's dick as he rode him through his release. The worship, it was totally out of control, powerful and pure. It slammed into Nergal with the force of a freight train. Nergal was unable to resist the call. He closed his eyes and took everything his lover gave him and tried to return more. He pumped into him, keeping him on edge until Charle was sobbing, begging him to stop. Only then did he give into his body's demands.

His boy was a sobbing shaking mess as he ground in deep and succumbed to his own release, feeling the pull of energy coming from his lover. Nergal hissed, throwing back his head, aware that his eyes were glowing but unable to stop them.

His tattoo, his marks of power, began to glow as his balls drew up and his orgasm was torn from his body.

He was wrecked. He shuddered as the energy slowly began to fade. Closing his eyes, he lay down beside Charle. They were both panting sweaty messes and Nergal breathed in the scent of the two of them.

He was perfect. Charle was perfect. Life was perfect.

All except for the lights that still flashed behind his closed eyes.

He opened them, hoping for a long look at his lover's face, replete and worn out from the sex, only to see that the glow wasn't behind his eyes.

It was flame -- all over his body. His tattoos were glowing and Charle, well, his boy looked like he was torn between fascination and horror. After a second, when Charle didn't go running off screaming into the night,

Nergal knew that he had to tell him the truth if he wanted to keep him.

"Don't panic. I can explain."

The look on his lover's face did not bode well. Damn it. Why did life have to be so complicated?

Chapter 5

"Um... you're glowing." Charle very slowly eased back from Abadon, trembling in sudden fear.

There was no way to describe coming down from the heights of ecstasy to land in some kind of horror movie special effect zone.

The sex was hot, no doubt about that. His ass was still burning in a pleasant kind of way. But the sight he was seeing now was enough to make it pucker uncomfortably as petrification set in. Was petrification a real word? He hadn't a clue but it fit the suddenly glowing scenario that was going on in this bed.

Speaking of being in this bed... Charle hit the ground with a thump, tangled in sheets, the panicky feeling in his stomach growing as Abadon turned bright red eyes in his direction.

"Holy shit! You're the devil!"

Can you get a social disease from fucking the devil? They'd used condoms but he had a feeling that a latex barrier had nothing on the Prince of Evil.

Oh, God. He'd fucked evil and liked it. He was so going to burn in hell.

"Oh." Abadon lifted a green glowing arm and stared at it for a moment before wincing. "I can explain --"

"Are you going to kill me?" Charle was scooting backward across the carpeted floor. Sure, he was leaving rug burn on his ass, but it was better than having your ass fried.

"Why would I kill you?" Abadon sat up and ran a hand through his wild sex hair.

Yeah, Charle had been all in that, pulling and tugging and now the man was going to eat his soul. How was this even remotely fair?

"Because... glowing... and... unless you're an alien?"

That was a little better than realizing that maybe he had just fucked the devil, but not by much.

"What?" He blinked and the red glow in his eyes faded so that more black showed. "I'm no damn alien. Really, Charle?"

"Well, it makes more sense than to say... I fucked the devil. You're the devil right? 'Cause normal people don't glow even after good sex."

Abadon growled and as Charle watched, the green glow that surrounded him like a halo seemed to fade into his person until only the wild runes and symbols he had tattooed on his body glowed.

"I'm... well, I wouldn't say the devil, per se. I would have to ask you which one you're talking about --"

"There are more than one? Oh shit! Catholic school had it all wrong."

"I'm not Catholic." Abadon snorted and when he made to rise from the bed, Charle let out a manly squeal and crab walked backwards until his ass hit the wall behind him. "Stop that. If I was going to hurt you, I would have already done so."

"You're not... are you feeding off of me? Holy shit! That is why you wanted to party with me. You took control of my mind --"

"Not one of my powers."

"You admit it! You have powers and you used them on me!"

"Only to prevent your stupid ass from overdosing or dying from alcohol poisoning," Abadon snapped. "And stop looking at me that way. You look at me like I'm going to kill you."

Charle felt his heart race as Abadon raised his voice. The man was looking more frustrated than angry, but you really never could tell with devils. Then again, what the fuck did he know about devils? He had never met one before.

"You're not out to destroy the world?"

"Why would I do that?" He rolled his eyes so hard Charle was sure he heard it. "Not to say that you people aren't due for a plague or something. A really good war would help thin out the stupid."

Well, he had a point there, but still. "What do you want?"

"Maybe to live?" He asked, rising to his feet. Charle held in a squeak as Abadon causally strode bare-assed naked across the room and snatched up his guitar. "Maybe I just want to do something I love and just exist."

"But the Bible --"

"I'm not the devil in the Bible, Charle. How dare you stereotype me like that! It's racist."

"What? What?" What kind of fucked up logic was this? He was the devil. The devil destroyed things and lied and cheated, and caused death wherever he roamed. "Not-- but --"

"There is more than one god in this world, isn't there?"

"Um..."

"What is a god, Charles?" He started strumming as he took a seat in the armchair near the bed. He looked down at the guitar before those red and black eyes seemed to latch onto his face once again. "You know the answer. What makes a being a god?"

"Um... worship?"

"Exactly, Charle-boy. The act of worship. And who do people worship... other than the gods in your holy texts?"

"Um..."

"Famous people, Charle. Hell, people worship money, influence, power, burritos, taco Tuesday, those stupid cats online... people worship many things in many ways, Charle. And among the most fiercely worshiped is..." He let his words trail off as he stared Charle down.

"Rock stars?"

"But you call us…"

"Rock gods."

"Precisely. You call us rock gods, lords of metal, any title you deem worthy to apply to us."

That made Charle settle down more. Really, he was sitting there on the carpet wrapped in a sheet and having a philosophical conversation with a god… or a devil. As he watched, Abadon broke into a guitar riff so fast that his fingers seemed to blur and the music he produced sounded so unworldly that for a moment all he could do was sit there and stare. As he wound down, Charle realized he had to ask. "So which one are you?"

"Pardon?"

"Which god or devil are you?"

"Still hung up on labels?"

"I have to know."

"Why? Scared for your mortal soul?" His lips quirked in humor and Charle huffed as he realized that he was being laughed at.

"Not funny. I think I have the right to know --"

"You didn't care when you were fucking my ass in that office."

Well, damn. Abadon was correct. He had been so ready to get his rocks off, to prove that he wasn't a boring, whiny, reliable stick in the mud that he really didn't give any thought to going out and doing something wild.

"That was different." Was he that selfish that he just went about his merry way using people and taking what he wanted from them? No. He wasn't that kind of person.

"Different because?"

"Because I didn't know," he grumbled. His fear was lessening as he sat there and watched Abadon play, totally in the buff and totally comfortable with it. "I don't know what that says about me --"

"It says that you're human, Charles Lexington. And if you really want to know, I really was called Abadon."

"The place of destruction in the Bible?"

"No, that place in the Bible was named after me. You have to go to ancient Sumerian texts to find me. My original name really is Nergal."

"I don't --"

"I suppose some could call me the devil. I was a war god." He began to play something that sounded dark and sinister but enthralling at the same time. "I was the god of plague, war, death, and disease. I was a fire god, the lord of the desert. People feared me. People loved me. People would drop to their knees and praise me if I quirked an eyebrow. I was a rock star, Charle-boy. People from all over brought me tribute. I was their savior, the guardian to the gates of the underworld, their salvation from the barbarian hordes."

"And... and you still exist?" Trying to accept all of this was giving him a headache. How old was Abadon anyway?

"I still exist because people never stop killing, never stop causing plagues, and still worship at the destruction they attributed to me. But you know what the scary thing is, Charle boy?" He stopped playing abruptly, slamming his palms down on the strings, enveloping the room in silence. "The scary thing is that I never did any of those things. Bring about plagues? Maybe they should have bathed more or not shit and pissed in their drinking water. Brought about war? Maybe they shouldn't have raped and fucked their way into their neighbors' camps, stole their daughters, burned their crops. But everyone needs someone to blame and if they wanted to blame me, who was I to quibble? They created me because they didn't want to take responsibly for their actions when they saw the horrible things that they had done. So they created me, breathed me into life, and guess what? They still do. They still worship me, Charle. And as a rock star, the worship I get is more focused, more pure. No one is tainting my tributes with fear or anger. They praise me for the skills that I spent years honing. I'm being worshiped for my own merits, my own human actions."

He paused in his speaking to stare into Charle's eyes. "Do you even know how good that feels? Sure the worship I get from most is self-centered and rebellious, but no one is blaming me for murdering their family when they set their deaths in motion by their own thoughtless actions. Now people want to be like me, not fear me. They want my music to lift them to the lights of heaven, not offer a blood sacrifice and revenge for something I had no party to. And then there is you."

"Me?" Really, how fucked up was this? Charles Lexington was starting to feel pity for the devil. How did that even work?

It seemed that Abadon… Nergal…had been created by the selfish needs of a people who didn't like the consequences of their actions.

He tried to picture that for himself, always being blamed, always being the guilty party when you, in fact, had nothing to feel guilty about. His life was hard but he hadn't been created to be a cosmic scapegoat. Damn, he realized that he held some sympathy for the devil.

"You, Charle Lexington. You went into the anonymous sex not wanting anything. You praised me for how I made you feel. I can't tell you how long it had been since I felt that. You made me feel alive. That's why I couldn't get you off my mind."

"You said you didn't know who I was."

"I didn't." The guitar went down and Abadon leaned back in his chair, still observing Charle. "I only knew that you reminded me of that someone, of a feeling… I shaved my body hair because I couldn't forget your smell. Your scent on my skin was hypnotic. It had to be gone for me to function."

"And the rings? I mean, you have some major hardware going on…"

"I'm a god, Charle. I can do whatever I want. After you left, I removed them. I could feel your tongue tugging on the rings… It was all I could think about, so they had to go."

"But you wanted to help me find myself."

"I didn't know who you were, but there was something about you, Charle. I wanted to help you find yourself, as you say, and use that experience to get over what I was feeling. I wanted to create music that made me feel… like I felt when we were fucking. I felt alive and torn and I didn't want to let you go."

"So you were falling in love --"

"I never said that."

"You just said you didn't want to let me go."

"That doesn't mean I was in love. Charle? What do I know of love? I had a crazy ex I had to damn near kill to get away from, but who would love me? Who could? I was an exceptionally good warrior who was elevated somehow by powers that I don't fully understand and I became their god. When did I have time to know what love is? Unless you think you were falling in love with me --"

"I didn't say that."

"So we're back to where we started. I didn't mean for you to find out this way. But there is something about you that makes me forget myself. I feel comfortable in your presence and what you give me… I just can't explain it, what you to do me… Your Windsong stays on my mind," he crooned softly and Charle was torn between laughing and crying.

"So you aren't a devil, you're a god."

"I am whatever you need me to be."

That was way too much… Charle didn't know what

to think or to feel.

He pulled the sheet around him, never having felt this vulnerable before. "What do you want from me?"

"I don't know." Nergal looked aggrieved. "I just... I... Can't we just see where this takes us? I want you like I have never wanted another person, Charle. I want to explore this thing between us, see where it goes. I'm not going to hurt you. You know that. I'm not what I once was, a god of destruction, the devil if you will. I'm just Nergal and I'm finding myself not wanting to let you go."

He was a god. Those words kept flowing through Charle's mind. Nergal was a god. He'd fucked a god. He just let a god wear out his ass in the most delicious of ways. He was once a god of destruction. He was ageless. He was a god.

Charle, when he set out on this wild ride, had had no idea what was in store for him. He didn't expect to do half of the things that he'd managed to do. He rubbed shoulders with the stars, he rode a mechanical bull. He got tattooed and pierced, for goodness sake. And now he'd had sex with a god.

What could he offer a god?

Sure, he'd gone a little buck wild while trying to prove himself to Nergal, but that really wasn't him.

He was up at eight and had breakfast by nine. He did laundry on Tuesdays and called his mom every Sunday. He was the one everyone called to fix last minute bullshit. He was the magical negro so many times that it got to be annoying when people called him because he was so reliable. He was polo shirts and long sleeved t-shirts with his hair bound up as tightly as his anxieties. He wasn't... couldn't be what Nergal wanted him to be. He was getting emotional over someone who didn't exist. It wasn't like him to fuck a complete stranger, to stare in the face of danger and laugh, to challenge those who could physically and financially break him. But that's what he had been this whole trip.

The man that Nergal -- Abadon--was attracted to was a lie. He couldn't live a lie. He couldn't be a lie.

"I--I have to go."

He looked up as the smile fled Abadon's face. He watched the lingering glow melt into nothing and felt an aching disappointment that he was the cause of it. He knew that he was the cause of it and yet, he had to persist in telling the truth. He could not live a lie.

"What?"

"I 'm... I'm not what you think."

"Charle --"

"No." He shook his head as he rose to his feet. "No, Abadon."

"Nergal --"

"Abadon. I can't be what you need. I -- I have to go."

He turned and fled. He couldn't stand looking at the pain he was causing the man a moment more.

But it was for his own good. He wasn't what Abadon thought he was and he didn't want to be the one left abandoned once again, when he realized that Charle Lexington was the world's greatest imposter... the world's greatest coward.

The door closing behind him was the death knell of his rebellious stage. Rebellion had come late, but it was merely a stage. Now it was time for him to go back to reality. The reality of being just plain old Charle Lexington, bystander, hanger-on, and definitely not the object of want for a god.

* * *

Charle had no idea how he got dressed, but he managed to do that and pack what was left of his belongings in total darkness.

He had no idea where the bus was parked, but he knew he had to get out of there and fast... before he turned around and...

"You hurt him."

Charle felt his heart leap into his throat as he spun to face a resigned-looking Apollon.

"I-- I --"

A little hurt now was better than major disappointment later.

"That is stupid reasoning."

Charle blinked, not realizing he had spoken out loud.

"At least you didn't say it was stupid." Then he stared hard at Ner--Abadon's friend. "Are you...?"

"Apollon, but you can call me Ent."

"I know nothing of pagan gods." Charle hung his head. He was torn between fear and depression and the depression was winning. Right now he really didn't care that he was on a bus presumably filled with pagan gods.

"Sumerian."

Okay, standing on a bus filled with Sumerian gods.

"You realize that I still don't know who the fuck you are, right?" Now he was cursing at gods... and frankly he really didn't care.

"Okay, smart-ass. I am Ent, god of water, intelligence, creation, and mischief."

"So you're a zany Loki."

"Like that bugger actually exists." Ent snorted. "More like he was a rough imitation of me.

"And the others?"

"Hash is Nabu, god of wisdom and writing, Python is Sin, god of the moon... the ever-changing moon..."

"Way to fuck up Romeo and Juliet," Charle muttered, making sure his backpack was packed tightly and his laptop case was in hand.

"Speaking of star-crossed lovers... "

"Don't go there."

"Abadon himself is Nergal, god of destruction, the forgotten one who always walks beside us, the most powerful of us all."

"Because mankind loves to destroy itself."

"Yes. Just look at yourself now. I bet he's getting a powerful buzz off this one... if he's not planning on hiding away or taking off to lick his wounds. His seven will murder us for letting this come to pass."

"His seven?"

"His Pleiades. His seven lawyers and agents. Can we say hard-asses? They're going to do their best to destroy us."

"But not me?"

"Squishy human? Nah, no sport in it."

It must still be the drugs, Charle decided. The drugs were still working their way out of his system. He was never doing drugs again. Hell, he might never drink again because right now he had just finished having sex with a god and was talking to another god while packing to leave a busload of still more gods.

This isn't what he had in mind when he'd decided he was going to become a new him. In fact, this wasn't what he had in mind when he came on this trip or fucked a stranger who turned out to be a god, or got tattooed or pierced or--

"You're afraid."

His whirling thoughts stopped for a moment as he contemplated the statement that Ent, the god of fucking mischief, just made.

Yes, he was scared. Not terrified, but scared. "I just fucked a god."

"True. We all got a buzz off that one."

"This isn't me. This is that damn voice in my head..."

"Which would be a part of you that you keep repressed."

"I... this isn't me. I don't do wild things or crazy stunts --"

"The several photographs that I and the general

public got of you wilding out says differently."

"I-- I don't know what happened... "

"You are growing up." Ent took a seat and stared at Charle as he began to pace, his bags in his hands.

"I'm a grown man."

"Who is running away like a child."

"That just got handed some uncomfortable truths."

"Oh," Ent purred. "Upset that your world order suddenly changed? Pissed off that your Catholic school upbringing missed so much?"

"I can't be what he needs me to be."

"So, you really just wanted a good hard fuck."

"No."

"But you used him?"

"No!" Charle was angry enough to stomp his feet and throw a tantrum like a child. But that would aid in nothing. "I may have started out wanting that to prove something to myself, but... but ... I fucking care all right. I care about him."

"Do you now?"

"He was... is nice. Okay? He has a huge heart. He took care of me like no one else could. I wanted him even before I knew that he was the guy I fucked --"

"That was you?"

"You didn't know?"

"What? You think that we sit around talking about how we gods got one over on the sweet innocent kid from Baltimore? No, no matter what you think of us, we don't do shit like that. It's uncool."

"You really didn't?"

"Well, if I had I'd have tossed you into bed with him and locked the damn bus door behind myself. You changed him. He said that there was something special about the one that got away and he was going to go back and look for you." He smirked at Charle. "Fancy meeting you here."

"That's not the point!"

"The point is you're everything he was looking for and now you're leaving him once again."

"You don't understand --"

"I understand that you aren't even going to give it a chance."

"He is a fucking god, Ent. You all are. I'm just human."

"And?"

"I'll grow old and die. I don't have any powers. I'm nothing special. There are millions just like me."

"And yet it was you he wanted."

"I'm not what he thinks I am."

"You're right." Ent rose to his feet. "You're a coward."

"What?"

"I saw you face fears head-on. I watched you stand up to Nergal the toppiest son of a bitch that I know, and you backed him down. I watched you do things it took even me years to want to try. But when it comes to your heart, you're flaking out. Why? Is it because the heart is something that can hurt you? Been hurt too many times, Charle? Too scared to try it again?"

"I'm not in love."

"Never said you were, yet here you are running from the possibility of it. Thus you're a coward."

Was he right? Charle couldn't think. He needed to get out of there. Was he running from himself? Was he really a coward afraid to be at least a little bit emotionally available? Damn it, he had to go. He couldn't *think*.

"I'm sorry," he muttered, turning toward the bus door.

"Coward." Ent stepped towards him and placed a hand on his shoulder, halting him. Was he about to get smote? Smited? Was he about to be *killed*?

Ent handed him a ticket.

"We're at the airport."

"What?"

"We're at the airport. When you went missing, Nergal canceled our remaining stop. He was either going to put you in a plane to save you from yourself or we were all going to be flying back to Europe so he could explain this god thing to you. Convenient, no?"

"I can get my own ticket."

"Take it," Ent insisted. "It's the least that we can do, springing godhood on you and all."

"But --"

"Nergal wanted to take care of you, protect you. At least let him see you home."

Nodding Charle took the ticket in hand.

"I'm sorry," he repeated, one more time.

"For what it's worth, so are we."

Then Charle Lexington, for the last time, left the building.

Too bad he left part of his heart behind, the part that had hope, the part that was open to the possibility of love.

Chapter 6

The boys of Abadon are an amazing mix of tenderness and excitement. They're brash, exuberant assholes and the meanest sons-of-bitches that ever graced a stage. They're relentless, unstoppable, and retain a wild, untamed spirit that is legitimately what rock and roll strives to be.

Hash on drums is not a man to toy with, yet he's wise beyond his years. His mind is a complicated maze of ideas that will have you turned around in your own head if you're not careful. Observant and judging at the same time, honest to a fault. Yet he's quick to come to the defense of those in need and those who are struggling. His intelligence is scary and he can cut you down with a glance, let alone with his words. He's a badass and the thinker in the band.

Python is one of the most sensitive men I have ever met. His curly red hair and his snake that perpetually hangs on his shoulders (the snake, who as of the time this report was logged, still doesn't have a name) makes him more than intimidating. Yet if you ask him about the misunderstood, the unwanted, those that society deems outcast, he will fill your head with knowledge that will shame you into silence. Python is understanding of change, embraces it in a way that is frankly terrifying, and expects that if you don't understand or accept, you sit back and keep your mouth shut. In his world people should be judged by their actions and intentions, nothing more. This huge mass of muscle and tattoo ink will break you. Step a toe out of line, intrude on the rights of others, become nasty for no good reason and he will strike as swiftly as the snake he's named for. No one fucks with Python. It is an unspoken rule.

What can we say about Apollon? First off, his voice is inhuman. No person should have a voice that can drop so low it vibrates metal. Combine that with his aristocratic looks and his wicked sense of humor, and you don't know whether to kill him or praise him for the levity he brings to the group. Apollon is the answer to a question no one asked, but one that we all should experience at least once in our lifetime. Yet he's the most insane asshole there. He will laugh at your misfortune if you brought it on yourself and revel in your fall back to earth as he destroys your ego. He will cheer to see you rise and laugh his ass off as you fail. It's all part of his unique charm.

That brings us to Abadon himself. The front man and bassist for Abadon is a man of layers. He's rough. Make no mistake about that. The man is harsh and rough and has so many sharp edges that one could injure themselves if not careful. He's demanding. He wants the best for his band and demands the best of himself. He's a hard worker who dedicates everything that is in him to his brand, his label, his people, and his fans. This reporter has watched him treat a terminally child like an equal, encourage the next generation of rockers who will be his competition, praise those who do the most minor of jobs, and yet lay out an abusive asshole with one punch. There are so many facets to his personality that a lifetime wouldn't be long enough to sort them all. His talent is amazing and his causal mastery of his chosen craft is astounding. If he has his way, this hiatus the band is taking to add to their sound, will be filled with self-imposed deadlines and the pursuit of excellence that has always been a hallmark of this band. He will make the best of his allotted time and when Abadon once again is up for public consumption, he will awe us, wow us, and leave us slack-jawed by the perfection and brilliance of his lyrics and music. Expect deep emotions, amazing synergy, and an irrepressible energy that will silence nay-sayers and ensure his place as one of the biggest rock stars on the planet.

Abadon is a Rock God. Long may he reign.

~Charle Lexington, *Excerpts from Sympathy For the Devil*

"Charle!"

Charle groaned as his boss popped his head into his office door.

"Yeah, Bob?"

"The magazine is going into triple print, and most of that is because of the in-depth article you wrote. For a moment there, I was concerned. You chewed them up and put them through the wringer, but in the end you were objective and you gave the readers something they had never had before, an intimate glimpse into the lives of Abadon." He raised his hands as if framing a marquee and Charle fought the urge to roll his eyes.

"More bands are requesting you. I've been on the phone with agents all morning. People want your honesty and your sense of adventure."

"And I'm sure the photos of me had nothing to do with that."

"I will admit, when they first started surfacing, I thought someone had photoshopped them. You came this close to losing your job." He snapped his fingers. "But then I remembered there was always a touch of wildness in you, Lexington. It's what makes you such a great reporter."

Or maybe it was that PFLAG and the LGBTQIAPK community had a field day with praising him for the I-don't-give-a-shit-what-you-think sexuality stance they thought he'd taken. He was a, for lack of a better word, rock star when it came to civil rights organizations right now. That the boys for Abadon were there beside him and it didn't taint their success any at all, was just another positive boon for tie-in business and made them even more of a household name. Could it be that other bands wanted in on that?

Charle said nothing. What could he say? The photos of him acting a fool were everywhere. *TMZ, The Chive, Out Magazine* -- they were all having a field day with the straitlaced reporter finally showing his wild side -- with the full support of his magazine. It was a good thing that Abadon was in disguise for some of the racier shots because the paps would never leave him or his one-time lover alone when they figured out that he'd gotten busy with the reporter. But really, it had been weeks and still more photos were surfacing. The one with him on the mechanical bull was interesting and the one with him shirtless on the table was getting him some positive attention. With the dick contest photos however, he had gotten offers from *Playgirl* and a few less legitimate magazines… There was only one reason he wasn't blowing up about those photos being leaked. It was the one thing he had done that had captured Abadon's attention from the shocked look in his distressed face and his one-time lover…

There. He thought the term twice now and still felt regret.

Hell, they only fucked twice and… and Charle was still infatuated. What the hell was wrong with him?

He sat back in his chair and stared at his boss, nodding every few moments to attempt to show that he was paying attention even as he was zoning out on Bob's droning words.

The man finally smiled at him and offered him words that made him blink and try to refocus. "So, you'll be there tonight?"

"Hmm?"

"Abadon. They're playing one last gig before they head back to Europe, and they're back in Baltimore. I figured I would send you, full circle and all."

"What?"

"They suddenly put the show they canceled back on and went on to rock the crowd in Texas. It has to be an advertising ploy because scalpers were having a field day jacking up the prices of those tickets. I hear they played three encores and didn't stick around for the afterparty. I bet you partied them to death."

He ignored his boss's leer with a patience born of someone who was expected to fix everyone else's problems, and stared until Bob got to the point.

"I want to send you in to cover this performance.

Rumors have it that they're going to introduce a new song in the style they're hoping to add to the new album. You've been brooding all day in here so I just want to be sure you got the memo."

Actually, Charle had been ignoring any memos from his boss. He kept sending him out to singers and groups that wanted to talk about his experiences with Abadon more than they wanted to talk about themselves. And they kept trying to touch his tattoos...

He didn't even realize when his boss walked away because thought of his tattoos... of the courageous lion on his chest. That courage was a lie, he was willing to admit now to himself, but it brought back the memories of what could have been.

As soon as he walked into the airport, he'd wanted to turn around and go back.

Ent's words rang in his head, and knowing that the rest of the gods in the band had probably put him up to it, meant that they carried even more weight in his imagination.

Of all the things he'd thought of, he didn't even have to picture the pain on Nergal's face as he walked away. The man... god... had bared his soul and Charle had just left, abandoned him. Like so many people had abandoned him.

He didn't know when his determination to fuck the man went from that to protective and then coveting. Okay, he just hadn't wanted to admit that he had feelings for the god. When he thought Nergal was an oddly named European man with an undefined accent, he was all for it. It was the thought of him being a god... of Charle being left behind...

Yes, he was scared of being left behind again.

It was stupid, but what could Abadon see in him? He was going to get old and die. Abadon was going to go away sooner or later, no matter how prettily he aged.

Then Charle would have to face the pain of falling for someone who was going to leave him... But then he was making decisions for another person... he was taking away his right to think for himself because he was afraid. He was an asshole.

He came to that realization even before he made it fully into the airport. He tried to turn around and go back, but by the time he got to where the bus was parked, Abadon was gone and so was the chance he had of actually making a relationship.

Relationship. That is what Nergal hinted that he wanted. He wanted to try. He opened himself up to the possibility and Charle had run.

Ent was correct. He was a coward. And now he had lost something that maybe could have been great because he didn't believe he was good enough. How Harlequin romance of him.

There was never any guarantee that a relationship was going to last and he hadn't even given it a chance.

If he had it to do all over again, he would have stayed on that damn bus. He must have sat and brooded on his sorry state for a long time because when he looked up, the time had flown and he was late getting to the venue.

Fuck it, he decided, resigned. He was going to do his best to get backstage to see Nergal. He was going to see if there was still any hope for them at all. He would get on his knees and beg if he had to.

He couldn't get the feel of Nergal out of his mind. He could not erase his taste, the sound of his voice, how he ran behind him, protecting him from all the stupid things he had done with a decisive lack of judgment that even impressed him.

Nergal had invited him to discover himself, had changed his world view, and the most awe-inspiring thing, didn't even consider his own divinity when he offered himself to Charle.

A god wanted him. The devil wanted him. *Nergal* wanted him.

If he had to, he would spend the rest of his life to make up his abandonment, but before that could happen, he had to get to The Stage. He hadn't any time to waste.

And after a speeding ticket, three near misses on the highway, and nearly giving an old woman a heart attack when he cut around her slow ass on a two lane side street, he was there... just in time to breathlessly catch the end of the song Nergal was on stage singing.

I have no idea what went wrong, I turned around and you were gone,

and the life I thought we'd share... well, I guess you just didn't care.

And in the back of my mind, I keep our romance on rewind, examining every single part, from the end back to the start.

I can't figure out what went wrong, so I try to carry on, but until my dying day, this pain won't go away.

You can blame me, that's a fact. I only want you to come back. But I only know you'll be a shell, and I would rather face the hell...

of living with you gone, I wish I never had you all along... but I can't lie to myself, my state of broken mental health leaves me playing the fool, as I playback all the things you do...

So I guess I know it's true...

there's no getting over you.

Can you feel me reaching for you?

I'd kill for one more sip... of life from your lips.

It's not a thing you can do to me, to cut me up worse to make me bleed.

I'd be a liar if I say, that come what may, that my heart is pure and true...

'cause there's no getting over you.

As the last word of the song filtered through the speakers, the whole club was filled with dead silence.

Abadon sang alone, an acoustic guitar across his lap as he sat on a high stool, the muscles of his legs bulging as he stared blindly out into the crowd.

It was like they had ceased to exist for him, like his song had transported him to a higher plane, to taken him places that he dared not revisit but couldn't help entering.

He looked sad.

And it was all his fault.

Charle Lexington stared at the strong but breaking man -- god -- centered in the middle of the stage, a huge spotlight shining on him alone, and wanted to do something rom-com girlie and throw himself on top of him and swear that everything would be okay.

But that shit only worked for movies.

And this was reality.

As he stared, the venue went from shocked silence and erupted into fervent applause as the Locusts hooted and howled their approval. Feet were standing, hands were clapping and nearly everyone was screaming.

The newer, softer sound put out by Abadon was going to be a blazing success.

And through it all, Nergal sat on the stage, looking lost, barely acknowledging his audience's response.

It was amazing that in three short weeks, Abadon had put together this song, polished it to the point that it brought tears to the eyes of some of their hardest fans. Abadon had a heart. And it was now exposed for all the world to see.

"Um --" Nergal went to speak, but had to clear his throat to get the words out clearly. "This one... I'm not sure if it's going to be on the new album or if this is a one-time thing."

He offered a wry grin to the audience as they booed and hissed, and begged.

His hair was for once, not a wild lion's mane around his head. There was no eyeliner or heavy stage makeup.

He was wearing a simple pair of dark jeans, combat boots, and a long sleeved t-shirt that bulged at the seams as it attempted to contain all the muscle therein. He seemed calm, resigned even. He looked just as powerful, but somehow contained in a way that Charle had never seen him. God, he wanted to touch him.

"It's called *Charle's Song.*"

He stood up and before Charle's common sense could override the tiny voice in the back of his head that he had been smothering into silence for weeks, he was racing to the stage.

Damnit, he was going to be the girl in an eighties rom-com.

His feet cleared the stage steps, he doubted that he was even touching ground, when he launched himself at Nergal. He saw peripherally that the band was watching him in approval, but that didn't matter.

Security went in to try and stop him, but he dodged like a NBA baller and pivoted like a NFL half-back... and then Nergal's arms were wrapping around him and the world disappeared.

"Charle," Nergal gasped just before he slammed his mouth down on his, taking his lips in a kiss so powerful Charle was moaning like a porn star and trying to climb the sturdy body that he had had the privilege of possessing before. There was so much to be read into the strange gasp of his name, but now wasn't the time to think about that. Now was the time to take, to give, to reassure through touch, it was a time for them to just be together, damn the whole world. It was time for them to reconnect and they were taking the opportunity that they made for themselves. It wasn't a guarantee that their relationship would work or even last, but there was the hope of a possibility that it would.

The Locusts went wild.

Rise By Sin (Sympathy For the Devil 3)
Stephanie Burke

Python is more than just a pretty face, more than the quiet guitar god from the band Abadon. In another time, in another place, he was pure Sin. While taking a break, the god of the moon stumbled onto the person who made his whole life complete.

Orion Bane was not like the other boys. In fact he was born a she, but he never let that get in the way of a good time. When his flirtations with the sexy redhead led to a heated night of passion, Orion was sure he had met the man of his dreams... but he never expected that man to be a god.

Nowhere in the stars was it written that these two should meet, but when lust meets understanding, love could happen, if Orion is brave enough to Rise by Sin...

Chapter 1
Some rise by sin, and some by virtue fall.
-- William Shakespeare

"Oh, for the love of prostate abuse and little fluffy kitties, make it stop!" Apollon threw himself rather dramatically onto the sofa in the communal living room as the sounds of disgustingly spectacular, backbreaking, bed-wrecking sex filled the air. "Did we have to pay a deposit on the mattress? 'Cause if they fuck it up, I'm not paying for it."

"I thought they were moving back to Charle's place after Hash threw a bucket of water on them," Sin grumbled as he determinedly rose to his feet. His snake, the as-of- yet unnamed snake, wrapped itself around his arms almost as if it needed the comfort, like the screams and yowls coming from Abadon's bedroom were striking terror in its cold little heart.

"They left," Hash, who was in the middle of unbinding his long black braids, muttered. "They apologized for being loud, reminded me that good sex is a building block in a solid foundation of a relationship, and rolled out to get kinky at Charle's place. His walls are insulated." He looked down at the waist-length mass of wavy hair in his lap and wrinkled his nose as he carefully untangled a lock of hair with a wooden rat-tail comb. "Then they came back to get more clothes for Abadon and *that* happened."

"Make it stop," Apollon whimpered, rolling to his stomach and covering his head with his hands. "I didn't do anything to deserve this."

"You encouraged their joining," Sin pointed out, adjusting his grip on the snake so that it mostly rested across his broad shoulders, its head curving to rest at the base of his neck. "So some of the blame can be laid at your feet."

Apollon lifted his head, his silvery eyes glinting at his friend in pained amusement as he whispered in his unnaturally deep voice, "You said laid."

Sin, better known as Python, awesome guitarist for the band Abadon, frowned at his long-time friend and fellow nearly forgotten god. "You're not funny."

"Yes, I am!" Apollon, also known as Enk -- god of mischief, creation, and water -- sat up in feigned indignation. "I am the funniest person you know. My sense of humor is legendary. I have been known to bring smiles to the..."

The screams from the next room filled the air.

"You like that, don't you? You dirty little cock-slut!"

They all froze at the unique sound of Charle Lexington, ace reporter for *Rolling Stone* magazine, dominating their friend and band leader Abadon, once known as Nergal, god of war and destruction.

"Fuck yes!" The lead singer's distinctive and loud voice, a voice that once boomed out orders to fighters on battlefields, mewled in delight.

"And I'm out." Hash was on his feet, hair flying around him as he all but leaped into his Chuck Taylors and fled the scene. "I am so out..."

Apollon was right behind him, trying to hold in his snickers as he shadowed his friend, leaving Sin standing there in shocked dismay.

"Hmm... I thought he would be the one to top," he explained to his snake as he too quit the room while a loud series of smacks and screams rolled through the closed bedroom door.

Shrugging, Python ran his hands through his bright red locks and made for the exit as well. There was a bar downstairs. He had no idea where the others went, but he deserved a drink.

"Daddy!" Abadon bellowed, and Python winced.

Maybe three or four drinks. After this, he deserved to

get a little tipsy.

* * *

Sin made it to the lobby before he realized that maybe he should have put more thought into his escape plans. With the breaking news of Abadon and his public declaration of love just two days before, their hotel had been swamped with paparazzi, protestors, counter-protestors, and screaming Locust fans. They had changed hotels twice, but the third time seemed to be the charm as there were no surprise people waiting for them in their suite. But that didn't mean they weren't waiting for them outside.

As he peered around the corner, he saw a crowd of no less than fifty people waiting, along with reporters and protestors.

Sighing, he made his way into the nearest bathroom, wondering where Hash and Apollon had disappeared to.

He sent out a quick flash of magic to ensure that he was alone before he pulled the flat bull-head pendant free of his T-shirt.

"Sorry, Snake," he whispered to his constant companion. "I know I promised you a day in the sun, but that will have to be for later."

Closing his eyes, he felt the pull of his powers as he called upon the transformative energy of the moon. Within seconds his signature bright red head of waist-length curls was muted down into a deep rich bloodred and straightened until it lay flat and heavy against his skull. His brown eyes deepened until they were nearly black, and his skin darkened into a deep tan. Snake, his ever-faithful companion, shivered and flattened and melded into his being until the large albino python was a very detailed and elaborate full-body tattoo. Her head now rested high on his shoulder while the rest of his colorful tattoos faded out of existence save for the crescent moon-shaped tattoo in the center of his chest.

He petted the snake's head once, feeling her wriggle in his skin with pleasure, before he turned to face the mirror.

While still a pretty large man at six feet five inches, he was no longer recognizable as the lead guitarist and rock god Python. Now he was merely Sin, eccentric intellectual who happened to love snakes.

He held out one hand, and in a flash a pair of squared black-framed glasses appeared. Smiling, he slipped them on and nodded at his overall look.

He resembled himself again.

Being the rock star was fun, and the worship he pulled from being in the spotlight was amazing, but sometimes he just wanted to lose himself in a stack of books with a hot cup of tea and his companion snake.

But he was in this thing for survival. If he wanted to live he had to maintain a steady flow of worship to prevent him from fading like so many of his comrades from days past.

It had been Abadon's idea for them to become rock stars, because such people were worshipped worldwide. Nergal, Enk, and Nabu had been friends of his for eons so he knew the plan was sound. And it was. Here they were seven years after Abadon burst on the scene, still growing their fan base and unstoppable. Now with Nergal's unexpected descent into love, the worship they received nearly quadrupled as more people joined the horde of Locusts, singing their praises or plotting their demise. Either way, it meant huge power boosts for them, and it was returning them gold according to the Pleiades, the Seven who still managed their careers.

They were due to leave America in a few days and head back to the Canary Islands. He was fine with the break, but The Seven had ideas to keep the momentum of Nergal's love life rolling in their favor. There would be a hiatus, but there were going to be exclusive music videos, interviews, webcasts, and personal pieces on each of them. They were about to be invaded, and Sin took it as par for the course in this era where just about anyone or anything could be worshipped. Even the cat with the grumpy face had a massive following that was soon going to send it the way of Bastet and other Egyptian cat gods that had fallen in and out of favor over the years.

What was it about humans and cats? That was why his animal companion was a snake. They were warm, silent, and arrogance wasn't in their makeup.

He gripped his bull-head amulet, a focus for his powers and a comfort to him since his inception, and contemplated the world he now existed in.

In some ways it was better than what he was born into, with hot water, reliable plumbing, libraries, and literacy, but in some ways it was more complicated as people took hard work for granted, ignored their fellow man, and communities online were more viable than the ones in which you lived.

"Progress," he muttered to himself as he gave his T-shirt one final tug and turned to exit the bathroom.

He slipped right by the growing hordes and made his way into the heat of a Baltimore summer afternoon.

His day was going to be just fine.

* * *

"Well, your mother so stupid, we told her it was chilly outside so she went and got a bowl."

Orion groaned as he threw the bar towel at the fool who was trying to throw up a "Your Mama" joke that old.

"I bet you spent all of the eighties thinking up that one!" The barflies broke into laughter, and Orion leaned his lithe frame against the bar.

"Let me get down on your level," he joked. "Your momma so stupid she put lipstick on her forehead to make up her mind."

The bar oohed and heckled the upstart, and he nodded that he had been bested on that one, but raised both his hands to show that he still had jokes.

"Your mama so fat, she got baptized at SeaWorld!"

To which Orion swiftly countered with, "Your momma so fat it took me three trains, two planes, and a bus to get to her good side."

The laughs came even harder, and Orion threw up his hands for some well- deserved high fives.

"Well," the contender tried the master yet again, "your mama so old her breast milk comes in powdered form."

That got more chuckles, and some joker put the discarded towel around his shoulders, rubbing his back as he danced in place like a pro fighter.

"Well, your momma so dumb she went to a dentist to get a Bluetooth!"

People were screaming in laughter, and Orion crossed one well-muscled arm over an equally developed chest and took a bow.

But the contender was not about to give up. "Your mama so fat, she has to wear six different watches to tell time, one for each time zone!"

Even Orion broke down laughing at that one, but he held up his hand and silence fell.

"Well, your momma so fat when God said let there be light, he told her to get her ass outta the way!"

There was a moment of silence before the whole bar cracked up. The laughter was so loud that several people in the Fells Point area came walking in to see what was going on, including a red-haired man who took in the proceedings with interest.

Orion smugly added, "I also could have tossed out, your momma so fat her Patronus is a cake!"

The contender took a bow, and the bar exploded in laughter once more.

"You win, Orion," he laughed, taking the towel from around his neck and handing it over. "That was a good one."

"And now, I have to wash my towel. You got it all stinky with those shitty jokes you were telling."

They both cracked up, and Orion pulled himself together enough to slide him a beer, to good-natured applause and heckling.

Competition over, the bar area thinned out, and a few of the newcomers, including the intriguing-looking redhead, came walking over.

"What can I get you?" Orion asked, tilting his head to the side and examining the black-framed glasses and the well-developed body.

"Hmmm. Well, what *can* I get you, Daddy?" he asked again, noting that though the man appeared to be no older than his early thirties, he had a distinctive air of a daddy about him. "See anything you like?" he flirted. "And the drinks aren't bad either…"

The redhead, despite this strange mien of respectability, immediately began to leer before pulling those glasses down his nose and offering him a huge wink. Oh, this was getting even more fun by the minute.

"What do you recommend?" He leaned on the bar, and Orion got a nice glimpse of a very detailed snake tattoo on his neck, and for a moment wondered how far down it went.

"Something tall, full-bodied, and racially ambiguous?" Orion licked his bottom lip and waited for a response.

"Oh," he purred back. "The house special. I'll take one of those, please." He pushed his glasses back up, and his whole face lit up as he smiled broadly, showing perfect teeth. "Just what is this delight to the palate named?"

"Orion Bain at your service." Orion offered him a

small bow. "Purveyor of fine wines, spirits, and cock… tails."

"Color me intrigued." He leaned in closer. "I'm called Python by most, but feel free to call me Sin."

"That is a pretty interesting pickup line, and I've heard a few." Orion chuckled. Looked like the daddy was trying to pull up some old school game. He was down with that. "Python for the snake tattoo, and I am guessing Sin for the red hair?"

"Something like that," he purred back, and suddenly Orion was struck by how beautiful this man really was.

Up this close, he could see that his eyes behind those studious glasses were the color of sherry or really fine aged wine that just made his hair seem richer. He wasn't exactly tan, but he wasn't redhead pale either. He was tall, that was for damn sure, but he wasn't trying to be intimidating or use it to his advantage. And Daddy was ripped. Orion could see the muscles shift and bunch under his T-shirt as he leaned farther on the bar, his gaze intimate, as if he was the only other person in the world.

"So…" Orion had to clear his throat and try again. The more he looked at Daddy McHottie the more he wanted to peel that T-shirt off and see what was underneath. "So what is it? A pickup line or your real names?"

"Both. Is it working?" He leaned closer and licked his lips, and Orion felt a flash of heat run though his body so fast he was sure his hair was standing on end.

"In ways that should make you nervous," he managed to get out, his smooth and cool departing as he fought the urge to drop his hands to his ankles and bend over to present. "But right now, all I can do is offer you a drink."

"I never get nervous." Sin-Python was cute, but with that accented voice he was pure sin. He leaned both elbows on the bar and looked up at him through the longest red eyelashes he had ever seen. Those damn things were like fans, and that look... Sultry was too weak a word to describe it. "But I'll take what you can give me. For now."

Orion gulped hard and forced a smile, though his knees were shaking and his thighs felt weak. He rested his hand on the bar, leaning closer, then pulling it back as a fine tremor ran through it. No one had ever affected him so strongly or so quickly since he first discovered his love of dick at age thirteen. "So what can I get you?"

"How about a Sex on My Face?"

Orion gulped.

"Can you do that? Or maybe a Cocksucking Cowboy? I hear that Baltimore is in the South, no?" he asked when Orion could only stand there and stare.

"Well, how about an Anus Burner? I've had one before and liked it."

He blinked innocently as Orion gripped the edges of the bar, arousal hitting him so fast he nearly passed out. "Anus Burner?"

"If you can't do that," the cheeky devil grinned, "I wouldn't say no to a Climax. You know how to give one, right? If not, I carry the recipe with me."

"Pardon me." Orion had to look away before he did something he would regret... like throw himself across the bar, shove Sin down on the floor, and actually take his face for a ride. He had to cool down fast.

He spun around and grabbed a bottle of cold water from the fridge, chugging half of it down as he tried to pull himself together enough to face Sin once more.

"Have I offended you?" That voice sounded more amused than concerned, and Orion turned around, the urge to laugh mingling with the urge to stick his tongue down his throat and take him up on what he was offering. "'Cause believe me, that wasn't my intention."

"I am far from offended," Orion placed his water

down and turned fully to face Sin once more. "Really miles away from it, actually. More like intrigued and excited."

"Oh, I like the sound of that." He was now resting with his elbows on the bar, chewing on his lower lip as those eyes examined Orion from the top of his spiky hair to his waist, all that he could see above the bar. "And right now I'm not talking about the drinks."

"Well, duh." Orion laughed, some of the tension building up between them easing. "I'd have to be stupid not to realize that kinky drinks aren't the only thing you are thirsting for."

"And you are anything but stupid." Python smiled, easing up the seduction factor a bit but adding to the adorableness that made Orion want to squee -- and still sit on his face.

"And how would you know that?"

"Oh, I notice things." Sin leaned back and began to read him like he was a national best seller.

"You adjust your speech patterns to fit those around you, meaning that you adapt to the people you like. You are open and curious -- you were testing my intelligence and tolerance with your earlier flirting and relaxed as you realized I was doing the same in kind. You sized me up one minute after I walked into this bar and decided I was safe enough to flirt with as I didn't come in angry, looking like I was carrying concealed, was generally accepting of people of different races -- your racially ambiguous quip -- also accepting of many socio-economic backgrounds because you recognize I don't care about the makeup of the clientele of this bar. I wasn't offended by off-color humor, genuinely enjoyed your joke war, and I am open and honest in my appreciation of you."

Orion blinked slowly and then grinned. This man was on point. He saw through some of his many and varied defense points and understood what was going on. He was either very observant or a serial killer... and his instincts were telling him that this man was as safe as houses. "Okay, but there are still some things you don't know about me."

"Small hands."

Orion lifted one of his hands up and arched an eyebrow at Sin, a new and uncomfortable tension filling him.

"What about them?"

"You are carrying twenty-inch biceps, a chest that I could build a house on, I'm sure that is a very tight eight-pack under the very tight T-shirt you are wearing, and I can almost taste how fucking hard you are right now. And your hands are smaller than expected."

"Fuck," Orion breathed, and stared. He just stared.

"Your hands are smaller, your hips are a bit wider, and your torso doesn't quite fit with the muscles you've built up."

"Oh, fuck," Orion breathed, eyes growing wider with every word he spoke.

"I don't care, just so you know. I don't give a fuck that you fixed what nature fucked up. I think you're one of the hottest men I've seen since I came to this town, and I want to strip you down and have you in ways that would make Ron Jeremy blush. How does that sound to you?"

Orion didn't know how to act.

He'd had several experiences where people found out, some good and some bad, since he'd transitioned fully as a teenager, but he had never been in a situation quite like this.

He didn't have to explain to a date what was going on between his legs, putting his safety and personal life out for public consumption before he started falling for the guy. He didn't have to explain that he was a fucking man with some bits that nature screwed up on. He didn't have to worry about a violent reaction or even worse, a disgusted one from a man he found hot. He didn't have to delve into his gender backstory and his whole life story to a near-stranger just to be open and honest about what could possibly happen between the two of them. Sin just... knew. It was scary and exciting all at once.

Sin was still staring at his face, reading him, he assumed, as he waited for a response.

"Where are you from anyway?" Orion knew his voice was sounding a bit rough, but this was a hell of a lot to take in. It was a notion, this easy acceptance, that was growing on him. Was this how cisgendered people felt when flirting with a stranger? It was... nice, but he still needed a minute. "I love your voice, but I can't place the accent."

"Originally, a small town in the Middle East and of late, La Gomera."

"The Canary Islands," Orion grinned as Sin nodded, offering a smile of his own.

"There... your intelligence," he pointed out. "Not too many Americans know of it."

"Well, I wanted to be an anthropologist, and I studied lost languages as part of my masters," Orion admitted with no small pride. And this conversation was giving him a chance to get his head together where Sin was concerned. With a few sentences Sin had effectively blown his mind, knocked his socks off, and had him hungry for more. This man was... unique. "The Whistle language?"

"Yes, I know of it and have learned a little," Sin admitted. "It was dying out, but now people are actively trying to preserve and teach it."

"For the future." This man was hitting his buttons in so many ways...

"And our future, Orion Bane? What do you think of our short-term future activities?"

"Fuck..." He ran one hand through his hair and stared at the man. He could be dangerous. He could be a kitten. He could be the daddy experience he'd always wanted. Damn him and his soft spot for the mature type. This man was well-spoken, highly intelligent, well-traveled, honest about what he wanted...

"I get off at eight," Orion spoke softly even as he was mentally making plans to actually sit on this redhead's face. "There is still a lot we have to discuss."

"Yes, I agree. Especially on one thing that is important to me. I need to know your boundaries and how far you want to go."

"And yours," Orion was quick to point out.

His snorted laugh was cute. "I don't have any."

He leaned on the bar again, getting as close as a foot and a half of laminated wood would allow. "At least none that I wouldn't be willing to try for my partner's pleasure."

"Eight it is, then..." Orion got out as his mouth went dry and began to water at the same time.

Damn, this man was hot.

His slow answering grin was just... fuck.

He turned to walk away, and Orion was taken with the tight twin globes of his ass as he moved toward the door.

"Wait," Orion suddenly remembered that he was manager of a bar and tending it was part of his job. "You still want that drink?"

Sin paused, and Orion sucked in a breath as he turned in the doorway. With the sun beaming in, it encased his tight body in a red-gold aura that obscured his fine facial features and made him appear almost otherworldly.

"I'll wait," he called back. "I don't mind having my Climax delayed."

He was in trouble. Orion knew that he was in trouble

deep.

    And he really didn't care.

Chapter 2

"Pete, take over."

Orion called over to his fellow bartender who was working the other side of the bar and made a mad dash for the back room.

What the hell had just happened? He needed some quiet to process this.

"Small hands, huh?"

He threw himself into his office chair and lifted those same hands up to the level of his eyes.

They were strong hands. Capable hands, really. The palms were calloused from carrying heavy kegs of beer and boxes of wines and spirits. The nails were cut short and functional, yet his fingers were rather short and thick. He didn't have piano hands; that was for damn sure.

His hands were designed for holding weight, cracking open jars, and typing on his ancient laptop as he pounded out essays after work.

They were for popping open a can of his favorite cheap beer, a hang-on from his undergrad days, and flipping people off when they deserved a good old-fashioned fuck you.

They were good hands.

There were a few cuts and scars scattered around his knuckles. Being the queer kid in high school hadn't always been easy, but those marks proved he knew how to kick ass when needed. He had bounced more than a few drunks out of his bar without the help of the bouncers on crowded nights or festival days.

His hands proved that they were capable and strong, but he never thought of them as small.

His hands were perfect for getting him off too, or maybe that was just experience. He had used his hands to pop one off whenever he felt stressed or in fits of depression, or when he was younger and thought that no man would want him or his body when they learned the truth. He was so good with his hands that he could get himself off five or six times in a row and made damn sure to teach all of his lovers those tricks while he returned the favor. His hands looked good wrapped around a dick, rather commanding actually, and they looked even better when he sat in front of a mirror, legs spread wide, and fucked himself whenever he felt like it. He was kind of kinky like that.

Sin said his hands were a bit small for his body. Oh, he'd pointed out a lot of things that Orion saw when he looked into his mirror, things that proved that medical science hadn't quite caught up to his needs, but the comment about his hands rang clear in his mind.

He twisted them around and stared at the palms, noting the nicks and the calluses... he needed some lotion for a few ashy spots... but he'd never really considered them before, not really. They worked, and that was good enough for him. His concerns had always been if his upper body was proportionate enough or if his packer was sitting properly in his jeans or if his light dusting of chest hair covered up the thin scars from his mastectomy. The visuals were important, but not as important as looking at himself and seeing the he that he had always imagined himself to be. There wasn't a feminine thing about Orion Bane from his well-maintained facial scruff to the thickness of his neck and body. He worked hard to make his body match his mind and soul and was damn proud of the results.

Now he ran his hands over his bicep and smirked a bit. He did have nice guns. He'd started working out as a teen when the hormone changes got confusing and his body grew restless. His parents got him a weight set and told him to do something constructive with all that energy that had him bouncing off the walls. It had become kind of an addiction with him. He wasn't a gym-

bro by any stretch of the imagination, but he didn't feel
right unless he did some kind of daily exercise.

Pumping iron had become his refuge, and with his
body type, it was easy to pack on muscle and transform
his body into what he imagined it to be. Bad day at
school? Instead of busting Billy's head to the white meat,
get on the bench press and do fifty reps. After a shot of T
when he started to have some serious mood swings?
Instead of ranting about how unfair his life was, get on
the bicep machine and do some curls. He didn't even
want to go into how many miles he ran on his various
treadmills. His parents replaced three of them just getting
him through his teen years alone. But the results were a
body he could work with and an inner core of strength
that led to an abundance of self-confidence in his life as
he truly began to befit his namesake.

Orion didn't have to change his name when he began
transitioning at the tender age of thirteen, right before his
breast buds got out of control and he started -- ick --
menstruation. His parents were hippy intellectual
snowflakes and laughed in the face of anyone who had a
problem with his name. Then the idiot who questioned it
was given a lecture on mythology that would put most
Greek scholars asleep. His parents liked to punish with
lectures because they said the trauma lasted longer. He
only questioned his strange name once when he was
seven and in Peru with his parents on an archeological
dig. A kid from one of the locals said his name was
stupid, and he asked his father why he was given such a
dumb name. His father had taken him to the top of one of
the sandy man-made walls in the early evening, and
there, under a sky unpolluted by civilization, answered
his question first by pointing out Orion's Belt.

"He was a mighty hunter and fought for love," his
father explained, pointing out the three bright stars that
made up Orion's belt. "He built Vulcan's forge with his

bare hands and drove all the wild and dangerous animals out of Chios for his love of the fair princess Merope. When the king refused to give his daughter over, he tried to take her. So her father got Orion drunk, blinded him, and cast him out near the sea. But Orion fought until he got his eyesight back, and the goddess of the Hunt, Diana, fell in love with him for his strength and perseverance. The two were to be wed when Apollo, Diana's brother, not wanting pure godly blood sullied, tricked his sister into shooting Orion dead with an arrow. I would assume she kicked the crap out of her brother when she realized what he had done, but she turned Orion's corpse into the stars and placed him in the night sky so that his light would always shine."

Orion had stared up at his white-haired father, lost in the romance of the epic tale of warriors and love. He was named after a real fighter, a champion who didn't even let loss of his eyesight slow him down.

"Fight, Papa?" he asked. Did his father want him to fight? "Fight for love?"

"Fight for what you believe in, for what you want, for what you need," he corrected with a smile. "We named you Orion because you are going to have some challenges in your life, my dear. Your mama and I had to fight so many people and so many attitudes to get to where we are now, and we wanted you to have that same strength. We always want you to fight for what you hold dear and let only your own decisions plot your course."

"I'll be strong," he remembered telling his father with a grin, jumping to his feet and dancing along that huge sandy wall with the moon looking down upon them, dancing under the warrior he was named after. "I will live up to my name with every breath. This I vow!" He had been rather dramatic as a child.

"There is another story too," his father told him as he pretended to fight off gods and imaginary monsters.

"About your namesake."

"Oh?" Orion wanted to know this story too. He had to know. After all, he was named after the guy.

"Orion became a mighty hunter and as his fame and strength grew, so did his ego and his arrogance. A tiny little one-inch scorpion put him in the dirt." That was his father, the perfect example of the stick and the carrot. "Don't get cocky, Spud. No matter how big you get, something small and insignificant to some can slam you face-first into the dirt."

His father gave him a wink and pulled a pipe from his pocket, not smoking it, but chewing on the tip as he stared down at him with amused green eyes.

"Fight for what you want. Defy those who oppose you when defiance is needed, but never forget that an inch-long bug brought down a near-god. Don't be a butthead."

So even as he took pride in his successes, he tempered that with the knowledge that one little thing could bring a house of cards that was his life tumbling down. He strove not to be a butthead.

When they made it back to the states for a more formal primary education, he never bragged about the places he visited though he was more than willing to show photos and tell stories of his family's exploits. He never bragged that he could speak four different languages -- French, Spanish, Arabic, and English -- because it was par for the course when you traveled for years at a time with famous archaeological parents who were always in demand worldwide.

He looked down at his hands and remembered being a shirtless brown-skinned child hauling rocks with other shirtless brown-skinned children as they worked under the hot sun in South America or in the deserts of Egypt.

His parents were older when he was born, his mother nearly fifty, actually. They thought that they were never to be blessed with a child, as his mom told him, until after a jungle fling in the rainforests region of Peru when suddenly the taste of mango set her stomach rebelling. "It was dangerous and fun, Poppe," she had confided, her dark skin shining bright in amusement. "Panthers, you know," she sighed in delight. "Back then, your papa and I could go three or four times a day without even trying. It's all the clean living, you know, that keeps the sex muscles operational. You have to put in the time to make a good sex life work. That and a lack of a gag reflex have always stood me in good stead."

Back then he was between impressed and disgusted that at near fifty, his parents had been actively screwing. It made him proud to think of his future energetic sexual exploits for when he was so old he was farting dust... and horrified him that near their fifties, his parents were fucking outside in the jungles, carrying on like Tarzan and Jane, leaving DNA everywhere.

His parents tended to overshare, but that was cool because they just wanted him to understand everything life had to offer. Knowing their intentions gave him the courage at the ripe age of eight to ask his parents why they were calling him a she when he was clearly a he.

"Wrong pronoun," he had shouted as he glared at them in defiance.

It had started with some missionary who visited the headquarters of the dig they were staging near the Temple of the Moon in Peru. His parents always told them that wherever there was a monument or ruin of any major religious importance to another culture, Christian missionaries would be as there as thick as flies on a fresh corpse. This one was there under the guise of offering aid to the workers when she noticed Orion running around with some of the local children in shorts, sandals, and tank top on a Sunday morning. She didn't even notice that nine-year-old Orion wasn't a native child until she ran up to her mother and asked if she could run and play football, the kind Americans called soccer, with some of the other children.

"She should be playing with other little girls," the woman insisted.

"Why would I want to? I'm a boy, and all the girls do is play with dolls, and I wanna play football."

"Well, isn't she precious... Exercise is important, but you can't allow her to go native all the time. She will have responsibilities to her family, and I think --"

"He," Orion boldly corrected the rude woman.

"Pardon me?"

"You're excused for getting it wrong." Orion offered her a smile. "When you make a mistake, you are supposed to apologize and seek forgiveness." He had nodded as his mother snickered and ran a hand through his tossed hair. Like what happened with a lot of kids, his mom just chopped it off in the front so that it wouldn't fall in his eyes and ran wild with a head full of bouncy curls.

"Yes, you can go and play."

"But you're a girl," the woman pointed out, cutting off his mother as if her point of view were the only one that counted. "You should be wearing dresses --"

"Wow, lady." He shook his head. "You are so wrong. You can't carry rocks in a dress, and why would I wear one? I'm a boy."

"No, you are --" the woman reached for him, but cut off when his mother's hand lashed out and swatted the missionary's fingers away before they could touch him.

"Who gave you permission to lay a hand on my child?" she demanded, her brown eyes narrowing in anger.

His mother's brown skin had darkened to a deep burnt sienna with exposure to the sun, and now it took a more distinctive red tone as anger rose up in her.

"She said --"

"I don't give a flying fuck if my child said she was an elder god returned to rid the land of the curse of man, you don't have the right to lay a finger on her."

"Him," Orion corrected.

"Him," his mother agreed, pulling him to her side. "You can take that and your charity and your good will and shove them sideways up your ass."

The woman gasped, outraged, and stared at the gaggle of female worshipers that came visiting with her, all tittering in outrage.

Orion covered his mouth with his hands and giggled outright in her face. "You said a bad word, Mama."

"It was warranted in this situation, for emphasis on how serious I am." She tore her glare away from the woman and stared down at her child. "You don't repeat that until you're over eighteen or out of my hearing, you understand, Orion?"

"Yes, Mama." He offered her up a huge smile. "And football?"

"Go and play." His mother added in a serious tone, his eyes twinkling. "Have fun."

"But she --"

"Since when does your opinion count for shit?" his mother asked as she shooed Orion away to his collection of waiting friends who were nearby kicking a soccer ball around. "This is grown-folk business, Orion, so go and play before you hear me use some more words forbidden to you unless you are grown and out of my earshot."

The words were said with such venom that the missionary backed off, and Orion took that as a cue to leave. He didn't think on it again until he was having his bath with his mother that night.

"So you're a boy now?" she asked as she scrubbed what had to feel like the whole of the desert out of his hair.

"Yes," he nodded with conviction. "When does my penis grow in?"

"It won't," his mother explained bluntly as she began to scrub behind his ears. "Your doctor told me you were a girl when I pushed you out." He wrinkled his nose because he felt another lesson on biology coming on. His parents always answered his questions, no matter how obscure or uncomfortable they were. "But it's starting to look like they got it wrong."

That night, and in the following nights, his mother asked him a series of questions which he answered honestly. *Yes*, he was a boy. He was old enough to know who he was. *Yes*, he knew he didn't really have a large penis -- he figured it would grow bigger like the rest of him did when he got older, and he wished it would hurry up. He wanted to pee standing. *No*, no one had told him what he was, he just always knew. *What do you mean his biology had gotten his gender wrong*?

It took him longer to understand that he wasn't going to grow a larger penis so he could pee standing up with than it took him to accept that his body was one thing and his mind, his personality, his soul was another.

When they made it back to the states, his parents had taken him to doctor after doctor until they found one that would believe them. After years of dressing and behaving as his proper gender, he started hormone treatments at the tender age of thirteen, just before puberty set in, with the warning that he might never be able to have children.

He'd never wanted snot-nosed rug rats anyway. He started his treatments, and then he had to deal with unreasonable anger, mood swings, crying jags for no reasons, a stunted period that horrified him, and changes to his mental state that were so drastic he was sure an alien was going to explode out of his head at any given moment.

Yet he was so happy that he was transitioning, that

his parents fought for him and understood what he was going through, that medical science was going to fix what biology had gotten wrong, that he took all those changes in stride.

Yes, he knew other people transitioning who had harsh beginnings and horrific tales of growing up different, but he had been doubly blessed in his parents. They supported him no matter what and made sure he had the tools that would survive being different in this world where not being what society dictated often led to frustration, anger, pain, and even death. They would have supported surgery if he'd taken that route, too, but left him free to decide what worked best for him.

And now he looked down at his hands and wondered how some sexy stranger who just walked into his life read him like a book, given his unneeded approval, and made no bones about wanting to fuck him silly, could make him look back on his semi-charmed life instead of how many condoms and how much lube he would need that night.

He leaned back in his chair and chuckled out loud. Sin, huh? The man really was hot. Orion had a thing for redheads and for big, tight muscles. Orion, who was pansexual more than anything, found himself itching to sit on that face and work those pretty lips against his front hole.

He fucking hoped Sin delivered on all that he promised, because there was no way that Orion was going to let this pass him by. He looked up at the wall-mounted Guinness clock and noted that it was a little after three. He had five hours to wait.

In five hours he was either going to have the ride of his life or would have to teach the gentleman a few things about his anatomy in order to get off. Either way, he was going to use Sin as a gigantic sex toy and would hopefully limp away sore and sated. Sin looked like his fantasy man. His personality was like icing on a cake. Who didn't like icing?

Chapter 3

"I can come four or five times in a row. Why fuck with perfection?"

Instead of a look of shock, Sin gave him the sexiest grin he had ever seen... a grin that was immortalized with a flash of Orion's camera phone. Sin blinked, and his sexy look turned questioning as Orion typed swiftly on his phone. Then Orion grinned up at him.

"This?" the bartender asked as they stepped out of the bar's doorway and into the street. "Just a bit of insurance. If I don't check in with a friend, the cops know who to start looking for."

Orion stopped walking, waiting to see what Sin had to say. He wasn't a huge fan of one-night stands, but there was something about this man that he just simply wanted. But he wasn't a fool either. Too many people went missing in this town. His friend Rachael knew he planned on hooking up with a sexy daddy, and now she had a photo of him in case something went wrong. "I spent too long getting my life in order to just give it away for a fuck."

"A devastatingly perfect fuck," Sin corrected with a grin. "Here." He rattled off a series of numbers that Orion was quick to type.

"What's that?"

"Personal cell phone number and the suite number where I'm staying. Send that to your friend as well, along with the name of my hotel. The Royal Sonesta Harbor Court on Light Street."

Orion whistled softly as he typed the name and number to send to his friend as well. That hotel was big bucks, right there.

"The Harbor View four-bedroom guest suite. Call them now and check to see if I am listed." Sin winked at him and handed him his own phone. "Use this one since someone will be willing to answer mine when you call. We can wait until you check me out. It's good to see you really are as smart as you look."

"Why, thank you, sir. You turn my head with all your praise." Orion relaxed as he leaned against the side of the bar front and made his call.

For a moment, he'd wondered if Sin would get angry at the safety net he'd devised for himself, but the man was in total agreement with him. That eroded most of the lingering doubt that echoed in the back of his head. He dialed the hotel number and after a few rings, it was picked up. One of the deepest voices he had ever heard outside of an opera house or a horror movie answered.

"Sin? Where are you, man? You disappeared totally. Not that you can't take care of yourself, but if you went off and found a kick-ass party, you had better be calling to invite us. We deserve it after putting up with the unintentional exploration into Nergal's love life. Rose and Jack weren't back at Rose's place, so he can draw him like his French women a few more times before we get together and decide what to do next."

"As in the Titanic?" Orion was amused, and he really didn't know why.

"Hey Sin," he called out, smirking. "Rose and Jack haven't gone back to Rose's place so he can be drawn like a French woman some more."

"Well, now," the voice purred. "This sounds like a party for one. Who are you, you sweet-sounding morsel? And after you tell me, can you put the soulless ginger on the phone? You better watch out since he eats soulful cuties."

"Well, since you asked so sweetly, my name is Orion Bane, and most certainly I can put the ginger on the line. I don't think he's soulless, though. I mean I'm the brightest, shiniest thing he's ever had the privilege to speak to, and my soul is still intact. Maybe he's consumed enough souls to be a real boy now, in which case I get to reap the benefits. Win for me."

The gravelly laughter was infectious, and Orion was grinning when he handed the phone over to his redheaded daddy.

"That was Orion, as he told you." Sin spoke as he winked at Orion, an amused look settling over his face. "Yes, he is as hot as he sounds, even more so when you can get past the glare of his pure soul. It's blinding, and I'm hungry."

Orion snickered as Sin nodded at what gravel-pit voice was saying, eyes never leaving his face.

"Safety check. He's as intelligent as he is smart. I gave him this number as proof and insurance." A pause and then, "Yes, very wise."

Orion crossed his legs and watched as people drifted into the bar, a few regulars nodding at him but most passing in and out, people out on a hot summer's night trying to have a good time.

"No, I'm not asking if he has an equally hot friend. And no, I'm not being selfish… and that would be a no. I am not sending you his photo."

"Oh, I don't care if you do." Orion snickered. "I'm beautiful, and the whole world should know it."

"He doesn't deserve to look upon your greatness," Sin explained, laughing at whatever his friend on the phone had said. "I'll call you when Orion and I catch a break," he sounded reverent as he ended the conversation. "I will probably be sore as fuck and half-dead to boot, but it is so going to be worth it."

If Orion was less self-confident, he was sure he'd have been blushing by now. But instead he took those words as a challenge and a statement of fact. He was going to fuck Sin's brains out, ride him hard, and put him away wet and wanting when he was done.

"Oh, I promise," he purred as Sin ended the

conversation.

"I expect to be walking with a limp, then… as proof." His eyes glittered oddly, and that strange accent was back in his voice. It must be a Middle Eastern dialect he wasn't familiar with.

"And if I want to be walking with a limp?"

"Oh, that can most definitely be arranged."

Orion felt himself grow moist at Sin's words. Goddamn, the man had no right to be so sexy. "My bike is over here."

Sin whistled as he circled the Triumph Rocket Three, one of the largest street-legal bikes. Orion's bike was a muted tangerine combined with a wave of cream over the tanks with custom black leather seats and the sweetest after-market exhaust system he had ever seen. This bike was obviously used, but at the same time was lovingly cared for.

"Nice," he breathed, and Orion grinned in pride.

"The only baby I'll ever have."

Orion handed the other man a helmet he pulled from his saddlebags while pulling his own from the helmet lock on the handle. It was a three-quarter mask à la Speed Racer and was painted to match the bike. The one he handed over was a solid black and was large enough to fit Sin's head.

"My dad likes me to take him out when he is here without his own bike," Orion explained. "I think he's old enough to get a trike, but the man says that's not real driving. I think seventy-four means three wheels, but he'd never talk to me again if I suggested it." Orion laughed.

"Adventurous parents?"

"You have no idea."

Orion climbed on and gestured for Sin to climb on behind him. "You ride?"

"I got a Speed Triple at home," he informed him as

he placed his feet on the foot pegs and wrapped his arms around Orion's waist. "I can't wait to get you on the back of mine."

What followed was one wild ride through the city, the bike vibrating between his legs with a hot ginger daddy at his back.

He could feel Sin's heat through his thin summer jacket and had to concentrate to ignore the thick thighs that bracketed his, the powerful arms wrapped around his waist, the hard wall of a chest at his back.

He was cursing and pleased at the same time that the ride was so short. Cursing because it was an exercise in control to keep the bike from slamming into the back of a car because he was turned on and pleased that the ride was so short because he was sliding around in the slick of his briefs.

He pulled up in front of his apartment with a sigh of relief. Having Hottie McHotness behind him was an exercise in torture he no longer had to endure.

Ignoring the helmets, he led Sin to his front door, and by the time he got it open, both helmets were off and their lips were fighting for dominance.

They tripped over the couch and paused to kick off their shoes as Sin demonstrated his strength by lifting Orion completely off of the ground.

"Fuck, you're strong, Daddy," he purred and grinned as he felt Sin shudder. "You like that? When I call you Daddy?"

"I'd like it better if you'd show me to the bedroom," he answered. Sin's fingers lifted up his shirt to get at the hot skin beneath.

His jacket fell somewhere behind him, and he pulled back to whip his shirt over his head. They were both hungry and trembling, eating at each other's mouths when through a series of grunts and pantomime, Orion guided them to his bedroom. Once there, he dropped his legs down from Sin's body and tugged off his jeans.

Knowing that Sin was watching, he casually kicked them off before strolling to the bed, his tight ass wiggling as he ripped the comforter and top sheet free.

He looked back at Sin, watching as he stroked the bulge of his dick through his jeans, those reddish-black eyes following his every move.

"I've been good, Daddy." He climbed onto the bed. "Can I have my reward now?"

The look in Sin's eyes guaranteed that his prize was going to be long, hard, and hot.

Just how he liked it.

"Come play with me, Daddy. I want to play."

Let the games begin.

* * *

Orion crawled to the head of his bed, his shirt long gone, posing in his tight whites like he was a model. His body was beautiful, and he knew it. He confidently ran his hands over his chest, his eyes staring straight at Sin's, daring him to deny he was walking perfection.

Sin licked his lips, unable to help himself as he let his eyes roam over Orion's body.

He wanted to be inside him as deep as he could get.

The man's chest was well-defined and hard, his rounded pecs showcasing hard brown nipples lightly ringed with hair. The scars of his top surgery were nearly invisible, and the time Orion spent in the gym was documented in the popping planes of muscle that made up his chest and abs.

There was a thin line of hair that started from his navel and disappeared into the tight waistband of his briefs. The bulge of his cock was solid and listed to the right. Sin let his eyes trail down to the thick thighs that had a thicker dusting of hair, and then slowly looked up back into those bright, hungry eyes.

"You are fucking perfect," he breathed, stepping

closer to the bed.

"You better fuckin' know it," Orion responded with a smirk, sitting back on his rounded ass and observing Sin carefully. "And you are far too dressed."

"I can fix that."

Sin gave no thought to his own clothing, tearing off his shirt and kicking off his shoes as he let his eyes rove over Orion.

"Tell me what you like," he asked, deciding now was the time to discuss things so later when they were in the act, a bad ouch wouldn't end the fun. He kicked off his shoes and stood back wearing only his jeans. "I don't want to make you uncomfortable."

"Well…" Orion purred, popping one finger in his mouth and sucking on it lightly as he let his eyes rake over Sin. "I like to fuck and I like to be fucked."

"No preference?"

"I like getting off with a partner, but I can handle myself just fine."

"And?"

"Are you asking if I get dysphoric?" he asked, tilting his head to the side. "Oh, you're so sweet."

"I want to get you off," Sin returned, unsparing with his jeans as he let the zipper down. "I want to make you scream my name as you blow, not because I did something that makes you want to kick my ass."

"I am not dysphoric, Sin. If you do something I don't like, I'll let you know. But as for setting the ground rules, I don't do water sports. I don't like pain. If you want to spank me a little, I am down for that, Daddy. But that's about it. I don't like to be humiliated. You call me anything but my name, you'll be calling a cab from the curb. I don't have a boy pussy or a cunt. If you gotta call it anything, it's my front hole and yes, it is about as hungry as my asshole. I like to get fucked in both, and I love to fuck. I have a drawer full of dicks." He pointed to his bedside table with a smirk. "You pick one out, and I'll make you see stars."

Orion's words went straight to his dick. Fuck, he loved a confident lover. And the way Orion was staring at him he knew this night was going to end with him getting fucked.

His hole twitched at the thought, and he felt more pre-cum slide from his slit. Tonight was going to be so much better than he could have imagined.

"You've been with a T-boy before?" Orion was asking as he casually sank one hand into the front of his briefs and pulled out his silicone packer. He placed it on his bedside table and turned back to smirk at Sin.

His fingers slid down, and his whole body shuddered as he tensed in pleasure, his head dropping back as he began to finger himself.

"Fuck," Sin gasped, slipping out of his pants and moving across the room in a matter of seconds.

Orion's whole golden body was shuddering as he dropped one hand behind him to support himself as his spread his thighs wider. He was moaning softly as his eyes slitted open and his gaze settled on Sin. "You're too far away."

In a flash, Sin was on the bed, reaching down to pull Orion's fingers free before he sucked the glistening digits into his own mouth.

"Fuck," Orion moaned as Sin sucked his fingers down as deep as he could, his chest rumbling in pleasure as he got his first taste of Orion.

"Delicious," he said after popping them free. "But I want to get it from the source. Can I?"

His dick was hard and throbbing, the foreskin pulled back from the plum-colored head. Already sweat was beginning to sheen his body, and the heady smell of Orion was beginning to fill the room.

"You're asking to eat me out?" Orion managed a

chuckle as he pressed his fingers to Sin's glistening bottom lip. "Fuck yeah, I want it. I want your mouth on my dick. I want to cream all over your face."

There was no stopping him after hearing that. Sin backed up enough to reach for Orion and pull him flat underneath him. He went with a small laugh, lifting his hips as Sin all but ripped his briefs from his body.

He spread his legs as his hands went to Sin's shoulders, tugging at his hair.

"It's so soft," he moaned. "And you are so fucking hard."

"All for you," Sin purred, pushing Orion's thighs wider as Orion slid down deeper into the bed, making a space for him to get between his legs.

Orion was perfection, his cock longer than expected, its small mushroom head glistening with his arousal. The lips of his labia were thick and surrounded the bright pink opening of his front hole.

His slick was leaking down toward his asshole, and Sin could only lick his lips as he thought of taking in more of Orion's spices right from the source.

He leaned forward, blowing cool air over him, just to watch that cock react.

"Stop fucking around and suck my dick," Orion growled, tugging painfully at his hair. Sin purred, tugging against his hold as he flicked his tongue out to lap at Orion's cock.

"Fuck," Orion shuddered, his legs moving until his feet were flat against the sheets and his thighs cradled Sin's head. "Damn, Daddy."

His words had Sin reaching for his own dick, gripping the base to stave off his own release. The things this boy was doing to him. He held his breath for a moment, fighting for control. Fuck, he had barely touched Orion and he was ready to blow.

After a moment he moved in closer, lapping at his

cock again before sucking softly at the mushroom-shaped head. His free hand slid up Orion's chest, caressing all of that golden flesh, loving the feel of his muscles wavering under his touch, driving his own need higher.

"You are exquisite," Sin murmured, lifting his head to slide up Orion's body, licking and lapping at his tight abs before he latched onto one nipple. He licked and sucked at the nub, loving the sounds he was drawing from Orion, who was whimpering and gasping, his hands dropping from Sin's hair to grip at his shoulders, the nails digging in deep, tearing at his skin. The little lines of pain only made Sin more eager to make Orion lose control. He wanted that body thrusting and thrashing beneath him. He wanted Orion covered in sweat and screaming until he was hoarse and could only whimper Sin's name.

He moved on from one nipple to the next, his fingers pinching and tugging at the wet one while Orion's legs jerked upward. His lithe hips were pushing up against Sin's own stomach, sliding his cock against Sin's abs. Orion whimpered at the pleasure that brought him.

Orion's eyes were closed and his mouth open as Sin tried licks and kisses up his chest and neck. He was trembling as he rose up enough to lick at his lips, tasting his name as Orion called out to him.

"You're beautiful," he whispered before thrusting his tongue in deep and tasting the pure fire of Orion.

He pulled back to attack his neck again, and Orion's hands were back in his hair. "You... you... tease," Orion managed while riding his stomach, his whole body quivering as he began to lightly sweat. "Daddy, please."

"Tell me what you want." Sin just wanted to hear him say the words.

"Daddy, please. Suck my dick." Orion looked up, high enough to see his face. Orion's pupils were blown wide with hunger, yet his gaze was strong and clear. This was a man who knew what he wanted and wasn't shy about asking for it.

"Anything you want," Sin promised, licking down his body again, stopping to again pay homage to his nipples before burying his nose in Orion's pubic hair, breathing in the primal scent.

He pulled Orion's legs off his hips and used one hand to push Orion flat to the bed once more. The younger man eagerly spread his thighs, exposing his need to his daddy.

His cock was even more swollen than before, and Sin could no longer resist. He dropped down, sucking his small cock deep into his mouth.

"Fuck! Daddy!" Orion screamed, his whole body arching up as more of his slick ran from his front hole. "Please, please, please…"

Sin began to suck at the tender flesh, careful not to pull too hard, while one finger began to tease at the slick pouring from his front hole.

"In me!" Orion was screaming, his back arching as he tried to fuck Sin's face, and Sin got his finger deep inside Orion's body.

Sin sliced his tongue over the head of his dick and sank his finger deeper, feeling his slick, silky walls quiver.

He pulled off long enough to groan, "That's it. Take what you want, baby," before engulfing him once again into the heat of his mouth.

"Yes!" Orion was screaming, his body tingling, his thighs flexing as he ran his fingers though Sin's hair, tangling the long red mass as he rode the man's face.

Sin pulled off to lick down at his hole, two fingers encircling his small cock and jerking it firmly, never letting the pleasure cease.

"Yes, Daddy!" Orion's head was thrown back, his chest rising up as Sin sank another finger into his front hole, spreading them and adding a pressure from the side that was making his baby wail.

Sin closed his eyes, savoring the thin slick as it flowed into his mouth, wetting his sheets and sinking into his hair. He was surrounded by Orion, by his scent, the feel of his hard body beneath him, lost in the fact that his beautiful man was giving his pleasure over to him.

His own dick throbbed as it pressed into the sheets, and he found himself grinding against them, trying to relieve some pressure so he could keep on making Orion scream.

"Suck me... please." Orion's voice was gruff and whispery and began to shake. "I'm so close, Daddy. Please..."

How could he say no to that? Sin gave his hole one last lick before taking his cock into the heat of his mouth once more.

He sucked harder as he slid three fingers in deep, pumping as hard as he dared, sliding his tongue against the head of Orion's dick.

"Yes, oh god, yes... almost..." Orion's words were disjointed, and his body was tensing as Sin worked him over.

His hips were no longer rocking and pumping. Instead he curved them up and held them still so Sin knew he was hitting all his baby's buttons just right. He redoubled this effort, and Orion began to pant and scream, his legs locking, his inner walls quivering until he exploded.

"Fuck!" Orion wailed, his cock growing hard in Sin's mouth as his inner walls flexed around Sin's fingers, making Sin groan as he delivered the first orgasm of the night to his baby.

Orion was riding his face, his own head thrown back as a red flush grew over his chest and face. Then he was moaning, releasing the tight grip he had on Sin's hair as his thighs fell open.

"Fuck me," Sin demanded and wasted no time going

to the condoms and lube that Orion was pointing to in his drawer.

He slid the drawer open and turned back to leer at Orion.

On a velvety-looking cloth lay at least six different dicks of varying size and colors. "I trust you have a harness for these?" he asked, his face shiny with Orion's release.

"Hell yeah," Orion managed, tearing his eyes open as he lifted his hands above his head, stretching like a cat as he let his gaze slide over Sin's body, finally resting on the long thick dick between his legs.

"You are so going to fuck me," Sin informed him, eyeing what had to be a nine-inch sparkly purple vibrator.

"After you do me," Orion grinned. "If you're up for it. Think you can fuck me into coming again, Daddy, and not blow your wad until I'm deep inside you?"

Sin's gaze trailed over his flushed, sweaty face, that hard body put on display for him, the swollen red lips, the eyes daring him to say yes...

"Challenge accepted," he muttered, grabbing the lube and the condoms. "But you better be energetic enough to give it to me hard. When I get fucked, I want it rough."

Orion's grin was answer enough.

Sin found himself covering that tight, perfect body again, relaxing as Orion reared up to grind the back of his head and pull him down into a deep kiss, first licking his slick from his lips.

"Fuck, Daddy, you feel so good." Orion rocked his hips up against Sin's dick, grinding into small circles as his arousal grew again.

Smirking, Sin reached out and spun him around onto his face. Orion squeaked but quickly got with the program as he slid up to his knees, spread his thighs wide, arched his back, and presented.

He paused as he saw the thin blue angel's wings tatted over Orion's shoulders before he ran his fingers over the stylized gothic-looking ink. The tattoo ran over his shoulder blades and down to his hips, somehow emphasizing the broadness of his back and the narrowness of his hips. As he ran his fingers over the perfect lines, the muscles in Orion's back shifted, giving the illusion that his wings were fluttering.

"Fuck, that's hot," Sin purred as he pulled back, opened a condom, and quickly fit it to his swollen cock.

He gripped Orion's thighs as he dipped his head low and lapped at his front hole.

"Oh yes, Daddy, put your tongue in me before you fuck me," Orion purred, wiggling his little ass and earning a sharp slap from Sin.

"Be still," he demanded, before popping his ass once more just to see his cheeks quiver.

Orion giggled but held still as Sin again dipped down low and lapped at his hole.

"Fuck, I am so ready to go again," he moaned, his fingers digging into the pillow as he lifted his head up enough to look over his shoulder at Sin and lick his lips. "You ready to fuck me, Daddy?"

"Whatever you want," Sin promised and slid up close to run the covered head of his dick against Orion's front hole.

"When you are done fucking me," Orion promised, "I'm going to suck your dick, Daddy. I'm gonna suck it good and bend you over like you have me and fuck you hard."

Sin reached down and gripped the base of his dick again, Orion's words sending his mind reeling and his body scrambling for control. His muscles tensed, and there was a hunger deep inside his body that made him want to slam into Orion as hard as he could and fuck that teasing smile right off his face. Instead he threw his hair back over his shoulder and leaned over to run his tongue along the lines of a wing, watching as Orion's head dropped onto his pillows and his whole body shuddered.

"Whatever my baby wants," he promised, straining his ass cheeks to take him all in. "Such a beautiful view you give me. For this, baby gets everything he wants."

He reached out and pumped some lube into his hand and hissed as he prepared his condom-covered cock. With a lube-damped thumb, he lightly traced Orion's asshole, watching as the hungry little orifice winked at him. "I am so going to fuck this hole too, baby," he promised as he fitted his dick to Orion's front hole and began to push in. "I am going to make all of this hot little body mine."

As he slid in deep, Orion made a whining growl as his body tensed up.

Orion was so hot and tight that Sin had to pause with just the tip of his cock inside Orion's body as the younger man's muscles went wild around him.

Orion was whimpering, "Yes, yes, yes..." as he spread his legs wider. Then, "Fuck, Daddy. You're so big."

There was no stopping him after that. Sin threw back his head, groaning as he slid smoothly, not stopping until he was pushed as far as he could go into his lover.

"Fuck!" Orion wailed as his chest dropped to the bed, leaving only his hips up, filled and still wanting more. "Big, Daddy! So big! Fuck me!"

Pulling out, Sin slammed back in at half-strength, and Orion screamed as his body tightened and he fell into his second orgasm of the night.

And Sin fucked him right through it, grinding his hips in hard and swiftly pulling back to set up a hard rhythm that had Orion tearing at the bed sheets and screaming his name.

Sweat poured down his back as he fucked him harder, his thumb slipping into his asshole as he began to push him hard.

Orion was wailing, his body shuddering as he threw himself back into Sin's thrust, another orgasm tearing through his body as he fucked back just as hard as he was being fucked.

Sin was cursing, his free hand at Orion's waist to pull him back harder as he squeezed his eyes and fought for control. He was going to fuck himself into oblivion inside his lover's body. He was going to pull out and flip over so he could get fucked... any minute now...

But he liked drawing those addictive cries from Orion as he spiraled into orgasm after orgasm, his body tight and clasping, then thrusting back -- until Sin knew if he stayed inside that perfectly delectable hole one second more he was going to explode.

He jerked out, ignoring Orion's cursing and flipped onto his back, one hand back at the base of his dick, staving off his growing orgasm as he squeezed his eyes shut and began to recite song lyrics in his head.

"Daddy?" He forced his eyes open to see Orion hovering over him, pouting. His face was flushed a deep red that went down over his chest. His nipples were hard peaks, and his thighs were shiny from his slick that freely ran from his front hole.

"You're fucking me, remember, Baby?" He moaned, arching up to pull Orion down far enough to take his lips. "Time to give Daddy what he wants."

The sensual languid look on Orion's face grew deeper as he reached into his drawer and pulled out a black leather harness.

Sin cursed and gripped his dick harder as he watched Orion stumble to his feet, his gaze on Sin's red-black eyes as he easily stepped into the harness and strapped it around his waist.

"Which dick do you want, Daddy?" he asked, running his fingers over his chest before they slipped down between his thighs, toying with his dick and slick swollen hole. "Whatever you want, Daddy. I'll make it good. I'll fuck you so good…"

"The purple one," Sin moaned, closing his eyes as he fought the urge to rip off the condom and jack off to the sight of Orion wrapped in tight black leather.

There was a teasing slide of latex on leather, and he opened his eyes to see Orion slipping a condom onto the glittering purple dick.

He moaned, spreading his own thighs and placing his feet flat on the bed as Orion climbed between his legs.

"You like getting fucked, Daddy?" he asked as he carefully lubed up two fingers, eyeballing him carefully.

"Like you, I don't play with my pleasure. When I want something, I ask for it."

That was good enough for Orion to lean in over him, taking his mouth into a deep kiss as he felt Orion's fingers press into his own greedy hole.

The burn was delicious, and he appreciated the fact that Orion was starting with one finger, carefully working him open.

"You're so tight, Daddy. You get fucked often?"

"Not as often as I would like." He purred as he gave in to the slight sting of being penetrated and spread open.

There was no feeling like it in the world, of being powerful and vulnerable at the same time. He looked up at the beguiling creature who was going to ride his ass and felt his heart turn over.

Orion was perfection, his hair a sweaty mess, his lips swollen from kisses and biting, his body quivering with anticipation. His eyes were shining as Sin looked from his face to where he was now adding a second finger to his hole, scissoring them, spreading him wide in anticipation of a good, hard fuck.

"You enjoying this?" he asked, hissing as Orion's wandering fingers tipped the bump of his prostate.

"Daddy, you got me off five times," he said, adding a third finger. Sin's hips shot up, and he let go of his dick before he began pumping the shaft and working the head himself. "I know I'm going to get off again just fucking you. You took care of me. Let me take care of you."

Before Sin could respond, the condom was whipped off his dick and Orion was sucking him in deep.

"Fuck, baby," he gasped, running his fingers through Orion's short damp hair. "Fuck." He closed his eyes and arched his hips up once more, helping Orion find that spot again.

Unerringly Orion found it, stroking it with three fingers as he prepped him perfectly, starting him out for his big purple dick. At the same time Orion sucked him down his throat, sealing around his length.

Sin whimpered at the expert blow job he was being treated to. He watched Orion's red lips stretched around the shaft of his cock and wanted to scream. Instead he closed his eyes and tried to hang on as Orion flickered his tongue over the head. He pulled off, teasing Sin's foreskin before snugly sucking him back down his throat.

Sin was massaging Orion's scalp now, his toes clenching as he grew closer and closer to exploding in his baby's mouth.

Finally, just as he thought he was going to blow, Orion pulled his fingers free and urged him over onto his stomach.

"Your ass is perfect, Daddy," Orion whispered as he leaned over him, pushing his hair off and nipping at the base of his spine. "You're so strong, Daddy. So solid. I know you can probably bend steel bars, but I know you would never hurt me. You got me off so good, Daddy. I can still feel you." He licked his ear, and Sin found himself arching up, offering his ass for the taking.

"I'm gonna be so good for you, Daddy," he whispered before he pulled back, and Sin felt the blunt head of his cock against his hole. Relaxing his muscles, he moved back, gasping as Orion slid past the guardian muscles before sliding smoothly into his ass.

Sin closed his eyes and moaned though the slight burn. He shuddered at the exquisite feeling of being filled to the brim.

How much he had missed this...

He closed his eyes and rocked back as he heard Orion gasp as his too small hands gripped his hips. And he waited.

Orion was not moving, not fucking him like he promised. He felt so good and full, and now he wanted more.

He looked over his shoulder and growled, "Fuck me now. Hard."

His commanding tone did it, and Orion pulled back and slammed, piercing him deeply, the hard, unforgiving shaft of his cock sliding along Sin's prostate.

Sin dropped his head and gave into being fucked, noting that Orion's cock was harder than any other that ever filled him.

His stomach grew tight, and the tension was back in his spine as Orion began to work him over good. The slick sound of bodies pounding deliciously into each other filled the air as their grunts and moans got louder.

"Yes, Baby, yeah," Sin's eyes were squeezed shut as he reached up and gripped the pillow tightly before he began to ride back, fucking himself on Orion's dick. His baby shuddered and wailed without restraint above him.

He reached down with one hand and gripped his dick, pumping it in time to Orion's thrusts.

"That's so hot, Daddy," Orion moaned as he began to fuck him faster.

He adjusted his hips and slammed into Sin's

prostate. Sin lost it as white lights exploded behind his eyes.

"Fuck," he roared as his whole body stiffened, and his load began to shoot on the bed beneath him, running down his fists as he blew his load. "Orion... baby," he gasped as he felt something he had never felt before.

It was like a shaft of white-hot energy, and it ran through his body, making his hair stand on end even as it increased the intensity of his climax.

It seemed to go on forever, and Orion fucked him right though it as his ass clenched around the firm dick in his ass and his body shook itself apart as pleasure tried to blow the top of his head off.

"Fuck!" he was screaming as he fell forward, his control slipping as a wave of energy engulfed him.

For a moment, everything was perfectly clear, he could see and understand everything. For one shining moment, he felt his heart lurch and his soul reach out to another. Tears rolled down his eyes as finally the pressure building within him popped, and his mind exploded with nothing to stop his ability to breathe, to see, to think, to control.

He felt his energy expand beyond his reasoning as a wave of power rushed over him again, causing him to collapse onto the bed as his body shuddered in release.

He couldn't breathe. It was too much, and then he heard Orion calling his name, fucking him harder before he stuttered to a halt and collapsed onto his back.

Finally Sin could take a deep breath, his whole body quivering at the powerful orgasm that had shaken his whole world as he felt Orion slide free.

His skin tingled... no, his skin was burning in a painful way, his hair standing on end as he felt Orion's fingers tease over his shoulders.

But Orion's fingers were holding onto his waist, so that meant...

Chapter 4

"That is new," Orion whispered as the huge snake tattoo completed its crawl off Sin's sweat-shined skin and wrapped them tighter together. Had he been drugged or was the sex so damn good his brain broke?

Some part of him wanted to run screaming into the night, but the other part -- the bigger part -- wanted to stick around and see what was going to happen. He was the son of people who made it their life's goal to discover and explain the mysteries that surrounded humanity, so it came as no surprise to him that he wanted to see where this was going.

"I can explain," Sin panted from where he lay facedown on the mussed sheets. "But first can you hand me a towel? I wanna get out of the wet spot."

Orion really should be scared. He should be terrified. If he had any sense, he would be running screaming from his own apartment. Instead, he was watching as the man... was it even okay to call him a man at this point?... changed his sheets with military precision.

"So," he managed as he sat at his desk chair watching, "you are a god."

Those were words he thought he'd never say outside of a sexual reference.

"Was a god," Sin said, tucking in the last corner and turning to face Orion. He was smiling again, and that daddy thing he had going was coming out in full force. "Wanna get back in?"

Why did he suddenly feel like a kid being tucked into bed? Orion shook his head and chuckled at the images that flashed through his head. But Sin rolled him flat on the bed, unstrapped his harness, bathed his hole tenderly, and plopped him on the chair to wait. If he had ever been curious about how it felt to be A Little, well, now he knew. But that kind of play really didn't interest him.

"I have a daddy, thanks," he offered as he rose to his feet, moving slowly as the light burn between his thighs reminded him of how he had been filled by this man... god... and before he went to his knees and demanded to be fucked as well. He was sore in a delicious way and really wanted to dive into that bed. But the man's tattoo had just popped out of his skin.

He looked at Sin, watching as the snake coiled around his body, though its head was lifted and its little black eyes were staring directly at him.

"And no, I don't want to get back in bed." He really did. Another round would be so good right now except for the... the thing. "So. A god?"

He reached for a robe that hung on a hook by the door. He cocked up an eyebrow as Sin frowned while he covered his body. "This is a conversation I don't want to have naked. In fact, this was a conversation that we should've had before the clothes came off."

"In my rush to bury myself into that delicious body of yours and immerse myself in your mind, I may have neglected to tell you a few things that could make you view me differently."

"Talk about a role reversal," Orion muttered as he reclaimed his seat on his desk chair and stared at the still naked god-man in his bedroom.

"Really?" He tilted his head to the side, and Orion resisted the urge to run across the room and run his fingers though all that silken hair again. He loved the way it looked like a fall of cool, colored water as it slid down his chest and across his bright pink nipple.

From there his gaze traveled down the light dusting of red hair and tattoos on his chest sown over the cobbled stone of his abs to his bloated dick -- that still wasn't fully flaccid yet. As if noticing his attention, Sin's cock gave a shiver as it began to grow hard yet again.

"Um... yeah." Orion ripped his eyes upward and tried to keep his attention on the conversation and not give into the memories of that solid flesh slotting itself so deeply in his front hole." Um... yeah. This is a conversation I usually have to have with my dates. You know, being open and honest?"

Sin flinched a little at that, his shoulders drooping a bit, but he nodded, accepting the blame.

"In my defense," he began, "I usually just don't go around telling people I'm a former god." He reached up to pet his snake on the head. "I would find myself locked away in a heartbeat."

"Fair point." Orion's eyes roared over his form once more, and his eyes got stuck on some very nice places on his body -- like those tight hips, that corded Adonis belt, those wide pecs with their pink nipples. "You need to put some pants on if we want to continue to talk about god things today," he muttered, shaking himself as he fought for control. He could feel himself growing wet and slick again and knew that a naked Sin was going to lead him right back into trouble.

Sin looked down at his swelling cock and then back up at Orion before he ran one hand over his hips and the area around him seemed to fold and grow wavy for a second before a pair of black lounge pants unrolled down his body.

"Oh, fuck, you are a god," Orion breathed, the situation becoming just a little bit more real to him.

"A snake popping out of my skin didn't prove that?" Sin tilted his head to the side as he examined Orion. "Your priorities are askew."

"My priorities?" he snapped, face heating as he realized Sin was right in a way. He had seen the snake pop out of his skin, felt it crawl over him, holding the two of them together. Yet it was instantaneous clothing that gave him a fright. "You may have a point. I should be running for the nearest church, screaming about getting blessed, and here I am drooling over your naked body, upset because you can instantaneously clothe yourself."

He had issues. Or maybe he trusted too easily.

"I mean, yeah, you are hot and all, but I really should not be getting led around by my dick..." He paused, narrowing his eyes at Sin.

"You really do look like this, right? I mean you aren't some purple-red slime monster with six arms, two heads, and three dicks, right?" Orion leapt from his chair and began pacing, as Sin, a half-grin on his face, looked on. "I mean, some of those depictions of gods were not... pleasant. Oh my god, you're not an animal, are you? Did I just fuck an animal? If you are some kind of walking snake, I am going to be so pissed. I am not into bestiality no matter how sentient and consenting the creature is. What have you turned me into? And you better not have five mouths..."

"I really don't look like this."

"I knew you were too good to be true." He winced and pressed the heels of his hands to his eyes for a moment, trying to gain some composure, before looking back up at Sin. "Okay. Show me. I am a grown man, and I can take it."

"Are you sure?" He looked amused. "I mean I don't want to scare you more, and I know how scary lounge pants can be."

"Are you trying to be a dick?" Orion snipped. "Because you are precariously getting close to dick territory."

"I'm just looking out for you." The man was definitely amused, Orion thought, so it couldn't be all that bad.

"Just show me."

And before he could open his mouth to say more, Sin waved his hand over his body and just... changed.

His hair, which was a deep almost bloodred, lit until it was a brighter shade of red with a few silvery highlights thrown in for good measure. It was also no longer straight. It curled and snapped with an energy all of its own. His skin darkened a bit more, and a wild array of colorful tattoos spread over his muscled flesh, spreading out from a half- moon tattoo that sat in the center of his chest. His face didn't change much, but the angles sharpened a bit and a near-blond scruff appeared on his chin and above his lips. His sherry-colored eyes brightened a bit, closer to a fiery red-brown, and his lashes grew longer and thicker.

Sin was pretty, and he looked so familiar.

"This is me," he offered, indicating that the changes were done. Orion ran his eyes over that face and body, noting the bulge shifting in his lounging pants as he moved.

"Um, your dick. It isn't crazy or anything?" He had to ask, and Sin smirked.

"No, I never mess with my junk. It's served me too well for far too many years to go fucking around with it."

Orion sighed and relaxed a bit more. He could probably handle two mouths better than he could handle a dick with a face. God, he watched too much hentai anime. But he still looked familiar. Sin reached up to pet his snake again when it hit him.

"Fuck me," he breathed.

"I just did. And you fucked me too, in case you forgot."

"Python! I know that name. Abadon! Holy fuck."

"Well, we did just fuck, and I am a god so…"

"Dad jokes," Orion groaned. "You are getting close to making dad jokes."

"Well, this isn't the most tolerable situation for either of us." Sin… Python… Sin sighed, shoulders slimming again. "I am not used to this happening."

"Sex with strangers?"

"Admitting who I am."

"So you do have a lot of sex with strangers."

"I'm a world-famous guitarist with a legion of fans worldwide. What do you think?"

"I'm thinking I should sit on your face some more." Orion flushed as the words just slipped out.

Sin grinned wickedly, this time showing off his perfect teeth. Okay, it was more of a leer, but it had no reason to be that attractive.

"I shouldn't have said that, and I don't know what I mean." Orion was exasperated and frustrated and at the same time fascinated. He would not be his parents' child if he didn't take delight in this situation at least a little -- and talk about an ego boost. He'd met and slept with a god. He had just fucked a god. He was attractive enough to catch and hold the attention of a god who let him fuck him into the mattress. He was a legend. Beyoncé had nothing on him.

"It is a bit much to take in," Sin agreed, moving to sit on the bed. "Wanna talk about it?"

"This should be a new reality show… *So You Banged a God -- Now What*?"

"For the record, I probably wouldn't watch it." Sin grinned up at him. "Most people get strange ideas about sacrifices and shit. I wouldn't want to see that. People are weird."

"Well, you do have a point there." Orion reclaimed his seat. "So?"

"So?"

"So what do I do with this?"

"I could try and explain. Would that help?"

Orion nodded. "It would. Help, I mean. Logic has to come into play somewhere, right? And you seem to be a pretty reasonable man… god… whatever."

"Fair point," Sin said. "So my real name is Sin. Some

call me other names, but I prefer Sin."

"This is sounding very familiar to me, but keep going."

When Sin tilted his head in question, Orion explained, "My parents are archeologists, with a specialty in ancient Peruvian cultures from my dad, and Middle Eastern cultures from my mom. The name *Nanna* stands out, but it's been a long time since I've brushed up on my ancient gods. I mean... how many of them are real?" Excited, Orion moved to sit at the foot of his bed, closer to the miracle he had just discovered. No one would ever believe him. His parents would go...

"Not my story to tell." Sin held a hand out as if to put a halt to his line of questioning. "So don't ask. But I can tell you that what gives gods life and power is worship. None of us are really sure how we came into existence, just that mankind had a need for us, and then we were there, sustained by their belief and faith. If we suddenly lose that faith or mankind forgets us, we just simply cease to be. Born from nothing, into nothing we return."

"Oh fuck," Orion blanched. "There are so many gods, so many lost ones. Were they all real?"

"Not all of us. Relax." Sin offered him a smile. "Your empathy is showing. But no, not all the old legends are based on actual gods, though quite a few are. Some were just people who did great things who had their stories embellished. That alone is not enough to make you a god. It can make you a hero, and heroes are always remembered. It is legends that never die."

"And you were a legend."

"That I was."

"So who exactly were you? I still don't place you."

"I am Sin, known as Nanna, god of the moon, father of the sun god Shamash, father of Ishtar, and some say father of Venus. I am known as The Great Bull, keeper of the cowherds, governor of the rising waters, overseer of the growth of reeds, keeper of fertility."

As he spoke, Orion felt his eyes grow wider and wider. Nanna. Of course. Sin was a big deal, a huge fucking deal.

"I am Sin. My standard is the bull represented by the crescent moon. I am over three thousand years old, and I cannot die. There can be only one."

And just like that, any heavenly notions he would have applied to Sin were gone in a flash. No, this man didn't just make a Highlander reference.

"How about if I take your head?" Orion asked.

"Why take it when I can just push down my pants and offer it?" He gripped the crotch of his pants and waggled it at him.

That tore a snort of laughter out of Orion, and any fear he had vanished.

"Oh fuck me," he groaned. "Are you sure you aren't the god of corn? 'Cause that was just juvenile."

Sin feigned a frown before he winked at him. "You were taking this a bit too seriously."

"I didn't know how else to take it," Orion grumbled. "And now I just can't picture you --" He shook his head. "-- godly."

"Oh, did I ruin it for you?" He simpered, batting his eyelashes. "Did I destroy your fantasies of screwing gods?"

"I didn't have any, thank you very much. How could I find screwing someone sexy when he was the subject of some elementary school student's term paper?" he grumbled.

"I don't know, but you find me sexy." Sin snickered, crawling across the bed toward him.

"No, I don't. I find you ridiculous and corny."

"You want to fuck me again."

"Well, before I could afford a decent dildo, an ear of

corn in a condom was pretty good to me."

"I'll be good to you," Sin promised, drawing closer, hovering over him as he slowly drew his body up and over his. "Let me be good to you? Please?"

Suddenly, Orion was breathless, his heart racing in his chest as he looked up at the beautiful rock legend straddling him. The desire in his eyes was real. He basked in the heat of his body as he waited for permission. "Do I get the full honey experience?"

"I'll let you sit on my face."

"Good enough for me."

The second round was about as thrilling as the first... and he only made one corn joke, so they both considered it a win.

* * *

It was morning, and Orion had the sudden urge to make pancakes.

Maybe it had something to do with the man who had fucked him no less than three times that night. Maybe it was the knowledge that was suddenly in his purview. Some gods walked amongst them and apparently used fame and social status to stay alive. He needed to know more.

"Madonna?" he asked as he began mixing the pancake batter while Sin lounged in his robe at the kitchen island watching him, Snake lazily sleeping while wrapped around Sin's neck.

"Human."

"Elvis?"

"Completely human... the putz. Never gave credit where credit was due."

"Do I know any people who are actually gods?"

"Frank Zappa."

"He's dead."

"No, he got bored with existence and moved on."

"Hmm." Orion nodded as he poured out the batter

to form the first pancake. "That makes sense. He always seemed a little... off."

"That would be accurate."

"But he had children."

"So did I."

"So that's why you have that sexy dad vibe," Orion teased, then sobered. "Where are -- I mean if it's not too much to talk about."

"I have no idea where my kids are or even if they still are. They are gods in their own right, and they have their own lives to lead."

"How can you stand that? I mean, my parents were old when they had me -- late forties and all, but they used to tell me that their greatest fear was dying off before I got to a point where I could live without them. I mean, I don't know how I'll be able to function when they do pass, but --"

"I may look it, Orion, but I'm not human. I was created out of human want and need, but I'm not human. I feel deeply, but I also know that existence is a perilous thing. I reared my kids to understand this. We're not afraid of nonexistence. We were never really born, so we can't really die. But we all know that our time, though seemingly infinite, is not. We have our duties to perform and our reasons for being here. When those duties are complete, it is our place to cease to be."

"So why are you still courting worship? It sounds like you don't want to cease to be."

"More like my duties are not complete, and I have no idea when they will be, so we all need the energy to be able to function until that time."

"God of the moon?"

"God of change, really," he grinned. "It's the order of things. Life evolves, adapts, and changes. It is inevitable as the tides rising or the moon hiding its face."

"That's insightful." Orion flipped the first pancake

and added another spoon of batter to his griddle. "I didn't expect it out of you, though I should. If I recall, Sin was also a god of wisdom."

"I am also a fertility god, which doesn't actually have a lot to do with begetting children and more to do with fucking over and over again until nature takes its course."

When Orion stared at him without saying anything, Sin offered up a sweet smile.

"I am the god of debauchery."

"That I believe."

"And has debauchery been accomplished to your satisfaction?"

"Well --" Orion snickered, flipping pancakes. "-- I am feeling rather debauched."

"I did wake up with you sitting on my face."

"You offered." The completed pancakes were plated, and Orion started another stack. "And instead of sitting there, you can pull a domestic and fry up some bacon."

Still grinning, Sin snapped his fingers, and a plate filled with perfectly cooked bacon appeared on the island beside him. "Any other requests?"

"Did you just -- I don't know -- magic up that bacon?"

"No. We just can't poof things into existence. I stole it."

"What?" Orion's voice hit a high note that hadn't happened outside of sex since puberty and before he started taking T.

"It's fine. I stole it from --"

His phone began to ring, and Orion grinned when Sin snapped his fingers and his cell popped into his hand.

"Show-off," Orion grumbled, before snatching up a perfectly cooked slice of bacon and taking a hearty bite. "A show-off and a thief."

"It's not stopping you from partaking," Sin pointed out as he answered, putting the phone on speaker.

"I know you stole my bacon, and you're a horrible person." The deep gravelly voice that Orion recognized as Sin's friend rang out clearly.

"You always have bacon about this time," he snickered. "And I know where you are so you can share."

"You could have asked."

"And what fun would that be?" he asked, picking up his own slice of bacon as Orion finished another round of pancakes and plated them up.

"Where are you? Are you still with Hottie McHottie getting laid?"

It was right around then that Orion realized that if these were the friends Sin trusted, then they had to be members of his band.

"Holy shit," he breathed. "It's Abadon."

"Why are you more impressed with that than with the knowledge that I am a god?"

"Well… it's Abadon," Orion tried to explain. "It doesn't make sense, does it? Now ain't that fucked up? I can't explain it." Really, he couldn't. God of the Moon fucking him into stupidity? No problem. Members of his band calling for a morning chitchat and calling him hot? He was ready to go on social media and brag to the world.

"You told?" The deep voice sounded more amused than angry, and some tension deep inside Orion, tension that he didn't even know existed, relaxed. "What is it about Baltimore? I need to get out of here before I start spilling my secrets too."

"You have no secrets, you loose hussy," Sin said. "You give them all away for free, Enk."

"Like you gave up the dick?" he teased back. "I know you gave it up. You got languid orgasm voice."

"Enk?" Orion muttered, going for his own cell phone. Dressed in a loose pair of sweat pants and socks, he had slipped his phone into his pocket after giving his friend the all clear and safe call that morning. Now he went to Google and pulled up Enk. "God of water and mischief," he spoke those words out loud before falling silent and straight into his research, bacon and pancakes forgotten.

"Are you giving away my secrets now?" Enk asked, still sounding amused.

"He knows about Abadon, and he's not stupid. He's an English Major with a minor in anthropology."

"Ohh, brains and sexiness. Do we get to meet him?"

"I don't know." Orion was vaguely aware of the conversation going on around him as he researched. This was rather fascinating, but that it was happening to him -- that was out of this world amazing. "Hey, wanna meet the guys?"

"Meet the guys," he muttered while going through the *Encyclopedia Mythologica*. "What?" he gasped as he digested what he had just repeated. "Do I want to meet the guys? Hell yes, I want to meet the guys!"

"Hell, yes, he wants to meet you, though I have no idea why he wants to waste his time like that."

"Fuck you, Sin," Enk laughed back. "You're just afraid that if he meets some real gods, he may just toss your ginger ass to the side and curse all the time he wasted on you."

"Right," Sin drawled as Orion stared in open-mouthed amazement. "So, three or four hours suit you?" he asked.

Orion nodded.

Three or four hours was good. They could shower, get one more round of mattress mambo in, shower once more, and make it to the Royal Sonesta with time to spare. "Sounds good."

"Okay, we'll see you around one for a late lunch. Are Nergal and Charle going to be there?"

"Yeah. We have some plans to make for our trip

home. And you know Abadon isn't going to leave Charle behind." Farewells were exchanged, and Sin ended the call before turning to look at Orion again.

"That was real? It wasn't publicity?" Orion asked as he picked up another slice of bacon, setting his phone and his research aside. "That Charle Lexington and Abadon thing?"

"It was real."

"He really went wilding out like that, and Abadon fell in love?"

"Not my story to tell." Sin picked up a fork and began digging into his pancakes with gusto. "But yeah, Abadon and Charle are totally in love. It was about time too. Abadon had been alone for so long. I was beginning to think he was doubting his existence."

"Will you tell me who he is?"

"Nah, you can ask him." He held up a piece of pancake, and Snake struck out, snatching the bit of breakfast pastry with every sign of enjoyment. "He'll probably tell you."

"Is that healthy for him?" Orion asked, wondering how his life had gotten so strange so suddenly. There was a god at his table feeding pancakes to his snake that was once a tattoo wrapped around his body. Real life was so much better than fiction.

"He's about a hundred years old, Orion. I don't think a little flour and water is going to harm him. I see to it that he is safe and healthy."

"So, is he really a tattoo?" Orion began to pick at his own food. "Sorry to be asking so many questions but... I mean, when will I ever get the chance again?"

"It's fine. Curiosity is sexy." Sin waggled his eyebrows, and Orion rolled his eyes in response.

"I'm beginning to think that you are the god of cheese and dad jokes."

Sin leaned in closer. "You know you like it."

"You know I do," Orion answered, leaning forward to press a kiss to his lips. "Now answer my question."

"No, he isn't a tattoo. We can't create life. Give the illusion of it, yes. Create it, other than through conception, nope. I found him in Nepal when I was passing through. I was with the East Indian Spice Company, and word had gone down that Nepal was going to be unified and declared a Sovereign nation. I had to go and see."

"Wait. You were with the East Indian Spice Company?" Orion's eyes grew wide.

"Um, yeah. They needed a translator, and I got bored. Britain owned the world then, so I was traveling around with those in power. It was safer and granted me easier access to see what was going on in the world."

"So, you weren't an officer or something?"

"Why would I want that?" Sin winkled his forehead. "The world wasn't a nice place, Orion. There was a lot of negativity going on. There was slavery and abuse. If I had become a soldier, I would have been expected to take part. I didn't want that. I just wanted to watch the tides of the world shift, as it were. I didn't want or need the attention, and frankly, I would have murdered somebody. The barracks weren't the safest places for a common man, and there would have been no way I could have bought myself a commission due to wealth or family status. I had money squirreled away, but in Britain it takes more than money to be accepted."

"That is… wow. You must have seen a lot of history."

"Been disgusted over a lot of history, you mean." Sin sighed but chomped down on another slice of bacon. "Remember that history is a work of art designed and painted by those in power. I could've been a soldier and been forced to kill or be outed. I could've tried to be some sort of gentry, but I am a foreigner and had to be able to move quickly without notice. I could've been one of the common men but scraping up shit off the streets to tan leather wasn't high on my list of things to do, and the revolution of industry was killing jobs left and right in England. Don't even get me started on the smells. It was cleaner and healthier for me to be a translator and guide. And since Nepal liked Britain, we were welcomed to explore. I was exploring near Tikapur Park -- it is really beautiful -- when a child offered to sell me something that no westerner had ever really seen."

He offered another nibble to his snake and grinned as it tightened in what appeared to be a hug before he struck out and snatched the bacon from his fingertips.

"Snake was just a tiny thing. I put him in my pocket, and when I got bored or lonely, I would take him out and scare the shit out of people."

The skin around Sin's eyes crinkled when he laughed, and he just looked all the more charming. Orion smiled before shoveling another bite of pancake into his maw.

"So, your snake is your emotional support animal," Orion summed up.

"I never thought about it like that, but yeah, I guess you're right. And there's no way I could let my emotional support snake die on me. So I keep him healthy, and he… calms me when I can see… well… life is a repeating cycle, the good and the bad. It… hurts, I guess that would be the best way to describe it, when I get lost in the largeness of the cycle and forget the everyday things, you know?"

He tilted his head to the side and tried to offer a smile, but Orion could see that there were dark shades in his red-brown eyes.

"You see too much," he whispered as reality, Sin's reality, slammed into him all at once.

How could this man remain sane when he was designed to cause change, yet see the same things happening over and over again? How could anyone sit back and watch people making the same mistake again and again for all of eternity or until you ceased to be? Orion knew he would probably blow his brains out if he was stuck in a grand cosmic Groundhog's Day for all of eternity. Just… fuck.

Even as these thoughts flashed though his head, he saw Sin reach up and pet his snake, and Orion watched as his muscles minutely relaxed.

"Damn, that is a hard road to be going down, Sin."

Sin's eyes snapped up to Orion, surprised.

"I mean, that is like being trapped in the worst time loop ever. I give you props for dealing as well as you do. I mean, a lot of people would have gone crazy. Oh. You said you were not human. Like us, but not."

That revelation was like a ton of reality bricks landing on his head. There was an inhuman god in his kitchen eating pancakes and bacon, petting his emotional support snake, after fucking him through the mattress.

Suddenly meeting Abadon wasn't as overwhelming as he thought. There was a miracle sitting in his kitchen, and all he could do was stare in awe.

Sin was doing his best not to get caught in the loop. Orion deserved more than that. He was spending his precious time with someone who should have scared the crap out of him. But his brave bartender just used reason and logic about the whole god thing.

He could imagine some people's reactions to having a huge snake pop off of the body of their one-night stand, but instead of running out, Orion Bane had questions.

Orion was unlike any other lover he had known... well, at least not for hundreds of years. The man was honest nearly to a fault about his wants and desires, and he made sure his lover knew each and every one of them.

He was demanding as hell, but gave as good as he got. He was confident about his body and the changes it had gone through in order to match his soul. He was as honest and open about that as he was about what got him off and what turned him on and demanded the same of the person he was pleasuring.

Consent was huge with both of them, with Sin because he honestly needed to know what Orion's needs were and what wouldn't trigger any dysphoria. He knew that he was down for just about anything... those years spent in a brothel in Pompeii taught him a lot. The Lupenare had been really eye-opening for a god of fertility. He'd like to think that he taught as much as he learned, but it was there that he learned the power behind honesty and individual wants and needs. He had done as much talking as he had fucking, and those lessons carried on to this day.

But to have honest and open Orion show some glimmer of understanding over the ordeal that his existence could sometimes become? It was devastating to him on a whole new level of honesty and understanding.

Even the members of Abadon, and admittedly his

beloved brothers, often failed to understand the full meaning of being the god of change. They had their own existence and reality to contend with, but the dark side of his gifts sometimes overwhelmed him.

He was happy, healthy, financially stable, and had a job he adored, but sometimes that just wasn't enough. He was lucky that he never started to doubt his own existence like Abadon, though he could understand why it had happened. Nergal was a god of destruction. He had to watch as humanity laid waste to each other in glorious Technicolor brilliance over and over. That was a lot of death, and it weighed heavily on him. Charle loved him despite him being a god, not because of it, and that was a major thing in the lonely one's life.

Sin had always thought that he was content in his position. He could watch the world change, he could travel, he could bring understanding and change where he saw fit to intercede, but he never thought of himself as lonely before, not even after Nergal found his one true love.

But now? Now with the understanding lighting Orion's eyes, he was beginning to understand a modicum of what his friend felt when he first met Charle.

For as he tried to get his mind out of the downward spiral that talking about his twisted existence would bring, he looked up and saw Orion's eyes. Not a glimmer of what it would be like, but understanding what hell part of his existence actually was.

It hit him like a blow to the heart.

Orion didn't pity him. He didn't envy him or show any fear of him and his collected knowledge over the years. He just seemed to understand the extent of his darkness that often made him feel his life was meaningless.

He was right, of course. His snake was of the emotional support variety, and he desperately needed that support to keep from losing himself in the darkness that constantly surrounded him. In the past, only the gentle touch and unconditional love of his familiar had pulled him through with none of his brothers being the wiser. Until now.

With that look on his face and understanding shining in his eyes, Orion offered up something he thought he would never feel again... the flash and power of true worship.

It slammed into him with the force of a speeding train, it vibrated his bones and rattled his nerves and filled him with a slow, glowing heat that started at his toes and trailed up his body until he could feel his face flush red with it.

It left him stunned and breathless, and a little in awe, if truth be told.

Sin suddenly understood Nergal a lot more than he thought he had before.

Sin knew that he was falling in love.

Who knew?

Wow.

* * *

Sin sat and stared at the beautiful, amazing, intelligent, hot, smart...

Sin sat and stared at Orion. He couldn't take his eyes off of him.

How had the fates conceived someone so perfect and then placed him within his grasp?

Right now, Orion was laughing and joking with his brothers, fitting in without trying.

He barely remembered the motorcycle ride here, though he had fond memories of the shower.

With Orion facing the wall, he had slowly slipped into his ass...

Orion had a shower chair. He said it was because he was lazy, then he hinted that it could hold up to five hundred pounds. That had him being flipped, and his tiny little asshole being prepped.

Orion had grunted and groaned and admitted that he loved his ass being played with as he suggested the shower.

Sin grinned at the memory of hot water and slick soap running over Orion's muscles, the way his eyelashes spiked up when wet and the expression on his face as Sin spun him around to kneel on his shower bench so he could eat his freshly cleaned ass good and proper.

His screams echoed in the shower, and again Orion proved that it was damn good being multi-orgasmic as he popped off at least three times before Sin rubbed up his fingers and opened him up for his dick.

In addition to a shower chair, Orion owned a handheld shower unit, which was perfect because Sin perched on his chair like he was a king as he slid Orion's tight ass down on his dick. With his back posed tightly against his chest, his legs wobbling, and his breath sobbing in his chest, Sin cruised up into his tight hole while he gently jerked Orion's small cock.

Orion screamed for more, tried to fuck himself down hard on Sin's dick, but Sin held him fast, not moving... just slowly jacking his dick and fingering his slick front hole.

"Please, Daddy?" Orion whispered, his head falling to rest on his shoulder. "I've been so good... please..."

That was when Sin had the bright idea to turn the handheld showerhead to pulse and spread that water directly on his cock.

Orion screamed, rearing up, trying to break his hold on him, but Sin was relentless. He held the hard flow of water directly on his cock as he began to bounce his baby on his lap.

The heat and tightness was amazing as his cock speared into flesh, filling Orion up.

Orion was swearing, screaming, tearing at his hair, and calling him every foul name he could think until he allowed Orion up enough to snap his hips, driving Sin's dick in hard.

Knowing that Orion didn't have a prostate, he was careful to circle his hips to stimulate all the nerves in his ass while he held that roaring water against his dick and over the sensitive lip that surrounded his front hole.

Orion was a crying, writhing mess as he gave one sharp thrust up, and he exploded into his orgasm.

He lost count of how many times he made his baby come sitting on his lap and begging as he was torn between the unforgiving water and thick cock stuffed in his ass.

He kept him there until the water began to run cool, then flipped them around, making Orion kneel on the bench as he fucked him hard until he blew his condomed load deep within his ass.

He had to carry Orion back to bed as the younger man could barely walk and was totally incoherent.

When he recovered, he reached for Sin and demanded a repeat when they got home before he moved his fingers down his chest to play with Sin's still-bloated cock and tender balls, sliding down in the bed to take him into his mouth and...

"Earth to Sin. Are you in there, Sin?"

Red-brown eyes blinked away the scintillating memory, and he focused in on his friend, Apollon, whose bright blue eyes shined with mischief.

"Back to Earth, are we?" he teased. "That looked like a very good memory."

"One of the best," Sin agreed, and almost against his will, his eyes went right back to Orion.

"You got it bad."

He looked up as his friend started snickering at him. Taking a seat beside him, Apollon -- Enk -- threw an arm over his shoulder as he watched Orion and Nabu engage in a conversation.

Orion was so engaged, his eyes lit up with knowledge he was acquiring, and he was just so damn beautiful. Even Charle and Nergal had taken a break from attempting to rip up hotel sheets and were listening to what Orion had to say.

"Your boy is pretty special." Enk sighed. "You were lucky to find him."

"Luck… fate… I really don't believe in it."

"I know, Sin." Apollon smirked at his friend. "You believe in what is tangible. He is very tangible."

"Very," Sin agreed as he reached up to pet his snake. "Scarily so."

"And he figured it out?"

"Well, my snake kind of popped out at an inappropriate moment."

Apollon stared at him for what seemed like an amused eternity before he began to howl with laughter. "He fucked the snake out of you?"

If Sin were any other being, he would be blushing hard enough to make himself pass out or at least achieve a nosebleed. But he was Sin, so he tilted his head to the side and offered up his most shit-eating grin. "Jealous?"

"Hell yes! I want someone to rock my world so hard I lose track of my power too, you lucky bastard."

"Luck again," Sin admonished, stroking his snake absently as he watched the others turn to them for a moment and just as quickly dismiss them and go back to their conversation, although Orion offered him a sassy wink before turning to engage Charle in whatever discourse they were having.

"So, skill." Apollon calmed his uproarious laugher into snickers before commenting again. "Is that why you have a stranglehold on your familiar?"

"Emotional Support Snake," Sin corrected, noting

that he was rather engaged in petting his snake. "That's what Orion calls him."

"And did he pop out before the debauchery was complete?"

"The debauchery was completed several times before I lost control," he admitted. "There is something about Orion…"

"Yes, I can see that." Apollon examined Orion from the tip of his stylish helmet hair to the bottoms of the thick black riding boots he wore. "So what was it? Afterglow a bit much? Tired from lying back with your heels to the sky and enjoying your pounding? Did he call you Daddy?"

"Yes and no. Yes, he called me Daddy, and I liked it. And no, he doesn't have daddy issues. Apparently his parents are still alive, if elderly, and they have a good relationship."

"So it was nothing he did."

"It was… Apollon, do you remember being honored by those who willed you to be?"

Apollon sat back and frowned just a little. "Vaguely. It was so long ago. I remember feeling as if I was floating, like I was riding a beam of pure light and everything was soft and warm." He turned his head to stare at Sin. "It was the first act of pure worship that I ever received."

"You feel that a lot?"

"I used to," Apollon admitted. "Kids, you know? Mischief is kind of their thing, and every now and again I get a powerful jolt of it. Why?"

"I think… I didn't get a lot of it. I mean every now and again, I get a flash of it and the memory…" He frowned as if trying to reconcile what he was trying to express with mere mortal words. "It was warm and light and safe." He turned to stare at Orion again. "What I got from him was damn near painful." He turned to look at his brother-not-by-blood again. "It was a fucking inferno,

- 226 -

Enk. What he gave me blew my control, and it made the cycles stop."

"Damn," Enk whispered, leaning closer to his friend. "What are you going to do?"

"I don't know. I -- I haven't experienced something like this before."

"You were mated and had children, Sin. You didn't feel this for their mother?"

"No. We mated, and I sired children on her because it was expected. She and I -- we had an agreement. We looked out for each other and we cared, but I've never gotten a rush like this before." All laughter aside, he looked at his friend. "I don't think... How can I..."

"You want more."

"I want more."

"So what are you going to do?"

"I just don't know." He dropped his hands from his snake and ran them through his hair. "Orion is -- he is like no one I've ever met before. He is open and honest about everything in his life. He's curious, but it's just for curiosity's sake. He has a thirst for knowledge but the intelligence to temper that with understanding. Most humans would have been running scared or trying to see what they could get out of me... all of us. And I say us because he figured it out. He was more impressed that we bang on instruments in front of large crowds than the fact that we were gods. It never even occurred to him. He just wanted to know more."

"A scholar," Enk decided, putting a hand on his friend's shoulder as if to comfort him.

"A scholar. Do you know how delicious that feeling is? I was explaining my need for my snake, and he understood before I could finish my tales. He just knew. How could a human just know? It's not like he understood, but he understood as much as someone who isn't faced with this situation can understand. It's intriguing."

"Maybe it's because he's had a lot to overcome in his life. Maybe he understands fate fucking you over and over... and over again. I have never envied your godhood, Sin. Of all of us, you had to deal with the most. It's unfair, and I understand why you don't believe in fate. But I do believe that we each get what we earn. Maybe it's life's way of compensating for all the bullshit you see, you know? Maybe it's time for you to have true happiness and joy."

"Like each of us is fated to find what, Enk? A temporary soul to be a balm to our souls? And then the torment as we watch them age and lose them once again?"

"So answer me this." Apollon sat back and turned Sin's head until they were staring deeply into each other's eyes. "Is it worth the pain you know you'll have to face to have this time of pure joy? If you don't have anything to fight for, to hope for, why are you fighting?"

"I --" Sin reached for his snake again. "I don't know."

"So do you think it is worth it to stick around and find out? Or do you want to let him go?"

"I don't want to let him go... not until he is ready to leave me."

"Then you want him to stay."

"I -- I think I do."

"So he is worth the fight."

"He is worth the fight."

"So are you going to ask him to stay?"

"How can I? I've only known him for a day."

"Like that ever stopped us from going after what we want? What is time to a god?"

"Hmm." Sin sat back and watched as Nergal strode over to them, a slight limp in his stride but radiating joy and afterglow.

"I like your human." He spoke as he gingerly took a

seat on the sofa beside Sin, taking up what space was left. "He's smart. Almost as smart as Charle."

"You're just in love," Apollon snickered. "And you know you can give your boy time on the bottom? It won't kill him."

"But it will hurt him. He was getting sore so I decided to let him get a leg up so he can heal a bit for later."

"Too much info," Apollon sang out, covering his ears with his hands, though he did leer at Nergal.

"Why won't you just heal yourself?" Sin asked. "That can't be comfortable."

"I like the burn." Nergal looked smug as he gave him his patented Abadon arrogant stare. "It reminds me that I'm loved."

"And it only took you months to come to that conclusion." Apollon sneered, dropping his hands to cross them in front of his chest.

"I knew I loved him... I just needed him to figure it out for himself."

"You whined like a little girl denied candy." Apollon laughed. "You locked yourself in your room and wrote sad emoji poetry. You downloaded every photo of lover-boy and pined over them. Your nose is so wide open we can drive a semi through it. You fell hard."

"Falling," he corrected, leaning back and crossing his legs as he got comfortable. "Falling, Apollon. I am still falling, and it feels so good."

"Tell me that when you can sit in a chair without wincing."

"He's got a big dick."

"I suggest you learn how to deep-throat it before we start recording. You'll have to sit for hours at the boards, and I don't want to hear you whining and complaining."

"Says the man who is not getting laid."

"Says the man who is content with what he has,"

Apollon corrected. "Who also has no problem sitting in hard chairs. That flight home is going to be so much fun for you."

"Is it worth it?"

Sin's serious question cut through the jesting between Nergal and Enk.

He stared at his friend, his eyebrows wrinkled as he tried to work out his own feeling in his mind. "Is it worth knowing that you will have to deal with human issues with Charle? I know you're going to say yes because you are in love with him. But I know you've given this some thought. Will it be worth it in the future?"

As much as Sin wanted to just beg Orion to stay, no matter how hard he tried to ignore it, the future spiraled before him, and it was filled with loss.

How would he react to Orion's first gray hair, to the wrinkles that would line that handsome face, to the voice that would grow cracked and weary with age? How would he stand up to his human's mortality and still just try to be happy day by day? How did one plan for that heartache?

"It's worth it," Nergal answered honestly. "I know that a mortal's life passes in a blink of an eye for us, but for every pain I have to deal with in the future, it's worth it just to have him in the here and now."

Sin took that in, staring as none of the joy on Nergal's face diminished.

"It can be hard when I think about the future, carrying on without him, but because I'm making the most of every moment I do have with him, I know that when I lose him, he'll be a part of my soul that will always warm my heart. I can think of him and have him back with me. I can lose myself in those memories and carry on, because it is what he wants me to do. I love him, Sin. And for a love like this, any bleak future is worth it just to have him now. He will sustain me and carry me for eons. I can't regret that or live my life thinking about the loss of him."

Sin nodded, wishing he could do the same.

But then, really, why couldn't he? He was the god of change. He tried to affect things where he could in humanity, to improve them. Who said he couldn't create a little change in his own life?

He looked over at Orion, and that warmth hit him in the chest again as his lover turned and smiled at him. It was a jolt that made his heart race and the hairs on his arm stand on end in a most pleasant way.

"A life time of that," he mused, a sappy grin spreading across his face.

Yeah, Orion was worth the fight.

Chapter 6

"No! You didn't jerk off to his T-shirt?" Orion roared with laughter as Charle Lexington told his most embarrassing story.

Hash, otherwise known as Nabu, walked over to join his brothers and bandmates on the couch, gossiping like hens, leaving the human actors the room to converse amongst themselves for a moment.

"He smells so good," Charle tried to explain. "And I was desperate. He kept walking around naked in front of me... and he smelled good."

Orion shook his head at the slim black man and wondered what he would have done.

"I feel you. If Sin hadn't turned up when he did, I would have gone home and grabbed my unicorn vibrator and an extra set of batteries."

That sent Charle off in peals of delighted laughter with Orion joining in.

"Oh my god, a unicorn?"

"Well, despite my nice STP packer, I don't actually have a dick big enough for a flashlight to jerk off with."

"Point." Charle snickered. "But a unicorn."

"Trust me on this one, horns and ears. They vibrate."

That sent Charle off again, and his laughter was so infectious that Orion once again joined in.

"You laugh, but that baby delivers multiples every time."

"Every time?" Charle stared at him in amazement. "Every time, really?"

"Every time." Orion snickered. "It was worth the cost. You get used to it looking so cute. It's really a nasty little bugger."

"And how does it compare to a god, if you don't mind my asking?" Charle stared at him in curiosity, nothing nasty on his face -- and Orion was really good at reading body language at this point in his life. "You're the only person who can even relate to what I am talking about. It's not like I can go around telling everyone I am fucking a god. I'd be in the nut house for sexual deviance before you can say god kink."

That made Orion snicker for a moment, but he pulled himself together before he decided how to answer this question.

"It's not too personal. I was just talking about my stand to pee fake dick and my favorite sex toy. I don't think anything will be too personal after that. Besides, you're the only one I can talk to about this as well."

He sat back in his chair, crossed his legs and decided just to be honest.

"He was the wildest fuck I've ever had."

"Always the quiet ones," Charle mused.

"He's not quiet in bed. He is vocal, and he does this thing with his tongue... It's hard to explain, but his lips on my dick sent me straight into orgasm faster than anything I've ever had, including my unicorn."

"I get that." Charle sat back and examined Orion. "I think that you are the only human being in the world who can relate. I mean, Nergal is wild in bed, but there is something more. It's like he knows what I want and worships me just because I'm me."

"No, I get it." Orion was quick to agree. "It's like all their concentration is on you, like the world ceases to exist, and all they want is your pleasure. It is... it blew my mind. I have never had an experience like that, and I've had my share of pick-ups and one-night stands. I've even had live-in relationships where my partner never tried so hard for my pleasure. It's unearthly."

"It's unreal," Charle agreed. "It scares me sometimes."

"What do you mean?"

"I mean having the weight of their experiences laid

on you in such a way that their only desire is to explore you, worship you. Sometimes I wonder if I can I compete. I know my history. Our generation didn't invent sex, or relationships for that matter, and here I am with someone who has eons of experience. I wonder what he could want with me -- but he never does. He sees me as I am, and he puts everything into bringing me joy. I am his sole focus. It's like he's lived all his life just to get the experience to be perfect to me."

"Like fate, huh?" Orion winked his nose. "But I don't think Sin likes the words fate or destiny. His godhood, for lack of a better term, tears him apart."

"God of change?"

"God who creates change to make humanity better… and yet no matter how much they change, they still destroy each other."

"Human nature." Charle sighed. "You can't beat that. It's what created Nergal. God of destruction, Abadon, the blood-letter. Isn't it amazing to think that the same beings who willed a god of destruction into existence also willed a god of change to help fix the destruction problem?"

"Maybe they realized they are trapped in a loop," Orion agreed. "Life was different back then. It was all life or death at any given time."

"And that begat needs."

"And those needs still plague the ones who are devoted to them till this day. Did you know that Sin gets depressed to the point where a human would kill himself?"

"What? Python, otherwise known as Sin?" Charle was shocked.

"Can you imagine seeing the people who you swore to help doing the same destructive things over and over no matter how much you gave them to effect a change? Can you imagine seeing a future of that looping over and over again?"

"Like some hellish Groundhog's Day." Charle shook his head. "No, I didn't know that. He can see all of that?"

"He can predict it because he has seen it so many times before. Can you imagine knowing that no matter what you do, you would get the same result time and time again and nothing can change it?"

"Definition of insanity." Charle nodded. "Doing the same thing again and again and expecting a different result. How is he not insane?"

"Well, he has the others in the band."

"So he isn't alone."

"And he has his snake."

"He never lets that thing out of his sight. We are still waiting for him to name him."

"It's his emotional support snake," Orion informed him. "He helps him break the loop when he gets stuck into himself."

"You've learned a lot about Sin in such a short time." Charle learned forward. "I've known them for a few weeks now, and you know him better than I do."

"I'm sleeping with him. And you are sleeping with Abadon."

"Honeymoon phase." Charle blushed. "He wrote me a song and everything."

"Well, since you are rooming with them, I am sure you'll get to know them soon enough."

"And you?"

"What about me?" Orion was confused.

"Are you going to travel with us?"

"Uh… haven't given it any thought. Why?"

"Well, you think Sin is special."

"Very special."

"So are you willing to give that up?"

"It's not like I'm in love with him."

"But could you be?"

Now that was the question. Orion stole another look at Sin and felt his heart beat faster as he took in the concentration on the redhead's face. He was listening to his brothers, a conversation between Nabu and Enk from the looks of it. He felt his breath catch when Sin looked up and offered him the sweetest smile.

"I -- It's a bit soon for that, don't you think?"

"What do I know?" Charle snorted. "I only wasted a month and a half of my life pining for the man I kind of fell hard for and did nothing about."

"You ran away?"

"With my tail between my legs. It's a big thing, you know? They are gods. They have forgotten more things than I can ever learn. They have seen more, done more than I can ever hope to accomplish. What is humanity in the face of that?"

"Yeah, that is kind of scary," Orion agreed. "But if you want something, you should be willing to fight for it."

"And that is what I did. I fought myself, the expectations of others, myself... yes, I said it twice because I can be kind of an asshole."

"And you got him?"

"I ran back and got him. I couldn't imagine facing my life without him. Look, we're humans. I'm a black man who writes for a rock-and-roll magazine. I am a gay black man who had to fight off the conventions of society who said I should act a certain way, love a certain way, dress and behave a certain way. I had to fight my own fears, and I have a lot of be afraid of. Hell, some cop could pull me over, think I have a weapon, and end me. We live in Baltimore, murder capital of the nation. I could get hit by a car or a stray bullet at any given time. I follow rock bands. A rabid fan could try to make me pay for spending time with someone they perceive as theirs and decide to make me the next star of a *Criminal Minds* episode. I could die at any moment, but am I truly living if I exist in fear? If I go tomorrow, I can say that I loved to the hardest and best of my abilities and that love was returned. I comfort myself with that whenever I start thinking about him being a god. Guess what? He's my god, and that's good enough for me."

"You make wise points," Orion agreed. "And I've lived my life for my namesake. I fight for what I want. I fought to make others understand I was born in the wrong body. I fought doctors who thought it was a phase. I fought literally in school when someone thought that they could beat me into being a girl. I fight the gay community who sometimes think that trans people are just confused. I have no problem with fighting if I think the fight is worth it."

"And do you think he's worth it?"

"I don't know."

"Good answer." Charle nodded. "If you had said yes, I'd have done my best to show you the door. I said take chances, not be an idiot about them."

That made Orion chuckle as he considered thin Charle trying to manhandle him out of the door.

"You funny."

"Well, this is my new family. I have to look out for them."

"I like that."

"And I would like to see more of you," Charle admitted. "You make Sin happy. I find that I want all of their happiness. They all went to bat for me and let me make my own mistakes. I've never really had family that cared like that."

"I -- I don't know what to say," Orion admitted. "But it's not like Sin is going to ask me to stay. I am a hookup who found out about his secret, and he's placating me and my curiosity."

"If you think that, then you really need to make your

way toward the door," Charle laughed at Orion's dumbfounded look.

"What?"

"He has never reacted that way toward anyone. I've seen him with groups and clients. I've seen him with his family, and he is treating you like you're already a part of it."

"He -- he is?" Orion got another look at Sin and found those red-black eyes glinting up at him. He gave him a stupid smile in return before turning to face Charle again. "So maybe there are some feelings there. A spark of something, mind you. Not real love or anything."

"But a possibility of it if you nurture that seed, right? Do you want to unearth that seed?"

"And that is the question," Orion sighed. "And it's not like he's going to ask me to stay."

"I think he is."

"What makes you say that?"

"The fact that he hasn't made any noise about putting you back where he found you, he keeps giving you googly eyes that follow you wherever you go, and he introduced you to us, his family, who he would kill to protect. He's going to ask."

"I don't know what to say."

"Better think of something. We leave in a week."

"A week..." Orion sighed. Only one week left with Sin... if he even wanted him for that time... which it seemed he did.

He had some heavy thinking to do.

* * *

Sometimes life moves fast; sometimes life moves very slowly. It was part of Sin's world, something he was used to. But right now he really couldn't recall where the time went.

There was a meal with Nergal and the others, and for shits and giggles they went out as the band Abadon. It was amazing to watch the paps as they surrounded the group, snapping photos and asking about their love lives. Orion was having a blast hanging on to Sin for a shot, then running over to Nabu to kiss him on the cheek to ensure that they all would be blinded by the flash. At one point Nergal took Charle under one arm and Orion under the other, and the crowd went mad.

His favorite had to be when Apollon got in on the act, dipping Orion back hard like a blushing virgin in a black-and-white movie, and laying a passionate kiss on his neck. Orion pretended to swoon and nearly threw Apollon off-balance as he struggled to capture all one hundred fifty pounds of muscle and amusement. The mischief was strong with those two, and Sin enjoyed watching as several different stories were spun and put out on social media.

They ended up at Stakes, a trendy steak house in the Inner Harbor, for one of the most enjoyable meals he had ever eaten.

It reminded him of the old days when his people would gather and feast to celebrate the spring or a bountiful harvest. It relaxed him and made his attachment to Orion that much harder to break. Not that he had any intention of breaking it at all.

Autographs were signed, and fans gathered everywhere they went, including a pit stop at Orion's bar. The owner was there and delighted was too weak a word for the man's attitude. Sin could see the dollar signs in his eyes as he swiftly called in more nighttime security and raved over the band. Photos were taken and autographed, and Nergal was nice enough to give a soundbite advertising the bar. They swiftly went through the listings of erotic drinks that Sin and Orion dueled over and laughter was the sound that followed them... laughter and the sound of screaming fans wanting to get into the bar that their idol endorsed on Twitter.

Eventually they had to sneak out the back with the owner's praises for Orion ringing in their ears.

Once out of view in an alley, the band did that magic disguise thing, and they calmly walked toward the front of the bar, the fans none the wiser about their escape.

They separated after that, and Sin found himself once again sitting in Orion's apartment, the enthusiastic young man sitting in his lap as they traded soft kisses and laughed about their evening out.

"Do you always do that?" Orion asked. "I mean I haven't had so much fun in ages. They kept throwing food at us and ignored the fact that we walked into a high-end steak restaurant in jeans."

"Privilege is power." Sin snickered. "That and we're worth a few billion collectively. Money talks…"

"And bullshit walks."

"You know that's right." Sin pressed a kiss to Orion's bottom lip, suckling at it gently before nipping it lightly and licking the sting away. "But no, we don't do that too often. That's why they make a big deal out of it when we do. We are known for wild after-parties and greenroom hookups. It's easier to just blend in and walk away in that crowd."

"And do you fuck a lot of them?" Orion's curiosity was showing as he sat back on Sin's lap, his ass rocking softly against the growing bulge in his jeans.

"Quite a few," Sin admitted, shrugging. "There was no reason not to take what they were offering. But sometimes it got to be a bit much, and I'd just walk away. It got kind of boring, you know?"

"Same old, same old?" Orion snickered.

"Well, same old dressed in new packaging. It was easy to see what they wanted. Sometimes it was to feel appreciated and sexy. Other times it was just to say that they did it, another check on the bucket list. And there were quite a few fanatics. We tend to avoid those. They can be a bit fucked up in the head. That's not the kind of worship we crave."

"So you fucked people for their sakes? That sounds... not right. Like you are letting them use you."

"Make no mistake, Orion, I fucked people because I wanted to. I try not to let myself be used for anything. Sometimes I could help someone by spending time, and sometimes it was just fun. But I get as much as I give. It wouldn't be fair otherwise."

"So... a lot of groupies?"

"Quite a few." He grinned. "And I don't discriminate."

"Do tell." He could scent that Orion was getting aroused by this conversation. He had a bit of a voyeur streak in him, and Sin found that hot. Orion leaned in closer, tugging at Sin's shirt until he lifted his arms and allowed Orion to jerk it over his head.

Sin hummed in amused pleasure as Orion began to toy with his nipples, flicking them lightly with his thumbnails, tugging at them before petting down his chest.

Sin closed his eyes, letting his head fall back against the back of the couch while he gently moved his hips upward, feeling the head of his dick dampen with arousal. He looked up at Orion and saw those beautiful eyes narrow in concentration, the pupils blown so wide with arousal the rich brown appeared black. Orion leaned forward and nipped at the side of his neck near his shoulder.

Sin cursed lightly and ran his hands up his lover's back, pulling him closer.

"I've had a lot of bodies in my bed, Orion. Race don't matter to me. That's a recent bit of human stupidity and won't mean a thing in the future. I don't give a damn about how big or how small you are. Your body is a vessel that transports your soul. I don't care about gender... There are so many beautiful bodies out there, why should I limit myself? It's all about the soul, you know? About their spirit and their attitude."

"So you have had trans people in your bed before?"

"Oh yes," he purred, tugging at Orion's own shirt until he managed to free him from the confines of cotton blends. Satisfied, he leaned forward and sucked one pink nipple into his mouth, laving it with his tongue.

Orion hissed and arched his back, his hands going to Sin's hair. He welcomed the painful pull as it went straight to his dick.

Sin let go of Orion's nipple to lick up his wide pecs to over his collarbone to his neck.

"One of the hottest experiences I ever had was with an asexual man who just wanted to dominate me for a time. I let him tie me up and do the most delicious things to my body with a vibrator, a hairbrush, and some silk ties."

"Fuck," Orion whimpered, jerking Sin's head up to take his mouth in a short, hot kiss, thrusting his tongue between his lips and taking Sin's mouth for his own. He pulled off to whisper, "Tell me more. I'm taking notes."

* * *

The sun was high when Sin next opened his eyes. He was overwhelmed but with a feeling of contentment that he'd never felt before.

Orion was nestled in his arms, his back to his chest, and his arms were wrapped around this amazing man, spooning him tightly as if he never wanted to let him go. He inhaled deeply, taking in the scents of the Egyptian musk shampoo he washed with, the slightest tingle of sex that remained after their hasty cleanup the night before, and the incredible woodsy smell that was Orion Bane.

He could gleefully wake this way every moment for the rest of his existence. The thought scared and comforted him at the same time. It was such a very human thing to feel.

He inhaled again and maneuvered his head to press a soft kiss to the back of Orion's neck and felt the delightful squirm as the muscled body of his lover settled closer, his perfectly rounded ass pressing into his groin.

"Keep that up, and I'm not going to let you out of this bed."

Orion's sleepy voice was soft and rough with sleep as he grabbed Sin's arms and pulled them tighter around his body.

"Like I want to go," Sin whispered back, pulling Orion even closer, one of his legs slipping in between the smaller man's. "Like I can ever let you go."

"You leave in a week," Orion purred, craning his head back to press a kiss to Sin's hair-roughened chin. "That means we have a limited time to tear up the sheets again." There was amusement in his eyes as he grinned up at Sin.

"Or maybe we could have longer," Sin tentatively offered.

His mind was screaming, "Abort! Too soon! What are you doing?" but he was running out of time, and damn it, he wanted to know if he could keep his Orion before he lost more of himself to the marvelous man.

"You planning on staying?" Orion twisted in his arms until they were facing each other, his tiny little toes on his perfect little feet pressing against him as he snuggled close. "You going to give me more time with you?"

"How about you come with me?"

The world seemed to hold its breath for Sin, tension and anticipation growing as he waited for an answer, as he suddenly began to silently beg the fates that he didn't really believe in to grant him this one wish... that Orion would say yes.

"What?" There was confusion in Orion's dark eyes as

he pulled back, putting a small but painful distance between the two of them.

"I want you to come with me." Sin reached out and took one of Orion's hands in his, pressing it against his heart. "I know we haven't known each other long and this is a big step, but I don't want to let you go, Orion. I want you to come with me so we can explore this thing we have."

"Uh…" Orion pulled back and sat up in bed, the sheets falling from his body, sending a suddenly bitter cold air that matched the coldness that was starting to overtake Sin's heart. "What?"

"I said --"

"I know what you said." Orion ran a hand through his hair as he stared down at Sin. "I heard you. But…"

"We could be great." Sin offered up his best smile as he sat up reaching for Orion's hand and flinching when he pulled back. "I mean," he stammered, his breathing increasing as he fought against the dark thoughts that were threatening to overwhelm him. "We can decide what this thing with us is together. I think we have something special, and I think we owe it to ourselves to see where it can lead."

"All I hear is I and me," Orion breathed as he frowned. "But what about me?"

"You missed the we. I think we have something growing between us."

"Genital soreness from how many times we fucked," Orion grumbled, rising from the bed and looking around his bedroom before he walked over to his dresser and pulled out a pair of loose sweatpants.

"We have more than that," Sin grumbled back, feeling a desperation he hadn't felt since he realized the people who willed him into existence no longer needed him. "We have something huge growing between us, Orion."

"I -- I can't -- What about my life here?"

"What?" There was a shrill tone in Orion's voice that set Sin's nerves on edge. He sat up fully, dropping his legs over the side of the bed, any warmth and contentment he felt upon waking dissipating as the sun's light went from comforting to harsh and glaring. "What about your life here? I'm not suggesting you stop living --"

"No." Orion pulled out a shirt and jerked it over his head. "You're suggesting I drop everything and run away with you. The real world don't work like that, Sin. I have responsibilities here. I have a job and school. I can't just drop everything and run away with you. I like fantasy as much as the next guy does, but the reality is I have things here I need to accomplish. I can't drop it all and run away with you."

"Oh." Sin blinked and blinked again, darkness starting to settle in his heart. He reached for his shoulder, for his snake, but it wasn't there. He looked around the room and found it settled in a small twisted ball in Orion's discarded shirt and pants, wrapped around the material like he usually was wrapped around his body.

A wave of his hand had his snake around his neck once more. The snake, as if sensing something was wrong, wound tightly around him, its forked tongue tickling his earlobe as Sin gently ran his hand over its body.

"I mean we barely know each other." Orion, who was looking more and more distressed, tried to explain. "We just met, and there are so many differences between us."

"I don't see the differences." Sin was finding it more and more difficult to talk and could feel his face slipping into a neutral facade, but he couldn't stop it. He couldn't throw on a fake smile or feign understanding. He didn't understand. Well, he did in a way, but... He thought they were growing something worth fighting for. He knew he couldn't fight on his own, but --

"There are a lot of differences," Orion tried to explain, running his fingers over his hair once more. "I mean, you are a god in a rock band."

"We are on hiatus."

"Still in a rock band, about to move to the frigging Canary Islands."

"Do you have a passport?"

"Yes."

"Then I don't see the problem."

"I have bills to pay, Sin. I have a job and school. I just can't up and leave on a whim."

"The way I feel about you is not a whim, Orion."

"Don't tell me it's love," he scoffed. "We haven't known each other that long."

"I didn't say it was love yet. But it has the potential to be." He tried to desperately explain, his words soft and low. "I don't want to let that potential die."

"It won't. I mean, we can call and we can email and Skype... and maybe before summer break is over I can come out and visit you..." Orion trailed off as Sin just stared at him.

"It's not the same," Sin whispered, and his snake wrapped more tightly around his neck. "I wouldn't be able to touch you, to hold you, to wake up every morning with you in my arms. It's not the same, Orion."

"You're asking a lot."

"I'm asking you to take a chance. Please." He held out his hand for his lover, hoping against hope that he would reach out and take it. "Give us a chance."

Orin stared at him for a moment, chewing at his bottom lip, before he turned and made his way out of the bedroom.

"I need some air," he called back. "I'll be back... Just... Stay here. I need some air."

Sin listened as he fumbled into some shoes and heard the quiet click as the door opened and swiftly shut.

The tension in him broke, and disappointment settled in along with the familiar darkness.

He inhaled and exhaled once before he dropped his arms to the side.

His attempt to get Orion to stay at his side wasn't good enough.

Of all the things he could change, he could never change himself. He was what he was, and apparently he wasn't good enough.

Chapter 7

"What the fuck was that?" Orion tried not to bump into anyone as he calmly walked out of his house and down his street.

He felt something for Sin, that was for damn sure, and he didn't mean the soreness between his legs. His hole had never been so well used before, but that wasn't the point. He was mentally rambling in run-on sentences, and he couldn't make himself stop. But really... What the fuck?

He felt his heart race as he began to pace. A few people walking down the street gave him odd looks, but he ignored them and they were forgotten as he pulled himself out of pace mode and began to walk down the street again.

He was scared.

What was he scared of?

He tried to put his thoughts in some kind of order, but logic was escaping him, and he was running on pure emotion and adrenalin.

"Stop this," he muttered to himself as he paused to actually see where he was. He was only a few blocks from his home and near a public park. He made for the nearest park bench and plopped his butt down though his legs suddenly started shaking.

What was he afraid of?

Was it of Sin?

"No," he muttered, gripping his hands and resting his elbows on his knees, letting his hands hang between his spread thighs. He wasn't afraid of Sin no matter what godlike powers he possessed. And he wasn't afraid of the rest of the band of gods either. In fact, they'd never come into his thoughts until he started trying to break down the conversation he'd just had in easily digestible chunks.

So what was he afraid of?

Maybe it was being in a different country with a man he barely knew with no safety net if things went south?

Well, the logical part of himself argued, it's not like he couldn't get a plane ticket home. And it wasn't like he didn't know the people in The Canary Islands and in, specifically, La Gomorra. His parents had several friends who were glad to help him with documenting the Whistle Language in the area that was dying off. So he wasn't really going to be out on a limb by himself.

Was it money? He didn't have the kind of money that Sin was rolling with, his more emotional side screamed in his brain. With all that money, he could easily be disappeared.

Unless someone was stupid enough to discount social media. In the past day he was sure his face had been plastered over every social media platform and linked to the band. If he disappeared, Abadon and the band would be the first people they looked at.

So what was he so fucking afraid of?

The sex was amazing. Having a person who understood him inside and out was something he thought he'd never have. His bandmates, the other gods, even the human Charle, were fun, intelligent people. He felt safe around them like he hadn't felt safe since he left his parents' house and started tackling life on his own terms.

So… was he afraid of being hurt?

Really.

He stopped shaking and sat back, dragging his hands over his face, and tried to organize his thoughts.

He'd never expected to have a relationship. Seriously, it had nothing to do with being trans and more to do with his lifestyle. He grew up roaming the world, being free of any real emotional entanglements other than his parents, and he thought that was how his life was going to be.

Not too many people would be able to take a partner who disappeared for several weeks at a time, going to god knew where, chasing obscure texts, and playing with dead languages. Only someone in academia would be able to understand that. All the single scientists and broken families he had encountered over his years proved that to be true.

Correlation is not causation, he reminded himself as he tried to picture a relationship with Sin.

It could be fun, he decided, thinking about all the bullshit they could get up to. Sin would be okay with Orion having to take off for academic lectures and trips. He would be doing the same thing when the band started touring again. He didn't have to worry about the man cheating on him as he'd already screwed the living daylights out of any given number of people through the years. He trusted him to keep it in his pants or to at least respect him enough to break with him before he dipped his wick into any willing honeypots.

But he barely knew the man... god... man-god person.

Fuck, again with the pronouns.

He needed advice.

He reached into his pocket, glad that habit had him sticking his phone in his pocket when he walked out. He didn't even have to look as he hit his speed dial and rang one of the most important people in his life.

"Hello, Orion." His mother's voice was light and smooth, her accent about as undefined as his race. "It's good you called when you did. Your father just took a Viagra, and we are having a bit of wine while we are waiting for it to kick in."

"Eww, Mom!" Orion winced. "I didn't need to hear that. And since when did Dad need Viagra?"

"He doesn't. A friend came into some, and we decided to try it out. It's perfectly fine, dear. We just talked to his doctor a day ago, had a checkup before we head out to Egypt again. Going to join up with Dr. Walters. You remember him? The one with the horrible halitosis? He is brilliant when it comes to North African studies, but really, I think he needs to get his teeth checked. All those bottles of mouthwash I leave in his office isn't getting the point across. But your dad's heart is fine, so we're going to see what we can do with an erection lasting more than four hours."

"Mom?"

"What? We have some weed to mellow us down if we get too excited. And I made brownies in case we get the munchies."

"I know way too much about your sex life." Orion wrinkled his nose at the thought of his parents getting it on like bunnies. "There are some things a son doesn't need to know."

"Oh, fuck you, Orion." His mother laughed. "You had better look to us as an example of what your future holds. From where I am looking, it's going to be a long, hard ride."

"That's what she said!" His father interjected from the background, and Orion was torn between rolling his eyes in frustration and laughing in amusement. He chose to chuckle a little because, really, that was funny as hell.

"But I'm sure that's not why you called across the country, dear. What can your magical manic panic mother do for you?"

"I just... I met someone."

"Good. If you get laid more, you'll be less concerned about your father's and my sex life."

"You volunteer that information, thank you very much." Orion snorted. "I don't have to wonder. You put it all out there."

"Neither here nor there." His mother chuckled. "So you met a nice boy. Good for you."

"Well, he's nice to me."

"You got a badass? Even better. Everyone needs a good bit of rough every now and again."

"Mother!"

"What? I'm only approving of you getting some variety in your life. You tend to go for the cute, stupid ones."

"Miles was a lawyer!" he grumbled, recalling one of his past relationships.

"Like I said, the stupid ones."

He had to laugh because despite having esquire after his name, Miles was kind of an idiot.

"So you got a smart wild ride, yes?"

"Not everything is about sex, Mother."

"No, but it is one of our basic needs. Along with a feeling of safety and security, trust and sex go hand-in-hand in a good relationship. Sex can be one of the foundations to building a strong healthy one. Just look at your father and I --"

"I'd rather not, thank you very much."

"We trust each other greatly, and we started with a strong sex life. It can be key in a relationship."

"And how do you know I am calling about a relationship?"

"You wouldn't bring up meeting a man if he was a hookup, dear. You'd just make him breakfast and put him out the next day if you decided to let him sleep over. That's your MO."

"I don't have a MO," Orion grumbled, all the while wondering if he did.

Did he love them and kick them out? No, he shook his head. All of his flings knew where they stood... though he'd never tried to kick Sin out.

"Nevertheless --" His mother interrupted his thoughts. "-- what is it about this young man who is scaring you into calling your mother early in the morning at your time?"

"Mom… he's famous."

"That's nice. So are you in some circles."

"I mean he is internationally famous, Mom. He's big."

"And yet he met you? Is he an actor? They're always filming in Baltimore. Did he see you on set or something and decide my child was the most beautiful boy he had ever seen?"

"He's a musician."

"Not one of those talentless hacks who use Auto-Tune, is he? I'd have to object to that."

"He's a guitarist in a rock band."

"Good with his fingers, then." His mother chuckled. "So what's got you tied up in knots?"

"He asked me to go with him."

"Where?"

"To La Gomorra."

"Excellent. Do drop in on Barbara and Stanton. I think they're still on the islands somewhere. It's been a few years since I saw them in person."

"Mother. He wants a relationship with me."

"So do you want one with him?"

"I don't know," he huffed. "That's why I am calling you."

"So do you or don't you?"

"I just met him."

"Do you or don't you?"

"So many things could go wrong. I could get hurt."

"So. Do you or don't you?"

"I want to, Mom. But I'm… scared."

"Of?"

"Of being hurt."

"Leave a trail of broken hearts behind him?"

"No."

"Stalkers?"

"No."

"End up on TMZ or World Star a lot?"

"No," he chuckled. "He and his group have been known to throw killer parties, but no, none of that stupidity."

"So you are just scared to try."

Well, that summed things up neatly.

"You can't be scared for the rest of your life, Orion, and you know as well as I do that life comes with risks. You have to experience it before you assume the worst. You get nothing if you don't try."

"But -- But what if he breaks my heart?"

"Are you in love?"

"Not yet," he admitted. "But I could fall really easy."

"So fall, my angel," his mother urged. "You have such beautiful wings. You can pull yourself up again."

"But I've never... Mom... I never considered falling in love."

"You were eight when you asked me when your penis was going to grow in."

Orion chuckled at that memory.

"You were nine when you told me you were in the wrong body and had researched what to do. You were twelve when you wanted to go on T and fix what nature fumbled. Your life has always been filled with risks, Orion Bane. You just never took a risk with your heart."

Well, hell. Again, straight to the heart of the matter.

"I just... I don't know what to do. Mom?"

"Do you think he is worth fighting for?"

"I don't know."

"Is he?"

He paused and considered the man he knew, the man who was waiting in his bed for answers, the man who had looked devastated when he refused to take his hand.

"I -- I think I am brave enough to... to try, Mom. I

think he may be worth the fight."

"You knew that already, dear. You just wanted to have someone to urge you into doing the right thing."

"You may be right, Mother."

"I know I'm right," she insisted. "And now I have to go. Your dad just went from half-mast to full-mast, and I'm about to get pounded like mochi."

"Mom! Eww!"

"Text us your important information, travel itinerary, your lover's real name and address."

"You wouldn't believe me if I told you."

"There isn't too much I'm not willing to believe," she insisted on a more serious note. "You take care of your health and safety, and if need be, you know we'll be there in a heartbeat to bring you home."

"I know." He smiled, knowing that his parents, even at their advanced ages, would move heaven and hell to get to them. "I love you, Mom."

"I love you too, angel."

"Give my love to Dad."

"As soon as he gives it to me."

"Mom!"

"Afterglow is calling. Love you. Bye."

Orion stared down at his phone for a moment, before snickering… and then his snickers turned into full-blown laughter.

His parents were crazy, but they were right.

This conversation with them reminded him that everything he'd ever wanted in life, he had to fight for. Why would a lasting relationship be any different?

If it didn't work out, he could always come home and appease his heart with the adventure he was about to have. If he did nothing, he would always wonder if he was too cowardly to fight for what he wanted.

He was going to fight.

He rose to his feet and rushed back to his apartment.

He had a conversation to have with a ginger love god, and he didn't have any time to waste.

* * *

Sin was dressed. He was dressed, and apparently his snake was going to be the only comfort he had for an eternity.

Oh, he would have his brothers, no doubt, but it looked like he had attempted to change his own future a bit too soon. How was he ever going to forget Orion Bane?

He didn't want to be there when Orion returned, didn't want to face that rejection again. He really had no right to ask a man he knew for days to give up everything and just take off with him. He was being selfish and unrealistic. He sometimes forgot that he was a privileged person in this lifetime, money and time not obstacles in completing his goals in life. He couldn't bring chaos in Orion's life. It was unacceptable. Even though he would never feel his white light again, it wasn't fair for him to push his wants on the man. Orion was young and still had so much life to live. He was right to be cautious.

He waited as long as his heart could stand, and then he walked out. There would be no goodbyes… he didn't think he could handle looking into those intelligent beautiful eyes and let Orion go without pressing the point and causing a breakup before they even started something.

So he dragged on his clothes, draped himself in his glamour, and wrapped his snake around his neck. He took one last look around the home of the man who could be the one… and walked out. He couldn't ask him to wait, and he didn't want to let him go. The best thing for him to do was leave.

He made it down the block when he heard someone calling his name.

"Hey! You ginger bastard! Where are you going?"

Sin froze, his eyes widening as he recognized the voice, heard the pounding of the footsteps behind him, and turned around.

Hair disheveled, panting, and looking excited, Orion ran toward him, waving his arms.

Unable to stop himself, Sin opened his arms and exhaled in relief as Orion's firm body crashed into his. He wanted to cry as he felt his lover's legs wrap around his waist, and Sin lifted him from the ground. Before Orion could speak, his mouth was taken, commandeered as Sin pressed their lips together, his tongue invading Orion's mouth and tasting the flavor of the man he thought he would never taste again.

He broke off the kiss when Orion pulled back and dropped his feet to the ground.

"You came back," he managed as his snake wound around them both, holding them together.

"You were leaving me."

"I -- I didn't know how to say goodbye," he admitted. "I didn't want to do that. I couldn't stand to watch you walk away from me again."

"I just needed to think," Orion explained running his hands down Sin's face gently. "I needed to reason some things out."

"So... You're coming with me?" Sin asked, his whole body relaxing as the darkness that threatened to swamp him fled in the light and heat of those caresses.

"I can't leave with you." Orion spoke softly.

Fuck. He felt his heart shatter once more.

Sin went to pull away, but almost as fast as his snake's strike, Orion reached out and grabbed both of his hands.

"I can't leave with you *now*. But I can meet you there."

Sin blinked as Orion's words registered. "But -- I -- I thought --"

"You think too much," Orion grumbled. "Leave it to the professionals."

When Sin continued to stare at him, the pain in his chest easing as his breathing steadied and his heart stopped painfully pounding. He wasn't going to lose Orion. He was going to experience someone new and for once change something meaningful in his life. He was going to attempt a relationship. His hands started shaking as the enormity of what he was doing sank in.

"You --" He choked up, had to clear his throat and start again. "You're going to meet me there?"

"I'm not a rock star." Orion pointed out calmly, but with excitement filling his eyes. "I have to close up the apartment, talk to my professors, put in for a break at the university... I have to get a replacement... fuck it. I'll have to quit my job. But I can't just pack off and run away with any Osiris, Anubis, or Sin, now can I? I'm human, and I have to make plans. I mean, I want to explore this thing with you, but I have to have something to fall back on if it doesn't work out... not that I am planning for failure. I always hope for the best but plan for the worse. It's the human in me. I can --"

His words were cut off as Sin reached out and jerked him into his arms, slamming his lips on top of his lover's.

Damn, when was the last time he heard those words? Lover. He had a lover. He had someone who understood him, who cared for him, who was willing to try for him.

He bent down and took his mouth again, his lips gently parting Orion's, their tongues battling as they both fought for control, and then Sin letting his mouth be invaded by his lover.

He had a lover now, someone who was just for him, someone who helped clear his head, someone whose pure want and need sent a bolt of power straight to his heart each and every time they touched. Sin finally had someone just for him, someone who made him... be.

Pulling back, Sin stared down at the bright, glowing man who filled his arms and rocked his world.

"Will you let me name your snake?" Orion asked, looking a bit dazed and sounding a bit winded, but still filled with amusement and life.

"No."

"But I'm your lover now."

"No."

"I'm your potential mate."

"No."

"I'll make you pancakes in the morning."

"No."

"I'll sit on your face again."

"I'll think about it."

Some rise by sin, and some fall by virtue, but if Sin's luck held, it wouldn't matter anyway. He was too busy basking in the act of falling in love to give a damn about fate.

Bang One Out (Sympathy For the Devil 4)
Stephanie Burke

One of the most revered rock gods, Nabu is known for his focus and wisdom, as well as his ability to keep his cool under pressure. But all the intelligence in the world won't help when your plane goes down and in order to save an innocent and rather sexy woman, you have to expose your deepest secrets.

This was to be one last job for Aika, then her student loans would be paid off and she could make her way out in the world as a writer and cartoonist. Being on the flight crew on a private jet is at least interesting and will give her a lot of material to work with… like the sexy-hot crazies from the band Abadon. But one of the super hot band members is destined to play a key role in her fantasies. What's a woman to do when the man she is crushing on big time happens to save your life and claims to be an ancient god at that?

Chapter 1

"Is that the Westboro Baptist Church?"

Charle's eyes were wide in shock as he stared at the group protesting outside the private airstrip they had booked for the trip back to the Canary Islands.

Among the Locusts carrying banners and cheering the band on, a dedicated group of haters were amassed. The men, some wearing khaki pants and white polo shirts, were carrying signs denouncing fagotry, women's rights, savage people, and rock and roll. According to one list that contradicted itself several times over, underneath the big JESUS LOVES EVERYONE line they were all going to burn in hell 'cause Jesus hates fags.

"I don't think that's what the good book preaches," Nabu muttered, shaking his head as he pointed to one poster that depicted him being lynched while the rest of the band served as logs that burned beneath his swinging body. "I don't ever recall anything about hanging people from their necks till their feet quit kicking."

"I am pretty sure they made that one up themselves," Apollon, who appeared strangely buzzed, noted. "I think they make up half this shit for jealousy, and the other half is because they want to fuck us. Oh, Charle," he interjected as he pointed from their limo window. "You're included in the debauchery now so look out, you gonna fry."

Charle's eyes widened as he saw a photo of himself engulfed in flames that looked like they'd started from his ass.

"Flames coming out of your butthole," he read the caption. "Only when we don't use enough lube," he commented casually, causing the other band members to snicker. "But Nergal always heals me up just fine."

"Overshare!" Nabu chuckled, the beads in his braids clacking as he shook with laughter. "More than I wanted to know… like we already don't know you switch off all the time."

"Making up for lost time," Nergal, the front man for the band Abadon and known publicly as Abadon interjected, pulling his lover closer and pressing a kiss on his forehead.

Charle smiled as he looked around at the band that was quickly becoming his new family. They were all brothers united by being ancient gods and using the success of their band Abadon to keep themselves topped up with godly mojo from the worship they received from their adoring fans.

"I am so glad that Orion missed out on this." He leaned forward and tapped Sin, known as lead guitarist Python, on the knee. "I'm not sure he's ready to run the gauntlet of stupidity without getting into someone's face about it."

"I'm sure he's watching this from his apartment." Sin paused in braiding his long red hair. "I expect to get a phone call any minute. He's going to be so pissed about this." He tilted his head to the side, one hand leaving his braid to pet his ever-present snake wrapped around his body, his emotional comfort snake. "And amused. I think he's going to laugh his ass off at this too. He's good at laughing at stupid people… in their faces. He's also good at throwing punches. I've never seen him do it, but the condition of his knuckles tells me that he's knocked out a few teeth in his lifetime. He doesn't deal well with ignorance."

"But any publicity is good publicity as long as they spell your name right," a giddy Apollon interjected. "And in your case, learn to pronounce your name, Charle Lexington. They keep saying you name like you were grilled over an open fire. Maybe that's why they drew you with flames… coming out of your butthole."

"If that were true, I'd have brought some hot dogs to

roast… or at least some marshmallows. It could replace your opening act; burning things with the flames from my ass. It'll be a hit. It's very rock and roll."

"In the anime world," Nergal pointed out, snickering. "If there are any flames coming from your ass, I'll snuff them out, baby."

"With your dick!" Apollon shouted, snickering at his own joke, the others nodding in agreement or chuckling along with them. The two were not very quiet about their sex lives.

"But my articles would get a lot more attention." Charle snickered. "More than they do now. Apparently there are a lot of people interested in the working dynamics of dating a rock star… and so many more stars are now willing to get interviewed by me because I haven't let out any of your dirty little secrets. Rhianna agreed to let me interview her next month because I've managed to maintain my professional integrity when it comes to ignoring assholes that criticize, and never allowing an interview to loop back into our personal lives. I think she has a lot of secrets she wants to keep and it's not my job to ferret out shit she doesn't want told. I keep it about the music and the artist's goals as an individual."

"That's a plus," Nabu, known as Hash and the drummer, added. "I can remember walking out of more than one interview because the one conducting it got really stupid about my past or kept harping on my race instead of my talents." His eyes narrowed as he began reading more and more of the negative picket signs. "Gods, these people need dictionaries. How do you misspell 'go back to Africa'? I don't even think that guy is with the church. He and his group are… Alt-right?"

He frowned, his dark brown skin showing a tint of red as his frustration with this stupidity increased. "You think they would have something better to do with their lives instead of becoming the equivalent of gigantic cockroaches of the world."

He leaned back and closed his eyes, making a visual effort to control his temper, Charle noted. Apparently Nabu didn't abide ignorance well. It seemed to affect him more than the others in the band. Maybe it was because he really wasn't a war god? He was a statistician and a god of knowledge, a master of the word arts who valued loci above everything else. It was one of the reasons he and Charle had become such fast friends. But that mess going on outside... Charle turned to stare out of the window once more.

"This stupidity defies logic," he muttered. "The haters are even hating themselves. I don't think the church people like the alt-right people much."

"I remember when skin color prejudice became a thing. It shocked me that people could be so stupid when we were dealing with, you know, famine, disease, pestilence, and death. Out of all the things they could fixate on, they bypass negative intent and actions while they jump straight to appearance. Humanity sickens me so much sometimes."

For the quietest member of the band, Nabu had taken an unfair bout of hazing from the community at large, some saying that it was wrong to have a black man playing in a rock and roll band, others saying that a black man should be supporting his own race by playing black music... whatever that was supposed to be. And then there were those who fetishized the man, not because of his talent or skill, but because of his skin color.

He was growing visibly exhausted.

"You were brought into existence because they needed intelligence, man." Apollon calmed a bit to lean against Nabu's side. "Just because they recognize the need doesn't mean they're going to follow through," he added. Nabu huffed.

"There will always be a selection of humanity that sinks to the lowest level," Sin agreed, offering his snake to Nabu, who reached out to pet its head, smiling a little as it nuzzled up against him, more like a kitten than a snake. "But there is always a larger selection who decry stupidity and embrace learning from each other instead of tearing each other down. You, who have seen more civilizations rise and fall than any one of us, know this to be true. When all of our temples were torn down and they attempted to erase us from history, the powers that be always venerated you and carried your writings and your wisdom through the ages, and insisted that your legacy remain. The fact that you still are one of the most powerful of all of us proves that there are intelligent people out there. They just have better things to do with their time than visually assault others with their bad spelling and lack of grammar."

That drew a laugh out of Nabu, who, after giving the snake one last pet, settled back in his seat as they drew closer to the private jet.

"Don't feel too bad." Charle tried to interject some levity into a dark situation. "You would really get pissed if some of these idiots started a letter writing campaign against you. I got a letter from the gay black men's alliance saying that I am a traitor to my race for publicly supporting a man who is not black. They misspelled traitor and alliance and used the same two misspelled words over sixty times in two paragraphs. I think they're jealous 'cause his dick is big enough to buck the stereotype and I'm getting it every night."

The rest of the band groaned but Nabu laughed outright.

"And you're forgetting the Locusts out there aren't taking any shit."

"Oh yes." Apollon suddenly giggled, turning to look out the window where an explosion of color caught their eyes. "Right in the daddy button, baby." He was visibly vibrating as more glittery colors floated through the air.

The Locusts were taking no prisoners. As the band watched, pastel pink and sparkly purple rained down on the protesters. Several glitter bombs had been deployed, much to the disgust of the protesters, and the air around them glistened like a beautiful rainbow. There was a scramble but either the police were reluctant to get glittered or they found it funny as hell. No one was really making any effort to stop the bombing. The glitter bombs weren't directed at anyone, just shot off in the air above, so it made it really hard to pinpoint who was shooting them off and at whom.

The Locusts didn't seem to mind at all, bathing in the glitter, and it had the added benefit of making the hate-filled protesters sparkle like tiny walking rainbows of peace. Some people were pointing and laughing while others carried counterprotest signs of their own offering to get the church members laid if it would calm them down. Pictures were being taken, and Charle's cell was blowing up with the numbers of his managers, friends, and social media sites' messages all but making his phone dance in his hands.

So far, the Locusts were winning when it came to sheer numbers and devious tactics, but it really was a bit too much attention for a single band and far too grand a send-off for a band that was taking a hiatus to produce a new album.

"This is far more reaction than normal." Nabu spoke softly as Apollon was reduced to giggles when more color erupted over the protesters.

"Keep in mind that the worldwide tour had been a rousing success, guys," Charle pointed out. "Two out of the four of you found your partners and that is awesome odds for love... not to mention it happened in such a short period of time."

"There is something about Baltimore." Nabu nodded in agreement. "This place is so strange, and I'm surprised we didn't run into any other gods. I mean, if an alien landed he would fit right in even if he had three legs and five arms. Hell, people would line up to take photos with him and sell them for a quick profit. I am sure there are a few gods floating around that place, drawing power from the oddity of it all."

"Baltimore is unique," Charle began, but closed his mouth as their limo completed the trip to the plane. The ever-faithful and slightly insane Max was there to open the doors and lead them to the ladder that would get them inside the custom, black-and-green Gulfstream the band owned.

"There are some storms from here to Cali," Max informed them as he swung open the limo doors and rushed them toward the plane. Once out of the soundproofing of the limo, Charle was almost smacked in the face with the wave of cheering and booing that immediately attacked them. It was like a wall of sound, closer than the jet noise, and it had them hustling up the metallic ladders and racing into the plane while the band waved and blew kisses at the crowd. Apollon was especially hyped as he jumped and waved, and basically clowned for the crowd who ate it up. Love him or hate him, Apollon was an unmistakable force, and his flamboyant personality showed no matter what he was doing.

"The pilot is going to drop down to the south to avoid most of the storms," Max continued as they made it into the relative quiet of the warming-up plane, and he slammed the doors shut. "It will put about an hour on your time, but your hotel has been made aware. You roll out from Cali to Canary tomorrow as planned. It should be a good, turbulence-free flight."

Charle was surprised to hear so many words -- so

many coherent words -- from the strange man. Max was their bus driver and apparently majordomo when needed, but no one looking at the wild-haired, tattooed wall of muscle would think intelligence was high on his personality scale. The many-times broken nose and the cauliflower ears gave away his past as a fighter, but his attitude was truly the scariest thing about him.

"Are you sure he isn't a god of something?" Charle whispered to Nergal. "Of bare-knuckle boxing maybe?"

"Nope. One hundred percent human," Nergal said with a laugh. "He just showed up one day and no one had the heart to tell him to go. He's just that awesome. Ex-military, we believe, but we never really asked."

"You were all probably too scared to tell him no," Charle whispered back.

"That too." Nergal snickered. "He might have a flaming sword strapped to his back via pocket dimension. None of us really want to test it."

The plane itself was beautiful, Charle noted as they moved forward. Having been on a few private jets himself, he was somewhat experienced in matters of comfort. It could easily sit eight people, and was designed to be configured into seating and sleeping areas as needed. The light tan interior was a startling contrast to the dark colors outside, yet it somehow made the place feel homey. The chairs were of leather and there was a door in the back that led to the galley and bathroom areas. There were a few flat screen televisions affixed to the walls, and the movable tables looked to be made of black marble. There were books and guitars mounted on the walls and a few exotic plants rested on counters. The jet was amazingly beautiful.

"This is nice," he purred, and Nergal laughed. "We spend so much time on buses that when we have to spend hours on a private rental plane, we want the comforts of home. Plus it's a neat write-off for taxes," he added and Charle started to snicker.

Who knew that a centuries-old god would be so fiscallyconscious?

"You laugh, but you haven't met The Seven yet. They're savage." Then he leaned in closer to whisper in his ear, "Later we can join the mile-high club..."

"I know you're probably a platinum member already," Charle pointed out, no stranger to his lover's past exploits.

"But we have yet to punch that line on your bucket list," Nergal pointed out, leering. "When the band goes to sleep, I say we make use of the bedroom in the back and blow a few more things off your list -- not that you didn't turn that list into Swiss cheese when you were playing hard to get."

"It worked, didn't it?"

"You don't see me bending over for any other man, now do you, lover mine?" he whispered back, dropping a kiss on Charle's nose as they moved further into the leather-clad, luxurious depths of the plane.

Charle was still chuckling when Max knocked on the pilot's door, and it swung open to reveal an amused-looking man in a pilot's uniform.

"Max doesn't fly?" he asked at large.

"He does," Sin answered as he moved into the plane and took a seat, tossing his completed braid over his shoulder. "But he wanted to stay back and fly with Orion. Orion just inherited a bodyguard he didn't think he wanted but really needs because people have started recognizing him from social media. Max didn't want anything to happen to him."

"That is awesome, Max," Charle praised the stoic man, who just grunted in return.

Charle was about to make a comment about him using up his store of words for the week when Nabu gasped. It was such an odd sound that everyone stopped what they were doing to turn to see what had caused him to start.

There, standing in a neat, black, hostess-pants uniform, was one of the loveliest women that Charle had ever seen. She was about average height for a woman, which meant she looked like a fun-sized candy bar standing next to all the tall, broad men onboard, yet she appeared comfortable and confident.

Her long hair was tied up in a loose bun at the back of her head, the silky-looking red-brown hair fitting her golden complexion perfectly. Her large, oval-shaped eyes were a deep mysterious brown that that showed her Asian ancestry, along with her gently rounded face and high cheekbones. Her perfect, cupid's bow lips were tinted peach and her makeup, while attractive, was very understated, professional.

No one noticed Max leaving because everyone was staring at Nabu, who was in turn staring at this unknown woman with stars in his eyes. If this were a cartoon he would be a wolf with his eyes bulging and his tongue dragging the ground.

The awesome part was that she was staring back just as hard.

She had glanced over everyone, her pleasant expression never changing until she set her gaze upon Nabu. Her eyes widened and she pressed a small hand to her chest and she just stared.

"Um," Into the silence, the pilot began to speak. "I am Major Tom Ruina, your captain for this particular flight."

His words pulled everyone out of their stupor, and they all took their seats. "The flight plan has been logged in and approved, your luggage has been stowed, and as soon as you all take your seats and strap in for takeoff, we can be on our way. Assisting me today as cabin crew is Aika Fujioka. Our flight time should be around six hours with our detour south to avoid the growing weather concerns, and I wish you all a pleasant flight."

Nabu was still staring at Aika and she was doing some pretty good staring back of her own before a voice broke the tension that was building between the two of them. "That's much better than Max's 'Strap your nuts in, boys, it's going to be a bumpy ride.' I like his spiel better."

Everyone turned to stare at Apollon, and he just shrugged, giggling a bit harder.

"Are you okay?" Sin asked as they all moved to take their seats, Aika moving toward the front with the captain, both disappearing into the cockpit after she shot Nabu one more look over her shoulder.

"I'm just buzzing today," he offered, shrugging. "Is it some kind of holiday that I missed? Children's Day or something here?"

"No," Charle answered, looking confused as he stared at his friend. "Why?"

"You give Nergal a sharp boost with your unconditional love 'cause that is worship in its purest form. Sin gets one when he and Orion are together or when a major change happens in the world... which is, like, daily. Nabu gets a hit when a novelist pens a best seller or some dusty hipster creates a masterpiece of poetry, or when someone reads our song lyrics and really gets the meaning behind the screaming metal and drum beats. I get a buzz when it deals with children, stupidity, holidays, and college exam times. Spring break and Halloween really get me going."

"Um... children?"

"Mischief!" Apollon exclaimed, throwing both hands in the air as he grinned at them all. "Children are naturally mischievous. When they get up to hijinks, I get a buzz and there are so many children in the world. Same for stupid people doing stupid things that aren't major enough to throw a buzz at Nergal. It's a minor form of mischief like the glitter bombs. Certain holidays get me too, some because they encourage mischief, but others because of family arguments and the inventive things people do to get out of going to a family function. College exams? The cheating factor is high. I'm not even getting into spring break, but it can make me jizz in my pants if I'm too close to Florida or Mexico. It's summer here so there might be a carnival or something in the area. I am getting a massive surge and it's making me... kind of giddy."

"Maybe the Locusts?" Charle pointed at the goings on outside of the window he was seated next to, which still hadn't fully dispersed. "Maybe they have some parting gifts for the plane."

"Maybe. If you find a lack of complicated solutions, go for the obvious one. Good going, little man. Now you're cooking with gas," Apollon agreed before suddenly spinning around to face Nabu, a teasing glint in his eyes. "So... got the hots much?"

"Shut up," the tall black man grumbled, pulling himself together as he took a seat across the aisle from Apollon. "I really don't know what you're talking about."

"You were staring... hard." Apollon snorted, making himself comfortable and strapping in.

"Really hard," Nergal pointed out, taking a seat beside Charle.

"She's pretty," Nabu said, a ring of finality in his tone.

"That she is," Apollon agreed as they all settled down and let Nabu's staring go. Charle was good enough to not even mention the blush that still tinted his cheeks.

"So," Charle spoke into the silence. "Why do you all strap in anyway? It's not like turbulence is going to knock you guys out."

"We need to fit in," Sin explained, before placing a

kiss on the top of his snake's head. "And there are too many questions if we don't act human enough."

"So we follow the rules." Nergal pulled him in for a quick kiss, ignoring the catcalls from the other members of Abadon. "We fasten seatbelts, we look both ways before crossing the street, and we always use protection." He leered down at his lover.

Chuckling, Charle snuggled into his lover, never feeling safer than he did at that point in time. He was traveling with centuries-old gods with amped up super powers. What could go wrong?

Chapter 2

They had been in the air for more than an hour, and Nabu knew that he was still blushing, damn it.

Aika moved in the kitchen area with a skillful economy of motion that drew his eye like a moth to a flame. He tucked several of his long braids back behind his ear and tried to expand his energy a bit to get a feel for her.

Almost immediately he ran into a blockade.

Odd, he couldn't get a read on her but he felt she was as interested in him as he was in her. That made him look back to her, to examine her closer, and found that she was staring at him intently.

He gulped and looked away, almost like a youth in the flush of first desire... which was absolutely ridiculous as he was several hundred years old and had screwed that many women -- and men -- to say the least.

But there was something about this one... The sensuality that she seemed to exude. Her desire for him was plain to see as her own cheeks flushed deeply and she licked her bottom lip.

She flashed him a grin and a wink as she went about her business, taking a cup of coffee to the pilot before looking around to see if she could get anyone else anything.

And since he was the only one awake... "You would slap my face if I told you what I wanted," he almost purred at her, then shot her a wicked grin -- more laughter than a serious flirt, just wanting to see what she was going to say.

"You'd be surprised" -- she leaned down to whisper in his ear before giving it a gentle nip -- "about what I'd ask for."

He jerked at her actions and looked up at her, surprise in his face. He hadn't expected that, even with his rather cliché comment.

"Really?" he countered, his voice growing husky as she rose up and tucked a loose tendril of hair behind her ear.

"Really," she purred, before turning and making her way back to the kitchen, an extra sway in her hips.

Nabu looked around the plane, noting that his brothers were seemingly all passed out; Nergal and Charle snuggled up together on one couch seat, Enk curled up into a ball on his seat, and Sin looking at him with intense eyes. Well, not all of them were asleep.

"I see change a-coming." Sin snickered as Nabu glared at him.

"You just want everyone to be happy now that you finally are," Nabu commented absently, his eyes on the back of the plane, the heat in his pants increasing.

"Nothing wrong in wanting to see your brother smile," Sin replied.

"But there is something about her," Nabu said. "I can't really get a read on her. I mean I can tell she's highly intelligent and motivated. She is creative and secure in herself…"

"And practically perfect in every way."

"Yeah." Nabu grinned at his brother. "She is and I know that she wants me. But her true motivations? I can't seem to get a grasp on them. I don't think she wants anything from me but a good lay."

"Same here," Sin admitted. "But that just makes her more intriguing."

"I think I want to know more," Nabu admitted with a wicked grin.

"So," Sin said, gently rubbing the head of his snake as it curled comfortably around his body. "What are you going to do?"

"I know what I want to do." Nabu grinned. "And it may be illegal in a few states," he decided, running his hands through his hair, tugging lightly on his braids as he examined her with eyes at half-mast.

"She is rather pretty," Sin whispered as he relaxed into the arms of sleep.

"And her mind, what I can glimpse of it, is beautiful. Creativity is buzzing inside of her and it feels like nothing I have ever felt before. Her sensuality is obvious and her body is just amazing but I want to see if the rest of her is as amazing as well."

After a moment of contemplation he began to feel a pull that was intriguing as much as it as annoying.

He glanced back toward the kitchen area and caught a glimpse of his goddess as she efficiently moved about the kitchen area, doing god knows what.

Her hips were rounded in those rather form-fitting pants that were designed to be benign but somehow looked rather sexy on her. Her breasts were bound in the company button-down and designed to look as sexless as possible, but it was having the opposite effect on his libido. Her soft-looking hair was piled neatly on top of her head, and he wanted to mess it up. He wanted to run his fingers through it and make it wild and untamed as he just somehow knew she would be.

Once or twice he looked up and saw her peeking back at him, the smoldering glances making his stomach soar and his pants tight.

Finally, he had to get up and make his way to the bathroom. Something had to give, and he would rather it didn't give in his pants. That was in no way, shape, or form sexy, and instead of looking like a perverted fool he decided to take care of his not-so-little problem in the bathroom.

He had just the image in mind to help him get off quickly and neatly, then he could go back to contemplating how to get Aika's contact information. There was no way he was going to be able to let her go and he would rather approach her in a way that would not embarrass them both -- like having his dick lead the way and the discussion.

Decision made, he rose to his feet and made his way back past the kitchen area to the rather spacious bathroom they'd had installed on the plane. His body throbbed, and his mind was set on giving himself relief.

* * *

Aika gave herself a stern talking to as she cleaned the counter. There wasn't a lot of mess; she'd just made one cup of coffee, but she needed time to pull herself together.

Tall, dark, and beautiful was looking at her, and it was doing things to her insides - pleasant, tingly things.

He'd been introduced as Hash though he needed no introduction. Not that she was a fangirl or anything like that, but you had to be deaf, dumb, and blind not to know who the members of the band Abadon were.

They worked hard, they played harder, and now she had drawn the interest of one of the more mysterious members.

Hash, with his long dark hair and dark skin, stood out from the rest of the band in more obvious ways than race. He was one of the main contributing writers and he always had a thoughtful expression on his face, as if he was constantly getting a feel of the space he was in.

Constant hyper-vigilance. She recognized it in him because she tended to do the same things -- especially when she spent so many hours in enclosed planes with strange men and women. One quickly learned where the exits and entrances were for self- preservation. She could deal with grabby people by simply avoiding them and offering them a professional attitude that acted as a barrier between her and the stupid, but she never forgot that some people thought that they were better than her by virtue of her job or her race.

She didn't get that feeling with Hash or the rest of

the band. Most of them had settled down right away, resting up for what faced them when they reached Cali, but Hash... he had been examining her, but not in a creepy way. He didn't have rape-face or anything; he just seems to be trying to puzzle her out as much as she was him.

Finally, she listened to the voices in her head that were urging her forward when she approached the man, flirting with him in an outrageous manner that was unlike her usual self. It was fun to catch him off guard and make him blush but his reaction had her stomach twisting in knots and her thighs rubbing together for control.

The man was seriously hot and the hint of surprise on his face was worth putting herself out there. That blush was beautiful, and to know that she could affect him in such a way... Damn, her panties were damp.

She had noticed the bulge in his pants growing and had to resist the urge to lick her lips at the sight. Yeah, she knew that erection was all for her and it made her feel proud. It was a dumb thing to feel anything over, a man's erection, but somehow she just knew it was because he could see beneath the outfit and the air of propriety she had to wear like a shield and saw that she really hungered for him.

Damn, that was new.

In all the time she had served as crew -- hell, in all the time she'd existed, she had never felt like this before. Her heart was racing and her palms were damp. She had to put her tea kettle down several times because her hands were shaking so badly.

Damn, that man was perfect. With his long braids and his broad chest and his... OMG he was coming her way.

Act natural, she coaxed herself, but failed miserably. Damn, that was a walking powerhouse of muscle. His arms bulged as he gripped the back of the chair and just kind of glided toward her.

How broad was his chest, anyway?

And those legs…

She held back a grunt, biting her lip as he shot her a heated look and adjusted his pants before he moved toward her.

The look he gave her could only be described as smoldering before he disappeared in the direction of the bathroom.

She contemplated his ass as he moved, how the tight, rounded globes of muscle wiggled when he walked, and felt something inside of her break. It might be her only shot at this but she was going to get her a piece of drummer because that looked like an invitation if ever she saw one.

Two seconds after the door closed she was tapping on it. It slid soundlessly open, and she slipped inside.

She didn't know who grabbed who, but suddenly Aika was pushing that beautiful man up against the bathroom door, rising up onto her toes and taking his mouth in a fiery kiss.

God, his lips were so full and soft…

She pushed her tongue into his mouth, knowing the she was being the aggressor and not really caring. He tasted like ambrosia.

His broad hands gripped her waist and easily lifted her as she tried to climb his body like a tree.

She wrapped her legs around his waist and groaned out loud as his hard cock pressed against her crotch, her definitely wet panties creating a fire that made her head spin.

"You're so beautiful," he breathed as he pulled back, his dark eyes sparkling as he looked down at her, hunger written plainly on his face. "Tell me this is what you want." How thoughtful of him.

"I want this," she managed as she trusted in his ability to hold her upright as she reached for the hem of his shirt and pulled it up.

Flesh, glorious flesh! His skin was tight and hot, oh so hot, and she ran her hands up his back.

"Fuck," he gasped before spinning around and placing her on top of the sink.

The room was larger than the average airplane bathroom but still it was a closeted space. He had to stoop over to kiss her again, his hands braced on either side of her hips while her hands went wild on his body.

No lie, touching him was like every fantasy she has ever imagined come to life. He smelled of vanilla and musk and something that couldn't readily be identified but, if bottled, would make a million.

His slim hips slid between her thighs and he ducked lower as she tried to work his shirt over his head.

Fuck, he was built. His chest was a dark wall of muscle, his tight abs tightened further as he stepped closer and reached up to cup her breasts.

"Uniform," she managed to gasp as his head dropped lower to latch onto her neck. He was placing very gentle, maddening kisses there, each one making her own stomach quiver as fire shot up her spine.

"Can't mess up the uniform," he purred before he pulled her to her feet and swiftly undid her uniform pants. They were carefully placed on the counter while he undid his own jeans.

Her panties were tossed to the floor as he gripped her hips and hefted her to the counter once more, pulling her to the edge.

"I'm going to eat you and then I'm going to fuck you hard," he informed her.

She nodded her head in agreement. This was something she hadn't expected but who was she to argue? If the man wanted to eat her out, she was going to have to take one for the team and just let him do it.

But first...

She tugged at his shirt, finally pulling it over his head before reaching up to do want she wanted to do since she met him... she gripped his braids and pulled him in for a kiss.

God, he kissed like she was the last thing he would ever do. He kissed like he was storming her castle walls. He kissed like a starving man in the desert and she was his first cup of water.

His tongue slid into her mouth, dancing over her teeth before teasing her own into s sensual duel.

She moaned into that kiss and tried to keep him there when he pulled back and dropped to his knees.

This could not be happening. There was a rock legend on his knees about to go down on her. She had to be dreaming. She wanted to pinch herself to be sure she was awake but both hands were buried in his long braids, holding on for dear life.

She looked down as saw his wide, muscular back, a beautifully designed dragon tattoo resting across his shoulders, that perfect ass displayed in his loosened jeans and bit her lip to keep in the scream she wanted to let loose.

She did, however, have to slam her fist into her mouth to hold back the wail as he dove right in.

This man was eating her like she was his last meal, his tongue dancing along her clit while his hands gripped her thighs, pulling them open wider.

He was grunting happily as she felt herself gush into his mouth. God he was so good and this was so hot...

"Hash," she whimpered as her head started to spin. His tongue was sliding into her body, his nose nudging her swollen clit as she felt her fingers curl and her heart pound in her chest.

She was going to die. Death by tongue fucking and it

was one hell of a way to go. She was trying to remain quiet and was grateful for the hard grip he had on her waist or she would have squirmed right off the damn counter.

He was that good.

She had to tell him. "You are -- fuck -- Hash -- so damn good... Ohh..."

Then she was pushing him away and hopping to her feet, surprised that her shaking legs could hold her weight after so many orgasms.

"I want to blow you," she told him, knowing her approach was kind of bad but not really giving a good goddamn at this moment.

"Who could say no to that?" He rose to his feet, his face shiny with her juices, his eyes lazy with desire.

She let her gaze rove over his body as he eased his pants down.

"No fucking undies?" she teased and he winked at her.

Hash was built on the large side. His cock was a bit darker than the rest of his body and he was uncircumcised. This was a new one on her but she was always down for a new adventure. She dropped to her knees and gripped him in her fist, her other hand reaching up to cup his full balls.

He groaned softly, spreading his legs wider to give her room to work as she ran her cheeks over his cock. He was hard and hot and smelled perfectly of man and musk and... candy? Candy or flowers, she couldn't tell, and really couldn't be assed about it at the moment.

She pulled back to lick at his flesh, moaning as his flavor exploded on her tongue. This was nice.

Her mouth began to water as she used her thumb and forefinger to gently pull back on his foreskin, exposing the blue-colored, heart-shaped head, slick with precum and looking quite vulnerable.

"SO pretty," she purred, and he chuckled as he carefully ran his hands over her face, urging her forward but not demanding.

She liked that. The man had patience. She could work with that.

She carefully sucked the head of his cock, letting her tongue play with the foreskin before sucking deeply.

"Fuck, Miss Aika," he moaned, and she almost choked on her laugher as she peered up at him.

"Miss Aika?" she pulled off to whisper.

"I'd call you Miss Fujioka but I think you'd think I was a nasty boy."

"Not nasty," she whispered, making her breath bathe his cockhead before she licked at the slit at the tip. "Very naughty."

Then she dropped her head, once more sucking him in as deep as she could take him.

"Fuck," he hissed, smooth muscles contracting as he leaned over her to grip the counter for balance.

This was fun. She suckled hard at him and swirled his shaft with her tongue. She was only able to get about half of him down before her gag reflex started kicking in, so she fisted the rest and tugged at his balls with her free hand.

His legs were shaking and his grunts were getting louder when he pulled back and jerked her to her feet.

Damn, he was strong.

He reached into a drawer built into the counter and pulled out a string of condoms.

"Come prepared?" she asked, cocking an eyebrow.

He was fun but this was a reminder that that was all this was. There would be nothing serious between them. This was a hook up and nothing more.

"There are newlyweds on this plane," he explained, laughter his voice. "After what they did to that hotel room, I said we would stock up any place where they're going to be for more than fifteen minutes."

Aika choked at that but broke off as he deftly unwrapped and pulled on the condom. She arched her eyebrow at that.

"Not my first rodeo," he said, bending down to take her lips in a swift kiss. "Better safe than sorry."

"Damn straight." Aika was just glad she didn't have to give him the talk about condoms or walk away if he refused to use one. Her life was too precious to play games with it.

Then she was being lifted back to the counter, Hash leaning forward to kiss at her neck as he positioned himself at her opening.

"You're very tight," he offered.

"And you're very big."

"I don't want to hurt you."

"You got me good and wet with your tongue. Ten out of ten would do it again, by the way," she snickered.

"Thank you, ma'am. You're a pleasure and a joy to eat."

"You got me so wet… just go slow."

She wrapped her hands around his head and gripped his braids tightly. He moaned, pulling his head down to feel the tug of his hair being pulled, so she tugged a little harder.

"Keep doing that and I'm going to fuck you through this counter."

"Promises promise," she breathed. Her heart was racing, her breath sounding like she was geriatric and she could feel herself dripping, she was so wet. This man was her every fantasy made flesh and she was about to have all her dreams come true. "Come on, drummer boy. Show me your rhythm."

"Anything my lady wants." He grinned before dropping one hand down to aid in his penetration.

Aika hissed, squeezing her eyes shut as she felt his

cockhead pop inside her body.

"F -- fuck," she whimpered. He was big as fuck. She groaned because it was a little uncomfortable but it felt so damn good at the same time.

Lately the only thing she'd had between her legs ran on batteries and wasn't this hot, this giving, this fucking huge.

She arched her head back as she felt his hands slide under her shirt, under her bra, and began to palm her breasts. Her hard nipples were pulled and teased as he buried his face in her neck.

"Damn, Miss Aika..."

He was sliding in deeper, splitting her open, and she absolutely loved it. Her legs found themselves around his waist as she urged him to move faster. He was a thick hot mass within her and she needed some friction fast.

He pulled back and slammed deep, burying himself inside her on the counter, and Aika jerked his head back with his braids as she panted for control. "Gods, so good," she gasped, her breath hitching as he began a hard fast rhythm. Within seconds she felt a tension build in the center of her being; her spine was tingling, her pussy burning as he began to worked her over.

He pounded in deep and swirled his hips, teasing her clit against his pelvis. Then he was sucking at her neck, her lips, nipping at her ear as her legs raised and wrapped around his waist.

"Fuck," he hissed, as if trying to muffle the sound as she began to come apart at the seams.

One hand dug into his back, the other braced on the counter as she forced herself upwards, wanting more of that delicious burn. He was giving it to her so good... She looked down, noticed his dark skin flushing red, and his muscles contracting as he moved. He was giving her an excellent visual, which only drove her lust higher.

"Harder," she gasped, as the thing within her grew

tighter and tighter. She was losing it! She relaxed her head and let her head fall back and fought the urge to scream, knowing that if she did everyone would know what they were doing.

That element of danger only make his fucking more delicious.

She was trying not to cry out and he was grunting as he slammed into her, his movements becoming more erratic as the tension between them built and built...

"Yes!" She was panting, uncontrollably. "Yes, Hash, yes!"

Lights were flashing behind her eyes and the room was spinning. She couldn't take it yet she needed more!

She was on the verge of screaming for her release when he dropped one hand between them and flicked her clit. That was all it took. She went off like a powder keg.

Aika felt her body tense and freeze as her insides began to riot as her inner muscles gripped at the meaty cock that filled her so completely. She threw back her head, a wail beginning but he slammed his mouth over hers, swallowing her cries even as he gave up on his own.

Hash thrust hard into her, getting as deep as he could as his while body began to shudder.

"Fuck," he breathed as she felt him fill the condom that separated them even as he relaxed against her, his mouth now taking hers in gentle sips and soft licks.

"Aika," he breathed, his whole body shuddering in the tight clutches of her body.

Aika's own orgasm was fading now, the afterglow starting to make her close her eyes and take a nap, but there wasn't time for that.

They were on a fucking airplane and she has just joined the mile-high club.

Damn, today was a good day.

Chapter 3

Hash pulled back and couldn't stop the stupid grin that spread across his face. "You are perfection," he murmured and Aika blushed a bit even as she pushed him back.

"Thank you," she breathed running her hand over her face before she let her gaze travel over his body.

Oh, he loved the looks she was giving him and wanted more of them.

She was beauty personified when she orgasmed, and her intelligence and sense of humor had shown through no matter what she was doing. He loved that in a woman.

"I only speak the truth." He pulled back fully to toss the condom in the trash and grab a few tissues to clean up with.

He stopped her from moving as he pulled his own pants up and pulled a soft washcloth from a cabinet beneath the sink.

She said nothing as he cleaned her up and helped her redress. She said nothing as he adjusted her own hair and made sure she didn't look like she just had a quickie in the bathroom.

"Aika," he began. Man, this was... not awkward... not at all. But he didn't want to let her go, to share her. He wanted to stay in a nice enclosed space where he could convince her to fuck the hell out of him again.

"This was just simply amazing." She spoke, her voice soft and rough, the hangover from her calling out her release. Damn shame he had to swallow the call. He would have loved to hear his name on her lips shouted from the rooftops as it were.

"I want more." There. He said it. Ball was in her court.

"I don't thin--"

"Just think about it, okay?" he asked, knowing that

this was a lot on her. It wasn't what he'd expected to happen and, of all places, in an airplane bathroom.

Finally after a moment of stifled silence, she went up on her toes to press a kiss against his lips, lapping at them before nipping at the bottom one and giving his strands a tug.

"I'll think about it."

She was gone in a flash and Nabu made his way back to his seat, a stupid grin on his face.

Aika was damn near perfect, and come hell or high water, he was going to get to spend more time with her.

* * *

Nabu knew something was wrong the moment when Apollon threw back his head, howling in laughter.

Usually, that was quite common but then no one had said anything to him.

Nergal and Charle were sleeping, snuggled together, their decision about joining the Mile-High Club postponed to a later date, much to the rest's relief. Sin was in the middle of composing love letters or some such shit to Orion, and Nabu himself was trying to get the image of the delectable Aika out of his head. He couldn't believe he'd been lucky enough to grab her attention or hot enough for her to drop her inhibitions and actually screw him in the airplane bathroom. Mile-High Club indeed.

The woman was very attractive, with those deep dark eyes and that pretty pouting mouth, plus there was some element about her that he just couldn't put his finger on, but it was holding his imagination captive. And her mind… Her intelligence was a bright beacon to his mind. Her potential for growth was astounding. She was one of the most unique individuals he had ever come across and he felt honored to hold her attention.

Right now, he knew she was thinking about him. He could feel the buzz of her thoughts, and more than anything, he wanted to share all that he was with her.

It was a sudden thing too, something that he hadn't been expecting. He cast his eyes over his brothers and understood the contentment they felt when they finally met their one. It was a feeling that made him want to do everything to keep her by his side... and that meant telling her who he really was.

There were repercussions to this action, but if he wanted to keep her, he had to be truthful with her. It was sudden and she might not accept it, but that thing inside him that powered his godhood demanded that he do this and soon.

He looked to his brothers, to garner their advice, then decided to wait until they landed in California. He could discuss it with them before he spoke to Aika. Until then, Nabu decided it was time to look over his brothers, especially Enk. He could feel something brewing in the air.

Enk was just sitting there dozing, seemingly full of energy from his earlier bursts of mischief, but he had largely settled down. His actions were troubling, his behavior so out of character. Usually Enk had a lockdown on his mischief... he was used to the surfeit of energy from humanity and especially from small children, so that a bump in the amount he received shouldn't have had him reacting like that.

Suddenly, as he examined his most complex brother, the hair on his arms began to stand on end.

"Enk?" He reached for his brother but jerked his hand away as Enk began to wail, tears running down his face as it went from its usual watered milk complexion to bright red, his eyes wide in panic. The others began to pay attention, worry plain on their faces.

Nabu reached for him again but this time Enk arched away from him, screaming as he threw his head back, his whole body shaking as the brothers leapt to their feet, and

Aika opened the door that separated the captain's crew cabin from the rest of the plane.

"Enk--" he began, his concern turning into horror.

"It's going to blow!" His body arched harder and a shrill scream rolled from his throat, his usually deep voice reaching octaves it wasn't designed to reach.

"Fuck!" Abadon grabbed Charle and tossed him to the center of the aisle as he stood over him, throwing his arms out and amassing a surge of energy from... he knew not where.

Sin was next to move toward Nergal, gripping his forearms after dropping his snake on top of the confused Charle, who tried to rise but was shoved back to the ground by an impatient Sin.

Nabu was the last to feel it, that surge of hate and anger that generally prevailed before a violent act. Destruction was never his main focus and the realization about what was happening almost hit him too late.

"Gentlemen?" Aika sounded nervous as she moved out of the cockpit and into the cabin. Without thinking, he grabbed her by the arm, ignoring her struggles, and propelled her forward and just in time.

There was a deafening explosion, one that caused Nabu's eyes to water and the top of his head to feel like it was going to pop off. There was a flash of light and suddenly a wall of orange fire raced towards him as he tossed Aika beside Charle. The smell of burnt hair filled the air, and Aika and Charle began screaming in fear as clouds seemed to form around them. The smell wasn't with them for more than a second because the plane began to violently jerk, sending everything that wasn't bolted to the floors careening across the cabin.

Adding his own energy to the bubble that protected the humans with one hand, Nabu grabbed Enk by the arm and threw the hapless god on top of the humans as the plane began to go down.

He could feel the air rushing out of the place where the cockpit once existed and mentally surrounded them all with another barrier of energy, doing his best to protect the fragile human lives in the center of their protective bubble.

Plane crashes were easy enough to survive for them, but the humans... He added more of the energy to the effort as the plane lurched again, the engine seemingly shutting down and the silence absolute save for the humans praying for their lives.

Then time seemed to speed up as they dropped into a freefall, and it took all their willpower not to slam up into what was left of the ceiling.

"Water!" Sin roared and Nabu could feel a portion of his energies seeking. Understanding his need, Nabu allowed a portion of his utilized energy to break off and go seeking with Sin's.

Instantly he knew they were in the mountains, that the trees would do them more damage than offer them aid, and that there was a body of water nearby.

He relayed this information and could feel as Sin flexed his power, and the levels of the water in the small lake in their path began to rise.

"Hold it!" Nergal bellowed and Nabu knew what he was attempting. He sent him a boost of energy and the trees that were not brushing against the bottom of the plane shifted, their branches growing thicker as they redirected the plane toward the water while slowing down their freefall.

Nabu looked down at Enk, and he managed to pull himself together enough to pull Akia and Charle into his arms, shielding them as much as he could.

Enk's body was still shaking, and he was mumbling and groaning, lost in an energy surge that left him damn near useless.

"Too much!" he screamed, as his body went into

convulsions. Nabu wanted to go to him, to help redirect the mischief energies away from him but he couldn't let his concentration lapse more than it had. But Enk looked like he was about to shake apart. Just as Nabu was going to risk assisting his brother, the convulsions stopped and Enk sank into unconsciousness.

Nabu threw his full concentration on aiding the rest of his brothers and felt more than heard Sin roaring as he threw the last of his energies into the water.

Looking out from the ruins of the cockpit, Nabu watched the water reach up, like a gigantic hand of blue and seafood and snatch the plane from its deadly path, and it was still not enough.

Closing his eyes, he concentrated on the dragon that rested along his back and with one final push, it exploded from his body in a wash of red flame. It shot from the destroyed cockpit and encircled the plane, shifting it, slowing it down as it beat massive wings of fire.

The cabin shook and groaned as it slammed to a stop, tossing its occupants around like toys being abused by a two-year-old in the midst of a tantrum.

Nergal threw himself on top of the humans, Enk, and the snake, protecting them with his energy and his own body, while Sin was tossed nearly out of the ruins of the cabin.

Nabu reached out and snatched him back as the plane settled into the water with a colossal splash as objects went crashing into them at a speed that would kill most mortals.

Nabu felt his divided energies give out just as he tugged Sin back inside, his dragon breaking back to his body as his strength waned. Instinct had him looking up just as a table top flew in his direction.

It was beyond him to even raise a hand to stop it. There was a rush of sound, a sharp, indescribable pain, and then nothing.

* * *

Nabu woke at once, aware of his surroundings and more alert that anyone had the right to expect him to be.

Still, he lay flat, chilly, and wet while counting the unhealed aches and pains that throbbed within his human body and the oddest acrid scent of burned hair.

Fuck. His braids. It had taken him a long time to grow them without magical aid.

It was Akia's voice, the fear in it that forced him to open his eyes.

"He may have a brain bleed or something," she was insisting.

"And what are we supposed to do about that?" Enk was glaring at her, rubbing his own forehead while he cautiously eyeballed the area they were in. "I know. I'll just whip out my phone and… oh wait. It got wrecked in the crash. So I guess I'd better put my two hands together and call for attention. No, I know. I'm a rock star so I'll just open my mouth and scream. I'm sure if I yell help loud enough, someone will be sure to hear and rescue us on the ass end of this fucking mountain."

Nabu choked on his laughter as he made a move to sit up, only to be waylaid by a pint-sized Asian woman with wild hair, and oddly enough, perfect eyeliner. The rest of her makeup was a total loss but her lines were crisp and clean. Absently, he wondered what brands she used, because it might be something they wanted to look into before they took to the road again.

"Don't move. You could be hurt."

Nabu shifted his gaze to the exhausted-sounding woman and really took her in. Her hair was a wild mass of damp tangles, what remained of her uniform was ragged and torn, and there were several bruises on her slim arms and hands. She looked like she had been ridden hard and put away wet.

"Well, if that wasn't the understatement of the year,"

Enk grumbled, his deep voice resonating pain.

He was looking no better. His usually shining platinum hair was dull and lifeless, his T-shirt filled with holes and his jeans wrecked. He was missing one shoe and was sitting crossed- legged, elbows on knees, his forehead resting in his cupped hands.

"Nobody asked you," Aika hissed back, cutting him a dangerous look with her narrowed eyes. "In fact, why don't you just be quiet for the rest of the time we're stuck here? It would make us all feel better."

"I'm fine," Nabu interjected before any more anger could be put out in the universe. "I just need to --"

"You need to lie down," Aika insisted, reaching out and trying to press him back to the ground. "You took a blow to the head and it took forever to stop the bleeding."

He blinked hard then flexed his energies only to discover that they were dangerously low. No wonder he was bleeding like a human. He had given just about everything in supporting his brothers' efforts to keep the humans alive in the plane crash and had nothing left to fix his form if he wanted to maintain this current appearance.

He rather liked this incarnation of himself. He was not about to let it go for some inconvenient bleeding.

"I'm fine." He meant the words too, though he groaned and huffed a little as he finally succeeded in sitting up with sore stomach muscles. "What happened?"

"Best that we can tell," Enk answered, rubbing at his own forehead, "there was a bomb on the plane."

"A bomb?" No wonder Enk had gone off like he had. The rush of deadly mischief must have had him paralyzed with the rush of feedback. "The fuck?"

"It went off in the cockpit." Enk finally looked him in the eye and Nabu had to resist the urge to go and hug his brother. He could read the guilt in his eyes that he tried to hide, but they had been family for so long that he had no problems reading it on his face.

"It wasn't your fault," he said, reaching out a hand, and was gratified when Enk reached out and gripped his hand almost painfully.

He sent his energies out searching and almost recoiled at the surfeit of energy coursing thought his brother's veins. No wonder his head was aching. He was overflowing with energies; energies that he had been too far gone to use to help them with the plane crash.

"Of course it's not your fault." Aika sighed, moving away from Nabu's side to sit close to them both but away far enough that she wouldn't be an intrusion. She was missing both of her shoes. "Someone else was responsible and we're just lucky to be alive."

"The pilot?" he asked and Enk shook his head.

So that was what the guilt was for. It would have been impossible for Enk to assist when a rush of energy hit him that hard.

"Again, not your fault," Nabu informed him.

"He likely died when the bomb detonated," Aika interjected, and they both turned to look at her. "The way I figure it, maybe it was someone on the maintenance crew?"

"There were a lot of protesters." Nabu nodded. "And if one of them worked at the hanger or slipped in, no one would've been the wiser. It's not like we received any recent death threats we had to be concerned about."

"They wanted to kill us, they really wanted to kill us and didn't care about who got caught in the crossfire."

Enk looked at Aika before turning back to Nabu. "This world is a sick place, man." His usual baritone voice was soft and vibrated with fury.

"Where is everyone else? Is Charle --"

"He's fine." Enk calmed his fears before Nabu did something stupid in a panic. "We're all fine. Even the damn snake is fine. Abadon and Sin are with Charle salvaging what they can from the wreckage. Good thing we had a water landing. It was hard but they tell me the trees kind of took the force out of our landing so that the plane didn't break up."

"How did we get out?"

"Charle grabbed cussing beauty over there --"

"Hey!" Aika's face reddened, and she actually did look like she was about to tear Enk's head off of his body.

"You curse like a sailor. Admit it." There. There was some amusement back in Enk's voice. "I didn't even know some of those word combinations. I am thinking you need to get her to help us with some of our lyrics." He chuckled, and a light blush heated Aika's pale skin.

"I may have let some choice words slip, but it was warranted. I had just survived the bombing and a plane crash." She turned to Nabu then, her face softening. "Thank you for saving my life. I was coming into the cabin to see if you needed anything when you grabbed me and threw me on top of Charle."

"I think I saw... flames," he muttered, recalling the moment he could feel the bomb go off and how the bright light that was Major Tom got snuffed out.

He shook his head and asked, "The others okay?"

"Yeah," Enk answered. "Bumps and bruises. Charle got Aika, Sin pulled me, and Abadon managed to get to you. Good thing we hit the water when we did because brother, you were on fire."

Oh yeah. Nabu reached up and touched the ragged remains of his braids and sighed.

The waist-length twists of hair were now shoulder-length, ragged, rough ropes that despite his water dunking still gave off the scent of burnt hair and crumbled like ash in his hands.

"You okay?"

"He's epileptic, isn't he?" Aika interjected.

"Something like that." Enk sighed, placing his head

back in his hands.

"No one knows about it. That's a shame you won't come out of the closet and talk about your condition. It could help a whole lot of people, bring awareness, donations for the epilepsy foundations..."

"Or I could get a whole new host of problems knocking at my door." Enk tiredly waved his hands. "End of discussion."

"But --"

"End of discussion."

Aika huffed but reluctantly nodded before turning to Nabu. "How do you feel? I think you got hit in the head with some debris from the cockpit, maybe what was left of the door. It took forever to get the bleeding stopped."

"So you said." He turned to fully face her and was struck with the knowledge that she was talking to hide her fear. She had to have something to do or she would probably break down gibbering. "How did you get it to stop -- the bleeding, I mean?"

"Abadon said to rub some of your burnt hair into it and it just stopped. It was amazing. I didn't know he knew about holistic medicine."

"He knows a lot of things." Nabu winced, reaching up to touch his temple and the hot spot of pain he had been trying to ignore. "And that's more ancient than holistic. It's an old military trick to stop minor wounds from bleeding and from getting infected."

"We don't have any bandages to cover it yet so no touching."

Nabu looked up as her hand gripped his wrist and pulled it away from the wound. She moved so swiftly and silently that he didn't hear her approach.

But now that she was closer, he could tell beyond the scents of fear, fire, and pond water there was the delicate scent of the woman that he found so alluring.

He looked up into her deep brown eyes, and she

stared back into his. He felt eternity in that gaze. The feelings were so intense he began to tremble and as was with his gifts, he just knew that she would be an important person in his life.

She stared back just as fascinated, her eyes shining, her expression confused but accepting as she brought her other hand up to cup his cheek.

He was about to open his mouth to speak when --

"Fuck! I am never going back into that damn pond. If the rest of you assholes want your stuff, you had better go and get that shit yourselves."

Abadon was back.

"You all are deceptively good at roughing it." Aika examined the rough campgrounds the boys from the band had thrown together in what seemed like minute.

They managed to salvage enough floating parts of the plane and some cut off bits of nature to create a large structure that they now all sat under.

There was a cheery fire blazing in what Abadon called a primitive fire pit, but that damn thing looked like a starter kit for an advanced outdoor grilling system. It had walls, air vents, a rotisserie-like structure that now held four rabbits that Nabu had snared with his shoestrings and some sticks -- that in itself was insane -- and it was burning smokeless.

The rest of them weren't slouches when it came to outdoor living either. Sin had produced a selection of greenery that included wild onions and edible grains, Apollon was somehow tickling fish out of the water, and after setting his snares, the concussed Hash had managed to set up a latrine area that would not contaminate the groundwater and would be practically odor free near their camping site and he had gathered leaves that could be safely used as toilet paper. He even wove a basket to hold them so that the users could carry it with them and not, like, wipe their ass with poison ivy or some such nonsense. He even saw fit to set up a bathing area off of a shallow part of the lake that remained amazingly warm for it to be in the mountains. He said something about it being a natural hot spring but they should wait until daylight to use it, just in case.

She was impressed.

She looked over at her fellow normal human, Charle, then realized he wasn't so norm himself. He had a successful career as a writer and the lover of Abadon. Riding in private jets and custom-made tour buses wasn't normal. Hell, even before Abadon he was one of the darlings of *Rolling Stone*, so he couldn't be actually considered normal. Yet he wasn't rock-legend famous so he was the closest person she could relate to. Besides, they both were getting sexed up by rock gods... Okay, *had* been sexed up.

What was she thinking? There was something about Hash that had her drooling. She might have been like a hundred other groupies if the tabloids told it, but she had to have him. And it wasn't a notch on her bedpost either; it was like something in her was drawn to him.

When she followed him into that small bathroom she had no idea he was going to so solidly rock her world. Even now after all that they had gone through, she could still feel a slight soreness that came with overworked muscles. She forgot how many orgasms he'd delivered, but the way he held her, the way he stared into her eyes, he had made her feel as if she was the only woman in the world for him.

And right now he was sitting near Abadon, who was turning a tree limb spit with ease, like he had been doing it his entire life. Charle was petting the emotional support snake, as he called it, and looking calm despite the near-death experience.

She had nearly died.

The thought of it sent her shivering again and seeking something to do or say so that she didn't have to think about it.

She had nearly died. If she hadn't stuck her head out to check on the guys, if Hash hadn't jerked her from the room and tossed her into the center of the cabin... If the trees hadn't help break their fall or if the lake they'd landed in hadn't been unseasonably high...

If, if if if... the ifs in her head threatened to overwhelm her. She started bouncing her legs just to try and burn off some of this energy... if only she had moved one second later, she would be as dead as poor Tom.

She looked around their campsite and noticed all the things the guys had managed to salvage.

There were some water bottles, some seat cushions, three suitcases, oddly enough, a few of the guitars that had been brought on in equipment bags, and some electronic odds and ends that were laid out on bits of metal they'd salvaged but were too small to use in making the ceiling that protected them from the gentle rain that now fell.

She was grateful for the warmth and light of the fire as the sun dipped down and rain continued to fall.

"I can't believe you snared Thumper." Charle was poking at Hash as the man toyed with the ends of his savaged hair.

It was the first thing she noticed about the tall man when they met in person -- not that he was black, tattooed, and massive and sexy as hell, but that his waist-length braids were beautiful. They were also fun to pull on to direct his fucking action… the harder she pulled the deeper he went, but those were memories for another time.

First she'd thought that they were extensions, but she recalled the photos of him climbing out of a pool with his long hair flowing behind him or the times in concert when he wore it out and head banged with the rest of them while banging a beat out on his drum kit.

Hash was a very memorable part of Abadon. Not only was he a person of color doing a job in a genre that was mostly composed of white men in this country, he did it with skill, style, and panache.

When she agreed to come on and be cabin crew for this flight, she'd immediately contacted her friends at the agency who had flown with them before and got as much information as she could.

According to the men and women that served them

before, Abadon was quiet and moody but respectful of them and their jobs. Python was obviously a depressed cynic who spent a lot of contemplating mankind and petting his snake, though he was quick with a quip and a kind word. Apollon was a serious flirt who never crossed the line with them. It was like he couldn't help himself and teased everyone up to and including the pilot, their cabin crew, and any other who happened to be in his line of sight. Yet he was the one who would get up and clean with the crew, made sure his family, as they referred to each other, was comfortable, was an insanely good tipper. Hash was the intellectual, they informed her. He was the one who went through books like most went through potato chips, and spent a lot of his time writing and perfecting lyrics.

All of the boys were considered hot but there was something about Hash that put him in the inferno category.

Maybe it was his dark, intelligent eyes or how he stuttered a bit when speaking to her, how he dropped his hands to cover the bulge of his hard-on when she passed by...

She didn't know but that sight of metal slamming him in the head and knocking him unconscious tore at her heart as much as the plane going down.

"Given enough time and energy, I could track down Bambi for you, Charle," Hash teased the reporter. There was a howl in the distance that made her shudder and draw closer to the fire.

"How about you go and get Cujo before he gets us?" Charle asked, leaning more against his partner, Abadon. They were too fucking old to be called boyfriends at this stage of their lives.

"That's more like Bolto..." Hash laughed. "But he's just looking for his family. He won't come near the smell of fire and he's miles away. Their howls carry."

Odd, but that seemed to calm Charlie down, she noted. "You trust his word?" She didn't mean to say it. It just slipped out but since it was out there... "Just like that?" Her words weren't delivered in a hurtful tone and the smile he shot her proved that no offense was taken. She was more amazed that he garnered that kind of trust. It made him more impressive in her eyes.

"No one I would trust more," Charle spoke to her softly before throwing a grin at Hash. "He's an intellectual."

Hash, she noted, rolled his eyes but he did move a bit closer to her. "Are you okay?" he asked.

"I'm fine."

"No, really." He tilted his head and she wanted to snicker as he winced and pushed back the remains of his hair. "That was a lie and not even a good one."

"It's just... the plane crashed," she pointed out, like he wasn't there. She needed to get her act together, big time.

"Yes. I'm sorry you had to go through that."

The fuck? She eyeballed him, suddenly irritated at his attitude... at all of their calm attitudes. There should be widespread panic and mayhem and instead they were trying to make a four-course meal out of wildlife and had set up amenities. Who takes time to look for toilet paper in a crisis? They were having rotisserie Thumper in a crisis! What the hell was wrong with these people?

"You were there, too," she pointed out, her eyes narrowing as he became the target of her sudden anger. He was the one who snared Thumper after all. "You all were there. We almost died. And now you're having a fucking party!"

"Not a real party," Apollon pointed out. "They didn't bring back any booze."

There was a moment of silence. Aika swore that the universal was holding its breath so that she could hear his smart-assed comment clearly. And that is what made her break.

"Fuck you!" she screamed, leaping to her bare feet on the hard-packed earth. Yeah, before Abadon started building his grill/fire pit thing he had used some metal to clear some leaves and tamp the earth flat before tossing dried grass around to absorb shock and moisture, he had said. At the moment she thought it was brilliant; now it was only serving to piss her off more. "And fuck you and your fucking rabbits!" she screamed at Abadon, who calmly stared back at her. And that really gave her temper ignition.

"What the hell is wrong with you people? We almost died and now we're having a barbecue! Someone died, for fuck's sake. A man lost his life. We were almost obliterated by a fucking bomb and you're sitting here making jokes? I mean, what the fuck?"

"Would you prefer if we wept and wailed and prayed out loud for help?" The redhead was talking as he sat there petting his snake, staring at her calmly... oh so calmly. "Would that make you feel better?"

And that shut her down a bit as her temper went from boiling over to simmering.

"We know that Major Tom passed." Hash sighed as he reached for her hand. She jerked it back, not done with her stress-relieving upset. "I wish I could have saved him, but there was nothing I could have done."

That was true. He was probably sitting on the bomb as it detonated, and she didn't really know him, but... "We're going on like he didn't even exist, like no one gives a fuck about him."

"We didn't know him," Apollon added, the humor gone from his deep voice and his bright blue eyes. "Did you?"

"Not really," she spoke softly. "But here we are, being..."

"All alive and shit?" Apollon snorted in her direction. "Should we throw ourselves in the water and drown for the lack of Tom? Should we starve? Should we not use what we know to survive and put ourselves in danger over Tom?"

"That's not what I'm saying," she snapped, growing angry again. "That's not what I meant."

"Then what should we do to make you feel better? Because this is all about you and how you think we should be behaving, right?"

"It's not!" she insisted, glaring at the blond. How she hated him --

"Then what is it about? So you feel guilty that you're alive, Aika Fujioka?"

She started in surprise as he spoke her full name.

"Yeah, we were introduced at the beginning of the flight. No matter what you think of us, we do pay attention. So what is it, Miss Fujioka? How should we be acting in your eyes? What can we do to make you feel better?"

And damn him for being kind of right because she didn't know what to do. Even in her worst imaginings, she never thought that she would wind up surviving a plane crash with a rock band or that they even had survival skills. She didn't know what to do or how to feel and she was angry. Someone had tried to kill them! Someone planted a bomb that would have killed them all. If they were going for the band then collateral damage didn't matter. They were going to kill people innocent of whatever shit they thought Abadon had done. How could they do that? How could they take a human life?

As the thoughts whirled through her head, she turned on her heel and stormed off. She couldn't look at them. It wasn't their fault, not even that asshole Apollon. She needed to get away, at least long enough to get her thoughts together.

Someone tried to kill them and yet they were still alive.

How was one supposed to act? Grateful that it wasn't them? Angry that people had little or no regard for human life? She didn't know... she didn't know... she didn't know...

God make me a rock, she thought, as too many conflicting emotions swarmed her.

She did the only thing she could do. She made her way into the darkness so that no one could see her cry.

* * *

"Did you have to do that?" Nabu snapped as he rose to his feet and glared at his brother. "Don't you think she's been through enough?"

"If she is going to take her emotions out on me, I'm not going to sit around and be her punching bag, Nabu. I didn't earn it."

"None of us earned it," Sin countered, sighing as he stared at them both. "None of us deserved it. And there was nothing that any of us could have done if we want to keep living this life."

"I would have done it even if we had to disappear and start again." Nergal glared at them. "Nothing hurts Charle. I am not giving him up."

That silenced them all and Charle flushed where he was sitting beside his lover before he sighed and rose to his feet.

"Guys," he stated as he dusted his hands off on his thighs. "None of you know what it's like to know that at any moment you can die." Silence fell hard. "None of you know what it's like being human. It's a scary thing."

"You weren't scared," Enk pointed out, tilting his head to the side as if trying to puzzle him out.

"That's because I know who you are and I have faith in you. I know that you wouldn't let anything happen to me so that gives me a layer of protection that most humans just don't have. Aika doesn't have that. Right now she's scared out of her mind."

"Where are you going?" Nergal asked as Charle started to walk away.

"To talk to her. I can get her to calm down and come back to the fire."

"No." Nabu spoke up and Charle turned to look at him, a question in his eyes. "I'll go. I need to talk to her anyway."

"About the growing attraction between you two?" Sin smirked as he pet his snake. "You know we all got a buzz from the bathroom sex. You aren't fooling anybody. You really like her."

"Whatever, man." Nabu wasn't going to blush.

"She's feeling it too," Sin sang softly as Nabu turned to follow Aika. "Maybe you should tell her --"

"No taking advantage of the 'thank god we're alive' sex," Enk called out, humor in his voice once more. "Not yet anyway. Wait until she is in a better state of mind."

"After she stabs you with a tree branch, I'm sure she'd be up for it," Nabu hissed at his brother before turning to follow Aika.

She was in pain and he wanted to help.

Chapter 5

Without even flexing his energies, Nabu knew where Aika had walked off to. She hadn't gone far, thank goodness, but was sitting alone under a tree, sobbing her eyes out.

"Aika," he called out softly. "Whoa." He held his arms out benignly in front of him as she started. "I'm just -- are you okay? Well, that was a dumb question," he finished slowly as he approached.

Her head was bent and her shoulders were shaking as she cried, her arms wrapped around her bent legs, her head resting on her knee. She turned to face him and even in the darkness of the forest he could see her eyes were red and swollen.

"Yeah." She sniffed, sitting up and wiping at the still flowing tears with shaky fingers. "It was a pretty stupid question."

Her voice was husky with her tears and he had never felt so helpless as he moved to sit beside her.

"What can I do?" he asked. "I mean, we have limited resources here but --"

"Can you turn back time so that the plane never left Maryland?"

"Of all the grand things I am capable of," he said in a light, joking tone, "power over space and time has never been a thing." He wasn't lying, because if he could turn back time, a lot of things in this world would be different. "But I give mean hugs," he offered. "And I mean there is no intent on the offer other than to make you feel better. Not that I am against naked hugs but I don't think that's what you need right now and I'm not that much of an asshole."

Snorting, she leaned against his shoulder and he tentatively placed his arm around her.

Her hair was a wild tangle and her eyes were still

running with tears as she looked up into his face. "I'm not mad at you guys for knowing how to survive," she began, sighing softly as she rested more of her weight on him. "I 'm just tired and frustrated. I'm angry and sore and I want this to be over. I just want to open my eyes and be in my bed and to know that this is all some major nightmare. I don't want to be here. I don't want to do this, Hash. I don't know how to do this and I want to skip ahead to the part where we're rescued. I don't want to be here."

"I don't think any of us want to be here," Nabu agreed. "I know I'd rather be in my own bed surrounded by my mini dragons and reading up on Norse epic poems."

"Mini dragons?"

"Oh." He chuckled a little, thinking of his charges. "I breed rare and exotic lizards. It's related to the crocodile skink but is much larger, and their plates and scales are dark but outlined in red-gold, as are their eyes."

"Crocodile skinks?" She thought for a moment then grinned, her tears easing as she began to talk to him. "Oh, the baby dragon lizards. You breed them?"

"Mostly for myself." He settled a bit more comfortably against the tree. "It's a hobby, and since I was a child, I've always been obsessed with writing and dragons."

"Like the dragon tattoo on your back?"

"Yeah." He grinned. "You noticed?"

"When we were getting you settled. So you're obsessed with dragons and you play drums in a rock band." She arched an eyebrow, facing him fully now, pulling herself out of her own dark thoughts. "How'd that happen?"

"Well, Abadon, Python, Apollon, and I have known each other since we were very young. We kind of supported each other though some difficult times."

"Your parents were friends or something?"

"We have no parents." Damn, Nabu thought, trying to tell the truth as much as possible. This is why they never gave interviews about their pasts. They never wanted anyone to go digging.

"You're orphans?"

"You could say that." He nodded. "We basically raised ourselves. After spending a few years traveling and learning, we still kept in touch and tried to meet up at least once a year no matter what. We're our own family, you know. Then suddenly one year Abadon decided it would be awesome if we formed a rock band. Lord knows he has the voice to do a lot of different genres, including opera, but we were all so angry and unsettled that heavy metal seemed the right choice. And here we are."

"So you guys just roamed the world until you decided to make a band? Where did you learn to play? I mean, that just doesn't happen overnight."

"Well, I've always played the drums." He was so not going to mention that it was a neat way of passing messages across a battlefield. "I think the guys picked up guitar on their travels. Python taught me so sometimes I'll play onstage. Apollon loves the bass because it reminds him of his own voice." He chuckled. "That man has such a deep voice." And he was also not going to mention that it was used to scare the shit out of people on and off the battlefield, or that he could use it to give nightmares to those he really wanted to annoy. "Abadon can play the guitar, the drums, the piano, the violin, the sax, and a few other instruments." And he'd been a bard and spy during the Middle Ages, using the drums to help Spartans before that to keep their marching in time on the battlefield. Piano and violin strings could be used as weapons, and the sax... he had an oral fixation.

"So you're all a very talented group of orphans,

then."

"Yeah." Nabu chuckled. "And I love poetry. What is a song but poetry set to music? And I love writing. But I've spoken enough about me." Because if she dug any deeper he would have to admit what they were or start lying, and he didn't want to lie to her. "What do you do other than make flights comfortable for pretentious rich people on planes?"

She snickered at that, her eyes clearing as her voice lightened. "I am an illustrator, a Manga-ka, if you will."

"No shit." Nabu sat up with interest. "You create Japanese graphic novels."

"For an American audience," she informed him. "You probably never heard of my work because I'm just starting out with a few companies. But I write *The Unholy Chicken Alliance*."

He was impressed. "The series about a group of sentient attack chickens of war taking over the planet with their attack Chihuahuas? That is some crazy shit, Aika. It's amazing. Oh hell! You're *that* Aika Fujioka. It is an honor to meet you."

She chuckled, almost shyly leaning her forehead against his shoulder. "I am the one who is honored. You know my work."

"I love your work. I am waiting to see what happens when the human spy is found in The Coop even though he is agreeing with the moral arguments of the Chicken Brigade."

"I'm not telling." She chuckled then groaned as her stomach growled.

"You need to eat."

"But it's Thumper." She chuckled. "He was my favorite in the movie."

"If you could have anything, what would it be?" he asked as he rose to his feet and reached down for her hand and pulled her up.

"Honestly, I started *The Unholy Chicken Alliance* because I love fried chicken."

Nabu stared at her for a moment before bursting into laughter. "You wanna eat your cast?"

"I know!" She laughed along with him. "It's awful, but when I was a child, I decided that the chickens were plotting to kill me because I wanted to eat them all the time. So I came up with this story about the chickens trying to get me before I could get them."

They were still chuckling over this as they made their way back to camp.

But all laughter ceased as a reasonably large chicken clucked and raced past them out of the forest.

"Um..." After shooting each other a look, they moved faster to the camp to find feathers flying as Abadon managed to catch the chicken... along with the two others that Python was holding.

"What the hell..." Nabu breathed before turning to look at a stunned Apollon.

"Don't look at me. I didn't do it," he insisted. "But I am very amused, nevertheless."

"Why are there chickens running free in the forests of... where the hell are we?" Python asked, looking at the stunned faces of their party.

"Um... New Mexico... maybe?" Aika informed them as she stepped further into the encampment. "That's where Tom said we were heading about twenty minutes before we blew up."

She winced at her wording but was staring at the chickens in confusion. There were now four of them...

"Free-range, maybe?" Charle reasoned. "Maybe there's a farm nearby."

"There is no farm anywhere near this area," Nabu grumbled, arching an eyebrow at Apollon, who arched one back and shook his head. "This doesn't make sense."

"Maybe there is a road nearby and a truck crashed

and now we have chickens in the woods in the middle of Bum-Fuck-Egypt?"

"Bum-Fuck-Egypt is a military holding in Africa." Abadon sniffed, giving the chicken a shake as it squawked at him. "Maybe someone lost these guys a long time ago and they headed toward the light."

"They're about to see the light," Charle added, licking his lips, then shrugging as the rest of the party turned to stare at him. "What? Rabbits are small and these chickens look meaty. I'm hungry and about to get hangry. I say we eat them. Any objections?"

Everyone turned to stare at Aika, who looked down at her belly as it rumbled emptily up at her again.

"I hope someone knows how to pluck a chicken." She looked up at the rest of them, this time her eyes shining in delight. "You're survivalists, apparently. Help me survive by cooking me a damn chicken."

It was at that exact point in time that Nabu fell in love.

* * *

"You guys really know how to party!"

Aika spent the night next to Hash after a delicious meal of roasted chicken and fresh fruit.

Charle called it eating naked, Abadon called it the old way of doing things. Aika was just glad that there was hot sauce in her overnight bag, one of the three bags they'd rescued. Eating healthy might be better received, she decided, if every meal was roasted over an open fire.

As for Hash, he was cutely protective of her. Maybe their bathroom tryst had been more than just getting off with someone you found hot. Either way, she was grateful the man stayed by her side, offering silent support. Apollon seemed to be okay on his own even if he gave the surrounding woods odd stares at times. Abadon had Charle tucked up against his side and didn't seem to mind their situation as long as his lover was next to him. It was disgustingly cute and it made her consider drawing a romance about the two of them. Python seemed to be okay as long as he had his snake with him, though he clearly was missing his lover Orion who he spoke of with a reverence that was mostly reserved for speaking about their gods. And she spent the night with the man who seemed to be more than physically attracted to her. He might be emotionally invested, if the night before was a clue.

And speaking of lover-boy...

Aika looked around to see Hash cussing as he was undoing what was left of his hair, the locks released from tight braids standing wildly about his head.

Apollon was pointing and laughing, braiding his own damp, long white hair into a single tail as Hash huffed.

"It's only hair, man. It'll grow back." Apollon was gasping in between laughing at the increasingly horrified faces Hash was making.

"It smells like burnt hair."

"It *is* burnt hair," Apollon pointed out, leaning back against a recovered cushion, his morning toilette done. He was wet from what looked like a good scrubbing in the lake and was shirtless, his pale skin nearly blinding her as the morning sun glinted off of it. "But I kind of like this Medusa-Grass hybrid thing you got going, Hash. Sure, you look like you were hit with electricity but you pull off the look with such grace and class."

"Get a tan, pale boy," she found herself defending her man... uh... Hash. "Or put a shirt on. You're blinding me with all that white skin."

"Ohh, feisty!" He laughed, turning to blink up at her. "You don't find my pale ass attractive? You haven't seen my ass so you don't know how beautiful it is but I really can't help the pale. I mean I try to tan but I have two looks, pale as watered milk or lobster red. I don't like the lobster red very much, so ... do you like a little milk in your coffee?"

"I like my eyes in working order." She snickered. Maybe he wasn't so bad after all. "If you would be so kind as to cover up? The glare is blinding."

"Well..." He laughed as he tugged on a damp shirt. "At least you didn't call me an albino. You would not believe how many people think I cover up red eyes with blue contacts. I can't help it if I look like the Aryan dream child. I blame genetics."

"You're impossible to insult, aren't you?" she asked, rolling her eyes as she moved to sit beside Hash.

She had taken her morning bathroom break and had scrubbed up as much as she could without heading to the bathing area. Her clothing from her overnight bag was hung out on various tree limbs along with the contents of the other cases, and none of her stuff was doing her any good. Her silk PJs were not exactly rough terrain gear and her fuzzy slippers were still wet. At least her undies dried quickly.

"You can only be insulted if you take offense at the words given to you," he pointed out as he buttoned up his shirt. "I choose not to be insulted but entertained. It's laugh or cry. Your boyfriend taught me that."

He shot her a grin as her face flamed in a hard blush. "He's not -- We're not..."

"You don't think we know what happened in the bathroom after we took off? We're not stupid, merely discreet."

"Oh, God --"

"Leave her alone, Apollon." Hash finally let his hands drop as he glared at his friend. "What happened was none of your business."

"Oh, I'm just teasing," he insisted as he settled back, his gaze jumping back and forth between the two of them. "I think you two are cute together."

"Still, none of your business." Hash shook his head. "Are you okay, man? This is not like you."

"I'm fine," he insisted, running his hands over his face as he sighed deeply. "Things are strange here."

"I forgot you were an epileptic." Aika nodded, relaxing. "I am sure that recovery after a seizure is hard."

"If you say so." He cut his eyes to her before looking around the grounds. "Do you ever get the feeling you're being watched?"

"Paranoia could be a symptom of a recurring attack," Aika pointed out, and they both turned to stare at her. "What? I read. I am a writer as well as a manga-ka. I research."

Apollon opened his mouth to respond but the return of the rest of their party caught his attention instead. "I'm going to see what they're up to." He rose to his feet and padded away, leaving Aika and Hash alone. "Maybe Abadon has an idea about communicating with the rest of the world."

"He's strange." She turned to Hash to see him staring at his friend in concern. "You could make him lie down --"

"No." He shook his head. "Apollon *is* strange. He always has been. I'm not too concerned." He ran his hands thought his loose hair. "But I am annoyed. Very annoyed."

"You lost your hair pulling me out of the fire," she pointed out, remembering how important hair could be to some black people, and she was sure Hash had always taken pride in his appearance, especially his hair. It was a tangled, singed mess and she felt guilty about it.

"So worth it," he purred, leaning into her like a huge cat, before lifting his hands to his hair again. "I should just cut it all off."

"Why don't you?"

"I don't have anything to do the chop with," he

pointed out. "And I refuse to let any of my brothers near me with sharpened metal from the plane. I love them but barbers they are not. I am convinced that they have long hair because they're afraid of clippers. You should see the split ends that Python sports. I am hoping that Orion helps cure him of that."

She snickered at the loving insults he was throwing at his band mates -- well, his family -- and ran her own fingers through what was left of his crowning glory.

"I could help with that," she offered. "They found my bag and in my toiletry case. There are scissors."

"If you have a razor, I'll take you up on it."

"Gonna shave it all off?"

"I don't do things by halves," he pointed out.

"I have a razor."

"If you don't mind seeing me naked again, we can do this right now."

"Oh." She felt her stomach tighten and her thighs quiver. "I think I can handle you naked."

"And now that the rest of them are back from the designated bathing area, wanna take advantage?"

"You know, I think I may want to." She grinned.

Maybe now it was time for the "thank God we survived" sex.

Yeah, she was really down with that.

Chapter 6

She dropped one of his shirts at the edge of the water as she stood and smiled at him.

"Am I gonna get a show?" he asked as he whipped his own shirt off his head and ran his fingers through what was left of his hair before he stepped out of his pants and turned toward her.

He watched as she lifted her hands and slowly unbuttoned the remains of her blouse before tossing it aside. Her bra was next to go, and Nabu groaned softly to himself as her breasts sprang free.

Damn, she was beautiful.

She undid her pants easily enough and stepped out of them as they fell around her feet. Her panties were kicked aside and then she reached for the small bag she carried with her. It was pink and black and held the implements of grooming she'd promised.

"Come to mama," she purred, and almost in a daze, he found himself standing before her.

She moved into the warm waters, waist high, and motioned for him to kneel before her.

"You know, this puts me in the perfect spot to --"

"Go down on me later," she cutting him off, giggling. "First, we have to handle that mop on top of your head."

"First things first, I guess," he agreed and spun around so that his back was to her.

"Is this going to wreck the water?" she asked as he settled down and waited.

"Nope. There is a current that will pull what's left of my hair out into the lake and it will break down naturally or be used by birds for nesting. That is why the heat of this spring stays consistent; there is a constant flow of fresh cold water from the lake itself as it circulates along the hot water that is coming from deep within the mountain."

"If you say so." She chuckled, her trust in him and his knowledge making his heart sing.

"I know so," he countered, looking up at her as she hovered for a moment, before bending over to place a kiss against his forehead.

"You're so smart." She ran her fingers over his face, touching his broad nose, pressing against his full lips until he sucked one into his mouth, his eyes smoldering. "I think I am in lust with your brain."

"The body is pretty good too," he murmured as he reached up and back to span her waist with his broad hands. "Nothing like the perfection you present me with but..."

"But first things first." She leaned over further and dropped a kiss on his nose before fisting the remains of his hair. "Let's get this taken care of before you service me like the goddess that I am."

"Yes, ma'am." He grinned up at her before resting his hands on his lap and preparing for a major change in his life.

She removed some things from the bag and tossed it back to the shore, then there was a familiar snipping sound and a weight was lifted from his head.

He closed his eyes and thought of the years he had been Hash, drummer and writer for Abadon. Losing his hair was like losing part of this identity. He really didn't want that, to give up the life he had made for himself, yet in order to continue living, he had to let go of was essentially his past.

Snip, and more weight was lifted, and he remembered growing out his hair in the first place. Sure, he could have used his energy to make it any length he wanted, but he grew it out in the human way for reasons that still weren't clear to him. He knew he wanted to know how it felt to learn patience, and growing hair was a good way to start. That was why he'd stepped out of his temple and began walking, learning about the people he had served and hopefully to learn more about his own existence.

Snip. Another lock and another memory.

He remembered it being the fifties, standing aside and watching the people he had helped advance destroy one another over something as stupid as skin color, and over more dangerous things like fear and want of power. Fear and anger were constant companions, and he'd learned more about himself than he had about society. Societies never really changed; they just kept coming up with new reasons to destroy themselves, and the reason began to be more and more lack knowledge.

Snip.

He remembered being a slave, being caught off guard and captured, as he wandered through what was the Ivory Coast of Africa, and brought to America in chains. He could have fought and escaped but the people he was chained to, he didn't want to see them dead and they didn't stand a chance on their own. They sailed over the bodies of those who came before him, of those who fought and lost, of those who were considered a nuisance and tossed overboard. He didn't want that to happen to these people as they huddled tougher, a dark mass of humanity afraid and being forced to go where they had never imagined. He stayed and encouraged them, helped them where he could, observed even as he was whipped and abused like them, until they landed on the isle of Jamaica and it all started again.

Snip.

He recalled the protests, the marching in the streets, the bite of the dogs as they demanded dignity and respect, would never forget the smell of burning flesh or the sight of bloated bodies hanging from trees. He had been filled with an impotent anger then, learning the depths to which humanity could sink and also the indomitable way they could rise as a minority of people banded together to risk life and limb to create balance and help those who were downtrodden. He stayed and learned of bravery and soul and sacrifice, and learned to start to like humanity once more.

Snip.

He had started growing his hair long when The Naturals, later called Afros, were in style. Each inch reminded him that he was connected to these people he chose to stay with, chose to fight with, chose to learn from and teach. There was unity, and it was glorious until it wasn't. He watched as drugs and guns invaded the streets and the tentative unity shattered under political machinations, and love turned to distrust.

Snip.

He trimmed his braids once, back in the eighties, when everything was wild colors and break dancing. He let it grow through crazy music, crazy colors, and the economy that rose until America was known as the country of excess and her dark past was starting to be obscured and hidden from those growing up.

Snip.

He let his hair grow long and wild until he decided to braid it once more right around the time his frustrated and tired brother found him playing the stock market and donating most of his earnings to charity, and told him he wanted to start a band, to keep them all going for the next hundred years or so.

Did he want to keep going? There were a few hundred times he wanted to give up, to fade away, but there were new advances in medicine and science, even as he watched society backslide into the fear and hatred of his early days in America. His curiosity about the future was more powerful than his anger and exasperation with the human race, so he picked up some drumsticks and decided to beat out the tribal tones of those who came before him. And he never looked back, never regretted staying, and until this moment, never cut his hair again.

Now he looked down at the ragged braids that flared around him and decided that maybe this new change would make a new era in his life. He would never let go of his past, but that didn't mean he couldn't dive headfirst into a new future.

"Almost done." Aika was talking quietly as if she somehow sensed how important this moment was for him, and he respected her for it.

She sprayed some shaving foam in her hand and spread it evenly over his scalp. The passing of her razor was an odd scraping feeling, but the heat of the water and the feel of her soft hips pressing into his back took his mind far away from his own musings and placed him firmly into the here and now.

She was humming softly as she rinsed the razor time and time again, and his hair disappeared into undertow to be washed out into the lake. Finally, she tossed the scissors and her razor to the shore and ran her hands over the top of his head.

"Smooth as a baby's bottom," she purred, then squealed in laughter as he spun around and rose to his feet.

Laughter died as her soft form pressed against his hard body, and her smile changed from amusement into something much more sensual. With her arms draped over his shoulders, she lifted her head and demanded a kiss that he greedily gave.

"Aika." He breathed her name as he slid his hands down her sides, his thumbs caressing the sides of her beasts where her hard nipples pressed into his chest.

She was so soft and sweet, a delicious little bundle in his arms and he felt blessed with the knowledge that this was where she wanted to be.

"You're hot with hair," she breathed against his lips and he bent down to press small, sucking kisses to her mouth. "Without hair, you're beautiful."

It was in her eyes as he pulled back to look down at her. He felt that blush again as a shift of pure energy slammed into him. His breath hitched, and he clutched her tighter to himself so that he wouldn't fall as the sensations pouring from her fed deeply into his soul. She just... wanted him.

He blinked back tears as he experienced pure worship, a kind that he had never felt before. It wasn't because she knew who he was, because she didn't. It wasn't because she needed anything from him; she could survive on her own and they both knew it. It was because she wanted him without any ulterior motives. She wanted him, to explore him, to share her body and her heat with him.

In all of his years he had never felt anything like this before.

His mouth slammed into hers, his tongue forcing deep inside her mouth to taste what she was giving. She moaned and went up on her toes to get closer, clutching him just as hard. Her nails dug into his shoulders as he moved one thick-corded thigh in between hers. Instantly she began to grind against it, stimulating her clit as her slick juices merged with the water on his leg.

His cock was thick and hard, pushing against her stomach as lust punched him in the gut.

He gripped her under her arms and pulled her up, breaking the kiss, biting at her long neck, sucking lightly to feel her squirm. Her neck was going to become his favorite safe spot, the skin thin and soft. He wanted to mark her there, mark it so that everyone who saw knew that she belonged to him. Yet he respected her too much to rush what they were doing. He wasn't a greedy teenager trying to prove to the world that he got laid, so after one last nip to her flesh, he lifted her again, higher until her full breasts were pressed against his face.

He wasted no time in burying his face here before tilting his head to the right and pulling one dusky nipple into his mouth.

"God, yes," Aika hissed, throwing her head back, and her hair tumbled down from the loose knot that held it on top of her head. Her hands went to his head and Nabu tried not to wince around his mouthful of nipple as her fingers dug into his sensitive scalp.

He sucked her hard as her legs wrapped around his waist and he felt the head of his cock pull free from its hood and press against her hot wet flesh.

He loved moments like this, when he felt this familiar hunger wash over him, when he knew he was doing exactly what they needed to get off. Aika was no exception as she ground her hips down hard against his cockhead and all but squealed her pleasure.

"So damn big," she was muttering as she pushed her breast deeper into his mouth. "Hash!"

He pulled back, arms trembling with strength as he sought to hold her upright and not give in to the urge to just to fuck her raw when she started making her demands. Damn, but he loved women who knew what they wanted.

"Oh, God," she gasped, as she writhed in his arms, his dick running along her swollen slit, spreading her hot slick around. She was so soft and wet, weeping and begging for it. It would have been so easy just to slip right in and fuck her standing... "Fuck the foreplay. I want action."

His deep chuckle had her squirming as he took her at her word and moved closer to the shore. "And if I want foreplay?" he teased, making sure his dick kissed her opening with every step he took.

"I want your dick in me," she breathed, grinning up at him, and he nearly tripped as one hand slid down his back to squeeze his ass.

"And if I want to eat you out?" he managed as he stepped up to the grassy lip of the spring. "If I want to do that?"

"Then who am I to argue," she swiftly countered. "I am here to fulfill your every need --"

"Bullshit." He chuckled as he placed her on her back in the soft grasses, keeping his body in the water. She dimpled up at him and spread her legs wide.

"Supper's ready," she teased, laughing until he dipped down low in the water and put his mouth to good use.

Aika barely held in a scream, her body tensing as he spread her thighs wider and lifted her legs over his shoulders.

"Yes," he breathed as he spread her legs to expose her swollen clit and her slick pink opening. She was glistening with need and her scent was just perfect -- female musk and flowers. It was a scent he was going to become addicted to, and he bent closer to inhale deeply.

"Hash," she panted, her hands going to his bare scalp as she pulled him toward her need. Eagerly, he gave in to her demands and slowly ran his tongue over her clit.

She squealed and clamped her thighs around his head, holding him against herself as he lapped harder using the rough side of his tongue. Her slick filled his mouth and he eagerly swallowed her down, moaning at her flavor as he dove down for a deeper taste.

He ran his hands up her tense body, cupping her breasts, tugging at her nipples as he began to feast in earnest, dipping lower to lap at her opening before coming back to suck firmly on her clit.

"Yes... There... Harder!" She was going wild beneath him, bucking and squirming, digging her heels into his shoulders.

His dick was a hard, swollen thing between his legs, and his balls were shifting in their sac as he dropped one hand down to stroke himself, to relieve some pressure as her cries made his whole body quake with need.

He sank his tongue deep inside her, fucking her this way while her fingers left his head to dip between her body and his mouth. With knowing fingers, she spread her labia wide, fully exposing herself to his hungry eyes as she fingered her own clit.

"Fuck yeah." He pulled back to breathe, watching as she roughly fingered herself, her hips bucking as he began to lave her from her opening to her teasing fingers. He dropped his hand from his burning cock and slid one finger deep inside her body, and she groaned for more. "Yes, baby. Fill me."

He nosed her fingers aside and took her clit into his mouth, lashing it with his tongue as he started her slowly, his fingers seeking until they found the swollen bump of her G-spot.

"Hash! Fuck!" she blurted as he fingered her G-spot while pulling hard on her clit. She wailed as a gush of her juices covered his face, surrounding him in the scent and feel of her.

He sucked harder, flicking the tip of her clit with his tongue, unhooding it before suckling the tender bud. She stiffened, the muscles of her abdomen going rock hard while her thighs tightened like a necklace around his neck, trembling harder as she opened her mouth and wailed her first release.

He slammed in a second finger, fucking her through her orgasm, drawing it out and raising her hunger again as she thrashed beneath him, her own hands going to her hair where she tugged and pulled as she lost control.

He could feel her slick inner walls grasp rhythmically at his fingers, milking them as he recalled the feeling of his dick trapped within her body. He wanted that feeling again.

He pushed her legs down and crawled up above her.

Instantly her thighs climbed around his waist, as her hands ran over his head once again.

"In me." She was panting even as she reached for her kit and pulled out a condom.

"You sure?" he asked, running one hand over his face, wiping away her slick juices that made his face glisten in the bright daylight. "I mean I can go down on you again --"

"In me," she demanded, all but throwing the condom at him.

Laughing, he tore the pack open and swiftly slid the latex down his dick, smoothing it in place as her fingers trailed fire over his chest as she explored.

His nipples were tugged and pinched, his pecs caressed, her hands running down his body past his cock to cup his heavy balls.

Damn, she felt so good.

As he leaned over her, her fingers went to his ass, cupping his cheeks and pulling him closer.

"You are perfect," he breathed as he positioned himself at her slick opening.

"Back at you." Her voice was rough from her groaning as she cupped a breast and offered it up to him.

"Perfect," he panted as he lowered his head to pull her soft flesh into his mouth. He sighed deeply as he slowly began to sink into her tight body while nursing harder at her breasts.

He didn't stop moving deeper into her silken flesh until his balls were pressed against her ass.

She was whimpering, shuddering as her nails dug into his shoulders. "Make me come again," she demanded.

Who could deny an order like that?

Nabu pulled back and slammed deep into her, hard. He cried out as fire shot up his spine and he almost lost it, coming right then and there, but he denied the rush, pushed back the feeling and set about bringing his lover off one more time.

He pulled back and slammed in again and again, harder, twisting his hips just so, grinding down when he was in as deep as he could go, and Aika was loving it.

He felt sweat bead up as he bent down to suck at her neck again, sucking just a small mark, eating at the salt of her sweat, loving the feel of her small, soft body against his.

His body was trembling, his hunger growing, the pleasure rising up in him from her... It was almost too much.

He was in heaven, he was burning, his mind was going white, and Aika was screaming for more.

He reached down and gripped her hips, pulling her up so that she slid down deeper onto his dick. She squealed as her hand dug into his shoulders and her legs locked around his waist once more.

Grinning, he leaned down and let one hand drop down to thumb her clit, circling it as he swirled his hips, slamming his cock into her G-spot.

"Fuck!" she was screaming. "Fuck, Hash, Fuck!" and she was gone, her inner muscles clinching around his dick, milking it, wringing every drop of pleasure from his body until he too called out and let himself go.

His balls slammed up against the base of his cock and he threw his head back, roaring as his cock pulsed and shot his release deep into her, stopped only by the thin latex between them.

"Aika," he all but whimpered as she became limp in his arms. "Fuck." He shuddered as he gripped her harder, feeling his legs go weak as his orgasm tore through him.

Aika was clinging to him, her sharp nails digging into his back.

He shuddered as his hips circled again, drawing out her own orgasm as she slammed her teeth into his shoulder, muffling her screams as he felt her walls spasm around his still-hard cock as another orgasm tore through her.

Then she was whimpering, her body going lax as he fell, still holding her so close it felt as if he was trying to merge with her permanently.

"Aika," he breathed her name as he tried to control the shaking of his limbs.

"Bacon," she gasped, chuckling a little as she leaned back and looked up at him.

Nabu looked down, a question on his lips when she ran a damp finger over face before running her hands over his seductive, bare scalp.

He shuddered again because of the sensitivity and waited for her to explain.

"The only thing that could make this better is if there were bacon waiting for us."

He chuckled at her voracious appetite and gave her a hard squeeze, loving the feel of her soft flesh pressed against his own. He wanted her to stay there forever.

"Bacon would be nice," he agreed before tangling a hand in her hair to pull her head back so that he could take her mouth in one more, tender kiss.

"Mmm, bacon," she agreed, nipping at his bottom lip before running her tongue over the slight sting.

Then she sat up, her eyes going wide. "I do smell bacon. What the fuck?"

Nabu felt his eyes narrow as Aika pulled away to look back toward their campsite.

If Apollon... no. His brother wouldn't expose them like that, not before he had a chance to explain to Aika. And Enk had felt he felt that someone was watching him... What in the hell was going on? Was there another god in the area? That would explain the chickens. There was only one way to find out. Back to camp they would go.

Chapter 7

There was no bacon, but there were people with attitudes.

Aika looked around at their campground as if wondering what the hell had been going on. "I smelled bacon."

"I, as well," Nabu commented, stepping beside the damp and unamused woman.

"Well, we have leftover chicken," Abadon grumbled, staring at a chicken leg in consternation. "I would kill for some bacon."

"Maybe it was some of the chicken fat or wood or some leaves," Charle offered, not looking happy at all.

"Or wishful thinking," Sin added with what looked like a tear in his eye. "I really love bacon."

"So there is no bacon," Aika grumbled, stepping up to the fire pit where the leftover chicken was heating on some stones. "After last night one could hope, but the chicken looks good."

"It's that or Thumper," Charle joked, making room for her at the pit. "We have two live chickens left." He pointed to the makeshift pen they'd created to hold the remaining cluckers. "Maybe they will give us some eggs."

"Need a rooster for that," Aika happily informed him, reaching for one of the remaining legs. "But I am so hungry that I ain't complaining about hot food."

Nabu walked over to Enk, as the man was unusually quiet and looking disturbed. "Are you okay? I know that was a pretty huge blast of energy --"

"Someone is fucking with us," he grumbled, opening his hand to show a slice of perfectly coked bacon. "And I don't know who."

"Fuck." Nabu sat beside him. "Can you tell if there is ill intent?"

"No, and neither can Abadon. So maybe the intent is

not to do us harm but... I am getting a low level buzz, Nabu. And I can't identify where it is coming from. One of us is out there in the woods fucking around. I don't like it."

"Hmm." Nabu closed his eyes and sent his energy out seeking, attempting to know. There was the plane settled on the bottom of the lake. Sin had done something to keep the remaining fuel from leaking out so the water was safe. There were indeed wolves cavorting around in a den about five miles to their north. There were plentiful rabbits and birds, a few deer, some coyotes that were further afield. A bear or three that were not interested in them in the least. They were miles away from civilization and there were no hikers nearby. In fact, there was no person for miles around.

Pulling his energy back in, he concentrated on the mountains that surrounded them and...

"Fuck." He winced as he dropped his control and slammed his palms across his face.

"Nabu --"

"It's one of us, but he is powerful," he managed through the pain spiking through his head.

"Who?"

"I don't know," he managed, wincing as he dropped his hands to stare up at Enk. "He is like us but different."

"His intent?"

"I don't know but we're in his territory. He's managing to block me and his energy seems to be as old as these mountains."

"I don't think it's ill intent," Enk decided, rubbing at Nabu's back. "If that was the case he would have caused us some major harm. Instead, he provided chickens and bacon. It's like he's trying to help."

"He needs to stop." Nabu sat up as the pain in his head eased up. "He's going to expose us before I have a chance to tell Aika what we are."

"So... you're gonna tell her?" Enk brightened at that. "You're going to come out of the closet for her?"

"I was never in a closet," he snapped. "That is for insecure humans who question their sexuality. But yes, I intend to tell her who we are, who I am."

"You like her that much?"

"I do," he admitted. "I understand what Nergal and Sin were on about now. This woman is special."

"And if she breaks your heart?"

"Well, I don't know that my heart is all that involved, but it is more than sex. Sex I can get anywhere. But Aika... her mind is a beautiful place."

He looked over at Aika and watched as she joked with Charle, nibbling on chicken and looking cute in his shirt that hung around her like a dress. She was like a bright ball of energy and intelligence even as she sat relaxed after sex and food. She really liked sex and food.

"She mentioned bacon," he recalled. "Right before we started smelling it."

"Is that so?" Enk tilted his head to the side considering...

"And she mentioned chicken last night, right before they showed up."

"So whoever out there is helping... her?"

"I don't know but that seems logical." Nabu turned to look at Enk as the man let out an unrestrained giggle. "Oh man, the opportunity for mischief just increased."

"One who shares your power base," Nabu decided. "Can you tell who? There are only a few of us who can absorb and use that energy."

"I don't know who." Enk pulled himself under control but shot his brother a serious look. "But you better think of how to tell her and soon. It seems that if whoever out there is intent on granting her wishes, she is going to learn by accident and that never works out well."

Well, fuck, Nabu thought. Looks like things were about to get really interesting. He only hoped that it didn't come back to bite him in the ass.

* * *

Aika was standing by a pile of twisted radio parts when Nabu walked over to her.

She turned to look up at him and felt her breath catch. He had been hot with his long braids flowing around his body, but now that he was clean-shaven and totally bald he was beyond beautiful. He had a rather concerned look on his face though, and she turned away from pretending that she had an engineering degree and faced him fully.

"Can we talk?"

Instantly, her heart dropped. Was this one of those "we need to talk" conversations that would leave her looking and feeling like a fool? Of course she kind of leaped at the chance to sleep with him; that was so out of character for her. Did he think she was a huge groupie slut now? Had she made herself a come-dump for his baser needs? Had she misjudged him all along? Why was she panicking?

"A -- about?" Keep it casual, Aika she told herself as she forced a smile to her lips.

"About some things that have been happening."

Well, that didn't sound too bad... what? What things?

"Um... okay." She tucked a tendril of hair behind her ear and calmly waited, hiding the slight tremble in her hands by tucking them behind her back.

"Why are you in parade rest?" he asked, amusement evident in his tones.

"It's comfortable for me," she spat quickly, feeling a flush suffuse her face. "You know, airline attendant training and all."

"Okay," he drawled. "But I would be more

comfortable if we sat over here."

He gently took her arm and led her to the banked coals of the fire pit. He would take her someplace far away from the others if he was going to break up with her and destroy whatever mutual fuck society they had going on. As it stood, Abadon and Charle were tinkering with what looked like a radio, Python was with Apollon, cleaning the last of the chickens and getting them ready for the night's meal. She relaxed even more.

"I really don't know how to tell you this." He sighed, reaching up to tug at his braids and aborted the movement when he recalled that they were gone. Instead, he ran his hand over his scalp and shot her a sheepish look. "I tend to forget they're gone. I used to tug at them as a nervous habit," he explained. "But that's not what I wanted to tell you."

"What did you want to tell me?"

"There is something about us that you need to know."

"Okay." She nodded. This wasn't going to be so bad after all. Maybe they were all secretly related... or they were all in one big polyamorous relationship and they wanted her to join.

She found all the guys hot but she would not be fucking Apollon. Something about him just rubbed her the wrong way.

Yeah, that they were all in a sexual relationship made sense. They were grown men at the height of their sexual prowess, living in close quarters and traveling in each other's back pocket. She could see how that could fit. And if they wanted to add her... OMG, it was her dream of a reverse harem! She had toyed with stories like this in the past but never delved into yaoi. She could get into it though... She could feel her stomach dip and her thighs tingle.

"So long as you're my primary. I mean I slept with

you pretty fast but that doesn't mean I want to sleep with the rest of them. And some of them I wouldn't touch with a ten-foot pole... Apollon... just saying..."

"Um, what are you talking about?"

Aika looked into his face and stuttered to a halt as she took in his confusion. His hand was frozen halfway to reaching for hers and his head was curiously tilted to the side.

"Um... your big gay relationship with the other guys?" Had she read the situation wrong again?

"Me? Have sex with them? Eww." He snickered, shaking his head as if torn between humor and absolute disgust. "That would be like incest. No. Just no." He shook his head, shoulders shaking as he apparently decided on amusement. "I've seen them screw too many times with too many different people to want to even get on that carnival ride."

Akia was pouty now. "Okay, I was wrong." She sniffed. "But it was an honest mistake."

"You got from I need to tell you something to big gay line marriage? Where did Charle and Orion fit in?"

"So you can stop laughing at me now," she grumbled, her blush heating up. "I am a writer. I have a vivid imagination."

"So am I... and my imagination isn't that good."

"Har-de-ha-ha," she grumbled. "So what did you want to tell me, anyway?"

"Um... I wanted to tell you what we are. We're gods."

She just stared at him.

"All those strange things that have been happening -- the chickens, the bacon... it's how we survived the plane crash." She nodded and stared. This was... well, it was.

"We're ancient gods."

Okay. They weren't sexual perverts in the most wonderful way possible. They were insane. "So... what meds have you missed?" she asked, trying to remember if any of her friends who traveled with them mentioned this little mental issue.

"I don't take meds," he snapped, sitting back and glaring.

"There is no shame or blame when it comes to mental illness --"

"I'm not crazy." Nabu frowned hard.

"So you're the one who got me chickens?"

"No." He shook his head. "That wasn't me."

"So you didn't magic up some chickens."

"No."

"So... can you magic us up a radio? I mean the chickens were nice but..."

"I could try, but electronics are different from living beings."

"So you can magic up some chickens?"

"No," he grumbled. "Not my godhood."

"Then what is your power?"

"My power base is knowledge. I know things."

"Can you guess what I'm thinking right now?"

"I am not crazy!" he all but shouted.

She jumped to her feet. "Okay. Calm down, big guy."

"I am calm." He sat back down and crossed his arms over his chest. "I am not crazy."

"You just said you were a god."

"I said that *we* are gods."

"So you're going to drag the rest of them into this?"

"Because we are."

"So... you saved us when the plane crashed?"

"I helped."

"How?"

"I got you out of those flames, for one thing."

"You threw me --"

"Do you really think a human could have survived

with a bomb going off two feet in front of them? And do you think it is possible for us to *not* be sucked out of the plane with the whole cockpit gone? We all should have been sprayed along New Mexico and dangling from trees like piñatas."

"Coincidence," she insisted, crossing her arms and glaring down at him. "A series of very *fortunate* events."

"Really? Coincidence is what you come up with?"

"Beats saying that we were all saved by gods." She waved her hands in the air. "Ohhh... godly powers, activate! Let's make this plane crash less crashy!"

"It's the truth!"

"Yeah, right. And a herd of Chihuahuas are going to come crashing thought this clearing at any moment --"

"Don't!" He tried to cut her off, but he was too late.

It started with the yipping. Then there were whines and then a howl that make the hair left on his body stand on end. Then there was only time to react. He jumped to his feet and leapt atop the stones that made up their fire pit. Aika screeched as he reached down and jerked her up as well.

"*Incoming!*" he roared, and the rest of the guys stopped what they were doing and ran for cover.

Enk and Sin emerged from the brush, and Sin immediate dropped to his knees and waved his hands. Water from the nearby lake waved and funneled in the bright light of the day, creating rainbow patterns as he formed a solid wall between them and the oncoming horde.

Nergal waved his hands and suddenly Charle was on top of the cover they'd created to protect the camp. He lifted his arm and pressed at the blazing green-and-silver sword tattoo that graced his forearm, the symbol of the band Abadon, and hissed as the tattoo appeared to fall from his body, forming very real, sharp steel.

Nabu himself ripped off his shirt and the dragon that

had existed for millennia on his back roared to life as a creature of fire and flame. The red-gold dragon surrounded them, creating an impenetrable barrier that could withstand almost anything.

He looked down at Aika's face, seeing amazement and disbelief there right before the horde invaded.

Three were dozens of them, fangs dripping with saliva, black lips pulled back in growls, large round eyes narrowed in defiance as they moved as one horrific creature from the depths of hell.

The Chihuahuas were here in all their ankle-biting glory. Teaming masses of them with their short, muscular legs and their curly tails raced thought the camp, barking and biting at everything they set their beady little eyes upon.

"What the fuck?" Aika got out before the pint-sized wall of miniature dogs slammed up against the barrier of Nabu's fire dragon and then scattered to race all about the camp, yipping and barking.

Nergal was swiping low left and right, trying to keep the tiny beasts at bay as they made a wreck of their camp. They avoided the blade and shot him baleful looks as they raced on to the water wall that Sin had erected.

"Do something!" Sin shouted at Enk, who, despite being bent over laughing, waved his hand, and about a thousand red rubber balls with feet emerged out of thin air. Which created more havoc as the squeaky balls danced amidst the squeaky dogs, and the hounds from hell gave chase.

It only took a moment but it seemed like forever as the balls finally ran back into the woods, the dogs in hot pursuit. The members of Abadon finally let down their guard; Sin's water flowing back to the river, Nergal disappearing his sword, and Nabu waving his hand as his dragon encircled them once more before merging again with the skin of his back.

Silence and devastation were left in their wake, slobber and tiny little footprints everywhere, teeth marks on luggage, and what food they had, gone. Nabu looked around at his family, at the traumatized look on Charle's face, and at Enk, who still couldn't stop laughing... then down at Aika.

But instead of the horror he expected to find there, he found amazement and of all things, joy. "Oh shit," she was mumbling, eyes wide and bright, mouth falling open in shock. "Oh shit! The fire and the water and the dogs and the dragon and... Oh shit!" Then she turned to look up at Nabu, her whole body trembling. "Do it again!"

Chapter 8

"Who in the hell let the dogs out?"

Enk was laughing too hard to be of much help and the rest were sitting in the midst of their ruined camp with a lot of questions and a hyper-excited Aika.

"So Apollon is Enk, god of mischief." She glared at the snickering blond. "Kind of a low-budget Loki."

She expected some degree of outrage, but he was still snickering at her.

"And Abadon is Nergal the god of destruction. Python is Sin, god of change, and *you* --" she turned to Hash -- "Are Nabu, god of knowledge."

"Yes."

"I fucked a god... holy shit."

"I know," Charle chimed in, giggling. "It has a tendency to make one feel special."

"Who else knows?"

"No one," Nabu spoke softly, his hand rubbing hers as she gripped it hard. "Only the people here... and Orion."

"He must be worried sick." She turned to Sin, who shrugged.

"I doubt it. He knows what we are and is probably putting his acting chops to good use. Besides, Max is with him."

"And does Max know?" She turned back to her lover.

"Probably. But we never told him and he never asked. Max is unique. He truly goes with the flow."

"So you really are gods." She chuckled to herself. "I can't believe it."

"It saved our lives," Charle pointed out from where he was nestled next to Nergal. Who knew Abadon was really Abadon. This was madness.

"And your power is knowledge?" she questioned.

"It is a powerful yet limited godhood," he patiently explained. "I can know certain things -- book knowledge, practical knowledge, but I can't tell you what the future holds. No one can really do that."

"So you didn't know the plane was going to crash?"

"If I had, I never would have let my family board." He shot her a concerned look. "What kind of person do you take me for?"

"An all-knowing, all-powerful god. Duh."

"Well, I never claimed to be all knowing or all powerful. We have limits, and when we cross them there are consequences."

"Like being drained to the point that you can't do anything to help yourself," Enk chimed in. "Or getting a power rush so great you pass out or have a seizure."

"So you're not epileptic?"

"I never claimed to be. That's all on you."

"And you're rock stars because --"

"A steady stream of worship," Nergal explained, finally saying something. "Without worship we would be nothing."

"You could start a cult, or a church..."

"And that would be false worship and doesn't mean a god-damned thing." He hugged his lover closer. "Worship freely given is what keeps us locked into this plane of existence. I like existing and I don't want to disappear like so many others of our kind."

"That is wild." Aika shook her head, still not sure she believed, although the proof was right in front of her. "And you all have to be as old as fuck."

"Watch that." Nabu chuckled, drawing her attention back to him. "We're sensitive about some things."

"Yeah, seeing that Nergal and Nabu are amongst the oldest of us..." Enk laughed.

"How old?" she asked. She had to know.

"Old enough to fuck without getting stuck." Enk

laughed as she glared at him. There really was something about him that put her off.

"Cute," she snapped before shaking her head. "And none of you is responsible for the chickens or the puppies?"

"Not us." Nabu let go of her hand and again made an aborted movement toward the hair that no longer existed before dropping his arm with a huff. "We're not sure who is."

"So you aren't the only gods left in the world?"

"There are hundreds of us," Nabu explained. "Some more powerful than others. Humans are strange and curious beings. If you worship something enough it transcends normality and becomes a god. We don't know how it works. Some things remain a mystery even to us, but we figure it's all about need and desire. And knowing that, we would be fools to think that we're the only gods in existence. We've stumbled across a few in our time, but mostly we do our best to avoid each other. Some are not so amiable and some are downright evil."

"That's... that's kind of scary," Aika admitted. She couldn't even imagine running across a supernatural being that had the power to destroy and the intent to do as much harm as they possibly could. The thought of that sent a chill through her blood. "And the one granting wishes?"

"Ancient magic," Nabu explained. "I know he's here somewhere, but I can't trace him. It feels like we're sitting in the middle of his seat of power. If he wanted us dead, we would be. Instead, he's granting the human wishes in the most mischievous way possible so I think he shares a power base with Enk."

"That would explain all the giggles and inappropriate laughter." Aika shot him a sharp look before she softened a bit. She could try and give him the benefit of the doubt. If he was constantly being overwhelmed then maybe that was a reason for him being such an asshole.

"Not as inappropriate as doing a complete stranger in an airplane bathroom," Enk chimed in, and any good graces she had for him evaporated.

"None of your business," Nabu snapped, and she turned to him in surprise. "Let it go, Enk."

"But --"

"Enk." His voice echoed in the clearing though she swore he didn't raise it at all. The air seemed thick and heavy all of a sudden and she shivered at the power in that voice.

"Whatever." Enk, finally humbled, shot the older god a sheepish look.

"That was out of character for me," she pointed, out hoping to defuse the situation. She didn't really like Enk, but she didn't want to be the reason he was on the outs with his family.

"Me too," Charle added, cutting the tension more. "I mean, Nergal was getting fucked by some other dude who couldn't hack it and I stepped in to finish him off, so to speak." There was a light flush to his deeply tanned face as he grinned up at his lover. "And you see how that worked out."

"You chased me until I caught you." The man bussed Charle's lips.

"So sometimes your first instinct is the correct one." Charle sighed.

"I could feel that what we had was just... it was pure enjoyment for both of us, no ulterior motives. You didn't care who I was. Something in me called to something in you and you were brave enough to answer that call."

Nabu's quiet tones reassured her somehow. She didn't know what it was, but everything about this man calmed her soul.

"If we were dealing with my grandparents they

would have said that the red string of fate has linked us." She nodded in agreement as he continued. "Do you know much about that particular culture?"

"Please." She snorted. "I was raised in Buffalo. You're lucky I can speak the language... kind of. But I researched the matter for my mangas. I always thought it was a beautiful legend."

"You appear very accepting," he mused, running his thumb along the back of her hand. "I wonder why that is?"

"I am a writer, even if my genre isn't as popular as some others in the U.S. And besides... Chihuahuas. It's kind of hard to disprove a pack of salivating ankle-biters. I mean, there are teeth marks on the luggage." That... and there was just something about this whole situation; there was something about Nabu. She really didn't know him like she wanted to know him, but maybe she would have a chance to.

"By the way, I'm really glad you're not crazy. I was thinking about taking my chances of survival out in the wilderness. It wouldn't have been pretty but I would have done it to get away from crazy. I saw *American Psycho...*"

His laughter made something inside of her lighten. She couldn't help but grin up at him as her heart began to pound. Damn, she pulled a god. A god wanted to be with her... he wanted to be with her... he'd told her their secrets.

As if someone would believe it, she chided herself, but there he was, Nabu, god of knowledge, and he was holding her hand.

"Can we talk?" he asked finally, and she nodded as he rose to his feet, pulling her up easily.

"You aren't going to tell me that I am a goddess or some such nonsense, are you? 'Cause if you are, I've been woefully underpaid. I still have student loans, and if we don't get home soon, my goldfish will be dead."

He snickered as he led her out of the clearing and their camp, not too far away but far enough to ensure some privacy. "No, I sense nothing godlike in you besides your ability to draw me in like a moth to a flame."

"And this isn't a break up thing is it? I mean, we really don't have a relationship... I mean this thing we have is amazing but it's only been two days... and I'm quite sure if you were going to dump me you wouldn't tell me your secrets..." *Shut up.* But she always babbled when she got nervous so...

"Nothing of the sort," he assured her. "In fact, I'd like to propose the exact opposite."

"I'm listening," she all but purred, her breathing calming down as her mind stilled. "What do you want to propose? And not marriage... 'cause I don't know you like that, god or no."

"Nothing like that," he assured her, chuckling at her words. "But I would like to continue seeing you. Aika, there is something about you that's undefined by man or by nature. You're beautiful inside and out and the joy you take when you're with me nourishes my soul."

"So you want to give this thing a chance?"

"I want to give us a chance," he agreed. "Orion and Charle dove right in, damn the consequences, but you aren't that type of person."

"Wild and adventurous?"

"No, you're more protective of yourself and your heart. I think Orion and Charle spent their lives looking for something to complete them. You, Aika Fujioka, completed yourself. You don't need me, you want me. And there is magic in that. It makes my heart take flight."

Damn, he was perfect, she mused, as she stared up into his large brown eyes. The sun was slowly setting over the trees, and in the distance the lake was beginning to light up in a brilliant array of colors. Yet nothing was more beautiful than the words that this man just spoke to her.

He saw her. He truly saw *her*. He saw the struggle she dealt with in her business, with her race and culture, with acceptance and how hard she fought to make a way for herself to stand on her own. He got that. And he was right about missing parts of her life. She really didn't need anyone else. She had more than proved that to herself over the years. She was confident in her skills, content with her personality, and at ease with her life choices. She really didn't need anyone or anything to make her feel whole. Having someone like Nabu, the god of wisdom, affirm what she already knew... that made her feel invincible.

"I'd like that too," she breathed, going on her toes to place a small kiss at his chin, his cheeks, and then his lips. "I'd like to get away with you," she muttered before her lips were taken in a kiss... a KISS...

"I can get us alone now," he panted, pulling back from her.

"With all these guys..."

He whipped his shirt over his head, and to her fascinated shock, his dragon exploded from his back in a blaze of red-gold flame to encircle them.

"My Lady," he purred as he stepped on the dragon's back and held a hand out for her.

Dare she live out the dream of every fantasy geek in the universe, to actually ride a dragon? If it was going to get her laid, then hell yeah.

She stepped on, the only heat she felt growing was between them, and in a blur of motion they were off.

Their clothing must have disappeared somewhere along the way because when the dragon stopped at a clearing that looked to be halfway up a mountain, she was completely naked and completely wrapped around her god.

He easily hefted her off the back of the beast of fire. She would ponder that one later when she didn't have sex-brain, and all but threw herself at Nabu.

"Your name is sexy," she purred as the dragon let loose with a puff of dark smoke before swimming around them only to disappear into the skin of his back, once again becoming an extremely detailed tattoo. "But not as sexy as travel by dragon."

"Oh I know," he purred back, reaching out and pulling her closer to him. She eagerly went, jumping up and wrapping her legs around his waist. It was a thrill to know he had the strength and power to toss her around yet would stop at her slightest complaint. This is what being truly wanted must be all about, she decided, when someone put your wants and needs above their own.

But then there was no more time to ponder because his mouth was pressed over her and she dove into the kiss with everything she had.

Her hands trailed over the soft skin of his scalp, tugged at his cute little ears, and drifted down over his broad shoulders and biceps. Damn, her man was built.

The hard wall of his chest felt so good pressed against her breasts... and his cock...

The man was truly blessed in the dick department and she could tell as it was pressed against her stomach and getting larger and harder by the second.

He broke off the kiss to attack her neck -- he must have some vampire in him somewhere -- and she decided to explore a little lower.

His cock was hot in her hand. He groaned as she palmed him, feeling precum drip from the tip as she teased his foreskin. Uncircumcised men were new ground for her, but she knew she would have fun playing with his foreskin by how he reacted whenever she retracted it.

And yes, there was the shuddering moan, the tiny grunt he tried to hide, his hands drifting over her ass...

The world spun, and she found herself lying on a bed of soft, fluffy clouds. His tattoo had more than one purpose, she divined, as she sank back into the softness of his design.

"This is nice," she whispered, looking up into his dark, glittering eyes.

She would miss being able to tug at his hair but the tradeoff was that nothing was distracting from his beautiful face. Nabu, god of knowledge, was handsome as fuck.

His hands trailed over her body, worshiping her as she threw open her arms and welcomed him.

Nabu trailed gentle kisses over her neck, nipping sharply then laving away the small delicious pain with his tongue.

"I will never get enough of you," he murmured as he rose above her, looming, giving her an open smile, his eyes filled with desire. "You're everything that I never knew I was looking for."

He tangled his fingers in her hair, pushing it back from her face before nipping at her bottom lip and then pressing his full soft lips against hers.

The kisses they shared were filled with longing and lust, but also possession, and for the first time Aika felt that she really didn't mind being possessed.

She reached up and traced his features with curious fingers.

"I want to sit and draw you," she breathed, her heart racing as she took the man between her thighs. "I want to draw you naked and clothed. I want to draw you with your drumsticks and with your brothers. I want to draw you in color and with your dragons and I want to know the real you."

"You think you can learn the real me?"

"I can damn sure try."

"How I want you to," he breathed before he took her

mouth again, filling her with his taste, pushing the fire he created in her to an inferno. Her thoughts were crumbling as passion began to consume her once more and she willingly threw herself into the flames.

Aika let out a small whine, arching her hips upwards as he began to caress her body with devotion and reverence. Nabu ground his hips down, settling between her legs as he began to explore her once more. His mouth was everywhere, trailing down her neck to her breasts, his hands cupping her ass and pulling her tighter to him.

Aika wanted to touch him more, to return the gentle caresses but she was losing herself in the lust that was rising within her. She could fell her empty pussy clench as she wrapped her legs around his waist and her arms around his neck.

His skin was soft, a startling contrast between the rock-hard strength of his muscles. It was just one more contrast between the two of them. She looked down and watched as her golden skin seemed to glow against his darker earth tones. Her body looked so slight, so delicate pressed to his that that itself was a turn on.

She couldn't believe it, but yes, here she was, Aika Fujioka, manga artist, part-time airline steward, Asian woman born in Akron, Ohio, who had a god for a lover who wanted to love her in return.

This was perfection.

"You are glorious," he murmured, running his hand down her leg and pulling it higher on his hip, pressing his cock against her wet slit.

Yes, she was slick and wet for him and wanted him inside her. She reached down and palmed him again, slowly working his cock, smiling as he shuddered and groaned into her neck. Heat was building between the two of them as he lifted his hands to cup her breasts, his thumb rubbing at her swollen nipples. Her god apparently was a breast man. He lifted her enough to get his mouth on her nipple and she hissed in pleasure, running her fingers over this scalp before drawing them down his back.

"You gonna let me eat you out again?" he asked, shooting her the nastiest look she had ever seen him give.

"Whatever you want," she purred, then gasped out loud as he immediately slipped his tongue into her body, his nose playing with her clit.

"Fuck, just like that," she gasped, her thighs clamping around his head to hold him there where he was making her dizzy with pleasure. "Nabu!"

"Say my name again," he pulled back to say before he was tonguing her clit and making her dance to his beat as he consumed her.

"Na -- Nabu," she whimpered as he slid two fingers into her hole, pressing up until he found her G-spot. "Fuck!"

He was going to make her come. She squeezed her eyes shut as he hummed in pleasure, the vibrations singing through her clit and sending a gush of heat from her body. Her eyes opened into slits as she watched him lift his fingers to his mouth and lick her glistening slick until his fingers were clean.

"Delicious." He smiled down at her before going to town in earnest, licking at her clit while his fingers worked her hungry hole.

"Nabu," she managed to gasp, and before she knew it, lights were flashing behind her eyes and her body was stiffening as she gave herself over to her first release. "So good…"

Then his hands were on her, spinning her around until she was on her knees, his hands pulling her hips high into the air as she presented a perfect target for his cock.

"How did I get so lucky?" he breathed as he covered her, his hands cupping her breasts, pinching and tugging at her nipples while he mouthed the back of her neck.

"You earned me." She giggled, though her laughter broke off as she felt him slide in close behind her, his cock head pressing against her labia before he pressed in, teasing at her clit. "No condom needed?" She gasped out the question even as she spread her thighs wide in invitation.

"Not unless you want them. I can't get you pregnant and I carry no human ailments."

"Good enough," she moaned, wiggling backward. "Get in me."

Her hunger had not abated with her earlier orgasm, and it was a fire that was again burning out of control.

Then she was whimpering, a bit sore from his earlier penetration, but it was a delicious sting that remained her of how empty she was.

"Nabu," she demanded. "Please --"

"You never have to beg," he cut her off as he carefully slid inside her.

Gods, the feeling of him splitting her open was sinful. She shuddered and whimpered, reaching back, trying to get him inside of her faster.

He started with a slow rhythm, pulling almost fully out before slowly swiping his hips on the grind in, awaking all her nerves in her body.

Electricity was zinging up and down her spine, and her thighs began to shake as she arched her ass up higher, wanting more friction more movement, more Nabu.

He began increasing his thrust, his thick cock spreading fire throughout her system. Before she knew it, she was slamming back, his hands on her hips and ass, slamming her backward into him.

The sounds he was making were just driving her desires higher as he began to lose himself in her.

"Aika -- Aika…" he was panting, breathing her name with each thought as he managed to always thrust into her, just trying to increase the sexual tension in her body.

She was whimpering, burying her head in the soft clouds as he worked her body over. Her eyes squeezed shut as she felt herself wind up tighter and tighter.

He was bent over her now, covering her, the heat of his chest making her feel possessed and treasured all at once.

"Gonna come," he finally gasped, and Aika was so out of it all she could do was grunt in encouragement. It was all she could do to prevent herself from collapsing under the sensual onslaught he was pressing on her body.

And she was almost there, she just needed… Oh God, his hand slid from her hip to between her thighs, his thumb circling her clit until she exploded.

"Nabu!" she wailed as she felt her body clamp down on his hard cock as lights exploded behind her eyes.

She felt him pull out and flip her over before he slammed deep in again, and she found herself screaming out in a fresh release even before the second one faded.

She managed to look up to see his face, lost in pleasure as he ground his hips deep, slamming into her as far as he could go before pulling out to slam into her again and again.

She was overly sensitive and loved the feel of him desiring her, seeking his own release within her. She threw her hips up, her legs around his waist, and raked her nails down his back.

"Aika!" he roared, her name echoing across the mountain as she felt his cock swell even further, felt the steaming heat of his own release fill her.

"Perfect," he was babbling. "My Aika. Fuck!"

He slowly collapsed onto her prone body, is hands pulling her head up to slam his mouth down on hers.

"Yes," she sighed as she kissed him back just as hard, releasing the taste of herself in his mouth even as he settled in beside her, pulling her close.

She could happily die here. This moment was perfect and the man who had given this to her was –

"Excuse me."

Epilogue

They both jumped as a voice from behind them caught their attention. In an instant the dragon appeared and was encircling them, a barrier of flame to protect them from the unknown thing that was all up in their business.

She looked at Nabu. Naked, he was on his feet, a sword of flame dancing in his hand. Protecting her.

"Whoa, there." The visitor threw up his hands in a manner that screamed defenseless, though even she could feel that wasn't true. "So jumpy." He shook his head, a long silky fall of dark hair dancing around his bare shoulders.

He was wearing some kind of beaded buckskin leather pants, and at his side hung… a pipe? Yeah, it kind of looked like an alto sax but much larger and with less brass, and it appeared to be made out of wood.

She looked up into his face and noted his Native American features and the muscular upper body… he was cute. but not god-of-wisdom cute.

"You!" Nabu's voice echoed through the mountain clearing, and she felt the weight of his word once more, though he came out of his defensive crouch. He was willing to fight off another for her, buck naked if he had to. Man, that was the basis for a good relationship.

"Me." The newcomer stepped back and offered a very Enk-like smile. Already he was giving her more reasons to dislike him other than destroying the afterglow. "I just wanted to check on you and see what you were up to so far away from the others."

"The other interfering god," Nabu grumbled.

"That would be me." He offered a little bow.

Okay, so he wasn't a crazy backwoods man who'd stumbled upon them while trapping his dinner. He was one of the gods. Some part of her told her to be very afraid -- the part with common sense, but another, larger part of her was fascinated. She wished she had a sketchpad. Naked, beautiful godlike people could start to be her new thing.

"Kokopelli at your service." He gave another deep bow before he rose to his full height, which rivaled that of Nabu's. "Glad to see you got off okay, and now I really want to know when you plan to get the hell off my mountain."

Mischief Managed (Sympathy For the Devil 5)
Stephanie Burke

Apollon, the stage name for the god of mischief Enk, only wants to get back to living his best life, but with fans out to find him, insane people trying to kill him, and Kokopelli, an even more persistent god of mischief, stalking him, the pale god can't catch a break.

Surviving is even harder for the god in hiding now that the FBI is asking questions about the plane crash, social media is amazed that the whole band Abadon survived, and their would-be killers are getting closer.

In the middle of all of this Enk discovers, despite his ominous past, even he can fall in love... which begs the question, can Mischief ever be managed?

Chapter 1

"So this is how we die," Sin grumbled. "Not in a bomb attack, not in a fiery plane crash, or even attack Chihuahuas... we drown in a sea of reporters."

Enk let out a chuckle as he stared at the hundreds of people staring back at them: screaming people, crying people, people carrying banners and holding signs and pushing against the human barrier of police and security that held them back.

He was about to say something clever about the dour nature of man when a figure tried to push through the lines, was actually allowed through, and came barreling towards them.

Sin suddenly dropped his Mr. Doubtful expression and pushed them aside to race toward the figure.

Orion gave one mighty leap and then he was in Sin's arms, hitting him with such force that Sin toppled back onto the tarmac with his lover straddling his waist.

The kiss Orion bestowed on him was almost pornographic and the reporters were eating it up.

Enk looked back at their ragtag group and didn't even bother to hold in a laugh. They were looking the worse for wear by design.

Dressed in tattered clothing and wrapped in metallic heating blankets, they all tried to convey a look of horror and relief instead of looking like they spent a week at a day spa. And it was hard because as plane crash survivors, they didn't really have it all that bad.

They'd had basically a hot tub, a decent amount of chicken, fresh air, sunshine, the intervention of divinity... more divinity than they thought they should have, really. Their stay had been made more pleasant -- and uncomfortable -- because of having yet another god in their midst. One too many maybe.

Enk thought back to the tall, dark-haired, self-proclaimed Lord of the Mountain and struggled to hold in another laugh lest he not be thought of as eccentric but just a mean jackass. But the whole "Get the Fuck off My Mountain" thing was kind of cute. Like the god of mischief who proclaimed it.

The new god had finally showed up for all of them. When Nabu and Aika wandered back into camp after the obvious fuck-fest they'd shared, Enk finally got an explanation for the power zinging toward him that had almost made him useless on this trip. They were on the property of another god of mischief, and this trickster was named Kokopelli. As soon as they told the rest what was up, Kokopelli appeared and demanded they leave.

"I want you off my mountain," Enk mocked, rolling his eyes at the unnecessary theatrics of the other god. No matter how hot he was, it was no excuse to be such an asshole.

"Oh, I'm sorry," he'd replied before anyone else could get a word in. "I didn't know this was protected territory when a bomb blew our plane out of the sky. So sorry to have inconvenienced you by surviving."

The black-eyed god just glared at him with his waist-length hair that was bobbed attractively in the front to frame his face, and the amazingly hot breechcloth that exposed some of the most muscular legs and calves that he had ever seen... and the brown leather moccasins on large feet--and you know what they say about men with large feet--and all the silver jewelry in the form of several pairs of earrings and those bicep cuffs and...

Okay, so he found the guy hot, but he was still an amazing asshole.

Then he had no further time for contemplation because the press was rushing them and demanding answers to their shouted questions, with their security barely able to hold them back. Finally Sin got off the ground with Orion and they were hustled into the air-conditioned comfort of the airport offices where they were to be bombarded with new questions from the FAA, the ATF, and all sorts of federal investigators from alphabet groups, all of which made him want to go back up on that mountain with the grumpy god.

Once they were all separated Enk found it hard to hold in his ire as he glared at the agents who were asking him the same questions over and over again.

"No, I have no idea who wants to blow us up," he snarled. "We only get a few dozen death threats a day… including that church and its insane followers, and the alt-right which is polite speak for Nazis. Did you go and question the Nazis, agents? I'm sure they may have a clue because they only threaten to kill us daily. Or how about some of those anti-gay groups that pop up like pimples on a teen? They are loads of fun and write the most intelligent correspondence like die fag, die."

"Are you gay, Mr. Apollon?" one bespectacled agent asked, and the rest of the room groaned.

"You do know this is being recorded, right, Specs?" he responded, narrowing his eyes at the man as he sucked at his fangs. "That you can get into all sorts of trouble for asking me that when it has nothing to do with your investigation, right? Unless you are in on it. Are you in on it, Agent Glasses? Did you help plant the bomb on the plane 'cause you hate the fags?" His words were hissed in a soft tone, a dangerous tone that many in the room recognized. "Do you think maybe a difference in lifestyle is a reason to murder someone like Major Tom?"

The recording was turned off and the baby agent rapidly hustled outside of the room while the others all but fell to their knees and sucked his dick to get him to accept an apology.

"I think we're done," he finally snapped as he rose to his feet. "You have no reason to detain me as I've answered your questions several times over without the appearance of my attorneys... much to their dismay. I am sure The Seven will be interested in what happened in this room. And until as such time as they contact you, I don't want to see any of you again."

No one stopped him as he made his way out of the room.

Now he was waiting in a VIP lounge, watching the reporters cluster from the vantage point of one-way glass. Sometimes it paid to be rich and famous.

"So, I take it we're here for a bit longer?" Charle asked as he moved beside the disgruntled man.

"California dreaming, living the life," Enk muttered shooting Charle a look before turning to stare back out at the gathered group.

"Well, bright lights, street magic," Nergal's lover chuckled. "Oh, and an extra special added conference just for us. I find that I am okay standing in the background and playing little traumatized lover. There has to be over four dozen news vans out there and that's not even getting into the roving reporters from social media. It's a circus."

"Well, we were thought to be dead." Abadon--as he was known when he was just the insanely popular frontman for their band instead of Nergal the god--leaned against the other side of the window. "We are like Lazarus coming from the pit to them. Some won't believe it and think it's a hoax or a damn good publicity stunt. Others will think it's a miracle and that we were saved for a purpose. All of them want to get a soundbite that will pay off their student loans."

"So, who's going to speak?" Enk asked, turning his attention fully to the room.

Nabu and Aika were sitting together on one of the leather sofas and Aika had a pencil in hand. The human was plucky, he decided as she looked up, saw him, and flipped him off. Good times.

He chuckled as Nabu nudged her and she gave him an apologetic look. Nabu reached up to tug at braids that were no longer there and substituted the gesture with a tug at his earring, but he kept smiling at his lover.

Orion was sitting on Sin's lap, swiping through an iPad. He was pointing out all the articles that had them pegged as victims of a conspiracy to wipe trans and gay people, plus their allies, off the face of the earth. And why not start with a world-famous band that represents everything they hate?

Sin was nodding attentively while running a gentle hand up Orion's back. The young man had hustled across the country to be with them after the press got several realistic photos of him looking devastated as he ran from the reporters. His "about damn time" comment to his lover made them all laugh. Orion knew they had survived, but had to put on a good act so the public wouldn't be too concerned when they made their triumphant return.

"I had to watch 'The Color Purple' and 'Imitation of Life' to be able to work up some real tears," he informed them. "You all now owe me for the trauma I had to subject myself to." Sin's kiss after that was enough to shut him up, but Orion did keep a digital scrapbook of all the news of their deaths and enjoyed teasing them with the damn thing.

Enk turned his eyes back to his brother and sighed, going back to sucking at his fangs. "I suppose it's going to have to be you and me? Or is it Nabu and I this go-round?"

"I think Nabu and you," Nergal said. "I'm going to be in the background comforting my lover and treating him like a prince after his harrowing adventures with us. I'll make a statement later. Sin is a no because he never deals well with the press. Glaring at them when they ask a stupid question doesn't help matters, and when you make the press look bad, they make you look bad. You and Nabu because you can sling shit like no one's business and it will make all the intolerant bastards look bad. You do know you look like the poster child for the Aryan nation, right? They all want to be Apollon."

"Fuck you, Nergal," Enk, who was Apollon for the band, muttered as Charle let out a gust of laughter that drew everyone's attention in the room. "I still get fan mail from those bastards and it really pisses me off. Not my fault I can't tan."

"Meanwhile I'll cuddle my little black bunny and make him feel all safe right behind you." Nergal's smile was menacing. "That'll piss a few of them off."

"I'll wear my trans pride T-shirt if that helps stir up some shit," Orion added. "Mom will be so proud. We have matching shirts. I'm sure she'll wear hers in solidarity."

"I can get up front," Aika added. "It's been a while since I heard the term 'yellow fever' but I know some asshole's gonna bring it up. Plus, this will be good for my sales numbers. I know artists are worth more after they've died, but a resurrection? Yeah, I'm gonna work this good." She looked around at all of their stunned, silent faces. "What? Why shouldn't I cash in on this tragedy? It's worth its weight in gold."

"Never let her meet The Seven," Nergal intoned and the others solemnly agreed.

"And I'm sure the world will be wild to know about my hair cut... it'll make a stunning story, I'm sure," Nabu added dryly, "where I can be the dashing hero for once and not the uppity Negro who should be rapping or acting security."

"Oh, I know that very well." Charle snickered. "What do we know about metal anyway? That's white boy music."

"Or hair," Nabu laughed. "Because obviously mine

was fake. That's why The Seven made me do that photo shoot with my hair down in the pool."

"The Seven?" Aika asked, curiosity obviously piqued.

"Our lawyers-slash-managers," Enk explained, turning to look at her. "Look, if anyone gives you any hassle, like these agents, tell them that you are represented by The Seven and they should leave you alone. I had to invoke their name when they asked me if I was gay."

"What the fuck?" Nergal growled and reached out to grip his shoulder.

"They didn't ask you?" Enk asked, looking around the room at the shocked faces.

"They apologized," he added. Then a mischievous smile spread across his lips, showing his fangs. "I think I know the sound bite I'm gonna give them."

* * *

"Prejudice, racism, anti-gay rhetoric, and transphobia nearly murdered us all and the only thing you ask about is about our sex lives?" Apollon, with his deep gravelly voice, was in full drama-lama mode as he stared out at the press. He sneered, showing his fangs as he locked eyes with the reporter who asked such a trite question. True to form, he all but snatched the mic from Nabu, who was about to go off on the reporter who'd said something about Aika being a secret lover they snuck on the plane. Now silence filled the room as they all stared at Apollon, shocked that he'd even suggest such a thing.

Yeah, right.

"You want to know who we were fucking... the agents inside wanted to know if I was gay, like that has any bearing on someone planting a bomb on our fucking plane, and you have the audacity to question us about sex when there are people out there who tried to murder us and did murder another, because our lifestyle doesn't fit their agenda… or our values are different from theirs, or because we don't hold the same opinions about stupid bullshit that this country seems to thrive on. Instead of asking why, who, what, and when, you want to ask me who I'm sticking my dick in. If you need to know so fucking badly, then nobody. I have not currently nor have I recently been sticking my dick in anything other than my left hand." He ignored the shocks and gasps and the faint buzz he was feeling and lifted the hand in question to wiggle it at the reporters. The Locusts in the back roared in approval.

"So now that that question is answered, maybe you might want to look into who is trying to murder us and apparently any innocent people around us, like poor Major Tom, our pilot. You remember him? Wife at home, father of three, dead for no reason. Until you start asking the right questions, fuck off."

Nergal moved to the front, easing Enk aside and took the mic from his hand.

He glared at the reporters and those watching at home with the same steely-eyed stare that had made grown men piss their pants on the battlefield.

"No further questions." His voice, not as deep as Enk's but just as powerful, resonated across the tarmac where the press conference had been established, driving all voices into silence.

Then as if planned, he spun on his heel and walked out, reaching out to snag Charle's hand as he passed. The others fell in line with their partners, leaving Enk the last one to exit the platform.

As he shot one last sneer at the gathered reporters who were still quite shell-shocked, he saw something that gave him pause.

Standing front and center just next to a reporter with round glasses… where he hadn't been before… was a tall, long-haired man with rich, ochre-colored skin, a smile that sent tingles down his spine, and dressed in a pair of linen chinos, ears encrusted with silver jewelry. Enk almost stumbled when the man winked at him and wiggled his left hand.

Apollon damn near ran from the platform, the buzz of energy zapping him, making him breathless and giggly.

Kokopelli was here. For the very life of him, he couldn't imagine why, but he was damn sure about to find out.

"Thank God we got a house," Enk rumbled to Nabu as they lounged in the entertainment room of the six-bedroom house they were renting for their extended stay in LA. The home in Pacific Palisades hung off of a mountain with a huge infinity pool out back, an equally huge deck that butted up against a flora-filled sheer drop off to the ocean, a private, six-car garage, and had the extra added benefit of about a hundred tall, bushy trees between them and their neighbors. The Seven had hooked them up nicely indeed.

Once everyone took possession of the place, Nergal and Charle disappeared into their chosen room and hadn't come down since. Thank goodness these rooms were better soundproofed than any at the hotels they stayed in or Enk would have been tempted to gag them both and hide the keys to the locks.

Sin and Orion were probably in the pool, hopefully doing nothing that would force them to chlorinate it later. Or they could be in the hot tub, but the location didn't matter. The two just wanted some quiet time together to giggle at how stupid the rest of humanity was and to finalize Orion's move to their island home.

Aika was in the room she and Nabu were going to share, fielding phone calls from her family and assuring them that she was still alive and kicking. And yes, she was dating the huge, pretty black man she was cuddling on camera. No, they had not been dating long and yes, she was going to be dating a rock star. Enk could hear her try to explain everything to her mother, who was understandably freaking out. Nabu, being the bright god of wisdom that he was, came down to the entertainment room to take cover.

And now they both were watching their press conference on the television with all the beautiful beeps in place to protect the delicate public from their profane language.

"Do you think they got my good side?" Nabu snickered. "I think they got my good side."

Enk answered, "I think they only started in on me because you called that one reporter an insensitive prick for talking about how awful it was that all your hair got burned off as a black man even if you're still kind of hot."

"I believed I called her an insensitive bitch and asked her why the color of my skin had anything to do with me almost dying. I know Aika said some unflattering things to her in Japanese because the only thing she knows how to do in that language is curse. I told her I'd help her remember more. She hasn't spoken it since she was a child."

Enk cocked his head. "I think Faux News just called us indecent human beings that they wouldn't welcome into their home."

"I think that's a high compliment coming from those assholes," Nabu said and laughed. "What did CNN say?"

"That they were shocked and appalled by our language but even more shocked and appalled by the reporters' questions and how the FBI and the FAA treated us. At least they asked about the bomb."

"How are you feeling, though?" Nabu turned to him. "I know it wasn't fun being on another god's turf. His energy seems to be as old as the friggin' planet. At least it's about as old as ours, and that's saying something."

"He gave me a buzz, the bastard," Enk grumbled. "I'm glad he directed the search party in our direction but I could've done with less of his sass when he was showing his ass. I'm still feeling the shock."

"I think it's because you switched your godhands of power, Enk. If you were still a god of creation, I don't think it would have affected you as much."

"Maybe," he frowned but offered his friend a smile.

"But I like who I am right now, Nabu. I wouldn't have my godhand back if you paid me in life points. I am much more comfortable dealing with mischief even when it lays me out on my ass."

"I think he was confused by how deeply his mischief affected you."

"I think he was an asshole. Did you see him at the press conference?"

"He was there?"

Enk nodded. "With a smile on his face, standing in the front row. Charming."

"I wonder what he wants."

"Who the fuck knows?" Enk rolled his eyes. "But we're off his mountain so he should be leaving us the hell alone."

"I think he's intrigued by you."

"I think you're pussy-whipped." He ducked when Nabu threw a pillow at him. The leather sectional they were currently lounging across was heaped with the things. "What? I speak the truth."

"I think you're about as big a prick as he was. Maybe it's a mischief thing."

"I think that you want everyone to be in love like you are," Enk countered, throwing himself at his brother, laughing as they began to wrestle, tossing pillows everywhere. "'Cause everybody needs somebody sometimes --"

"Maybe I was just worried about you," Nabu countered, reversing their position so that he was on top of the pale god, pushing his hands over his head and getting in his face. "Call me crazy, but I'm concerned about you."

"Don't be." Enk laughed, bucking up, trying to dislodge him. "I'll be fine. I'm always fine. And as the oldest out of all of you --"

"Hey!" Nabu flicked a finger and a small burst of

power stung him on the nose.

"Okay," Enk, still chuckling, corrected. "As nearly the oldest out of all of you, I'm the one most likely not to be whipped by the genitalia of my love partner." He then proceeded to make a cracking whip sound until Nabu picked up a pillow and slammed it into his face.

They were still rolling around the huge couch, laughing, when the gong that was their doorbell sounded.

"Since we're at an unknown location, it may be the FBI again." Enk sobered as he crawled away from Nabu, his usual sleek hair a wild platinum rat's nest about his head. "I'll go and scare them off with my disgraceful unidentified sexuality."

"They may know something about the bomber," Nabu pointed out, rising to his feet to begin putting the pillows back. The gong rang again. "It may be good information. Stranger things have happened."

"What good information do you know comes knocking unexpectedly at your door at ten at night?" Enk paused to ask before a slight giggle escaped his throat. "Unless it's a pizza delivery guy with the wrong address. I think a lot of porn starts that way."

"Just answer the door." Nabu laughed, reaching up to tug at his missing hair and hastily tugging at his ear again. "It may be important..." He trailed off as he tilted his head to the side. "What the --"

"Fuck," Enk snarled, before he giggled and took off running.

He reached the front door just as the gong rang again and flung the damn thing open.

"What the fuck do you want?" he demanded and held back a frustrated snarl as none other than Kokopelli was found standing on their doorstep.

"As your friend stated, you intrigue me," the other god responded with a grin as he ran his hands through his loose hair. "I love the new look, by the way. It's very… well I wouldn't say hipster but something close to the opposite of that. Mind if I come in?"

The door slamming in his face was his answer.

"Was it something I said?" Kokopelli called out, and Enk crossed his arms and waited. There had to be some reason for the trickster god to have followed them here and he wasn't letting him inside with his family until he discovered the reason why.

* * *

"FBI?" Nabu asked, walking around the corner, pausing at the incensed look on Enk's face.

"I wish."

"You wished for the return of the assholes who made your life a living hell?"

"Yours too."

"Yeah," Nabu agreed. "But as a black man living in today's climate, I'm very used to dealing with all kinds of assholes who like to try and prove their balls are bigger than mine. So what's got you wishing for such ignorance at our doorstep?"

"Kokopelli." Enk glared at the amused look on his brother's face.

"What?"

"Koko-fucking-pelli. He just rang the bell."

"He found you."

"Us. He found us and I want to know why."

"Well, you'll never find out if you slam the door in his face."

Enk was still not amused.

"He wanted us off his mountain, we're off, and now he's following us? I wonder what he's up to? What the hell did we do to offend the god of the mountain… except survive?"

"He didn't feel angry, Enk, just disturbed. Confused. And he made sure we got off the mountain safely. Maybe he's just interested in what happened or maybe who caused the crash."

"And now he's here instead of fucking with the FBI or the FAA? I don't think so, Nabu. He wants something from us."

"From you, maybe." Nabu chuckled and Enk shot him the evilest look he could. "I don't feel any interest in him for the rest of us."

"Can't you flex your might and discover what the hell he wants?"

"You know it doesn't work that way with other gods," Nabu said. "I can feel if his intent is to do harm, and it isn't. I can get that he is curious, but it is all singular and directed at one person. Congratulations. You have a stalker."

"What the fuck is wrong with him?" Enk grumbled, moving back to the entertainment room and hopefully some mind-numbing diversion from the haunted fish tank. "Out of all the gods roaming around..."

"There aren't that many of us left," Nabu pointed out, reclaiming his seat and snatching up the remote before Enk could grab it. "And I don't think his interest runs into offing other gods. He could have attempted that on his mountain, and as that mountain is his power base we would have had a hard time stopping him."

"So why follow us?"

"Maybe he was entranced by your deep blue eyes?" Nabu laughed, flipping through stations until he came across some reality show.

There was a man making love to his car. Really, he was fully dressed but he was humping it hard, caressing it with sweaty palms that made smears across the pale blue paint job, licking the back window and fogging up the glass.

Both Enk and Nabu tilted their heads to the side, trying to understand what they were seeing before Enk shook his head and got back to the matter at hand.

"He didn't get close enough to see the color of my eyes," he continued with their conversation. "He just bellowed he wanted us gone and *boom*, here comes a rescue worker who followed a hunch to find us."

"After you talked trash to him. And then the circus started. But you forget, Enk, your eyes glowed. When we appeared back at the campsite, I saw your eyes were glowing because you could feel his energies. Don't deny it. It's something, after all, that you two have in common."

"If he wanted to get to know me he could have asked and I could have told him to fuck off right then and there."

"But he didn't, you didn't, and I think he's interested in you."

"I can't have that." Enk shook his head. "I just want to be left alone."

"And you know we rarely get what we want in life. Most of us just barely managed to hold on enough to find a reason to exist. And we found our perfect partners. Maybe The Fates have that in store for you."

"Fuck The Fates," Enk snapped, turning to glare at Nabu. "And I have no reason to seek a reason to exist. I'm so fucking awesome that the rest of you should be able to feed off my aura for years."

"Until The Fates you want to fuck send you someone who's more than a match for you, you stubborn ass. Maybe finally The Fates want to make up for what you were forced to leave behind. And what better way than with a brand-new lover? You know, the best way to get over a lover is to get under a new one --"

"Isn't your girlfriend calling you?" Enk interrupted him.

"No. She's still arguing with her mother."

With a snap of his fingers, Enk sent the nearest cell phone tower crashing to a halt... along with the power to the whole neighborhood.

"Well, now she isn't." He grinned when they both could hear Aika cursing like a sailor from the bedroom she shared with Nabu.

"You really are a dick," Nabu grumbled, rising to his feet to go calm Aika down.

"And I hope you know what to do with yours to keep her happy and rampage-free."

He chuckled softly as the collective irritation from the neighborhood gave him a jolt of power. Nabu flipped him off before exiting the room.

"I just want to be left alone," he muttered out loud to himself. "I'm doing just fine on my own.

He didn't believe in fate. And if he thought he heard laughter, it was probably just noise from Nergal and Charlie's rooms.

Those two had the most interesting love lives…

Yes, that's all that laughing noise was. Charlie and Nergal getting it on.

He even ignored the shiver that went down his spine. He was fine. They were fine. Everything was just fine.

* * *

I can't do this anymore…
I'm done keeping score
Damn all your questions and your apologies
Your hang-ups ain't got shit to do with me

I can't do this anymore…
What the hell am I fighting for
This is more than a battle between us
This is outright war
And baby, I can't do this anymore.

Kokopelli listened as the deep, gravelly voice sang into the night, the lyrics haunting him just a little. Enk was sitting on the balcony, head tossed back, pouring his soul out in his lyrics. Kokopelli had to admit to himself one of the reasons he had followed these beings out of his home and back into civilization had been his curiosity about the blond one.

Enk really didn't seem... right was not the correct term at all. He seemed different than the rest, leashed-- like he had diminished himself.

Kokopelli had been around for a number of years, and never had he felt a force like the four beings working together when they saved the humans in the plane that crashed. It was stunning to feel and had awoken him from a dead slumber, but it was the actions of the one called Apollon that drew his intent the most.

He could read the energy used and knew that that one had actively contributed less to the rescue operation but appeared so powerful that he could have brought the plane down safely on his own. Yet he had only supplemented the energies of the others, bolstering them to allow them to do their tasks. When the humans were safe and he acceded to the female's wishes, he felt the waves of mischief that would have only bolstered his energy levels but had sent Enk spinning off in a spiral of energy that he could barely control.

And now, three days after he'd had the door slammed in his face, Kokopelli still didn't have answers to his questions.

The others were amused by Enk's stubborn insistence not to speak to him. They had even come out and thanked him for assisting with keeping them fed, though they mentioned they could have done without the canine intervention.

They were curious, but once assured he wasn't out to harm him, they just let him be, too involved with their human lives and maintaining their secrets to pay him any attention.

Now here he was, camping out in the trees near their

chosen home, becoming more and more intrigued as he observed this fellow god.

Enk was mysterious but very protective of his chosen family. He was beautiful in a cold, aristocratic way, an untouchable ice prince who was as pale as he was stubborn.

Now listening to that voice boom, Kokopelli felt a growing sense of helplessness from the emotion evoked by his song.

Unable to help himself, he pulled out his favorite duduk, his Armenian flute, and began to play an accompaniment to the mournful music, adding emphasis to the words that Enk sang, highlighting the sense of loneliness and gloom.

His fellow mischief-maker paused for a moment before he picked up where he left off, singing with even more power and emotion, if that was possible.

As the last words trailed away, Kokopelli stepped forward out of the trees to look up at the balcony where Enk sat alone.

Kokopelli stared up at the other god, entranced by the moonlight reflecting off his pale skin and white hair. He resembled his past, when gods with immense power walked the face of the earth proudly, caring for and disciplining humanity as they needed.

Bright blue eyes stared down at him, and he opened his mouth to speak when a splash of cold doused him from head to toe. He sputtered, nearly choking as the unknown liquid burned his eyes and instantly turned his favorite leathers into a cold heavy weight that wanted to drag him to his knees.

He swiped at his eyes and stared up in disbelief as Enk looked down at him, snickering in amusement as the… chicken soup? He had been doused in gallons of cold chicken soup? What the hell!

He didn't even realize he screamed that until Enk

answered, nearly choking on his laughter.

"Get the fuck off your mountain? That's what you said to us? You're a rude, insensitive prick and I don't think I like you... despite how well you play."

"So," he called back, amused despite himself. The god was holding onto a huge grudge. "You like the way I play?"

"You're an asshole!" Enk called back in a sing-song tone. "It doesn't matter how good you are on that thing."

"So you think I'm good?"

"What the fuck do you want? You wanted us off your mountain and so we're off. Now you come sniffing around here --"

Enk's words stuttered to a halt as Kokopelli flexed his magic and flew through the air. Within seconds he was on Enk's balcony, in his face, cold wet noodles dripping from his hair, a carrot slice behind one ear.

"I want my questions about you answered," he purred, enjoying the look of shock on Enk's face.

The blond's blue eyes went wide for a moment, then narrowed with intent.

Before Kokopelli could make another move, there was a rush of wind and he felt something grip his hair.

He let out a yelp, though he would never admit it to anyone, and found himself flipping backward over the balcony, only to fly about twenty feet until he splashed into the deep end of the infinity pool.

Looked like Enk had some magic of his own to flex.

"And clean my fucking pool!" he called back as Kokopelli kicked his feet to pull himself to the surface of the water despite wearing what now felt like twenty tons of leather. "I don't think my filter will like chicken chunks."

Treading water, Kokopelli began to laugh as a shaft of mischievous energy struck him in the chest. "I take this to mean you like me a little?" he called back. Even from this distance, he could see the smirk on Enk's face, and his shoulders shook as he held in a laugh.

"Now why on earth would you think that?"

"You tossed me to the pool and not the concrete!" he called back, genuinely delighted.

Enk flipped him off before he turned and made his way back into the house, slamming the door behind him with a wave of his hand.

Enk was getting more and more interesting, Kokopelli thought. He not only felt of mischievous energy, there was something else there too... something powerful but muted.

It only served to interest him more. What was going on with the handsome man? He was going to stick around until he found out.

* * *

"Romeo, oh Romeo --"

"Shut it," Enk grumbled and the rest of his assembled family burst out laughing.

"I can't believe you threw the soup!" Aika managed while trying not to fall out of her chair. "I made that to cheer you up!"

"It worked." Enk grinned widely, showing off his fangs. "Oh how it worked. I'm feeling so much better now."

It was becoming a joke with them, the god of mischief who left his mountain home to stalk him in the hills of California. Only... he wasn't laughing much.

"Why don't you just talk to him?" Orion offered from his perch on Sin's lap. Sometimes he felt that they had a kinky Daddy thing going but Sin was quick to assure them that wasn't it at all. Sin just liked Orion's weight on his person, especially in the shower -- which was something Enk really didn't need to know about.

"I -- don't know," Enk finally admitted. "Maybe I think he needs to learn to ask instead of demand."

"I thought he asked that first night." Charle leaned closer to him from where they were all gathered in Enk's room, arrayed on the many pillows that surrounded his fireplace in the seating area. "When you slammed the door in his face --"

"He demanded, like he demanded we get off of his mountain."

"To be fair," Nergal interjected from where he was plastered to Charle's side and Enk just hoped they didn't start going at it in his room -- "we were in his seat of power."

"That's no reason to be an ass." Enk sniffed.

"You're always an ass." Aika dimpled up at him and he sneered in return. They didn't really hate each other; they'd learned over the past few days that they loved needling each other up. When you found someone who could give as good as they got, it almost became a challenge of one-upmanship. So far Aika was winning due to a weird sketch she had put on her website about living with rock gods who were glorified babies… well, at least one of them.

"I have invited many gods into my temples," Enk informed her archly. "Some in need of healing and some in need of correction, and yet I have never treated one so inhospitably before, even within my seat of power."

"You threw me out when we first met," Sin pointed out.

"You brought floods and I had just had the temple floor cleaned."

"It was the rainy season."

"Semantics." Enk sniffed, waving a hand as he took a seat on a huge pillow closest to the fireplace.

"You know," Aika interjected, "I have never heard of a god named Enk. What are you god of, precisely?"

"Mischief and mayhem," Enk answered brightly. "And don't you forget it."

"And you had a temple?" she continued with her questioning.

"All of us had a temple at one point or another. Some of us still do."

Aika, Orion, and Charle froze at that.

"You... you have a temple?" Charle turned to his lover Nergal, excitement in his eyes. "I wanna see."

"Most of my temples were destroyed a long time ago," he admitted. "Though some of them haven't been discovered yet and no, we are not going to go and visit them. The last thing I need is for someone to start saying how Abadon is starting to believe that he really is a god. I am sure that will go over well with the church set."

"Even more so than your blatant bisexuality, use of drugs and alcohol, and all those demonic tattoos," Charle teased.

"You forgot to mention my uppity black homosexual lover who is the progenitor of fake news and the nail in my coffin holding me in my hand basket to hell." Nergal nodded sagely.

"Hand basket to Hell... good song title." Nabu laughed as Aika elbowed him. "What?" he asked. "Too AC/DC?"

"Just a touch, yeah," she snickered. "But as the only straight one in the band --"

"I've had male lovers," Nabu corrected.

"How could I forget? And as hot as I think that is... and you are going to have to tell me about your hook-up with that British actor..."

"My lips are sealed... but I can give you details with the names omitted to protect the guilty --"

"Awesome, and I want every detail, but that's not the point. They consider you the only straight one in the band and that's good even if you're black, they say... and they're confused about Enk."

"What?" Enk sat up and honed in on Aika.

"Confused about me? They've reported on my lovers in the past."

"But you are like their Aryan poster child gone astray," Charle said. "You would not believe the questions they ask me about you that get stuck in the crazy person file. Some KKK motherfucker even wanted us to know that you are their perfect mole and when activated you will kill us all in our sleep and bathe in our blood because of all the gay sex and fraternizing with the impure."

Enk stared at him for a full minute before he exploded in laughter.

"No, what? Really?" he shouted, throwing back his head and laughing so hard tears ran down his face. "This... This is what I get for... for asking The Seven to keep that shit away from me?" he roared. "Aryans? Really?"

"Although the guy who wrote it mentioned butt sex so much, I think he has a major crush on you."

And that sent him off again until he rolled off his pillow and was choking for lack of breath.

"After all that," Nabu snickered, "maybe an infatuated god who shares your godhand isn't that bad."

"All things considered," Enk agreed, calming at last as everyone gathered themselves and prepared to go to their own rooms.

"I did like the flute though," Sin added as he rose to his feet, never losing his hold on Orion, who just turned and wrapped his arms and legs around his lover as if the show of strength was a huge turn on for him. "It blended well with your voice. You should sing more."

"And you know why I don't." Enk sighed as he rose to his feet.

"Still, think about it," Nabu added. "With us doing Nergal's ballad for Charle and changing up our style a little, it could be an awesome thing."

"Do I look like The Edge to you?" Enk snorted. "Every once in a while popping up to do a solo to prove I can do it? I think not."

"I feel numb," Aika sang as she followed Nabu out of the room. Charle and Nergal said nothing, too involved in staring into each other's eyes as they also left the room. "Oh, ohhh oh!"

"Fuck you very much," Enk called back and snorted as Aika began to cackle.

With his growing family gone, Enk settled back on his pillow and flicked his fingers at the cold fireplace. Within seconds, he had a low fire burning as he settled in to contemplate his life.

He had no temples left that could be considered seats of power. He made sure he destroyed them all when he--

Cutting off that thought he just sat quietly and stared into the flames, contemplating his life and what he had done to survive, what he had sacrificed…

Well, it really wasn't an unwilling sacrifice, was it? And his life was so much richer now.

So lost in thought was he that he didn't even notice the slow, mournful notes from a flute echoing softly in the night, lulling him into sleep.

Chapter 3

"Follow me till you love me," Enk grumbled under his breath as he stared from the glass window of the pub he was currently sitting in, out at the faces that tried to peer into the darkened glass, cameras at the ready.

He'd only wanted to get out of the house for a little while--there were too many lovey-dovey relationship things going on and he needed a break. He managed to slip out of the neighborhood without anyone being the wiser as to who he was. He could change his appearance like the others but for him it took a lot of effort and concentration so he relied on subterfuge.

The Seven put them up in such an exclusive area because the security was so good and paps weren't allowed to troll the area. So it was nothing for him to braid his hair into a single tail, slide it under his shirt, toss on a hat, and drive his nondescript but bitchin' Camaro into the market area to have a little alone time.

The problem was his damn voice.

He silently made it through two shops, looking for the perfect jewelry to fit his despondent mood; he even considered getting another piercing at some bougie upscale overpriced place when he stopped to ask the tattooist a question. He was considering a tongue ring, *really* considering getting some form of body modification that he could control, when a patron recognized his voice.

"It's you," the wide-eyed jail-bait had gasped, whipping out a phone and starting to record before he could even blink. Man, the youth of today might not be all that impressive intellectually in some eyes but they could work a mighty fast recording device.

"It's always been me," he spoke in a low voice, hoping not to attract any more attention but the young bitch opened her mouth and squealed.

"And, I'm out," he called to the tattooist, who was

torn between looking excited and angry that his own privacy policy about disruption was being flouted... but way too excited because he could see dollar signs for business recognition and product placement...

Yeah, he had to get out of there fast.

Spinning around, he swiftly walked -- no matter what the footage showed, he did not run -- to the nearest dark space that would not allow an overly excited teenage brat who had no sense of discretion--and the crowd she was gathering--to follow.

Enk ran to the nearest pub. And now here he sat in a dark corner, ignoring the looks the other patrons were shooting him, the nervousness of the waiter, the huge grin of the manager as he called in extra security to limit the number of people who suddenly wanted a beer at nine in the morning, and the scowling bartender who had to keep up with the demand for libations from people who just wanted to be close to the mega star who had just cheated death.

Fuck. His. Life.

He was contemplating how to make it out the back without notice and calculating how fast he would have to run to make it to his car given its distance from the pub, when the chair in front of him was pulled out and a heavy body dropped into it.

"Hello, gorgeous."

"And the last thing I would ever need just sat down," he grumbled, looking up into the grinning face of one of the last beings he ever wanted to see. Remembering his fantasy, he held in a blush. "Of all the dives in the whole of this town you just happened to walk into mine."

He felt the buzz of mischief energy as Kokopelli grinned at him, showing all his perfect white teeth. "You are hard to miss."

"But did you try? Did you really, really try?" The

sarcasm was thick with him that day and now he had a target to take out his ire on.

"Not really," he offered as he rested both elbows on the table and propped his chin in his hands as he examined Enk. "I see no reason to hide the fact that I was following you. I do feel the need to explain."

"Really?" Enk grumbled, feeling his temper rise. "Today of all days when I am trapped in this place by those idiots outside? Today is the day you decide to come clean with me?"

He sat back in his chair and spread his arms wide, ignoring the buzz of conversation that picked up when he didn't immediately call for security to remove the dark-haired stranger. Someone tried to pull up a cell phone for some quick video, but a member of the security staff quickly stood in their way, blocking the camera access.

"Well, I'm all ears." He stared Kokopelli right in his big brown eyes and waited.

"I wanna get next to you--"

"Yes, I know. You proved that by stalking the hell out of me."

"Yeah, that was a bit… high handed --"

"You think?"

"But," he continued as if Enk wasn't rolling his eyes at him, "I had good reason. Something about you tripped my magic and I had to discover what it was. I think I finally have."

"Oh, and what is it that you think you know?"

"While you were within my seat of power, I noticed that you have no natural ability to regulate any energy from our shared godhand."

Enk blinked at him and sucked at his fangs, but said nothing, waiting for the other god to continue.

"And that you feel… incomplete, I guess is the best way to describe it. You feel incomplete or not fully developed. My energies want to seek out and help fill that void or repair that damage or --"

"So you want to fix me?" Enk interrupted, knowing that the hissed words came out harsher than he intended, but the huge flash of fear nearly made him faint. This god was too close to the truth. Energy bounced through his body, making him shake before he could get it under control once more. "There is nothing wrong with me, *Loco*pelli. You're crazy as hell if you think for one damn moment --"

"There it is again," the other god interrupted him as he leaned in closer. His brown eyes began to swirl gold and green and Enk realized that though his seat of power was hundreds of miles away, the man still could use the mountains as a connection and a conduit of his power. "That feeling that something inside of you is twisted -- no, forced. Your power was originally not your own but you adopted it and adapted it to suit your needs. Only a powerful god could do that, Enk. And it's really odd that in all the pantheons I studied, I have never run across a god named Enk."

Enk lurched to his feet and took two steps away from the table. His gaze tore around the room desperately before looking back into those brown, swirling eyes. He had to get out. He felt trapped. Suddenly the dark wasn't such a generous friend that helped him hide; suddenly it felt more like a trap.

Ignoring the noise that picked up with his movement, the late security guys that were headed in his direction, the concerned look on the bar manager's face, he spun in a circle, eyes wide in terror.

He had to get out.

Almost blindly, he headed for the swinging doors that led to the back kitchen. There were laws against exiting through the kitchen, right? Safety rules and all that, right? Right.

He had a destination in mind and some of the fight-

or-flight panic receded as he moved.

Waiters, staff, cooks, they all got out of his way as he barreled through to the back. He ignored the sudden bright light and smell of grease and garlic that permeated the kitchen as he looked around for a back door.

The exit sign caught his attention and in a flash, he was moving through the back door.

It swung open with a metallic *clang,* and the smell of the dumpster teased his nostrils as he moved through the wet alley toward the main street.

"There he is!" someone screamed, and Enk looked around wildly, hair flying in his face and obscuring his view for a moment before the masses began to descend.

There were screaming crying fans, reporters with microphones to shove in his face, women with great swords tattooed on their bodies, people shouting obscenities at him, men praising him, and a single sharp shaft of mischief energy so powerful it nearly brought him to his knees -- just like what had happened before the plane crash.

He could not hold back the uncontrollable laugh that rolled from his throat as he was surrounded. Cell phones were in his face, reporters followed, microphones in hand and the bright lights of their cameras blinding him, and he wanted them all to go *away*. He wanted to scream that there was danger, to flee, to get himself somewhere safe but that shaft of energy held him immobile.

The energy came harder, nearly knocking him over, and he knew that this life as a rock god was about to come to an end. Someone was going to kill his body and there was nothing he could do. An overload of power -- no, this wasn't mischief, this was chaos, keeping him vulnerable and defenseless and he...he was going to die.

He closed his eyes, really all he had full control over doing, when the shot rang out.

He wanted for the bullet to tear into his flesh, to end

this existence, but instead of pain, the hard, wet, filthy concrete came up to meet his face.

There were screams as people began to run and duck behind garbage cans and dumpsters; the reporters were shouting and madness erupted all around them.

Enk lifted up his head, his now filthy wet, white hair staining his face, and darkness suddenly covered him.

"Stay down!" a familiar voice shouted and then there were still more screams as he was lifted to his feet as easily as if he was weightless, and then hands were pulling him through the screaming throngs of people.

He rallied as he tried to keep moving on his feet. A jacket had been tossed over his head, and a powerful calloused hand was gripping his. He could no longer smell the garbage and the stink of fear and humanity that had nearly overwhelmed him.

"This way!" the voice shouted again, and Enk used his free hand to push the jacket back far enough to see Kokopelli in front of him, waving his hands and creating mayhem before and behind them.

Boxes were exploding, plants were falling off of stands, bikes went flying into the paths of those who gave chase, a flock of seagulls swooped down out of nowhere and began blessing those following… and by blessing, he meant that they were shitting on heads and cameras.

Police sirens were ringing in the distance as they raced down another street, some followers still hot on their trail.

Damn! Some of those people must be experts in parkour, he thought, trying not to giggle as he watched photographers and paps duck, jump, and dive around, under, and over obstacles that were thrown into their paths.

As they neared the end of the street, he could hear the loud clomping of horse hooves as a beautiful palomino came seemingly out of nowhere and began racing beside him.

Rescue? Really? He was going to be whisked away on a horse by a Native American deity?

No. The horse, still outfitted in its formal dressage, turned and began racing towards the followers, scattering them like bowling balls hitting pins.

He was jerked to a stop as Kokopelli stopped at one of the largest, most bad-assed looking bikes he had ever seen. The monster was a solid matte black with silver accents. That had to be a car tire on the back and the tank up front was fucking massive. The front forks were fucking pillars, the fairings were designed to look nearly like a screaming face in the front, the front fenders nearly nonexistent. This monster of a bike was designed for speed or cruising at its master's whim.

Kokopelli all but threw him on the bitch seat before he climbed on front. Enk felt a small shaft of energy flow through the metallic monster, and then they were roaring down the street.

Enk squeaked and grabbed onto Kokopelli's waist as he buried his face in the man's broad back, the stores and cars around them blurring.

Even with the jacket tucked between them, Enk could feel the power in the body of the god riding before him, feel his energy as they streaked down streets and up hills, could feel the magnetic pull of this being's energy.

And the powers-that-be help them all, he could feel an empty part of him, the part that he had ignored or tried to fill with drink and sex and sarcasm, throb to be filled by this god.

Then there was the mother of all erections that was pressing uncomfortably against the seam of his pants.

His magic wanted him. His body wanted him. Kokopelli was delving into secrets best left alone, and Enk's body wanted him.

Enk whimpered as he realized he was in real trouble.

He lifted his head as Kokopelli's dark laughter ran over him as they sped away, cutting through traffic like it was standing still, heading back toward his house. Power and control...

Yeah, he was in deep trouble.

Chapter 4

"So... now you are trending."

Those were the first words out of Nergal's mouth as he pulled up in front of the house.

The gates had scarcely closed and he was still trying to devise a way of climbing off of the back of the bike and hiding his erection in the borrowed jacket when Nergal appeared seemingly out of nowhere.

The look in his eyes was... dangerous. His arms were crossed over his chest, emphasizing the tattoos on the bulging muscles of his arms, his stance wide and protective, his eyes containing barely leashed anger. Worst of all, Charle was not at his side. This was the dangerous god of destruction, and he was in full-out protector mode.

Kokopelli, for all his shenanigans, realized that he had entered dangerous territory. He gave Nergal a respectful nod while maintaining his stance. It was more of an acknowledgment of power than any giving away of authority, and for some strange reason, Enk found that incredibly hot.

"Trending?" Enk swallowed his arousal and gracefully slid from the back of the bike, managing to keep Kokopelli's jacket before him. He considered it a win.

"On Instagram, on Twitter, on Facebook, on MySpace --"

"Do people even use MySpace anymore?" he interrupted, looking puzzled. Really? Had the Internet come full circle when he wasn't watching?

"Apparently," Nergal grumbled. "Someone has an illegal download of Charle's Song tracked over a film of you dodging a horse and running down an alley."

"So much for some quiet time," Enk grumbled as Kokopelli climbed off the bike after dropping down the center stand. "And that is depressingly fast."

"You." Nergal tilted his head to the side, his eyes glowing green as he examined Kokopelli from the top of his silky-looking hair to the tips of his worn motorcycle boots. "I don't know whether to thank you or to kick your ass."

"You could try." Kokopelli flexed his fingers, and a gold aura of electric energy surrounded his palms. He flexed his fingers, making the energy spark.

"Bitch, please," Nergal sneered, flexing his fist in response and with an audible *whoosh* of displaced air, a pair of brilliant, curved Saracen blades appeared in his hands, glowing green and charged with destructive energy. "The mountains may contain your power base but this fucking city was made for me."

"I think you both need to stop!" Enk called out, beginning to tremble as a shaft of energy slid though him, making his knees weak.

He was ignored as Nergal moved in closer. "You wanted us off your mountain; we left. We didn't complain about the fuckery you caused with attacking ankle-biters and the chicken-run for life. That was your area and we were intruding. We didn't say anything when you accosted Nabu at his most vulnerable with his human mate, knowing that you spied on them being intimate, because again, we were intruding. Unintentionally, but still intruding on your territory. We didn't say a damn thing when you dropped the media on our heads like a fucking jackass before we could get our newest human acclimated. And now you follow us here where someone tried to murder us and did succeed in killing an innocent."

"I didn't --"

"I didn't say you did," Nergal spoke over him as he lazily spun the blades in his hands, making the hilts dance in his palms, circling them hypnotically slowly, which was more powerful than swinging them around rapidly like in the movies. "But I can't say that your timing for this psychotic flirtation is ideal. Someone or several someones are trying to kill us. Those someones don't care who gets in their way. So let me pose this question to you." Nergal leaned in close, knees bent, arms in a ready stance as his eyes focused fully on Kokopelli, green energy bleeding from their depths. "What the fuck do you want?"

"Him." Kokopelli flicked his wrists, and his energy dissipated as he moved to stand down from his ready stance and left himself open to attack, trusting that Abadon would do him no harm. "I just want him."

"Oh." In a flash Abadon's weapons were gone and a decidedly sly grin grew across his lips. "Well, okay then."

"Okay then?" Enk sniffed. "Like you have the right to give me away."

"I am not trying to give you away." Nergal snickered. "I just want you to get laid."

"Hey!" Enk responded but Kokopelli snickered too, earning a nasty side eye from Enk. "I can get laid all on my own, thank you very much. You just want me to fall in love because you are."

"I just want you to take a chance."

"I take plenty of chances, Nergal."

"With your life, yeah, but not so much with your heart."

Enk glared.

"I am not trying to tell you what to do but you've been alone for a long time."

"By choice."

"See? Choice is the word, my brother. You have choices and you never take them."

"Go back to your lover and leave me alone, Nergal."

"Yes, I will. Because I know I don't have long with my lover and I want to enjoy every moment I have with him. Human beings's lives pass in a flash and I don't want to miss a thing. You, on the other hand, have an opportunity to have someone in your life that will last just a bit longer."

Enk fell silent at that. He was right. Nergal, Sin, Nabu... they were all existing on borrowed time with their lovers and they knew it. Kokopelli though... they might not be in a relationship, but at least he wasn't going anywhere anytime soon.

"And you" -- he pointed to Kokopelli -- "that is my brother. I love him like my right arm and I will always look out for him. His whole pantheon will. He will always be a part of us and nothing will ever stop that."

"I understand." Kokopelli nodded as he turned to look at Enk. "He's special. I'll take care of him as I've already proved. He has a vulnerability about him."

Nergal was nodding seriously. "But if you harm him in any way he does not clearly and eagerly consent to" -- Nergal growled again, his eyes flashing green -- "I will end you."

"Like you could." Kokopelli snorted and Enk groaned out loud as Nergal leaned down to stare into his face.

"Oh, I could."

"I could own you. You are still on my territory, Nergal." Kokopelli waved his arms around to show he was speaking of the huge expanse of mountains that the property sat on. "And I have nothing to fear in my own house." Kokopelli sneered and Nergal threw back his head, his laugh echoing over the hills before he dropped his head and stared directly into Kokopelli's eyes.

"Bitch, I eat gods."

His laugher then grew in power and strength until the earth beneath them shook. A green glow suffused his body and the very air stood still as all noise ceased to be. The sudden silence was unnatural and horrifying as the birds, the bees, even the sound of far off traffic ceased to be.

The smile on his face grew, and in an instant Nergal became Abadon, god of destruction. His face elongated, his teeth grew into fangs, his jaws dropped and expanded.

Watching it was like watching the natural laws of physics twist and turn into something disgusting and impossible. It happened so fast. In an instant, Abadon went from a rather striking man to an unholy beast, a perversion of nature, a hell spawn too disturbing to even try to describe.

Kokopelli gasped and took a step back as Abadon's laugher grew in strength. His eyes all but disappeared, rolled back into his head, and his nails became like claws -- no, like talons.

It was a face that Enk hadn't seen in eons and it was one he never wanted to see again. He reached out and grabbed Kokopelli by the shirt, drawing the stunned god back and placing himself in the line of danger.

He opened his mouth to speak but the opening of the front door cut off his words.

"Baby?" Charle's voice rang out, curious and innocent and in an instant, there was a *whoosh* of displaced air and Abadon was put away and in his place stood the arrogant and sarcastic rocker known to his family as Nergal.

"Just finishing up a conversation," he cheerfully called out as Charle moved to his side. He dropped one heavy, tattooed arm over his lover's shoulders and turned to stare at Kokopelli. "I hope we understand each other."

Shaken, the other god nodded mutely while Enk rolled his eyes at his brother. "I can take care of myself."

"I know you can." Nergal winked at him. "But you don't have to."

He turned and placed a kiss on Charle's forehead

before turning to steer his lover into the house.

"I think I felt an earthquake," Charle muttered as they disappeared inside.

"This is Cali," Nergal teased. "It's been two hours since their last natural disaster. Besides, I always make the earth move for you."

Charle's answer was cut off by the closing of the door, and Enk turned to look at Kokopelli.

"You okay?"

"He -- what -- What the fuck was that?"

"You've met the real face of Abadon and survived to tell the tale. Congratulations. Not many can say that they've had that particular pleasure."

Kokopelli's still-wide black eyes looked over at Enk and he shrugged.

"Really?"

"He's my brother and a little overprotective of me."

"Why?" Kokopelli was bringing himself back to normal, his shock wearing off as color returned to his skin and he began to relax. Birdsong filled the air once more.

"That is a story for another day," Enk hedged but then smiled up at him cheekily. "So... you want me?"

"And your erection says you want me," his potential lover shot back.

"Well, it was a damn good stiffy before Hurricane Abadon dropped in on us."

"I consider myself sufficiently warned," Kokopelli admitted. "Has he... He said he's eaten..."

"You don't want to know," Enk solemnly informed him. "He is a god of war and destruction. As he said, he can draw his energy from anywhere. And what we had to do in our distant past is just that, distant and past."

"But --"

"Trust me." Enk placed a hand upon Kokopelli's chest and felt his own heart skip a beat at the feel of hard, muscular flesh. "You don't want to know."

"I'll take your word."

"So -- you want me?"

"I do."

"You followed me from your mountain because you want me."

"I was curious at first. You are... different."

Enk nodded slowly. "That I know."

"And then I began to learn about you, I heard you speak and your sense of justice firmly matches that of my own."

Enk nodded, humming under his breath as he moved closer. Maybe he would get a kiss out of this.

"And then I heard you sing."

Enk looked up at him as his head tilted to the side. "My voice scares people. It's not pretty or smooth. It's rough and too deep."

"And when you sing it is filled with experience and pain. It touched part of my soul; it drew out emotions that I usually don't pay any attention to. It caressed me from the inside out and I began to crave hearing it."

"So, my voice changed your mind from curiosity into desire?"

"That and you showered and put on clean clothing. You clean up well."

Enk snorted at him as the other god pulled him close.

"Your voice made me want to see if I could get you to scream in my bed."

He reached out and gently cupped Enk's face in his hands, moving slowly in case he disagreed but Enk leaned into his touch. They were about the same height, Enk noted, before he felt Kokopelli's lips press gently against his.

Soft, was his thought before he pulled back to nip at Kokopelli's bottom lip. That made him smile and Kokopelli took advantage by pressing in for a deeper kiss, Kokopelli's tongue sliding neatly between Enk's own lips.

Enk moaned softly, fisting his hands in the other man's hair, marveling at its silky texture before he tilted his head to the side and deepened the kiss. He chased Kokopelli's tongue with his, savoring the taste of him. He tasted of spring water and sunshine. It was a taste that never failed to make him hard and hungry.

Kokopelli stepped closer, dropping his hands from his face to grip him by the hips, pulling him in to his own erection.

Enk stepped even closer, the blood rushing through his veins as he pulled back to stare at the other male. His skin tingled, his breathing grew harsh; he could feel his blood rush down to his dick and his semi became a full-blown erection.

"Kokopelli," he pulled back to breathe, tugging at the fistful of hair he had in his hands, pulling Kokopelli's head back and exposing his vulnerable neck to his biting kisses. He wanted to mark the darker man, then take him somewhere and fuck him through a mattress or any other object strong enough to withstand their rutting.

"Call me Koka," he breathed, shuddering and grinding his hips against Enk's and panting at the contact.

"My room. Right now."

Kokopelli didn't bother asking if he was sure, not that Enk was going to give him an opportunity to think about what getting involved with him meant.

He was damn near racing to his bedroom and the very comfortable bed there.

Finally, after a good long time, Enk was going to get laid.

Chapter 5

"How long has it been?"

Enk didn't know how it had happened, but it seemed that suddenly he was naked on his back across his bed with one of the hottest males he had ever seen standing over him, a hungry look on his face while stroking a healthy erection.

Oh yeah, he was about to get fucked good.

"Since I bottomed?" he asked.

The other god nodded, a wicked grin on his face as he reached back and waved a hand, braiding his long fall of ebony hair. "Yeah. As delicious as you look, I want to make a meal out of you but I don't want to hurt you."

"Why, Kokopelli --"

"Call me Koka," he reminded him. "I don't like my full name when I am fucking. Most can't make it past the first syllable anyway and I don't want you coherent enough to pronounce it."

Enk narrowed his eyes as he ran his gaze over Koka's body. Damn, that boy was built. "You talk a big game," he breathed, his heart fluttering madly in his chest. "You better deliver."

"Everything you ever dreamed of. Now answer my fucking question."

That rough edge to his voice… yeah, Enk liked that. He was down for a little rough trade. "I've not bottomed in so long that I am nearly a virgin again."

"Then I'll be gentle with you."

"You do that and I'll fucking kick you out of this bed. If I'm going to be fucked, I want to be fucked, Koka." He purred the name. "And if you can't handle that then I'm glad to take over and take my shot at that bubble butt of yours. You have a fine ass, do you know that?"

"All the hiking in the mountains that I do." He preened before waving his hand, and a rush of cool, prickly energy washed over Enk. At his questioning look, Koka grinned. "Just cleaning you up because I intend to flip you over and eat your ass like I'm starving. Unless you object…"

"Fuck," Enk breathed, then he was flipping over on his hands and knees, presenting his ass to be taken.

"Get on with it!" he growled, looking over his shoulder at his lover through his long fall of silvery-white hair. "Dinner is served."

Laughing, Koka moved in close, climbing up onto the bed behind him, his large warm hands gripping Enk's ass cheeks and spreading them wide.

Enk couldn't help it. It had been so long since he had this done to him properly that he was already shaking in anticipation. He let out a small moan as Koka gripped him tightly, and he felt fingers dig into his soft flesh.

"You're pale everywhere," Koka purred as he ran his thumb over Enk's quivering hole. "I mean really, there is no color variation at all. You are as pale as snow all over."

"Yes, yes, I know." Enk didn't mean to sound impatient but…Damn. That motorcycle chase and someone shooting at him…and that kiss acted like foreplay to him. Adrenaline was still rushing through his body and his dick was hard enough to pound nails. He needed to get fucked. "Now give me what you promised."

Koka's warm breath across his delicate skin sent shudders through his body. He had to lock his arms or fall on his face, so great was that shaft of pleasure. And the other god hadn't really touched him yet. The actual act just might kill him.

"Fuck," Enk breathed as Koka's tongue made a brief pass over his quivering hole, the pleasure so unexpected it nearly knocked him on his face. The second, longer lick had him crying out loud and writhing so hard that Koka had to tighten his grip on Enk's hips to hold in him place.

Then Koka began to eat at him in earnest, switching from broad licks to teasing laps that teased his puckered opening. Enk dropped his head to the sheet, his head rolling from side to side as Koka pressed closer and boldly sank his tongue inside of him.

"Koka!" he cried out, his hands tearing at the bedding as he arched his ass up higher.

Koka eagerly lapped at him, teasing his tight muscles, coaxing them to relax as he made the most obscene smacking sounds. Enk knew Koka was grinning with his enjoyment of the act as he spread Enk wider.

He pulled back and Enk felt one thick finger slide inside. Enk began to curse in long-dead languages. He felt a wave of energy pass over him again and now two of Koka's slick fingers were teasing past the guardian muscles of his hole, spreading him wide and stretching him out properly while his tongue danced between them.

Enk felt his toes curl as he pushed his ass back hard. Damn it, he wanted to get fucked. He needed to feel Koka pressing in deep, splitting him open and easing the hunger that had begun to gnaw at his insides.

"Fuck me!" he demanded and slammed his ass back as Koka pressed his fingers inside again.

"In due time," Koka had the nerve to whisper, and Enk jumped as a loud slap landed on his ass.

"One day," Koka breathed as he sat back and slid his finger in, "I'm going to turn you over my knee and spank this ass red before I fuck you through the mattress."

"You wish, Little Mischief," Enk growled. "Because if I don't get fucked soon, I'm going to kill you."

Any other words he could have said froze in his throat as Koka reached around and gripped his hard dick. Enk closed his eyes and bucked as Koka's slick hand began to stroke him too softly to do anything other than drive him mad.

"I like little deaths," Koka said, slamming all three

fingers deeply inside, grazing his prostate. "Almost as much as I like the feel of you dancing on the ends of my fingers."

As he spoke, he rotated his fingers until they brushed his prostate again, this time sending a jolt of electricity through them to his button.

"Koka!" Enk roared, curling in on himself then thrusting his hips wildly as the other god tightened his grip around his dick and stroked him firmly.

"If it's been awhile," Koka said as he sent another shockwave of pleasure through his fingers, "I want you relaxed and ready. Therefore, you are going to come on my fingers before I make you come on my cock."

"I-I --" Enk was rapidly losing the ability to form words. He was sweating, shaking, barely hanging on as Koka tried to finger fuck the life out of him. The periodic jolts of energy to his hole made him squeak, as well as make other embarrassing noises he'd never made before. The hand pumping his dick was just perfect, the right amount for tightness and speed. He closed his eyes as his muscles tightened, arousal burning in his brain, his body losing control at the hand of the other god.

Enk lost himself in the feelings that Koka was forcing on him, and then Koka's tongue was back, swiping over his hole, licking inside of him.

Enk broke.

"Kokopelli!" he roared as the climax shook him. The wet heat of his lover's mouth, his slick hand -- it was too much. Enk found himself spraying his release over the sheets as his heart tried to leap from his chest, and his brain exploded.

He was a shaking mass of quivering flesh as Koka flipped him over onto his back. He forced his eyes open and stared up at the grinning face staring back at him.

"Part one," Koka purred, his face flushed with hunger. "You taste sweet like candy but you were able to say my full name. I've gotta fix that."

Before Enk could complain about over sensitivity, Koka slipped down and began to lick at his still bloated dick. He closed his eyes, arching his hips up, and his hands went to Koka's shoulders.

The man was licking his dick and stomach clean of his release, the hand gently stroking at his base while the other toyed with his balls.

Enk spread his legs further. What else could he do? He relaxed into the pleasure that the other god was giving him and felt his cock start to swell once again.

He closed his eyes as the wet heat of his lover's mouth enveloped him, Koka's tongue flickering at his head. He didn't have a foreskin, not liking the look of his pale penis covered, and enjoyed the faint hint of pink at the heart-shaped head. Koka seemed to like this too because he tongued the slit, his fist stroking his shaft as he slobbered all over the head, sucking him down like a sweet treat.

Enk purred, nice and relaxed as the fingers returned to his hole to find him gaping slightly and eager to be filled. He clenched down on those fingers, riding them as lust began to fill him once again.

"Oh yeah," Koka said, pulling his mouth from Enk's cock with a *pop*. "I think you are ready --"

"Been ready, you twat," Enk managed before spreading his legs wider. It had been too long since he felt like this, this loss of control. He wanted to be drilled and filled right now.

Getting the idea, Koka gripped his legs and placed them over his shoulders as he bent him nearly in half. Enk reached up and grabbed fistfuls of his hair as Koka positioned himself and then slammed in hard.

Electricity shot up his spine and Enk arched his back as he screamed his encouragement.

This! This is what he wanted. He wanted to be

ridden hard and fast. He wanted to feel this fucking every time he sat down in the next week.

Fuck, he hadn't been able to do much with Koka's body, but for the next round he was going to teach that bastard to play with him.

But for now, he spread his legs wider and held on as Koka fucked him good.

He forced his eyes open and stared up at the face growling down at him. Koka was simply magnificent, with his bronze flesh glistening with sweat, his powerful body working above him to bring him the maximum pleasure, his muscles bulging as he adjusted his hips just so and --

"Fuck!" He was striking his prostate dead on, sending jolts of energy through his fucking dick into his body, gripping his hips just right --

"Right there," the bastard had the nerve to breathe as he began to work him over good and true. The room was spinning and Enk had never felt so taken as the other god loomed over him, protective and demanding, as he fucked the taste out of his mouth.

Enk tried to throw his hips up, to meet him thrust for thrust, but Koka was just too damn good! He gave up and just let himself be ridden as he felt his dick swell to its fullest and his balls slammed up against the base of his cock.

His second orgasm tore through him like a hurricane. Fire and lightning flashed through his body as he threw his head back and screamed.

His hole clamped around the hard cock pounding into him, milking it with uncontrollable spasms as all thought melted and his body went completely limp. He was barely aware of Koka shouting his own name before his hot seed filled his body, soothing the ache of his rough taking.

Koka collapsed on top of him, and Enk couldn't find

it in his heart to complain, and in fact found his weight comforting.

He managed to throw his arms around the other god as he moaned and shuddered through his own release.

This was perfect. He could feel the beating heart of... he could smell the scents of spring water and mountain air... he could taste...

Damn it. He was catching feelings.

His realization made him jerk a little and Koka lifted his head from his chest to stare at him, a question in his huge, dewy brown eyes.

Groaning, Enk let his dead drop back and tightened his arms around his Little Mischief.

Maybe he was catching feelings but at that the moment, he was too busy after glowing to really give a shit.

* * *

"And you have no idea who was shooting at you?"

"You got me out of bed for this bullshit?" Enk was not happy. According to his plan, he had two more screaming orgasms due and deputy-do-nothing was ruining his plans.

Koka snorted at his side, sitting there unabashedly bare chested and smelling of sex musk. Or maybe it was arousal? After all, Nergal had jerked him out of bed while he was doing his best to blow Enk's mind with the dirtiest, sloppiest blowjob ever.

Who had been getting his knob slobbed? The same guy who had two thumbs and didn't give a shit about the po-po. This guy, Enk thought, mentally pointing the thumbs in question at himself.

"So you have no idea --"

"If I had an idea of who was trying to murder me, I would be in a police station and we would be having a very different conversation. So, you tell me, Agent. Who is trying to kill me?"

There was a beat of silence while Enk began to braid his tangled white hair, sex hair really, into some kind of order. He too was bare chested, all his pale flesh on display, as he crossed his legs in the loose sweatpants he wore.

As it was past noon, Nergal and the rest of his brothers were all in similar attire, but with shirts on because the rest of the household was awake and aware, and none of them had been about to get their brains screwed out. Enk had been, in fact, having his dick swallowed to the root while Koka was licking his balls at the same time... a neat trick he was sure the other god would not mind him practicing until he too learned how to do it without choking, when Nergal banged on the door and informed them that the FBI was back and wanting to speak with them.

The humans were not involved in this conversation, as they had nothing to add about the band's past. Excused from the rest of this part of the interrogation, they were busy on social media, gathering up what they could from Enk's posted flight from the paps and the unknown subject, yes, the unsub, and making notes about what they had observed. How police procedural could you get? The humans, with the help of The Seven, were also fielding a lot of questions from concerned friends and family as they tried to assure everyone that they were fine. There was also a growing movement that wanted to know who the dark-haired indigenous man was who'd been seen running with Apollon. They were hedging their answers now, not really knowing what announcements about the other god were going to be made and generally just trying to keep the personal fallout minimal.

Now the preternatural ones sat staring at The Agent, the same one with the glasses who'd asked the inappropriate question at the first interview. He was once again asking his inane questions while his partner glared at him and offered a "what-can-I-do?" look at the band.

"So if you knew --"

"I would boot my foot up his ass with extreme prejudice." Enk stopped messing with his hair to glare at the dark-suited man. "A person has died, Agent. More people were put into harm's way.   Innocent people. People who aren't involved with the band. That makes that person -- or persons, because I have no doubt that there are more than one -- very dangerous."

The Agent, Enk decided he was going to call him Kip. Every Kip he had ever met was an asshole in glasses. So Kip and his partner stared hard at him, sending a little buzz of energy in his direction. He smiled, showing all his teeth, and sucked at his fangs before he continued to plait his hair as he responded.

"Oh, if I knew, I wouldn't kill him, but I would make him wish he were dead."

"Are you admitting --" Kip began but was cut off by the bored-looking lead singer.

"Wow," Nergal stage whispered, which for a band front man used to playing for crowds of thousands was like shouting in a quiet room. "I thought they said they were going to keep the stupid one away."

Both agents turned to glare at him, though Agent Two looked to be holding in his amusement. They had names but Enk found himself too antagonistic to give them the dignity of remembering them. He is Dale, Enk decided. Dale was a good solid name for someone stuck with an asshole.

"Oh, did you hear that? I thought I was whispering." Nergal tilted his head to the side and offered an obviously fake tooth-filled smile. "My bad, homies."

Sin snickered while Nabu straightened up, annoyance plain, and began to question their methods.

"Is this how you solve crimes?" He went to tug at his hair, hissed, then ran his hands over his bare scalp, still getting used to the lack of hair thing. "Because I have to tell you, what I saw in the remake of *Get Smart* was more effective than asking the same questions again and again and expecting a different answer."

"We are trying to uncover motive." Dale took control of the conversation, such as it was. "We have to examine every piece of information we get, no matter how insignificant."

"Like asking us if we know the parties attempting to slaughter us like cattle?" Nabu asked. "Because from where I am sitting, it sounds like victim blaming."

"We are not blaming you," Dale insisted, looking down at the recorder that the whole band insisted must be used to record every moment of this conversation to send to The Seven. "But we have to know if this was a stunt gone wrong."

Silence fell like a lead balloon.

"Are you accusing us of manufacturing this… this murder as what? A publicity ploy?" Enk's already deep voice dropped several octaves and right into the demonic realm of sound.

"No," Dale denied. "But we have to ask because --"

"Because of instead of finding bullets and casings, trying to pull fingerprints, searching through the security camera footage and film posted to the Internet to find faces that appear repeatedly when we are in public, you would rather blame us for creating some murderous publicity stunt. That would be really easy, wouldn't it Agent?" Enk hissed as he rose to his feet, the look he gave the two agents promising death if he had his way.

"We would --"

"Never insinuate," he cut them off. "But yet you sit here and insinuate. Let me be the first to tell you two gentlemen that Abadon has not, not now, not ever stooped to the level of high school hijinks to gain publicity to boost sales or to deflect from the latest scandal we ourselves created. We are rockers, Agent. Which means in very small words for you to understand, we play the fuck out of our instruments and sing the hell out of our songs and we own our scandals. Our talent stands for us, gentlemen, and not in any cheesy gimmicks that we could craft. So no, we did not plan our plane blowing up and no, we didn't plan on me being shot while I tried to run from people who won't give me a moment of peace. I understand that us coming back from the dead makes for exciting press, but finding justice for Major Tom kind of supersedes that issue, don't you think?"

"Sir," Dale began again. "We would not think that of anyone, but there are very real questions we have to ask to determine who the guilty party is. We are in the business of saving lives, and to do that we need all the information we can gather. No matter how uncomfortable the questions may be --"

"Uncomfortable? How about plain rude and disrespectful," Enk snapped, sitting back in his chair as Kokopelli wrapped a dark, muscular arm around his shoulders. "Like asking me about my sexual preference."

Enk turned to stare at his lover and at that arm wrapped around his shoulders, and was struck by the contrasts in their skin tones. He looked so very pale when pressed against the darker-skinned Kokopelli. It was a stark contrast, and he smiled as he decided he liked it. He really hadn't paid any attention to their contrasting skin tones before, but now when faced with others who were outside of his family, it was obvious, and it was cool.

"Yet, we have to ask." Kip took up the conversation thread again and offered a weak smile. "So if you would be so kind as to answer the question --"

"I could have sworn he already did," Nabu pointed out. "And his answer stands for the rest of us. Now if you are done wasting time --"

"And you" -- Kip cut Nabu off and pointed, rather rudely, to Kokopelli -- "I don't remember you being part of the band."

"Because I'm not." Koka turned his eyes away from Enk's to pay attention to the agent.

"Then who are you?"

Enk would have panicked slightly before making something up. After all, if he told him that his new lover was the god of mischief and specialized in knocking women up, they would have him doing drug tests from here back to Baltimore, but he didn't have to say anything. Nabu spoke up.

"He's our flautist."

Both agents turned to stare at him and Koka offered up the biggest shit-eating grin he could muster.

"You do know what a flautist is, correct?"

"He -- he plays the flute?" Dale asked while Kip just looked skeptical. They both ignored Nergal's 'skin flute' barely disguised by his coughing. "He doesn't look like a flute player."

"And how is a flute player supposed to look?" Koka asked, arching one dark eyebrow while tossing his long dark hair over his shoulders. It had to be godly energy that made that man's hair fall, silky and smooth down his back, and not have it looking like Enk's hands had just been fisted in it while he fucked this face. "I know it's a far stretch from the noble savage stereotype... or the alcoholic fresh off the Rez stoner, but we Indigenous Peoples do play flutes and other fine instruments, if that is where our talents lie. It is one of the earliest instruments mankind played after drums. And I am so very good at what I do."

"We would never believe in stereotypes," Dale was quick to explain. "It's just -- in the footage you are the unknown element who is not here with Abadon, and you whisked him away on the back of a motorcycle."

"Instead of a horse, yes." Koka smirked at him.

"Sir --"

"But there was a horse there," Enk pointed out, snickering. "He just didn't go all Tonto on it to get me out of there."

"And I think we're done." Nabu rose to his feet, shooting the agents a nasty glare. "In fact, if you need to have another conversation like this with us you will inform us so that we can have legal representation present in person or via video conference. The Seven would welcome the opportunity to stretch their wings again. You know, two of them were with the CIA before they changed career paths and I think another one was an agent with Interpol. I am sure we can all have a wonderfully informative conversation without the insinuations and questions about sexuality. I remember your question, Agent." He cut off the agents as they opened their mouths. "And I am aware that Apollon is the only one who had to answer such an asinine question."

Silence fell again.

"Well, that is that." Enk rose to his feet, tugging Koka with him. "I trust you can see your way out."

"You never told us your name," Agent Kip stated, turning to Kokopelli. "We need to check out your flautist."

"Koka," Kokopelli offered. "Koka Four Feather," he offered with a grin. "I am well known in some circles."

Then Enk was tugging him out of the room and back to the bedroom. They had been interrupted after all, and he wasn't done getting sexed up right.

* * *

"Oh fuck, oh fuck, oh fuck--"

Koka had his eyes closed, his head thrown back, and was having problems remembering his own name.

Somehow Enk had managed to swallow his whole

dick down his throat and was licking his balls as he swallowed around him.

That took talent and skill… and a lack of a gag reflex.

He looked down at the white head bobbing in his lap and had never felt so vulnerable or so powerful at the same time.

Enk was on his knees gobbling down his dick like it was his last meal. Koka was sitting on his bed, doing his best not to blow in three seconds like an untried boy. His toes curled, his hands fisted in Enk's silver hair, and his hips were rhythmically pumping, fucking his lover's eager throat. And Enk was moaning like a whore as he fisted his own dick in time to his head bobs.

Koka let his head fall back on his shoulders as he prayed for strength. In all his years and in all his orgies, he had never felt this way. His heart was racing, his body sweating, his muscles straining to hold him upright. He would give the god between his legs anything if he but continued on.

He spread his legs wider as he felt fingers leave his balls to tease at his hole. Fuck yes, he needed it. He dropped back on the bed and placed his feet at the edge, opening himself as wide as he dared, inviting his lover to play with his body.

Lover. Yes, Enk was his lover. He was irritable and harsh, snarky and sarcastic, and the most beautiful thing he had ever seen.

Koka had wanted him from the moment he glared at him on the mountain when he made his demands to get them gone. He had recognized a kindred spirit with the other god, but he was just settling down for the summer and didn't want any excitement to upset his calm.

But it was something about those big blue eyes and the odd buzz that surrounded the other god that eventually drew him off of his mountain to follow him here and into the circus his life had become.

He hadn't expected press conferences and snipers when he went after Enk. He expected an explanation of why he was so drawn to the man... and then he heard him sing.

The pain in him was a palatable thing and it touched a part of him that he rarely could feel anymore: his heart.

And then to see him all cleaned up and shining in the sun like a preternatural pearl... he was hooked. It was impulse that made him follow the other god into that pub and sit down at his table, but it was pure lust that had made him make a hard play for Enk.

And then getting him away from the shooter had made him feel needed like he hasn't in a long time. Facing down the more powerful Nergal had only stirred his hunger for the pale god even more. And taking him for the first time... the male really tasted like candy--like sugar and honey and a touch of tart lemon. He had never experienced anything like it before and instantly was hooked.

And as sweet as he tasted, the other god was as prickly as a cactus, and that just made him more exciting to be around. No one knew what he was going to do next and that just added spice to his sweet and made him about perfect.

Now all that perfection was his, his fingers weaving a spell to clean Koka up and slick him up as he pressed into his hole.

"You like playing with energy, do you?" Enk asked, pulling back to tongue at the slit of his cock's head. Koka forced his eyes open and looked down to see his lover's tongue just circling as his fingers teased at the muscles of his hole.

"What --"

Fire hit him all at once. Every nerve ending lit up and he could only scream as Enk sent a bolt of pure power through him.

"Fuck! Fuck! Fuck!" he managed as Enk waved his hands and suddenly the sheets wrapped around his wrists, pulling him to the top of the bed while the blankets slid around his ankles, pulling his legs up and back, leaving him completely open to whatever Enk wanted.

It was scary and exciting and fun, and so arousing that he almost came right there on the spot. Closing his eyes, he had to fight for control, breathe through it until he could open his eyes and look at his lover without spilling.

"I like this body, Little Mischief," Enk said, his own erection bobbing as he climbed up onto the bed. "I like it a lot. So powerful and lithe."

His fingers were dancing over his chest now, plucking at his nipples before drifting over his chest and pressing down into his skin, lightly dragging his nails over his flesh.

Koka gasped a little at the sting, his hips shifting upwards as his hard cock rolled, caressing his belly, still damp from his lover's mouth and the precum he was leaking like a faucet.

Another wave of Enk's pale hand showed a long, thin, vibrating dildo in it and Koka licked his lips in anticipation. His lover was kinky as hell. He loved it.

"I don't want this hungry little hole to get lonely waiting for me to come back," Enk explained as the fake cock was slowly pushed into his ass.

Koka whimpered at the feeling of penetration, and the sensations of being split open and spread out. But as he relaxed into the feeling, the vibrator began to expand and widen in his body.

"Fuck," he hissed, as Enk dropped over him and began nipping deliciously at his neck.

"If you are good enough," Enk purred, before fire shot through Koka's body when Enk nipped hard at his nipple before laving the pain away.

He closed his eyes as the vibrations steadily increased while Enk began to play his body. His nipples were lovingly tortured, his sides raked hard enough with his nails to leave the most beautifully sensitive welts. His thighs were massaged as they flexed into his lover's touch, and finally his hair was fisted, his head pulled back as his lover took his mouth.

He moved as the sugary lemon flavor of Enk filled his mouth, and his tongue teased his in a game of chase. Fingers caressed his face and ran over his neck, making him moan his lover's name.

Then the vibrator grew larger and he was cursing him instead.

Koka jerked in his sheeted restraints as the pleasure became almost unbearable. His dick was throbbing, his hole was stretched and filled, although the fake didn't have anything on the real one. His gaze traveled down his lover's pale body to his pale cock that only had a hint of color at the tip. But it was wet and hard and looked like it would feel perfect in his ass.

He wiggled down, clenching on the vibrator, only to have it shrink and still in his ass.

"Oh, come on," he complained, his body quivering in arousal. He needed to be fucked and he needed it badly. The tension within him was almost painful, and his partner just hovered above him stroking his cock.

"Poor Little Mischief," Enk purred. "You need something, baby?"

"You in me!" he all but roared, then groaned as his cock was once again swallowed by his talented lover.

Enk's tongue was dancing all over his sensitive skin as he swallowed him down to the root. He began humming as the vibrator again stretched him wide and began pulsing in his ass.

Again and again, Enk did this to him, teasing him to

the point of rapture and then pulling back to watch him squirm until he was a sweating mass of flesh tied to the bed.

"Please," he begged, his body curling into the pain/pleasure Enk was giving him by tugging at his balls while he lapped around the dildo that Koka was alternately loving and hating. "Please, Enk--"

"What I wanted to hear."

He screamed when his lover ripped the toy from his body and then roared as it was replaced with real, hot, hard flesh.

Immediately, Enk began to pound into him as he leaned over and began to fuck his mouth with his tongue. Koka was filled with cock, filled with the flavor of his lover, his muscles jerking against the bindings in his need to get his hands on the other god.

He wanted to pull him closer, to wrap his body around him and never let him go, but the bindings were too strong. He was trapped, taking what his lover was giving, and Enk was giving him life.

His hips were grinding as he bottomed out, running his shaft against his prostate on each thrust. The fullness was intense; Enk was bigger than he looked, and his cock was splitting him open perfectly. Enk's hands were still roaming his body, his fingers plucking at his nipples, making him hiss and jump while his mouth sucked heat into the sensitive nerve endings of his neck. He had never been so thoroughly taken in his life and he wanted it to never end. He reveled in his ravishing and called out to his lover for more.

"Whatever you fucking want, baby," Enk responded, his pale body glistening with sweat as he worked him over.

Enk wrapped his muscled arms under his back and pulled Koka to his chest as the bindings fell away. Koka found himself sitting on his lover's lap, Enk's cock buried deep within him, while his legs wrapped around his waist.

On his knees, Enk was leaning back and slamming his body upwards, each thrust making Koka's head spin and light flash behind his eyes. Koka's skin was bursting, too small to take in all the ecstasy he was being given and he felt like his heart was going to shatter. His breathing was rasping in his chest as his release began to build within him.

"Fuck, baby," Enk whispered as he began to pound him harder. "Give it up to me. Come on. Give it all up."

He was crying, whimpering, tugging to hold on to his lover, his control shot when Enk twisted his hips just so, causing the head of his cock to hit Koka's prostate dead on.

That was it. Koka threw back his head and roared as his body went into spasms. His muscles tightened, his legs locked around Enk's waist, and his ass clenched around his lover's dick as his release spurted between the two of them.

And Enk was riding his body, drawing out his orgasm, fucking him through it before he gasped, closed his eyes, and Koka could feel him swell even larger before his own release filled him to overflowing.

Panting, Enk dropped him back to the mattress, his boneless body covering him as his body gave in to the need to rest and recuperate.

"You nearly killed me," Koka managed as he tightened his legs around Enk's waist, not letting him pull out despite his shrinking erection.

"Complaining?" he asked, and Koka smirked up at him.

"What do you think?"

"I think you better get some rest now," Enk whispered, taking his mouth in a gentle kiss. "In thirty we get to do the whole thing over again."

And Koka smiled, knowing that he would give his partner a performance that would bring him to his knees. But first, a nap was in order. "I want to take you to my mountain, Enk. I want to love you in the seat of my power, to cover you with all that I am."

He closed his eyes and snuggled down into the heat of his Enk.

Finally, his life felt in order. He never noticed the look of concern and guilt that flashed across his lover's face.

* * *

"I can't say for sure," Nabu groaned, looking at the security camera that led to the front gate. "But I do believe the FBI and the FAA set us up."

The alarm on his phone had gone off, and since he was the closest to the security office, he was the first one there... staring in disbelief at the screen.

Everyone was now gathered around the monitors, staring mutely at the dozens of people who now lingered outside their temporary home. There were fans, reporters, paparazzi, and, of course, protestors, all in living color, all right outside their door.

"Fuck," Nergal groaned, shaking his head at the mass of humanity milling outside of their gate. "Well, at least the landlord can charge more to rent this place out when we leave." He tried to find a silver lining in this dark cloud. He failed miserably. "Home once occupied by the controversial rock band, Abadon, who were actively trying to be murdered by unknown subjects that the FBI can't find."

"Set us up?" Orion asked before he glanced, backing into Sin. "Really?"

"What better way to draw out a killer than by giving them a hard and trapped target," Nabu answered. "This is some totally fucked up shit."

"They did it or they have a leak," Sin said. "What are

we going to do now?"

"Camping sounds like a nice idea," Koka offered, smiling at the gathered men -- and lady. "I know you all can protect yourselves and your lovers, but I can hide you from human detection."

Silence filled the air.

"Kokopelli," Nabu began but the god of mischief interrupted.

"Look, call me Koka. My name is a mouthful. And you guys need a break and I can at least give that to you." He hugged Enk to him, ignoring the annoyed huff the other god let out. "I mean I managed to hide from your detection until I was drawn out by a dark siren's magical voice..."

"Sex makes you stupid and sappy," Enk grumbled, "But it's not a bad idea." As he spoke the alarm tripped as someone tried to scale the back fence. The security team, alerted the moment the alarms were tripped, signaled that they were on their way, and the guy stuck on the fence -- he looked to be trying to take photos with a cell phone.

Suddenly, getting away from it all didn't seem so bad.

Chapter 6

"This isn't a cabin in the woods," Enk pointed out, looking around the five-bedroom chalet that Koka had led them to. Upscale was the only word that came to mind.

"I spend seasons sleeping here, recharging," Koka responded. "What did you expect? A two-room hovel?"

"And this just travels with you wherever you go?" Nergal asked, looking round with interest.

"It goes where I go, so long as we are in the mountains, and as long as this is a mountain range that has pictographs created to honor me, yeah."

"Jealous." Nabu chuckled as he strode into the room with Aika at his side. "We have to rely on The Seven to appropriate accommodations for us."

"They like to spend our money," Nergal explained.

"And they want us to live large since most of our temples have been destroyed," Nabu added as he and his lover moved out of the way to let the others in.

"This is what I call glamping," Orion cheered, dragging Sin in by the hand.

"Glamping?" His lover asked, tilting his head to the side. He was absently petting Snake, who had made an appearance when Koka led them from the back of the house after the police and security team cleared out the trespassers. It was interesting to open the gate and step into the woods only to be instantly transported to the front steps of this place.

"Glamorous camping," Orion explained. "The only camping you will ever get me to do. I am not one for roughing it, unless you mean Motel Six. They always keep a light on for you."

Enk ignored the rest of them as he examined the great room, noting its many beautiful Hopi adornments.

"That is a Kachina doll," Koka explained as he

pointed to the small, carved wooden doll with a solid black face and elongated eyes wearing loose linen pants and displaying an enormous pair of eagle wings.

"It's beautiful," Enk whispered, a feeling of reverence overcoming him as he stared at the small doll.

"They were given to young girls to teach them about the immortal beings."

Enk raised an eyebrow at him.

"Well, you won't find one of me. I'm not that arrogant. But they were here to teach about the beings that control the rain and the important aspects of life, and were messengers of the gods. They were given to young girls at birth, and it was supposed to teach them our ways and how they were supposed to behave."

"Messengers." Enk shivered in delight. "So they were your little spies."

"How can you attribute living emotions and thinking to an inanimate object?" Koka teased.

"It would fit in with your mischief godhand."

"And yours." Koka began to dig again. "I mean, didn't you have anything like that in your pantheon?"

"No." Enk shook his head. "That is why it was an easy role for me to fulfill." He spun around and threw his arms over his lover's shoulders. "And now I don't want to talk about it."

"But I can help you learn to control it so you aren't so incapacitated by the powers... especially the chaos."

"Don't want to talk about it."

"Enk --"

"No." Enk pulled back and glared at a sheepish-looking Koka.

"Okay. I know I push."

"Then you know you need to stop."

"Scout's honor." Koka held up two fingers in a Webelo position.

"You were never a scout. You specialized in

knocking up young women."

"And men," he said and snickered. "But that's beside the point. I mean, they named so many badges after the fictional, watered-down version of what I and my people did that I think that we should all be honorary Eagle Scouts."

"No lie there, brother," Enk agreed, taking his hand and pulling him toward the stairs while the others explored his home. "You sure you don't mind us invading like this?"

"Nah. I'm cool with it. Besides, the only being ever to come here and admire what I have done was my wife."

Enk froze. "You are mated?" His heart dropped. He all but threw Koka's hand away. There was no way on this fucking planet that he would be the other man, the reason for a break up, the side bitch, the dirty little secret --

"We split ages ago." As if aware of his thoughts, and definitely aware of the tension, Koka reached out and reclaimed his hand. "It was amicable and we just decided we were too much alike to really be happy with each other. No balance. So we severed our bond and parted as friends. Mana still comes to visit occasionally but she has this thing going in Vegas. She's a madam, you know. Wet dreams for men are her specialty but she runs her ranch with an iron fist. Sometimes when she's had enough of humanity, she brings herself and whatever lover is stoking her fire at the moment and we all chill a bit."

"So do you still --"

"Nah. That boat sailed centuries ago. She's just a good friend."

Enk relaxed and offered up a smile to his lover. "Cool to know. I just have this thing about adultery and wives."

"Because you were married before, right?"

Enk frowned at him. "I don't wanna talk about it."

"Fine," Koka said. "Not my business." He looked a bit disappointed for a moment before a genial mask slid over his features. Enk hated that mask and really hated the fact that he was the one to make him use it.

"But -- but I will discuss it with you one day," he conceded, all the while screaming at himself. What the hell was he doing? Was he even ready to consider something long term? Kokopelli was a damn good lay and knew how to give and take, but was that worth creating a relationship over?

He could almost hear Nabu saying that the being had followed him from the mountains because he was fascinated by him. And that he was equally fascinated and that they had comparable godhands...

He looked up, realizing that Koka had been kind of hurt, and cursed himself for hurting him.

With stunning clarity, he realized that the other god actually cared for him.

He knew that there were others who cared for him, like his brothers, but they were few and far between. Their human counterparts liked him, but they liked him because of his connection to their lovers rather than having any real regard for him. Except maybe Charle. He had given up some good advice to that young man, who had taken it to heart, and look at him and his lover now! But really, he hadn't had anyone care for him like a real lover in so long he didn't even know how to recognize the sensations. Groupies and short-term hook-ups didn't count. It had been so long since he genuinely had someone care for him like...

Now was not the time. He shook his head as he smiled back at Koka.

"So -- got a bedroom in this place?"

"Got five and the master is in the back." He purred, stepping closer and bent low to run his nose along Enk's sensitive ears, inhaling his scent.

"I say we leave the others to their own devices and you give me the private tour."

"That sounds like a plan," Koka said before turning to the others and calling out, "Your company is welcome and all of that. This is the house. There is food in the kitchen. I'm going to fuck Enk now. Please make yourself at home."

That laughter of his family almost made Enk blush, but the rush of heat that came at Koka's words drowned out anything but desire.

"Yeah," he breathed as Koka tugged him up the stairs. "That sounds like a plan."

* * *

"Are we ever going to leave this bed?" Enk asked, sweaty and wrecked as he panted beside a whimpering Koka. "Not that I'm complaining."

"Can't think," Koka complained. "Just got my brains fucked out."

Enk manage to gather enough energy to laugh at that. Swiping his sweaty hair out of his face, he decided, ugh, that was going to require a washing.

"You seem your usual self to me... and if brainless is your usual state..."

"Fuck you." Koka rolled over to throw his arms around his lover, pulling him close to his side, despite their sweaty skin and the heat they managed to create.

"See me in fifteen." Enk laughed, giving up on his hair to cuddle. The Fates must be laughing because he was seriously cuddling with his lover. In the three days since they'd come here, they had barely left the room, only seeing the others for an occasional meal and to shower and change the sheets. They were more content to lie back and make meals out of each other while the others frolicked in the woods that Koka controlled and got fat off of never-emptying cupboards of food.

There was no WiFi, no Internet, and no way of

communicating with the outside world. Just the way he liked it. This was a real vacation, and although the outside world was waiting and they knew they couldn't hide forever, they could spend some time just being themselves without the scrutiny of the public eye.

Nabu would let loose his dragon and travel with his lover to beautiful, scenic areas that she could photograph with her phone and draw. He was sure they were screwing like bunnies out there too, but he had no room to talk. He and Koka had done little else.

Sin was fond of watching sunsets with his lover when he could pull Orion away from Koka's library and artifacts. Orion was photographing what Koka allowed and taking notes to continue his education later and to tease the hell out of his parents with what he could touch and fully experience and they could just drool over.

Nergal was a bit uncomfortable with being in the seat of another god's power, but Charle… The way that young man's eyes lit up just being around him, the way he would watch intently as Nergal sang quietly to him of love and loss and of hope… yeah, Nergal was willing to swallow down a lot to continue to see the love light in Charle's eyes burn brighter.

Enk was aware that they had to go back soon, not just to avoid becoming suspects in the investigation themselves, but to actually see if they could discover who was really behind all this latest stupidity in their lives. One person was dead, and he really didn't want anything to add to that body count.

But for now, he was going to lie back and enjoy himself, relax, and let someone really care for him. It was a heady experience.

"So" -- Koka began, just as Enk ran a hand through his tangled hair, flexing a little bit of energy to straighten out the knots in his silvery-white hair as he did -- "can we talk?"

Enk's heart slammed into his chest and his stomach seemed to drop out.

No one wanted to hear those words on a lover's lips.

"Well, that killed the mood," he managed through nearly frozen vocal cords. Was this it? Had he begun to open his heart and trust the other god only to have his affection thrown back in his face? Was he not clear that he was falling in love with the big idiot --

Falling in love? Nope. He wasn't in love. It was a phase, a reaction to having a lover with some longevity -- was he skin hungry?

He was definitely not in love.

"It's nothing bad." Koka pulled him back as he sought to climb out of the wreck of the bed and away from those arms that were holding him down to hear what pain his mouth brought. At his words, though, Enk eased back a little. Time to grow up and see what the other god had to say and not assume.

"Okay," he slid back in. "But it better be important for you to harsh my buzz like that. I was after-glowing."

"I-I just wanted to talk about... about the gap I feel in you."

Not this shit again.

"I am fine, Koka."

"You could be hurt if you get a sudden burst --"

"It's fine." Enk knew his voice dropped deeply but he really didn't want to talk about it. Ever. What he had done... true, it'd had to be done, but that didn't mean he had to tear open his soul once more just to fix him. Fix him? Fuck, he deserved his pain.

"This is dangerous," Kokopelli continued, and Enk felt revulsion for himself, frustration, anger at his lover, mingled with the small desire to just tell him everything and maybe let him help correct his absorption problem.

But he was a murderer. He'd gone against his own godhood, and no matter what the reason, that was taboo.

He should have given himself to the void.

"Enk, I really care about you --"

"Do you?" Enk hissed. "Because if you did you would fucking leave this alone."

He deserved his pain. It was his burden, his penance to bear.

"Because I care, I can't."

Koka reached for him but Enk jerked back so hard he nearly fell off the bed.

In his mind, his uncleanness would taint the other god.

He didn't pay attention to how Koka's face fell or how he flinched, his eyes filling with sadness.

"I - I need to be alone."

Before Koka could say anything else, Enk rose to his feet and grabbed up the first clothing that he saw. Absently he threw on the pants, his own slim-fitting jeans, and the shirt, one of the tunics that Koka had taken to wearing on their expeditions out of the bedroom when they ran around his house and the protected zone.

He spun on his feet and, barefoot, made his way to the front door.

"Enk!" Nergal called out, but the stricken look on the man's face froze his words.

Enk walked past him.

He was going back to their house to think.

He had a lot to digest and really, he didn't know what he was going to do next.

* * *

"What did you do?"

"Nothing!" Koka shot back.

"You had to do something! I've not seen him this upset in a long time."

"We had a disagreement."

"About what?"

"None of your damn business, Nergal. Some things

are private."

"And some things will get your ass kicked." Nergal glared for a moment, then relaxed as he studied the other male.

He… he was hurting. He looked frustrated and confused and concerned. These emotions went deeper than a simple hook up. If anyone understood that combination of emotions, it was him.

"You're right. It's none of my business, but maybe I can help."

Koka stared at him, hard, for a moment, before he seemed to shrink into himself. "Okay. We had an argument… well, more like a heated discussion about what I am allowed to do."

"So you had a fight."

"Hard to fight when your lover walks out on you."

"Lover?"

"Yes, lover," Koka snapped. "It was stupid and I don't understand it, but it was a heated disagreement."

"So fix it!" Nergal said shortly, shaking his head at the stupidity of them both. It was clear that matters of the heart had come into play and the two idiots were fighting what was happening.

"I don't know how!" Koka roared back, his chest heaving as he stared at the other god. "I don't know what to do or what I did wrong. I don't even know why I give a fuck at this moment."

He ran his hands through his hair in frustration, eyes snapping with a light that showed his lack of control at the moment.

Nergal sighed and shook his head. Idiots. The both of them. He really didn't want to get involved, but there was at least one thing he could do.

"Look, he told you that his godhood was adopted and assumed, but you don't know what he gave up to receive it. And you don't know that you are the only person outside of those of us who were there that knows that much of the truth. That means something huge and if you are too blind to see it, then maybe you aren't the one for him."

"I don't know if I am," Koka admitted finally. "He just makes me so angry."

"Then why are you still here?"

Koka, who had begun to pace, stopped cold.

There were just the two of them in the room, the others asleep or out and about in the protected territory. It was just the two of them and the perfect time to have this out by Nergal's estimation.

"What do you mean?"

"I mean," Nergal said, stepping closer to him. "What are you doing there? Why are *we* here, for that matter? Why are you protecting us? You don't have to, but you offered us shelter and a way to get away from what's happening in the mortal world."

"It's Enk..."

"True, you followed him here, you stalked him here. I get it." He waved his hands at Koka as he spoke. "I get it. You are a god of mischief and I bet you got a nice rush out of fucking with us and especially him. He should be like you but he's not. He feels certain things more intently, more destructive things. He fascinates you because of that but what else?"

"He's... beautiful."

"Yes, he is. But it's more than that. If that were the only reason you were hanging around then you would have been gone the moment you fucked him. Yet there you were, associating yourself with us in the middle of a human investigation, helping us out by giving us a reprieve, and here you are right now, pulling your hair out because he refuses to let you deeper in his life. It could be obsession, which I understand but will get your ass kicked for playing with him like that. Or you're developing very real feelings for him."

Kokopelli stopped moving and frowned at Nergal, who in turn offered him a very toothy smile and laughed as the other god flinched.

"That is disturbing," Koka muttered, shivering. "You really don't need to show me that face again."

Nodding, Nergal assumed his normal visage and patted Koka on the shoulder. "You have deeper feelings for our God of Mischief than you thought. Congratulations. You're a real boy now."

Koka glared. "Okay. I admit I am... I do... I care about Enk more than I thought I could care about anyone. I mean I was married and we were too much alike to be of any use to the other. She was more like my sister than my wife."

"That Enk would understand as he was once married."

Kokopelli blinked in surprise before nodding as if something was cleared up in his head. "She was disloyal?"

"You have no idea. Why do you ask?"

"I ask because he had a really interesting reaction when I told him I was once married. I thought he was going to do me harm before he listened long enough for me to explain that we were no longer bound."

"You can say she was disloyal." Nergal nodded. "It's a minor explanation for what she did but it fits. And if you want to know the rest, go ask him. Not my story to tell."

Koka sighed and turned to look at all the wonderful artifacts of his people he had saved over the years, the Kachina figures that dotted the walls and recessed shelves in his home. Then he turned to face Nergal again.

"Patience, huh?" His words were soft with understanding. "I guess I pushed too much."

"You push when you care. Believe me, Enk knows

this well."

"So... I guess I better go and --"

Kokopelli froze, his whole body shivering before a look of horror crossed his face. Without a word, he raced out of his house and into the trees.

A second later a feeling of dread covered Nergal and he gave a battle cry that had not been heard in generations as he raced out after him, knowing his brothers would follow and would be battle ready.

Chapter 7

"I don't need fixing."

Enk stomped through the trees, finding the passage back to where he was before all this madness had started. He could feel the energy trails that Kokopelli had laid down as they moved to his home. Once he passed the last trail, he was once again standing in his own backyard behind the pool and the fence that kept out the wildlife and stalkers.

He really didn't want to delve into his past at any given moment but he really didn't want to go into why he was a god of mischief at the moment. He was too... confused was just as good a word as any.

He liked Kokopelli. He liked him in a way he had not allowed himself to like anyone in a long time. He had a lot of pluses going for him.

He was handsome as hell, he was an incredible fuck, and completely uninhibited in the bedroom. He was moderately intelligent, nearly as old as he was, and he was long- lived, a god with similar powers that wouldn't age and pass on like the other's partners. That meant Enk wouldn't get his heart ripped out over an accident or untimely death. He and Koka had time and opportunity to plan and work out what relationship worked for them. He didn't expect Koka to leave his seat of power and travel with them to their home base in Europe. That would be stupid and selfish on his part. It wouldn't work for the both of them so their relationship would have to be very open. Koka would understand that, and it would essentially mean any time they spent together would be time that they both craved and cherished. There would be no one higher in his esteem or his heart if they decided to make a go of this.

And in the interest of honesty, Enk would have to inform him of his past and why he was reading like a shattered god not quite put together well enough to handle all aspects of his godhood.

Sooner would be better than later.

He paused, his hand on the back fence as he wondered if it was worth it.

Was it worth ripping himself open and spilling his guts to a being who might very well reject him? That would leave him by himself to piece his insides back within his own body and stitch it all back together alone.

He thought of the possibilities with Koka. He did, in fact, play a mighty fine flute, and after following through with what he'd told the FBI the god did, in fact, have a totally separate career that he used as a front. He was listed on the credits of several famous artists' albums, from Aerosmith to Snoop Dog. He had no set genre and even had a few solo albums under his name so the two of them meeting was not too far fetched an idea for anyone to believe. Koka was stable and didn't need help with maintaining his own human facade or controlling his own godhand. Koka was honest to a fault sometimes, and yes, he had to admit, cared for him.

So maybe after all of this murder business was over, they would sit down together and have a long chat about his past. It might end in heartbreak or it might end in a higher relationship, but either way, Enk would never know unless he took a chance. Was Kokopelli worth taking a chance on?

Probably, was his sarcastic answer, and even with his cynical nature, it pulled a smile from him.

So he would talk to his short-term lover, possibly make him a long-term lover, and then maybe he could try to feel normal again.

Ninhursag would not, after all this time, defeat him. Maybe this would pull the last vestiges of his wife's betrayal from his being and he could go back to living a normal existence.

He stepped out of the woods and palmed the bio-lock on the back fence.

Just as it clicked open a jolt of chaos energy went though him so powerfully that he began to spasm.

Fuck, he thought, just before he was slammed in the back with a bolt of electricity that threw his body into spasms.

"Didn't mean to do that, brother," a voice he didn't recognize whispered in his ear as he was dragged forward.

He wanted to get up and beat the shit out of the person who had him, but he couldn't move. It wasn't the electricity that had caused this; it was being so close to such evil chaos.

It was about then that he realized maybe Koka had had a point about fixing that aspect of his existence.

He forced his eyes open to look around and saw three other men racing into the yard, carrying heavy-looking sports bags.

"We have to save you from yourself. Those unnatural men you side with, you associate with, are going to bring you to your end. Butt sex. How can anyone find that acceptable?"

There was that phrase again. Enk's mind flashed back to where he heard that stupid turn of phrase before and remembered the picket sign, and the letters he'd received from a man that seems to be obsessed with butt sex.

There were no such things as coincidences. These had to be the idiots who'd planted the bomb on the plane, and that meant that there had to be bombs in those bags.

"I know that the nigger is with the slant-eyed bitch, but races shouldn't be mixing like that either. It upsets the natural balance of things so that means they have to go as well. You don't sleep with your pets. You bring them to heel."

Homophobics and racists, Enk thought, trying to make his body move but to no avail. The moment he had freedom of movement back, the son of a bitch was dead.

"But there is a chance for you," the man continued as Enk was dragged back out of the fence and into the woods that surrounded the back of the house... so close to the lines of power that Koka had laid down.

If he could touch one of those lines, the chaos energy would, like electricity in a circuit, follow the path of least resistance and flow from him, draining him of his dangerous present and giving him the ability to move again.

"We can get you out and get you safe. You don't need them anyway, Apollon. You are a god and you should be worshiped as such. You should have good, clean, white women laid at your feet. You should be a beacon to your people, your pure people. You are superior in every way and with you as our figurehead, they would have to sit up and listen."

He was dragged a few inches more and gently laid down in a patch of grass, his fingers just inches from a power line.

He had to get them to move him further, to do something, to move him closer to that line. So he marshaled his energy to force his lips to move.

"Fuck -- you," he managed to say loud enough for the man to turn and face him, and Enk got a look at the enemy.

He was an unassuming man in a suit, wearing a round pair of glasses and had the most nonthreatening look he had ever seen on a human.

It snapped into place. The guy with the picket sign, the reporter from the reps conference, the man with the mic shoved in his face at the pub. His stalker was that close and he never knew. So this was the butt sex man. Enk was not amused.

"Excuse me?" The man didn't sound like a raving lunatic or a rabid racist. He sounded like a college professor or someone trying to sound smarter than they really were. It was almost amusing, yet disturbing to hear the words butt sex roll from his lips. "I am doing this for your own good."

"Psycho," Enk managed to spit and the man narrowed his eyes at him.

"I am doing this for your own good. I am here to save you."

"Fuckin' fag." Enk grinned to himself as the man went red in the face. Maybe Nabu was right about the guy's latent homosexual tendencies.

"What did you call me?"

"Fudge packer." Enk smirked at him, speaking becoming a bit easier. Maybe being close to Koka's line of power was helping.

"Stop."

"I bet you like taking it up the ass." He panted. "If you wanted it so bad, Abadon would break you off a piece."

The man's face went so red it was almost purple as he calmly stepped up to Enk, drew back his foot, and kicked him as hard as he could in the side.

It hurt like hell, with chaos energy filling him, but it also had the benefit of shifting him an inch closer to the power line he'd felt.

"You" -- kick -- "do not get" -- another kick -- "to call me names."

The idiot was breathing hard, his hands fisted, his eyes narrowed with an insane hatred. "No one calls me names!"

And all through it all, he never screamed. He never cursed. He just kicked Enk closer and closer to the power line until one last kick rolled him over onto his face completely.

His hand flopped out, his palm connecting with the line, and in a flash, the destructive energy flowed from his body in a rush, fleeing to a being who could control, master, and even welcome the energies. Kokopelli would be coming, and with him, his non-human family.

"So much fucking better," Enk purred and the kicks stopped. He heard the man back up, probably shocked as the strength of his voice, but his next action made the man squeak.

Enk lurched to his feet, almost as if being tugged upright by unseen hands, and spun to face his attacker.

"Hello, little psycho." In control as long as he stood on the power line, Enk waved his hands over his face, lifting his clothing and hair, flicking away the soil and leaves from his person. The move was magical, ethereal, inhuman, and enough to send his tormentor mute with open-mouthed horror. "It's time to play."

* * *

By the time Kokopelli rounded the corner of the fence that protected the property, Enk was chasing a man in a torn suit and really, he was doing more toying than chasing.

It was like watching a cat bat a mouse around. The man would run toward the fence and Enk would flex his power, sending the man tumbling ass over heels into the grass and trees that backed up to the band's property.

The man would recover enough to scream in terror, though no sound left his throat, and try to run again.

"Keep running, asshole!" Enk was laughing as he gave chase and knocked the man into some suddenly appearing and conveniently placed mud. "You're gonna tell me what I wanna know... eventually."

The man gave another silent scream and tried to run in the opposite direction. Mud-splattered, tattered and torn, he was the definition of not having a good day.

Koka was about to sit back and enjoy the festivities

when Enk asked something that made his blood chill. "Where are the bombs and how many assholes are in my house?"

"What?" Koka raced to Enk's side where he now had the silently blubbering man hemmed up against a tree. "Bombs?"

"He fucking tased me." Enk was panting, angry and magnificent, his bright blue eyes flashing as his energy pulsed around him. "He let those assholes in my house and I think they were carrying bombs."

Koka turned to look at the man, his eyes narrowing in confusion as he tried to recall where he had seen him before.

"This is our assassin?"

"This is fucking butt sex man," Enk roared, waving his hand and removing whatever he had done to silence the man. "This little bitch tased me from behind and now I think he knows he bit off more than he can chew."

"Please!" the man blubbered. "I didn't know! I didn't know --"

"That they were going to try and kill my family? That you already murdered an innocent man? What the fuck didn't you know?"

Koka could feel the rage inside of Enk building dangerously and knew that it was a type of destructive chaotic energy that would incapacitate him. He had to get him to calm down.

"That -- that you are a demon!" the man wailed, and the slow smile that spread across Enk's handsome face was enough to send shivers down his spine.

"You know nothing of demons, little man." Enk hissed, his voice sounding like the low tones of an engine burning underground. "But I guarantee I will show you if you don't start talking."

"Apollon," Koka spoke softly to him. "Would you like me to handle this --"

"It wasn't supposed to be like this!" the man wailed and Koka looked around nervously.

"I can talk to him... get the information before he lets everyone in the house know what's going on. They could detonate the bombs."

"They can't hear anything beyond the gate." Enk cut his eyes at Koka. "I know what I am doing, Mischief. This ain't my first rodeo."

Deciding that backing off would better his chances of keeping Enk calm, Koka lifted both hands in surrender. "Whatever you want."

"I want this bastard to start talking."

Before anything else could be said, Nergal, Nabu, and Sin all bounded through the trees, eyes glowing and bodies pulsing with power.

"What's the plan?" Nergal asked, taking in the scene with cynical eyes.

"Bombs in the house and I don't know what they plan to do. So I am trying to extract information from butt sex man."

"This is butt sex man?" Nabu asked, stepping closer and staring down at the cowering human who was trying to curl himself into a small, unnoticeable ball and failing. "Dude, you are one sick asshole."

"And he let people into the house. I suspect bombs. That seems to be the tools of cowards and bullies."

"Well," Sin pointed out. "He did try to shoot you, so --"

"I think it was one of them in the house," Nabu interrupted, reaching out to the man and watching as he cried harder, cringing away from his touch. "This is some seriously fucked up shit."

"Can you glean what is going on?" Nergal asked, crossing his arms and looking from the house to the blubbering man. "If there are bombs, are they on a timer or are they set to detonate when we enter the property?

How powerful a payload are we talking?"

Humphing, Nabu leaned closer, grasping the man's chin when he tried to pull away and demanding in a voice almost as deep as Enk's, "Look at me, human."

Almost as if compelled, the man complied and Nabu examined his eyes for a few long moments.

"There are four of them," he informed the others. "And they have bombs placed around the outside of the perimeter. They can't enter the house because of the biometric locks we have in place, but they seem to have enough explosives to send this house sliding down the mountain and into the ocean."

The man looked even more frightened, crying harder as the acrid smell of piss filled the air.

"Oh for fuck's sake," Nabu cursed, jumping back.

"Plans?" Nergal asked, looking at his brothers and the amazed-looking Kokopelli.

"How?" Kokopelli asked, looking at Nabu. "How did you tear that from his mind?"

"He offered it," Nabu explained. "I am the god of knowledge. I can glean people's intent and their desires, but when someone shoves the information to the forefront of their brain, plucking it from their minds is cake. It's very useful on the battlefield."

Koka nodded at that, looking around at the others. "What do we do now?"

"We could call the police," Sin offered, looking out into the distance. "But they may detonate the bombs at the sound of sirens. If we tell the police to come in silently, they may not believe us. If we tell them about the bombs, they will send in a SWAT team along with the bomb squad and that will force their hands into setting off the bombs. If they come in silently they may get a negotiator in place, but these men seem more fearful than fearless and they may set off the bombs then."

When Koka stared at him in confusion, Sin offered

him a smile as he tucked long strands of his red hair behind his ears. "God of change. I can see the possibilities of any action but also have an understanding that no one can accurately predict the future. I can see what might occur and shift variables into place in my mind to see how a course of action could play out."

"I never asked what your godhands actually were," Kokopelli finally admitted. "You are all war gods? You have to be war gods to be able to react this fast and with surety." He looked at Nergal, who offered him a grin.

"I fucking eat people but you already know that. Right, Koka?"

Koka blanched a little as Nergal waved his fingers at him.

"And if we intercede?" Nabu asked Sin, bringing them back on task.

The man tried to rise to his feet, but Koka waved a hand in his direction, and he went flying into a tree that opened its arms in welcome. Literally. The tree grew wooden arms and they wrapped around butt sex man, tentacles of branches and leaves wrapping around him, holding his arms and legs in place, and gagging him. "The smell was bothering me," he explained when they turned to stare at him.

Enk snorted, then tried to look serious, as this probably wasn't the time or place for humor... but he couldn't help himself, Koka knew. When he started chuckling, Nabu spoke again.

"You are going to have to stay behind." He pointed to Enk. "This close to this much chaos... you may fry your brain."

Enk open his mouth to complain, but Nergal cut him off. "I know you are a powerful warrior, and in any other situation I'd want you to take lead. But this may be too much for your system, and if you overload you could do yourself and those humans around the house massive harm. And I don't think you can live with yourself if you do that. You are already steeped in guilt. I don't want to add to that."

Enk stepped back and nodded, dejection in every line of his body.

"You know you did good," Nergal continued, bumping the pale man with his shoulder. "You got free because I'm going to assume they did something to you to get those assholes in and to keep you here with butt sex man. You got a warning to Kokopelli, which got us all here. You gathered our means of intel so we know what's going on inside the fence. You did good for someone who has been avoiding battle for generations, Enki. Now let us help you. That's what family is for."

"When you put it like that," Enk -- or was it Enki? -- muttered, nodding and stepping back.

"That's because you know I'm right." Nergal grinned.

"With Nabu and Sin providing you options and backup --"

"But that still makes me right."

Koka could feel the manic energy in Enk powering down as the banter with his family calmed him.

"I'll stay here too." Kokopelli nodded when they turned to him. "I'm no war god but I know my strengths. You go in and do what you have to do and we'll wait here."

He tentatively leaned against Enk and was gratified when he didn't pull away. In fact, he leaned back, offering and taking support.

"Sin?" Nabu asked, reaching up for his hair, flinching when nothing was there, and tugging on his ear instead. "When do we intervene?"

Sin closed his eyes for a moment, then smiled.

"Accurate number?" he asked Nabu, "And location?"

Koka felt a wave of energy float over him before Nabu began to speak. "Four, and the idiots are situated on each side of the fucking house."

"Detonators?" Nergal asked.

"Can't get much from them at a distance but from what I pulled from butt sex man, they each have a detonator. I can't tell you the yield on the bombs, but I can tell you that they learned how to build them on the Internet. Expect shoddy workmanship that may blow up in our faces."

"Duffel bags," Enk added. "I got the impression of duffel bags."

"Bigger than a pipe bomb then." Nergal grunted. "Sin?"

"Shock and awe would make them set the bombs off. We go in with stealth. They are afraid and nervous. Go for knockouts. As much as I would love to just kill the sons of bitches and get it over with, the human police would come down on us for that. I know it would be easier to destroy them, but we are living human lives now."

"Two in the back!" Nabu called out and grinned in triumph when the other two groaned.

"No fair," Nergail complained.

"Called it first," Nabu countered, sharing a high five with Sin.

"You're ridiculous," Enk called out and Koka looked at them all like they were insane.

"Is this fun for you?"

"It is now!" Nergal laughed. "We have a plan. We can act. We can flex our energies in a way that we haven't done in a really long time. And if it wasn't for the threat of unintentional death, I'd bring Charle down to watch. But humans... Very delicate."

The others nodded in agreement.

"Aika would probably love to follow and take notes

for future graphic novels."

"Orion would just want to watch shit blow up," Sin added.

"Your humans are as crazy as you are," Koka decided after a beat of silence. "All of you." He turned to Enk. "Butt sex man?"

"Don't blame me; he's obsessed with it!" the pale being pointed out, and Koka found himself smiling and shaking his head at all the mischief potential that surrounded these four.

In the end, the others silently stalked off, leaving Enk with Koka and the tied up butt sex man.

"So." Enk turned towards Koka. "Can we talk?"

"Her name was Ninhursag. She was my wife." When Koka remained silent, Enk tossed him a look that had the god of mischief waving a hand and creating two very comfortable looking seats. "You don't look shocked." Enk sat into the chair made of the softest moss he had ever felt.

"Nergal and I had a talk."

"Of course." Enk rolled his eyes. "He's a mother hen."

"I would like to know why. I mean it's obvious he cares for you like a brother, but his level of protectiveness over a god... is unusual."

Enk patted the seat next to him and Koka sat, his eyes intent on his lover, while he complied with his silent request.

"She thought she knew everything." He lowered his head and crossed his hands in his lap, his silver-white hair falling in his face. "She was a goddess of fertility... of summer... of a mountain, believe it or not."

"Probably why the things I do don't shock you too badly," Koka said, and that got a smile from Enk.

"Too true, but unlike you, she thought that mankind was corrupt and needed proper guidance."

"Okay." Koka nodded. "I have often felt the same."

"Yeah, but did you ever want to destroy all of mankind and turn them into beings with no free will? How do you feel about slavery, Kokopelli? Because that's what my dear wife wanted to do."

Koka stared at him in shock. Slavery? But they were created to serve mankind.

"So don't even attempt to compare yourself to her." Enk slumped a little in his chair.

"That would have started a war." Koka finally spoke, horror chilling him. "One of our kind attempting to usurp mankind's free will? All of the pantheons would have revolted."

"And there are enough of our kind who felt the same as her, so it would not have been a war with just her. Those who found truth in her words would have taken up arms against the rest of us. We would've slaughtered each other with humanity as collateral damage."

"We would have destroyed the world," Koka breathed. "Because I would have been there fighting for humanity."

"And that is exactly what she wanted." Enk looked up at the sky, his eyes looking lost before he turned to face him. "And she would have found a way to birth the next generation, even if it meant her death."

"If she was dead --"

"She was a goddess of creation, like I am a god of creation. From her body would have sprung forth the seeds that would infect this planet. Because if she didn't destroy mankind in all of its glorious differences, continents, and races, her offspring, sprung from her mind, would have."

"Racial memory?" Koka asked, blanching.

"Racial memory with the ability to slip into worlds of humanity and influence them. What Hitler did would have been a party compared to what she would have planned. Wholesale slaughter without any guilt or recriminations. She just wanted humanity dead and gone and she would have done it by any means necessary. And we would not know where her offspring or their progeny were hidden until they started mass destruction."

"They could hide..." Enk's mind unraveled at the sheer numbers.

"No one would be able to find them until they started their agenda. Sleeper cells, if you will, that would have lasted for generations, planting seeds of discord, racism, hatred, and fear. We would not have known until it was too late."

"Fuck." Koka sat back and contemplated that for a moment. Humanity would never be safe. Anyone from any pantheon would never know until it was too late and then their actions would have been reactionary. Millions would die before they could stop this madness and then it would start up again at any time or place. How many of their kind could hide within humanity?

"The only way to stop them would be to wipe out all of humanity and start again." Koka looked disgusted even as he said the words.

"Which would fit neatly with her plans." Enk nodded at the horror on Koka's face. "Either way, she would win. Humanity would be destroyed at her hands, at the behest of her offspring, or we would have to kill them all to stop the pain, torture, and suffering that was sure to come."

"Was Hitler --"

"No." Enk let out a harsh bark of laughter. "But he reminded me of her... in the end. He was just a very good manipulator who had the ability to use people's weakness and fears against them. He made thousands kill millions and never got his hands dirty. But if he were hers he never would have been caught."

Koka shuddered at that, unable to imagine that level of evil... but Enk could. He had been married to her.

"But you stopped her. A creation goddess? That would take some power."

"Power that none of us possessed alone," Enk admitted.

"But you-- what were you?"

"I was called Enki. Or sometimes Ea, Nudimmud, or Ninsiku... I've had a lot of names and a lot of titles. I was called shaper of the world. I was to teach mankind what they needed to know to survive, to be civilized, to become more than what they were."

"Which is why the Kachina so fascinated you."

"I thought they were amazing," he offered with a smile. "I am a god of creation, keeper of greater magics, but I could not stop her. She was too powerful."

"She had the ability to bring about new life."

"I am not a fertility god, Koka. I cannot top the ability to bring life. Only one well versed in the intricacies of death could do that and even then her total destruction was not a surety."

"Abadon..."

"Yeah." He nodded. "Nergal knew he could kill her but not stop her life from reforming in her children, who would, in all intents and purposes, be human."

"With an evil seed for a brain."

"He was not powerful enough to endure that... on his own."

"How --"

"Nergal has always been a close companion to me. When I discovered her plans -- the bitch did like to talk after really good sex. I have no idea why she thought I would go along with this. Her pussy wasn't that good."

"You fucked the truth out of her?" Koka held in a smirk at his lover's words.

Enk snorted. "In fact, I had no idea what was going on in my own temple. She was preparing to bring in the summer and when she was happy she was beautiful... undeniably so. She belonged on her mountains, her seat of power, and when she was in them, she flourished. She was irresistible."

"And you didn't resist."

"Why should I?" Enk narrowed his eyes at him. "She was my wife and I thought our lives were perfect. When she started speaking of her plans, I knew there was no way I could stop her alone. With the help of Nabu, we devised a plan that would ensure her total destruction. He is the god of wisdom. Sin was able to give us insight into how our actions would affect humanity. So with the help of my brothers, we devised a plan that would stop Ninhursag."

He flicked his tongue, and the fangs that Koka thought were just another aspect of his lover, popped out. As he watched, the set of teeth whirled with power and then enlarged in Enk's hand. When the transformation was complete a broken, spiked crown lay in his hands, the centermost jewels... well, he didn't know what they were. They looked like fire opals but sparkled like cut diamonds.

"A visible standard of my power," he explained as he stared at the shattered crystals in his hand. "A tool that can be a conduit of my power."

"What did you do?"

"I am a creation god and a part of creation is death. Yet alone I was not powerful enough to wipe her out of existence." Enk held up his hand. "You ever wonder why I am so pale?"

"I assumed it was something you chose to do."

"No." Enk shook his head. "My skin was gold, Koka. It was a rich golden brown, the color of crushed amber in fertile soil. My wife was my sun and I looked as if I worshiped at her altar. I looked as if I bathed in her rays and absorbed her glorious heat." His smile was sad as he looked at his own arm. "After I did what I did, my power broke. I lost my color, Koka. I became a non-being that should not even exist."

"What did you do?" This was more serious than he'd thought.

Enk drew in a deep breath before he exhaled sharply. "I poured all that was me, all my energy, my power, my very soul such as beings like us possess, my very godhand onto this crown and bestowed it upon Nergal."

The silence that filled the woods was scary, but not-- almost like the fates were holding their breath and shocked at what they heard at the same time.

"You-- you gave your godhand to someone else?"

"Not just my godhand. I gave all that made me, my future potential -- everything that I am, I poured it all into this crown, shoved it on Nergal's head, and broke when he did something that abused my very nature as a being of creation. I helped him kill my wife."

"Enk --"

But Enk pulled away, shaking his head. "Let me say this before you speak." At Koka's nod, he continued. "I knew that just killing her would not stop her. So what if we were early? Her offspring would still be formed from her dead body, seeds that would scatter the moment her body touched any part of the earth. So I had Nergal do the unthinkable. I had him consume my wife."

Tears filled his eyes and a look of sheer horror crossed his face. "Because of me, the god of destruction took on new meaning, Koka. Because of me, Nergal had to eat the body of another god and then used our combined powers to totally devour her existence, her being, her godhand -- everything that she was." He was shaking his head... no, his whole body was shaking. "I had him consume her soul."

Koka reached out and grabbed his hand, holding on tightly as more words poured from his mouth.

"I remember the pain -- her pain, my pain, the pain of my godhand being torn and abused. I remember the others holding me down as I screamed my voice into what it is today, as every bit of color drained from my body, as I became a blank being who could claim no existence. I was ready to fade away, to join my wife in nothingness when Nergal begged me to return. He loves me, you see," he explained using his free hand to wipe his tears away. "Not like a lover or a parent, or even a child, but as a true companion, an equal, a brother. He didn't want me to die for my sacrifice. He felt that I would be rewarded instead of punished. He all but willed me back into being. He shoved my broken crown upon my head and threatened to devour the world of humankind if I died because of them. That was stupid enough to make me laugh through the pain… and with that laughter came the knowledge that some part of me was not broken. I still have a minor connection to a godhand. Mischief."

"Enki was a god of mischief?" Koka smiled.

"A very, very… *very* minor one. One that I never really exercised. I was too busy teaching mankind to be civilized."

"And it was not broken?"

"Nor was it fully developed. But it was all of my godhand that was left, and because of my brothers I grabbed onto it with both hands. It was tattered and torn, but it was enough to anchor me into this existence."

"And did it ever heal?"

"I can never again be complete. A god of creation who was instrumental in a major destruction? But it was solid enough for me to make a link to those who loved mischief making; therefore, I still exist."

"But only certain aspects of mischief?"

"Anything that is bighearted and not mean-spirited. Practical jokers, those who tease their friends and loved ones, those who want to lighten the spirit, those I feed from. But if anything musical, anything designed with ill intent, anything chaotic or destructive comes near --"

"It overloads your system, incapacitating you."

"Broken." He nodded. "Like my crown."

With a flick of his fingers, the crown shrank once more and he popped it neatly into his mouth. When he smiled, Koka could see the fangs had proudly returned.

"So broken that I can no longer hold color in my skin… any color. I wanted an Abadon tattoo. They helped create a sword design and yet I can't even get the ink to stay on my skin. It fades."

"Your whole aspect changed." Koka was awed. "Do you know how incredible you are? What you sacrificed…"

"What almost happened under my watch…"

"The way I see it, your wife was responsible for what happened to her and for what she almost did to you. She would have surely destroyed you. That's why she kept her plans secret. If you had known, you would have stopped her much sooner. You did nothing wrong and yet you sacrificed the most for humanity… and they don't even know."

"I know." Enk sighed. "And now you know. You can't fix me, Kokopelli. I am unfixable. So if you want to walk away, I understand. Nothing you or I could do would fix me. I am as I am."

"You are not broken."

"I am --"

"An asshole. A brave, amazing, powerful, caring, unapologetic asshole, and mine."

"Koka --"

"Like that would drive me away. So too much chaos makes you high? Stick with me and I'll absorb it for you. Because after hearing this, I have to tell you I want you more than ever."

"Kokopelli --"

"You think something like pale skin and spasms are going to keep me away from you? If only, it makes me want you even more. You are like a mystery, an enigma that will take me centuries to figure out. And being who we are, I think we have the time."

"You mean that?" Enk looked a little shocked at his worlds. "But I thought --"

"What? That I wouldn't want you because you have imperfections? We all have imperfections. I am impatient, stubborn, love to drink and party, and I tend to sleep winters away."

"And your website sucks." Enk laughed, reaching for his lover. "We're going to have to get The Seven on that. You can't be associated with us and have a site that bad."

"Whatever you want." Koka snapped his fingers, combining both chairs into one moss-covered loveseat. Then Enk was in his lap, his pale hair creating a world for just the two of them. He had just taken his lips in a kiss that was guaranteed to lead to some woodland fucking when a crash made them both look toward the fence that surrounded their property.

Before they could say anything, sirens sounded in the distance and Nergal, chipper as a puppy, bounced back into the woods behind the house.

"That was so much fun!" he crowed. "I scared one of them so badly, he pissed his pants too."

At that declaration, they all turned to look at the man who was still bound to the tree. Tears were running down his face and he stank of pee, but he, through his crooked glasses, stared at them as if they were monsters.

"Oh, him." Koka groaned and waved his hand. Butt sex man fell to the ground and immediately scrambled backwards.

"Demon!" he screamed. "You're all demons!" He tried to get away but a tentacle rose out of the ground and wrapped around his ankles, effectively hobbling him while making him face plant directly in the dirt.

"Like anyone is going to believe the unstable man who planted bombs in my house," Nergal said. "The story is we were leaving to go on a hike in the back forty to clear our heads. You opened the gate and we didn't lock it. We saw this one sneaking out back and did a little sneaking of our own, knocking them out 'cause we couldn't make it back to the house. We got them tied up but you noticed the bombs and made sure that we got out and called the cops."

As he finished speaking, Sin and Nabu rounded the

corner, looking just as gleeful.

"I got them to knock each other out," Nabu crowed. "I scared them into running into a wall. One dragon roar and *blam!* Blood and snot everywhere. Two for one. Then I put them in pink ladies' panties, thongs of course, and painted their toenails pearly pink. When they are strip-searched, they are going to have a lot of explaining to do."

"I just hit mine over the head with a rock. What?" Sin asked when they gave him funny looks. "It was quick and to the point."

"Right!" The others laughed at him as their very two favorite agents rounded the corner at a run.

Butt sex man started blubbering about them being demons and about the trees holding him hostage, but when they turned to look, they only saw a woven belt wrapped around his legs, keeping him in place, and Koka and Enk sitting on two tree stumps.

Along with the other three, he was taken into custody, an immediate psych eval ordered, while the agents got on with their questions.

It was going to be a long day.

Epilogue

"So," Enk said as he glared at the gathered reporters waiting at the airport for Abadon's final press conference before the band headed home. "Now you know what happened."

He and the other members of the band were sitting at a nine-foot table with their partners sitting next to them.

Nergal and Charle were making kissy faces at each other and generally being cleanly sweet and disgustingly adorable. They didn't care who was watching as they traded small, pecking kisses and facial caresses. Of course the world was used to seeing the two of them being outrageous. They leaked their own edited sex tape before anyone else could, though most of their bodies were hidden. There was just a lot of humping beneath rainbow sheets and gigantic stuffed green guitars. Overnight, those guitars became almost as valuable as their stuffed swords of glow-in-the-dark green dueling guitar T-shirts.

Orion and Sin were practically sitting in each other's laps, Orion in his blue-and-pink trans-pride chest cavity T-shirt, a shit-eating grin on his face and Sin staring out at the audience. Snake was wrapped around Orion's neck, and Sin absently reached up to pet it every now and again. In his hair was a long pink-and-blue braid, put in there by Orion at the beginning of the conference. In fact, he had pink-and-blue bracelets that he would toss to reporters when they asked a stupid question... which meant his supply of one hundred was almost gone and several idiots were holding multiple bracelets with confused looks on their faces. The watching crowd loved it.

Nabu and Aika were sitting close together, holding hands above the table. Nabu answered a lot of questions and sometimes pointed out stupid people who needed to be slapped in the face with a pride bracelet, which Orion gleefully provided. Nabu was still bald, getting used to the new look. In fact, several modeling agencies had already approached him about representing him in future spreads. He was still dithering about it, but The Seven were ecstatic. It meant more income. Aika was excited about the prospect too, offering to be consultant on every shoot, picking out the best photos with her eye towards art, and thumbing her nose at the world that had issues with their relationship. They were often called the straight members of the band, which made them laugh hysterically and ask if a watching security officer was into threesomes. Of course they got his number... in front of the TV cameras no less, and a promise to hook up before the band left American soil for some time. Aika was taking notes with her free hand and drawing caricatures that were devastatingly humorous and nasty about the watching reporters... especially the two from Faux News. Everyone knew they were going to end up on her website and the Locusts could hardly wait. There was even talk of her creating a limited edition T-shirt of the band at a later date. Her career was going well and her talent was being recognized by a wider audience.

As for Enk, he was sitting in all his pale glory, hair flowing freely with his boyfriend sitting beside him.

Flautist Koka Four Feathers was a bit of a surprise to the rest of the world. No one had any idea that Apollon was in any kind of relationship. Rumor was that the two of them had been spotted on secret dates and that is what sent their supremacy stalkers into a murderous rage, killing their pilot and attempting to pop a bullet into Apollon's head. It had led to the four of them stalking the lead FBI agents' offices, entering the local headquarters in the guise of repairmen, and listening to the complaints of an agent that the band referred to as Kip long enough to get their address and find them on their property.

The FBI was embarrassed. Agent Kip apologized

because of all the negative media he brought the alphabet agency with his inane line of questioning while missing the same face popping up close and personal in at least two separate occasions. Of course this meant that he could lose his job or even better, wind up in a remote FBI way station in Alaska... there were FBI outlet branches in Alaska, right? But in the end, the unsubs were arrested, the bombs defused, the evacuated people allowed to return home, and some justice was obtained for Major Tom.

Now after the conference, the band was returning to their hotel and in the morning, Max would be back, flying them and their lovers home.

"I have one thing to say in closing." Enk grinned at his brothers and they all leaned back and waited for him to get the last word in. "Hatred brought us to this tragedy. Hatred and stupidity cost a man his life, almost cost the lives of my brothers and their lovers, and almost made Abadon legends the hard way. Some say we are heroes for taking down our would-be killers. But I say fuck that. We ain't no heroes. We are fucking legends. Heroes are remembered but legends never fucking die. And with that said, I want the world to know that we do what we want. We pay our taxes, don't break many laws... many" -- he chuckled -- "and we deserve to live our best fucking lives to the fullest. If you have a problem with our gender, our sexuality, our choice of partners, then fuck you. We share a lot of things about our lives with you but we don't live for you. I know I speak for everyone when I say I am whatever the hell I want to be and if you don't like it, fuck off."

The Locusts roared in approval, cheering his name.

"You don't like what we have to say, then fuck off somewhere else with your money. We don't want your money. We don't want anything to do with you and your asshole way of thinking. There is more to life than opinions and when the fuck did your opinion mean more than the lives of other people? And still we are made out to be the bad guys? To those who believe that shit, fuck you. We make music for humanity, for real people who have heart, for people who want happiness and a fucking future with no more of this bullshit. We make music for people who believe that there is a future, who are tolerant even when they do not agree with someone else's life, or lifestyle. We make music for people who have souls. And for the rest of you fuckers who want to try us, go ahead. Abadon ain't going anywhere and certainly not because of anything you think or say or feel. For the ones who follow us, who read about us, who support us… Hey, we can't love you more. You made us what we are, and what we are is fabulous! People want to call us Rock Stars but we are fucking bigger than that. We are Rock Gods and don't none of you sons of bitches forget it."

The Locust roared their approval, chanting "Devour! Devour! Devour!" as the band and their partners, as one, rose to their feet and exited stage right.

* * *

The sales of their next album skyrocketed, once again cementing their places as rock gods for the ages.

Author's Note

Sympathy For the Devil is dedicated to my pretty Mommy, the woman who always wanted to break free. Mommy had so much fun helping me decide which misadventure Charle Lexington was going to get into. She had more fun helping me design Abadon. My Mommy never got the chance to do a lot of the things she wanted to do, she became an adult at the age of six, but she never lost her innocent curiosity about the world. I love you, Mommy. You never understood me but you always loved and supported me in my wild adventures... and joined in for quite a few of them. I miss you, Mommy. There will forever be a hole in my heart where you once fit, but I know that you will be forever in my soul. I love you.

Stephanie Burke

Stephanie is a USA Today Best Selling, multi published, multi award-winning author, Master Costumer, handicapped, wife and mother of two.

From sex-shifting, shape-shifting dragons to undersea worlds, sexually confused elemental Fey and homo-erotic mysteries, all the way to pastel-challenged urban sprites, Stephanie has done it all, and hopes to do more.

Stephanie is an orator on her favorite subjects of writing and world-building, a sometime teacher when you feed her enough tea and donuts, an anime nut, a costumer, and a frequent guest of various sci-fi and writing cons where she can be found leading panel discussions or researching varied legends and theories to improve her writing skills.

Stephanie is known for her love of the outrageous, strong female characters, believable worlds, male characters filled with depth, and multi-cultural stories that make the reader sit up and take notice.

Stephanie at Changeling: changelingpress.com/ stephanie-burke-a-30.

Changeling Press E-Books

More Sci-Fi, Fantasy, Paranormal, and BDSM adventures available in e-book format for immediate download at ChangelingPress.com -- Werewolves, Vampires, Dragons, Shapeshifters and more -- Erotic Tales from the edge of your imagination.

What are E-Books?

E-books, or electronic books, are books designed to be read in digital format -- on your desktop or laptop computer, notebook, tablet, Smart Phone, or any electronic e-book reader.

Where can I get Changeling Press E-Books?

Changeling Press e-books are available at ChangelingPress.com, Amazon, Apple Books, Barnes & Noble, and Kobo/Walmart.

Changeling Press, LLC

ChangelingPress.com